THE SEPA

Simon Robson was born in 1966 and grew up in Wiltshire. He studied at Cambridge University and trained as an actor at RADA. He has since worked extensively in the theatre with such companies as Shared Experience, Method and Madness, Bristol Old Vic and the Manchester Royal Exchange Theatre, where his first play, *The Ghost Train Tattoo*, was premiered. He is married to the singer Sophie Daneman and they live in London with their two sons.

Simon Robson © Scott Marshall

SIMON ROBSON

The Separate Heart

& Other Stories

VINTAGE BOOKS
London

Published by Vintage 2008

2 4 6 8 10 9 7 5 3 1

Copyright © Simon Robson 2007

Simon Robson has asserted his right under the Copyright, Designs
and Patents Act 1988 to be identified as the author of this work

First published in Great Britain in 2007 by Jonathan Cape

Vintage
Random House, 20 Vauxhall Bridge Road,
London SW1V 2SA

www.vintage-books.co.uk

Addresses for companies within The Random House Group Limited
can be found at: www.randomhouse.co.uk/offices.htm

The Random House Group Limited Reg. No. 954009

A CIP catalogue record for this book
is available from the British Library

ISBN 9780099507581

The Random House Group Limited supports The Forest Stewardship
Council (FSC), the leading international forest certification
organisation. All our titles that are printed on Greenpeace approved
FSC certified paper carry the FSC logo. Our paper procurement
policy can be found at www.rbooks.co.uk/environment

Printed and bound in Great Britain by
CPI Bookmarque, Croydon CR0 4TD

To Sophie

Contents

The Separate Heart

They made a striking, but pleasing, contrast, the two women seated at the kitchen table. The younger was dark, with short, bobbed hair; the other taller, with long hair that had once been golden but was now streaked with grey. She looked distinguished but faded, like a prophetess from the weathered frieze of a Greek temple, perhaps temporarily unemployed and wandering through suburbia looking for divine trade. Golden sunshine streamed over the garden fence and through the kitchen window, catching the dark girl full in the face; she squinted, as if she were unaccustomed to being so in the spotlight; the statue kept in shadow. The two women, without being aware of it, composed a well-balanced picture: one was born golden, the other had gold thrust upon her. The sunlight, where it fell, divided the table neatly into two.

Emma, who was squinting at the sun, was just married. The delicate, nervous hand that tucked a stray strand of straight black hair behind her ear wore an unscratched wedding band; Harriet's fingers, which were longer, which gardened harder, wore no rings.

They were sitting in the kitchen of Martin and Emma's new house; Harriet was their neighbour, and this was the first time the two women had exchanged anything more than a smile over the garden fence, the newly married couple having moved in only the week before.

Two cigarettes were smudged out on a pretty blue and white china saucer on the table between them. They lay there like a preliminary exchange of the vows of sisterhood. Now the two women were debating whether to have another.

'I didn't expect to find in you a partner in crime,' said Harriet from the cool comfort of the shadows; she turned the packet in her outstretched hand, as if she were about to perform a trick with it. 'I thought you were a timid little thing when I saw you arrive.' She smiled playfully. 'Not that I was spying.'

'Oh,' said Emma, 'I would have been curious, too.'

The older woman's hand ventured from the shadows and into the sunlight; Emma's went out to meet it and took the offered cigarette.

'I said when I married Martin I'd stop,' said Emma, like an acolyte brought up before the prophetess for questioning.

'Why, does he disapprove?'

'Oh no. Quite the opposite, actually.'

'Really?' said Harriet doubtfully.

'I know it sounds silly, but . . . well, he said that cigarettes gave me mystery.'

'The implication being that you lacked it otherwise?'

'I'm not mysterious,' said Emma, simply, casting a half-reproachful glance at the sun whose brightness was, she felt, interrogating her. Harriet watched her new friend's discomfort for a second, and, as if she was satisfied on a particular question which she had been debating with herself, stretched out her slender arm to her self-conscious host and lit her cigarette for her.

'You are an honest girl, I can see that. If we're to be friends,' Harriet said, lighting her own, 'we can at least share a vice together. Besides,' she went on, blowing the smoke from her mouth as if it had failed to please her and she were dismissing it, 'everybody is mysterious. And we don't need other people, least of all the superb male of the species, reassuring us of it. It is true whether or not . . .' – more smoke dismissed – 'doctors, or artists, or psychiatrists or . . .' – she suddenly smiled kindly, playing to what she rightly perceived as her new friend's strongest suit – 'husbands . . . tell us.'

Emma recognised her cue and seized the moment with relief. A sort of blindness descended on her when conversation took an abstract turn. It made her dizzy. Phrases such as 'the superb male of the species', which she knew were ironic, or meant to mean more than one thing, made her panic. It wasn't that she was stupid, it was just that she wished, well, that things would mean just one thing at a time. And in this instance her fear was compounded by having known this woman for only an hour. She wanted to return in kind the compliment of being treated like a sister at such short notice. But she could not; at least not in abstract kind. All she could do was seize this last comment and run with it as she knew best, enumerate her husband's virtues, tell the tale of his proposal, the ordeal of the wedding and the relief of the honeymoon. Emma was not so naïve as to think these events fascinating to a stranger; but she was naïve enough to be surprised that she still found them fascinating herself. Harriet watched her steadily – watched rather than listened; her face softened as she watched the younger woman talk on; she was very still, in contrast to the nervous movements of the other talking; one might think she was about to stretch out her hand and stroke the other girl's face and console her over a sadness that only she, Harriet, really understood.

Emma was unaccustomed to talking about Martin, and she found the experience of doing so made her miss him. She didn't want talk, she wanted him. His relegation to the third person made him feel too separate, and this made her anxious. Her too nervous temperament forbade her the luxury of making in words a still and concise version of him with which to satisfy herself. She always came up short as far as words were concerned. And talking to this woman made her miss him even more.

Emma was a modest girl. Those who knew her believed she was the least vain person they had ever met. She always seemed cheerful and hopeful, and did not have the vanity that can accompany certain sorts of unhappiness. She had every right to regard herself as pretty, but never seemed to find any reason to enforce that right. Her dark hair looked as if it had been bobbed for convenience, though she could not have chosen a prettier style; her clothes looked accidental and her face looked as if it was a relative stranger to the mirror. Even sitting as she was, with the spring sunshine on her, she seemed to succumb to the sun as to an unnecessarily extravagant gift; she seemed embarrassed on behalf of the giver. Perhaps it was simply that she was happy and did not wish to be seen to flaunt it.

But Emma was not timid. She had had, in her past, an unerring sense for those turning points in life when things are transformed; she had known when they were and looked them in the eye. At such moments she could decide for herself with the objectivity of a third party the best course of action. At such moments she could be surprisingly stubborn, and showed a tenacity that could be explained only by an unclouded conscience and a very clear sense of what she wanted. Very soon into her relationship with Martin she had made it clear, simply and unambiguously, that she was not interested in a brief love affair. That was not her style. Beyond a certain point some clear commitment would be necessary. Martin, for his part, was impressed by this, not so much by the sentiment as by Emma's manner of expressing it; it was clear she demanded of him that he commit himself without her having to be seen to be demanding it. This flattered Martin; it was as if she offered him a way of being a better person and at the same time made it look like his idea. Martin wasn't a particularly bad person, but who can resist the lure of seeming to be a better one? She forced him, without ever confronting him, to prove his good intentions without suggesting they were anything but exemplary already. The happy result of this, probably unconscious, ploy was that instead of suggesting they move in together, as she had expected him to do, he asked her to marry him.

So it was that barely a year later they were the new owners of No. 1, Milton Cottages. Emma was only sorry that Martin had been collecting the last of his things from storage when their new neighbour came to make their house-warming complete.

The owner of No. 2, Milton Cottages was not the longest standing occupant of the terrace, but she was certainly the most popular. The six little houses, all more or less identical, had been gardeners' cottages to the local estate, and the owners of the other four had all lived in them since the estate had been broken up and sold thirty years before. Harriet, who lived alone, enjoyed, even in her forties, the role of youngest and most energetic member of the community. She was their unelected and adored champion, who zealously guarded the interests of the two retired couples, the widow and the widower, who occupied Nos 3 to 6 inclusive. She guarded them principally from the more modern and wayward influence of the Close, a rather amorphous warren of family homes that surrounded the Cottages. Under her protection there were no teenage drum-kits, no drunken student parties, no Coke cans in the gutter and no unsightly satellite dishes. But she never made herself unpopular; even among those over whom she ruled she was liked, for all her puritan credentials. The women secretly admired her single status and the men were provoked by it; either way she got what she wanted. If she had ever married, not only would it have been the most shocking thing ever to have happened to the Cottages and the Close, it would also have been the most disappointing, to male and female alike.

So when the end cottage became vacant, and a couple of newly-weds ten years younger than herself arrived it was, well, a change, and one which Harriet accepted graciously. No doubt like all those in positions of political power, she wasn't without moments when she wished the responsibility would be lifted from her shoulders, and a young and energetic couple might be just the people to do it. Besides, it would be a challenge to take a young couple under her wing and deftly weave them into the social fabric of the Close; provided they didn't have a screaming child with unseemly haste. First she would make friends with the wife. The husband looked broad-shouldered and foolish; she would deal with him later.

'Your kitchen is quite different from mine. Older,' she observed.

'Is it?' said Emma. 'It has all its original features.'

'Yes,' said Harriet, laughing unexpectedly, 'you can call them original, or you can just call them old. Like me! Which would you call me?'

'Oh . . . you? You . . . are original.'

But Harriet seemed more interested in asking questions than hearing the answers, for she went on –

'You know how lucky you are to have got this cottage. There was a positive feeding frenzy when it became available. Word is, the previous owners took a shine to you, and that is as good a reference as you could hope for. We are like peas in a pod, we six cottages . . . all alike and yet so different. Unique . . . as we were saying before.'

'Were we?'

'But you . . . you I think are going to be the nicest of all. You . . .' Harriet looked at her again as if she were an appraising older sister. 'You . . . will become everyone's favourite.'

She stubbed out her cigarette as if she were dispensing with smoking in preference for friendship.

'Emma . . . I'll shock you a bit from time to time. I'm afraid I'm practising becoming one of those dreadful old English clichés – the ageing woman who speaks her mind. You mustn't mind me. Ask anyone from the Cottages or the Close and they'll tell you I may be mad but you can trust me with your life. You hear? And don't go worrying that having an energetic neighbour means I'll be poking my head over the fence every five minutes to gossip. You have your fine husband and your fine cottage and you'll want yourselves to yourselves.'

Emma smiled at this, partly from the kindness of the sentiment and partly from the idyllic portrait of the life she was so happy at the prospect of living.

'And by the way,' said Harriet, smiling, 'the walls are thick.'

'Oh, we don't play loud music,' said Emma, pleased to be able to promise something in return.

Harriet looked at her neighbour and decided she liked her new protégée very much.

'Besides . . . it will be a welcome change . . . a capable man about the place.'

With this innocuous blessing on Martin and Emma's arrival, Harriet knew all too well that she was offering her companion the opportunity to ask a certain question that would have to be asked eventually, and she would rather be asked it at her own instigation than be the victim of a tactless enquiry later on. And sure enough, she saw Emma struggling with the correct words, giving her time to prepare her answer:

'You . . . are . . . I get the impression . . . Do you live . . . Are you alone, Harriet?'

Harriet liked her the more for her awkwardness, but could not help smiling at the bluntness of the final phrase. It was also the first time that Emma had called her by her name, and for some reason it surprised the older woman. She sat back in the shadows.

'I have a cat,' she said.

Emma said nothing, not sure whether she was being teased or put off the scent of something more shockingly original. This time Harriet came straight to her rescue.

'No, I don't have a man, darling, if that's what you mean. I *assume* that's what you mean. And I know it's not fashionable to believe women when they say this, but . . . I don't really want one. I've stopped seeing the fact as interesting, or sad, or quirky, or remarkable in any way. Just don't have one. Don't blame you for having one. Don't want one myself. I've become attached to my solitude . . . married to it, you might almost say. And what began as a marriage of convenience has turned into a most satisfying love affair.'

'With . . . with your solitude?' queried Emma, uncertainly.

'Yes,' said Harriet, beginning to tire of her matinée audience, 'but I have a cat,' she repeated, like an echo.

There was a pause. Harriet hummed a little tune under her breath. Then she said, 'Welcome to Milton Cottages, dear Emma. Remember . . . if there is anything you want . . .'

She got up.

'What's his name?' said Emma, feeling she'd not contributed enough to the conversation, and so carrying it on beyond its natural end.

'How do you know he's a he?' said Harriet.

'I don't.'

'Well . . . *he's* a monster.'

'How funny. What's his name?'

'Teddy. Throw him out if he comes pestering, will you? He'll probably be over the fence to check out the strangers. He's territorial. Just send him back. And don't go feeding him or anything like that. He's fat enough as it is.'

'Oh I wouldn't do anything like that.'

'Don't, there's a love. Oh look!' she said suddenly. Emma jumped and stood up and followed Harriet's gaze, expecting to see at least the garden shed on fire. 'Look at the sunlight on your garden! What potential that garden has. Your predecessors had no passion for gardening. Have you?'

'It's my great plan for the summer.'

'Good for you. You'll learn. No, they weren't gardeners, but they had hearts of gold. Hated cats, though. *He* was allergic, I think. Yes . . . hated cats but hearts of gold,' she repeated, like a catechism.

And then, standing in the sunlight, her long hair that had once been beautiful golden again, she lifted her chin and laughed a good-natured laugh, with which Emma, with her pretty, dark, bobbed hair, attempted to join in.

A few days later, as Harriet had predicted, Emma had a visitor.

As each day passed in her new home, *their* new home, she felt more and more as though she belonged. They had married before Christmas, honeymooned before New Year, house-hunted for the rest of the winter and moved in in spring. So now, after Martin had left early to go to work, Emma would go around the cottage opening the windows, and feel the contrast of the sharp spring air to the close body-warmth of the bed that still clung to her. It made her want to laugh. And slowly, all around her, as the morning matured, she would sense the house warming up; new curtains just put up would blow proudly in the breeze, and that breeze in turn would bring in the public domesticity that the spring entailed, the sounds from distant houses now released into the warmer air travelling further, urgently linking house to house: washing-up, a dog barking, a lawn-mower being cleaned ready for the first cut, windows opened in image of her own; everything gave of spring a public dimension, and Emma lapped it up gratefully; its very sensuous appeal seemed designed to effect a welcome more winning than any visitor. Its public-ness was in delicious contrast to her private moments after breakfast when, with a cup of hot, milky coffee and a forbidden cigarette in hand she looked out at the garden and felt so happy she thought she would cry.

So she was sitting over the same pretty blue and white china saucer for an ashtray, when she heard a curious sound from the guest bedroom upstairs. A double thump, percussive, loud then soft, as if something had been dislodged and fallen and hit the floor but not broken; a sound that belonged somewhere between human agency and the fall of a leaf, neither meant nor accident. Just loud enough to make your heart jump in reciprocal rhythm. A double thump, like a heart; loud, then soft. Then . . . nothing. Just a long pause, and then a ginger head emerging, as of something returning from temporary eclipse, filling a void that was not a void until filled, and then seemed retrospectively an answer to a question that you could not remember asking, but you knew you'd wondered at . . . namely – the meaning of that pause; and it was, of course, his conjectured progress down the stairs, unseen, perhaps urgent, perhaps casual; meaningful only after the confirmation of his ginger head, fat, blinking, slow. From his size the double thump was the sound of his jumping from the windowsill, front legs then back.

'Teddy,' she said, involuntarily, with an ease with which she herself was surprised. She felt a part of herself insist she acknowledge that she had been waiting for this visit. Harriet's abstract conversation she had found exhausting; she had felt she could not keep up, and this cat, in her imagination, would be the concrete half of her neighbour, the true welcome.

Most un-Harriet-like Teddy wandered fatly towards her without looking at her, brushed her legs once and with the slow-motion fall of a redwood which the lumberjack stands back from and which seems such a fittingly portentous tribute to his having cut it down, Teddy began to tilt, and relinquishing himself with great trust to gravity, fell over, rolled on his back and thrust out one paw in a pose of melodramatic *noli mi tangere*. Then he purred, which, in a cunning reversal of traditional cause and effect, *made* her stroke his tummy. He purred louder, closed his eyes and put his head back. The weight of the whiskers gently pulled the mouth a little open, and Emma could see the white incisors, precise and shy as little crescent moons set off against the abstract ginger blur of his coat; a lion in miniature, a dwarfish primal terror in his aspect. Then he opened his eyes slowly, registered the pleasure, and closed them again, his little oriental face instantly peaceful in the opium den of her love.

'Teddy,' she said again, happily.

Then she remembered Harriet's words – 'throw him out, will you?' she'd said. *Will you* was slightly old fashioned, a mixture of assumed intimacy and aristocratic petulance. '*Throw him out, will you?*'

Emma stopped rubbing his belly. Teddy righted himself and looked her in the eye as if he were surprised at her having forgone something so pleasurable as giving *him* pleasure. He licked his paw, rubbed his ear and looked around with the plump, easy manners of a fat millionaire. A cat that could afford anything he cared to buy. It was a commonly accepted courtesy that one didn't throw millionaires out of one's house, even fat ones. Least of all fat ones, for in their fatness they proved that wealth had not made them vain and image-conscious; they were good-humoured livers of life, with as much love to offer as appetite to assuage.

Then, like a society débutante who realises she has remembered a matter of etiquette only seconds before committing an unforgettable *faux pas*, she read in his look her final duty as hostess. She glanced at the fridge.

Now Emma was in a crisis of conscience. She had never had a cat before. But she had also never had a neighbour, at least not in the grown-up, neighbourly way she had now. Emma was, as we have said, modest, and she was honest. She also could not bear to be the cause of anyone's unhappiness. The transgression of boundaries, the taking of liberties, the modern, casual commerce of affection and betrayal had made her loathe her teens and twenties; this safe place with Martin was what she had waited for. She looked at the cat and felt a foolish ache; that cat didn't care two pins for what she thought, he just wanted some milk. A whole orthodoxy of human expectation rose up in front of her to do with cats: centuries of required behaviour. The true weight of history. She felt cross with herself for taking herself so seriously. She blushed.

If Teddy had been more cat-like, less fat, more disdainful, aloof, haughty, preoccupied, with more of the independence that makes it so easy to turn from cats to the easier affection of dogs or lovers, it might have been different. But she felt that if she denied him she would be less of a person.

She sighed. She had never given a cat milk, or made feeding-time small talk, the 'what have we got heres?' and 'this is what you're after, isn't its?' that were the cat lovers' stock in trade; but she knew, instinctively, how to do it. Like an old hand she went to the fridge and took out the milk and repeated the put-upon owners' mannerism, immemorial as an ancient dance – of making a show of begrudging the concession, a physical shrug, a theatrical deflation of posture meant to betoken the melodrama of *effort* expended on behalf of another; an acknowledgement that concurrent with the gift of milk is the recognition, the ulti-matum, even, that the world could not always be providing cats like *you* with food unearned, prey provided *gratis*, gifts given outside of the law of the suburban jungle. She took down another one of the pretty blue and white china saucers and with a pang of conscience poured a little milk into it. Then she put it down. Before the china touched the floor the ginger head softly but firmly nudged her wrist and, like a bouncer at the bar, muscled in and made room for himself. His welcome was complete; he drank silently to their new-found friendship, and to Emma's new life.

About two hours later Teddy was gently ejected from the

spare-room window through which he had climbed (having reached it by, in turn, climbing out of Harriet's upstairs window and crossing the roof) and the window was locked behind him.

Emma loved Sundays.

She loved to lie in late, and watch Martin while he slept. He worked hard, and on Friday nights he liked to drink with what he called his business associates. On Saturday morning, then, he was apt to be ragged and uncommunicative. But on Sunday mornings his skin was clear and he slept deeper and dreamlessly; but for the delicate shade of weekend stubble on his cheek he would have looked boyish; instinctively his arm would stretch out over her in his sleep, and Emma would feel its weight and stare up at the ceiling in a gentle paralysis of happiness. The permanence, the very slowness of sleep, as of time thrown away with such profligacy, enchanted her; even modest Emma, in those first Sundays in their new house, felt some inner swagger at the sight of him. She felt, in her thirties, and in marriage, that she had been excused the endless challenge of her twenties: how to escape causing people, men, unhappiness; those who wanted too much or too little; those driven by desire, and those by disappointment. From the male manifestos to which she had signed up, seen implemented and lived under, she was finally emancipated; and she felt the man she watched sleeping knew this. Not in so many words, they never spoke of abstract things, but simply by virtue of his seeing how happy she was.

He turned in his sleep and pressed his face against the cool, cotton, wedding-present pillow, and Emma smiled, as though his cheek were pressed against her own.

From next door came the now familiar double thump, and the

same silence afterwards, the unknown whereabouts, the gap between the thought and the word, the nail and the scratch, the kiss and the sigh. He was probably inspecting the last of the boxes Martin had brought over from her old flat the day before. From round the bedroom door came the round ginger face, and in one jump he was on the bed, imperiously aboard them, like a seagoing cat aboard an unsteady boat.

Martin looked up sleepily.

'Cat,' he said croakily. 'There's a great bloody cat on me.'

Teddy settled between them.

'It's Teddy. This is Teddy. He comes sometimes during the day,' said Emma, half frightened. She'd told Martin about Harriet's strict injunction.

Teddy started to wash his face and Martin looked down at him distrustfully, as if he might be being taken in by a particularly cute cat act.

'Saw old Harriet a couple of days ago over the fence,' he said, properly waking up rather reluctantly. 'Said her moggy had been going AWOL. Asked if he'd been here.'

'What did you say?' said Emma, trying to sound offhand.

'Give us a kiss,' he said.

'Martin? What did you say to her?'

But Martin was kissing her neck.

'Martin?' He broke away and sighed. Teddy watched and blinked slowly.

'I said . . . no sightings.'

Emma leaned over and kissed him. He put his arm around her and she snuggled into his chest.

'We shouldn't pinch her cat, Em.'

'I haven't.'

'It's all she's got, old Harriet. All on her bloody own, and only an old moggy to keep her company. You mustn't do it. Eh, big fat puss,' he said, eyeing Teddy who in turn eyed him. The two males stared each other out. 'Don't want to piss off your owner, do we? Posh bird like that, you never know what they'll do. She might call the cops . . . she's scary.'

'She's not,' said Emma, unconvincingly.

Martin turned his head and looked at her face framed by her dark bob in turn framed by the soft, white pillow. he pushed Teddy gently aside and pulled her towards him. Unperturbed, the ginger puss seemed to accept his exile to a far corner of the bed, curled up and went to sleep.

Over the next few weeks, Teddy became an even more frequent visitor. It seemed to be out of Emma's hands. He had become so quickly part of her happiness with Martin, such a token of their new life together, she could no longer extricate Teddy from her gratitude for that life; it would have seemed churlish. Every morning after Martin had gone to work, she would open the spare-room window and go back to bed and wait for the tell-tale sound. Before long she would not need to wait; he himself would be waiting impatiently on the roof for admittance.

Emma had not forgotten her promise to Harriet, but the memory of it provoked no longer guilt but anger. She was angry with Harriet for placing such an arbitrary condition on their new friendship and she was angry with herself for having made so much of it. She was sure any other person of ordinary morality would not so much have ignored Harriet's request as placed it confidently in a file under the heading *things necessarily out of one's control*, and *things it would be absurd vanity to think about too much*. And this sense of her own moral squeamishness, compounded by the fact that she was equally unable to obey her over-zealous conscience and turf Teddy out, did cause her shame. Her solution was to trust Teddy; she came to prefer his moral arbitration to either her own or Harriet's. And in a sense this was not wholly out of weakness or convenience. Emma had a weakness for other people's judgements; she wanted a world in which everybody was right. Even Teddy.

So often it is the very promise that is made at the beginning of a relationship – in this case Harriet's promise not to interfere with their wedded privacy – that is broken first. But Harriet was as good as her word. She never forced her advice or her extensive local knowledge on them. If they asked a question about their neighbours, the name of a trustworthy plumber or the whereabouts of a good pub for lunch, she would tell them casually but carefully, wink at them, impart information she subtly implied was not available to all-comers and then briskly continue about her business. She was a little rough with Martin, whose boyish, urban charm she liked to mock, but she knew how far to go; her reward was to be promoted, in his private terminology, from 'scary' to 'bonkers'.

Emma, however, remained in awe of her. Not merely the Teddy business, but Harriet's social persona was intimidating. She had such a firm grip on the political machinery of the Close, and on the personalities of the eccentric inhabitants of the Cottages, and this grip was made all the stronger, it seemed to Emma, by her coolness to the idea of attaching herself, profanely, to any single person, male or female. A cooler woman would have seemed to have absented herself from life. Harriet seemed in the thick of it. She controlled the interests of a large, devoted, suburban congregation; she was charming and firm with them, and within the certainty of the boundaries she herself imposed upon them – she rarely had friends for dinner in her own house, for instance, or stayed very late at other people's – she was superb. Since the transgression of boundaries could be said to account for a large proportion of the misery in this world, it explains why Harriet exuded a kind of bracing certainty, an old-fashioned first-thing-in-the-morning wholesomeness. It was this that cowed Emma. It made her fear the great happiness she felt with Martin was in bad taste. Socially she felt helpless in her friend's hands. The only consolation being that they felt safe hands.

In keeping with what Emma felt to be the unspoken timetable of their arrival in Shakespeare Cottages, they invited Harriet to dinner. She stood in their kitchen, slightly too tall for the room, drinking wine and observing, from a great height, Emma frying onions. Martin wasn't yet home.

'I allowed myself the luxury of coming half an hour early,' she said, watching Emma's cooking with approval. Harriet looked like a member of the Bloomsbury Group moonlighting as a home economics teacher. 'How marvellous of you to cook.'

'I'm not very good at cooking,' said Emma.

'Nonsense. You are good at everything. If Martin doesn't tell you so he must learn to. I will defend to the death your right to be confident.'

And with this strange comment she went to the window and looked out.

'Time to garden, Emma.'

'Pardon?'

'Time to garden. These weeks are vital, darling girl. Now is the time to decide whether you rule the garden or the garden rules you.'

'I keep meaning to but . . . other things detain me.'

'Like what?'

Emma paused, guiltily, a flash of ginger in her mind's eye.

'I don't know,' she said.

'Time to garden.'

Emma hoped she wouldn't say that phrase again.

'Do you think Martin might help out Captain Mike?'

Captain Mike lived at No. 5.

'He's a rum old stick but he needs his hedge trimming and he'll kill himself if he goes up that ladder. Do you think your Romeo can handle him?'

'I'm *sure*,' said Emma.

'Captain Mike used to work at Kew. We'll get Martin's hands dirty if it kills us, won't we?' She winked at Emma conspiratorially. Emma took guilty pleasure in Harriet's sketches of her husband's inadequacies. Emma was hardly ever ironic herself.

'He's something of an expert gardener, and a hard taskmaster,' said Harriet.

'I wish I was an expert in something,' said Emma, as ironically as she could, just to prove she could join in. 'I can't even fry onions.'

'You, my dear, are an expert in having everything and still being nice. You're not ambitious, you're not greedy and you're not gauche.'

Emma had, at various times, accused herself of being all three of these things, and to be absolved of all of them at once was a little too thrilling. For some reason the good opinion of this woman was very important to her. The compliment made her feel gauche, greedy and ambitious. She blushed and sighed, pushed a stray strand of hair behind her ear, and tried to look as if it was the heat from the pan that was a little too much.

'Having what one has always wanted,' Harriet went on, lighting a cigarette, 'is apt to make people a little hysterical, I think. There is embarrassment in an embarrassment of riches. People getting more of what they have already – eventually it is self-destructive, don't you think? They come to have an appetite for appetite itself . . . they have to, because their original appetite has faded, and they can't remember what it was they wanted in the first place. It has become objectless and has nothing left to feed on but itself. Self-devouring. But you . . .' she smiled warmly, genuinely indulgent of her shy friend. 'You are good. A doting husband, a pretty cottage . . . and you are pretty yourself . . .' Her voice trailed off into a sort of soft incantation. She looked at the sun setting over the back garden. 'Perhaps you will have children . . . yes . . . you will guard your hearth, and that is how it should be. Good for you. Good girl . . . you're happy.'

'Yes. I am happy,' said Emma, though the smell of burning onions might have contradicted her.

Then, before she could elaborate on her happiness, or qualify it on account of the onions, the deep, bold voice of Martin was confidently preceding him, and the women turned to see his broad shoulders fill the frame of the door. He would have seen two quite different reactions to his arrival: on Emma's face there was undisguised relief; Harriet exhaled cigarette smoke in a manner very like a sigh.

But the evening progressed very promisingly. It was true that Harriet's responses to Martin were unpredictable, but it was soon clear that she had no intention of denying Emma the pleasure of being a hostess for the first time. Emma saw this and was grateful. New onions were fried, a fresh bottle of wine was opened, and both in the kitchen and then around the dinner table the three of them worked away at the boundaries between them, conscious that they were eating together for no other reason than that they shared just that, a boundary. Harriet decided to treat Martin like an errant puppy, one minute she teased him, the next she scolded him, all mock-stern; Martin looked bemused, played along and decided he was being far more entertaining than he could ever remember being before. He did drink rather more than was usual, more even than on Friday nights with his business associates. But Emma was delighted. Harriet was far more forthcoming than she had expected her to be. They were told about her parents, both of whom were dead, about some of her growing up as an only child in a grand house; she even told a number of stories against herself, just to prove that she didn't spare herself whilst putting the world to rights. It seemed she had been left a quantity of money on the death of her mother, had bought her cottage and settled down to busy, independent, thrifty solitude.

'It's not fashionable nowadays to find good deeds and social-ising a respectable way of life. People think it's somehow politically incorrect. But I don't discriminate. I deal with down-and-outs and I deal with the middle classes. As long as you do some good.'

'Abs-a-bloody-lutely,' said Martin.

'There's only one true evil in this world, in my humble opinion, and that is introspection.'

'Why hasn't an extremely glamorous woman like yourself, Harriet, ever married?' said Martin, taking another large gulp of wine; his capacity to provoke their guest had gone to his head; he looked as if he might be about to go too far. Emma glanced at Harriet nervously.

But Harriet, as she was apt to do, suddenly laughed a good-natured laugh and for a moment Emma felt it would all be all right.

'Isn't it time you were in bed, little boy?' said Harriet.

Martin looked wonderingly and a little drunkenly at Emma. 'Why won't she answer my question?'

'Just because we did it, doesn't mean it's natural,' said Emma.

Martin thought about this, giggled, and said, 'Well, I'm normal . . . I mean natural,' got up, and went into the kitchen.

'Introspection,' repeated Harriet.

'Yes,' said Emma, bracing herself for philosophy.

'There's no time for it, and people forget that fact until it's too late, and suddenly their life's over and they've spent half of it thinking about what goes on in their heads.'

A voice piped up from the kitchen, 'Oh, I quite agree.'

'Will you put the coffee on, Martin?' said Emma.

In the kitchen Martin was pulling himself together. He drank a glass of water and then reached for the coffee-pot high on a shelf and caught with his sleeve a small, blue vase of Emma's. He watched, numbly, as it fell; he'd barely brushed it and there it was, falling past his face, on its way to the stone floor; not there yet, not there yet. He seemed to have missed the point of impact; now there was sharp, smashed china spread out star-like from where it must have hit.

'Fuck,' he said, simply.

'What's the matter?' said Emma.

'I'd say that was pretty bloody obvious, wouldn't you?'

There was silence. At the table Emma could not help but feel that some prejudice of Harriet's concerning Martin was being gloriously fulfilled and that a bit of her would be pleased to see him being drunk and rude. Emma expected this idea to make her cross; but instead she just felt sorry. She could not tell why.

Then, as if Martin had heard the voices in Emma's head thinking these things – or so she thought afterwards – his voice came from the kitchen, loud and sober.

'We've seen your cat, Harriet. Lovely bruiser, isn't he?'

Harriet looked at Emma.

'Have you?' she said.

'He's a bruiser,' repeated Martin, still from the wings.

'He's a naughty boy, if he's been wandering. Bruiser or not.'

'Boys will be boys,' said Martin, entering, with another large glass of wine in his hand, then taking his seat. Emma looked at his face with dismay; he was smiling, but a frown flickered across his forehead. For some reason it made Emma want to cry.

'I tell Em to throw him out,' he said.

There was a pause.

'And does she?' said Harriet, not looking at her friend's pale face.

But Martin just snorted and took a gulp of wine.

'Eventually.'

It is impossible to say which, of Martin and Harriet, was most keenly alive to the multiple betrayals contained in that one word. It is possible that both of them had, at that moment, omniscience. The one, drunk, was drunk on behalf of his own weakness; the other, seeing his drunkenness, and seeing that the word came from weakness and not particularly from malice, was nevertheless merciless in her prosecution of it. Turning from him with disdain, satisfied he could provide no further useful information, or embarrass himself further, she looked to one side and said quietly:

'Emma, darling, you must turn him out if he comes. I made

an express request. The only one I believe I have made of you. I don't understand. I was absolutely clear on that one, neighbourly point.' She paused; she looked as if she wished she were somewhere else, as though the room were suddenly too small for her, or she too tall for the room; then she said, in the same quiet tone, 'You have so much. Everything. I just have my cat. I thought we understood one another.'

Martin giggled.

'He's a fat boy,' he said, sensing he was no longer the focus of Harriet's interest.

'Yes,' said Harriet, changing her tone, and even smiling. 'Are you a fat boy, Martin?'

'Not if I can help it,' he said, looking down enquiringly at his stomach. 'There's a gym at work.'

'I didn't think you got that doing the herbaceous border.'

'Em's department,' he said, and looked at his wife, genuinely sorry now for having landed her in trouble, desperate to make amends. But she only turned to her stately neighbour.

'I don't think of myself as having everything. He . . . he came in through the open window. I didn't tempt him. He's an animal. He's free. My house isn't a fortress.'

After this speech no one spoke, and the pause did Emma no favours. Martin giggled, and Harriet's cool brown eyes held Emma's in their steady gaze. The absurdity of what she had said started to work on Emma. Like an adolescent about to turn on their parents for the first time, with vocabulary still unformed, and a new species of anger, unlike any they have ever known, rising in them – who, day by day have felt themselves pushed closer and closer to the invisible line, the crossing of which is to cross the threshold of adulthood – so Emma held her breath, and waited for the moment of rebellion to break over her like a wave.

But she didn't have time to rebel. From upstairs came the familiar double thump on the floor. She had forgotten to shut the spare-room window. For a dreadful second she thought she might cry out.

She neither knew nor cared if her companions at the dinner table knew the meaning of that sound; she herself felt as if she knew nothing else. No one else existed except herself, and of herself only her guilt had any meaning for her. She believed that in the wake of that noise, that signature sound, she would actually pass out of consciousness; as if something had shifted in her unconscious, something beyond social knowledge, something that this dinner party was forcing her to accommodate in her life; some dreadful adult reckoning which she was unqualified to negotiate. Whatever it was she might have said to Harriet in the previous moment's rising passion was replaced by a living reality, it was embodied, made fact; the Philosopher's Stone of circumstance had turned the base metal of her adolescent ravings into living gold . . . living, feline, ginger gold. Her feelings were made a fact, and the fact damned her. She felt faint.

Could she have seen Harriet's face she would have seen on it no flicker of expectation. Only superb sang-froid. Perhaps she had not heard it at all.

Then, like a great actor, who plays, unbidden, even by his own will, the self-deprecation that adds genius to a vainglorious entrance, Teddy put his fat ginger face around the corner of the door, and purred.

'Fatty!' cried Martin. 'Our old fat friend.'

In spite of Martin's genuine pleasure at seeing the cat, Emma's hatred of her husband at that moment seemed permanently to forbid love, to make any future happiness impossible.

Teddy circled the dining-room table, rubbed against Martin's leg, jumped into the spare, fourth chair, turned a circle on the spot until satisfied, and having made up the quartet, went to sleep. It was a scene-stealing performance at the end of which Harriet gave a low, appreciative laugh – a keen but joyless approbation, as from a seasoned connoisseur of the drama, a critic for whom the *form* of greatness has long since overtaken any appetite for the *content*.

'It seems you've stolen my boy,' said Harriet, matter-of-factly, lighting a cigarette with surgical precision. And then, as if purposefully allowing the emotion of the moment to brim over, she said, 'Oh Emma . . .' with a tone of such reproach, but cross and smiling, like a disappointed older sister. And like a sister, the smile betrayed a forgiveness the words didn't have. This forgiveness was terrible to Emma. It spoke of a love born out of pity, and Emma hated to be pitied. Wasn't it the very fear of pity that had got her her husband? Had she not made it clear that she would not be a discarded lover, and hadn't Martin seen this and responded? She had ensured that rather than be pitied she would be loved. It was brilliant of her. And now her triumph lay in ruins.

There are certain photographs of groups of people, perhaps less common in these informal times than they used to be – seated at formal dinners, in deckchairs on the beach, attending academic functions – in which, in spite of the fact that the subjects are already in immovable poses, they have clearly been told to stay still for the camera, and consequently appear as if they were giving a demonstration of stillness. And this double stillness is particularly touching because one sees in these photographs how hard true stillness is, and puts us in mind of the other, rarer genre of photographs, which are also less fashionable than they used to be, and which are the true masters of stillness, namely photographs of the dead.

So these three sat, each imagining their individual unhappiness was being seen by somebody, seen as by a camera, for which they would stay still until the moment was over, and for which this double stillness was a double sadness and a testament of their faith to whatever creed they lived their lives by. Only Teddy sat with the stillness of the dead.

Then, as if the moment were by common consent over, Emma began to clear the table, and went through to the kitchen. She paused a moment by the sink in case she was about to cry, and then continued. She could hear voices from the table and consoled herself with the thought that at least Martin was being a good host.

When she went through with the coffee they were sitting in silence. Harriet refused coffee on the grounds that she would never sleep. There was a pause, and Harriet stood up to leave. Emma rose to accompany her to the door, but with a gentle but non-negotiable downward pressure on her shoulder with her hand, Harriet kept her hostess in her chair. The front door slammed. Teddy looked up briefly and went back to sleep. Husband and wife were alone together.

'You shouldn't have told her about Teddy.'

'Really sorry, Em. Really am.'

'It made me look terrible.'

'Me, too, though. How did it make me look? I was the one out of order, making a joke out of it and everything. I tell you, she's bonkers, Em.'

'No, she's not.'

'She is. It's serious stuff. I tell you. Serious, serious stuff.'

And having discovered this phrase, and seeming to take a shine to it, he repeated it to himself a couple of times and then lapsed into silence.

When Emma suggested it was time for bed, Martin declined her suggestion that he accompany her. So she went alone, cried into her pillow for some time and drifted off to sleep. Teddy let himself out of the spare-room window. And Martin sat at the dining-room table, poured himself another glass of wine and pondered something Harriet had said to him while Emma had been in the kitchen.

Over the next few weeks Emma applied desperate remedies to her situation. To her it seemed she had a choice: either to concentrate on the fact that Harriet was absurd to have taken the whole matter to heart and to defend on philosophical grounds Teddy's right to find love where he chose, the rights of a free animal in Nature etcetera etcetera . . . or to take herself apart and honestly admit that, philosophy aside, she *had* caused distress and had a duty to alleviate it as best she could, however absurd the circumstances. She took the latter course. She kept the upstairs spare-room window tightly locked and she denied herself the garden. She would go nowhere where she might meet him. Harriet's cat would become Harriet's problem. If her neighbour was determined to project on to an innocent cat such an essence of possession that he became indistinguishable from her, just as slaves once took the names of their masters, so be it; Emma would un-christen Teddy and let him be only Harriet; she would shut her door to both if either found her culpable. How this patently absurd situation had come to have such a potent sway over her life she could not say. But she was convinced that its potency was not of her making.

April and May passed, regular sun and rain fell on the little back garden and soon it had grown over. Her grand design was never put into operation: the garden was to have been her joy, but now the summer progressed in her absence, it took on a life of its own. The borders thickened with weeds and ivy swallowed up the climbing roses on the walls. All the sounds of summer that were to have filtered through the house as those of spring had done that morning Teddy had first visited her, went unheard. The extrovert sounds of children playing, paddling pools, Wimbledon, barbecues and croquet on the lawns of the Cottages and the Close found no way through to the hermetically sealed sadness of Emma's heart.

Harriet made no direct reference to what had happened. If anything, during this time she grew more friendly. They carried on as though the dinner party had never happened. But she did begin a sort of game with Emma. She would paint, almost with an artist's attention to detail, vivid portraits of Teddy sitting on the roof of her house looking wistfully up at Emma's window. She would describe, laughing, how he pawed at the window to be admitted, until Emma had no choice but to smile, too. She would enjoin her to laugh at the male species generally, that could pine so melodramatically at being slighted by a woman. And finally she would congratulate Emma on having touched so robust a heart as Teddy's, that she'd had Teddy marked down as a one-woman cat . . . and so on.

The most curious thing about these exchanges was that it was not possible to say with any certainty that Harriet meant them unkindly. Emma was kept in a position of never knowing whether Harriet was, in her own way, trying to let Emma off the hook by making a joke of it. A joke, in fact, that might even be against Harriet herself. She had looked at Emma forgivingly that night. It might be that Harriet was trying to assimilate into her life a lesson, just as Emma had been; a lesson about love. Or it might be that Harriet was trying to destroy the life of her neighbour. Or both.

Perhaps the greatest change, at least outwardly, since the dinner party, was Martin's attitude towards Harriet. Whereas he had before been charming, in his boyish way, or pretended to be intimidated by her, he now seemed actually hostile. He bore her repeated requests for DIY assistance next door with greater and greater ill-humour. When Harriet's car was off the road for a week and he was left to drive her to and from the railway station, she became 'that stupid head-case', and he expressed a desire to 'kick that bloody cat' if he ever saw him again, since it was through the cat they had come to know Harriet. Emma pointed out that strictly speaking the opposite was true. Martin just ignored this. His wife began to fear he regretted their moving into Milton Cottages.

But slowly Martin cheered up. Through Harriet's elaborate network of contacts, of favours done to the less fortunate and introductions to the more interesting, he found himself in a world all too eager to use a personable, strong, capable man. Being called over to cut down a hedge ended with a gin and tonic in the garden; changing the oil of a distant neighbour's car with a beer; with his assistance Captain Mike managed to pay his council tax for the first time. Under Harriet's careful tutelage he became a great favourite. The Prince of Cottages and Close.

As for Emma, she looked back on the few weeks when she had had Martin and Teddy to herself, curled up together on a Sunday morning in bed, as an unspeakably happy, never-to-be-recaptured time. Now she seemed to have lost both of them. Having shut the door to the cat, she had lost her husband. He, in turn, seemed to have lost his boyishness, drank less often with his business associates and became quietly efficient in everything he did. Only once did he look out, in Emma's presence, at the jungle their garden had become, look at her with a frown, and seem to be about to say something, doubtless about why she had never ... but he'd stopped himself.

Teddy still came and sat and looked up at Emma's window, and Emma knew that Harriet knew, and Harriet smiled as if she knew everything, and from this knowledgeable roundabout there seemed no escape.

Then one evening in August Martin came home early from work. His boss was going to Tuscany the next day, and in a holiday mood had allowed the whole office to stop work at four o'clock. So the sun was still high over the mass of green that had once been their garden when Martin swept through the door and found himself a cold beer in the fridge. Emma was sitting at the kitchen table smoking her teatime cigarette.

'My, you're early,' she said, looking up guiltily. She no longer liked Martin to see her smoking.

'Thank God. The Hendersons want me to help them with the pool, and it's no small job. Old Jacky must have read my mind.'

'Jacky?'

'John Fisher. My boss. Let us off an hour early.' He swigged from the bottle. 'Come by later, have a swim.'

'I might.'

'Go on.'

'I might.'

'Suit yourself. There's virtually only the Hendersons left. The rest have gone.'

It was true. In August the Close was deserted and dusty. What few children had not been taken to France or Italy, the Lakes or the West Country roamed the streets sulkily. Whichever family stayed put became, for a brief, unnatural honeymoon period, the most popular in the area. This year it was the Hendersons. They had a pool.

Martin was going out the door when Emma said, 'Harriet wants you to call round. She asked me to tell you.'

'For fuck's sake, why won't that woman leave me alone? We should never have moved here, Em.'

'No,' said Emma.

'Only joking. But she is a bloody liability. Plumber fucked up her mains.'

'You don't know about plumbing.'

'Bloody learning though, aren't I?'

And he went out, carrying his bottle of beer.

Emma put out her cigarette in the saucer whose blue and white design was almost completely obscured by ash, and looked out of the window. The sun would be up for a long time yet. It cast dark, velvety shadows in the unkempt borders, and the dandelions and borage grew as lush as hothouse specimens. Then in amongst the deep green she saw a flash of gold.

It gave her no pleasure to see Teddy hunting in the undergrowth. She saw him, registered his presence, as of a memory of something she had learned to do without, as a reformed smoker watches other smokers; as if they might be in a cage at the zoo; an exhibit.

We are all human beings and we are all foolish, she thought. There was Harriet, a woman who had eschewed intimate relationships with men, who prided herself on her independence, and what had she done? She had simply transferred her possessiveness on to a cat, and had behaved as ridiculously as any neglected wife. What a shallow anthropomorphism to think that Teddy had wandered next door for anything but a saucer of milk.

And yet Emma had bought into the whole business and herself behaved as if she'd seduced the poor woman's husband. 'Yes,' she said to herself, 'it's me that's been the most absurd.' She had not guarded against the eccentricity of other people, and so had become eccentric herself.

Out in the garden, Teddy pounced, and Emma watched as he suddenly stood still, his head buried deep in the grass. Between the leap and reappearance of his mouth with or without his prey there was that same dreadful gap, that moment of conjecture that is like madness, as there had been between the peculiar noise of his arrival through the window and his appearance at the table that night of the dinner party. Once again Emma watched, paralysed. Teddy lifted his head; he had a shrew in his mouth.

Suddenly she was out of the door running, shouting and waving her arms, quickly knee deep in the long grass, the lush vegetation slowing her, as if she were running in the sea; but she struggled on till she was nearly upon him. Unperturbed and uninterested, Teddy looked at the approaching chaos of arms and legs and with a nimbleness that belied his size jumped in one bound across the garden fence with his prey. Emma reached the spot still struggling to articulate the horror of bloodshed in her garden, breathless and keening like a madwoman. This was it, the dreadful moment that she had felt upon her when, sitting opposite Harriet at the dinner table, she had felt so powerless under the cool stare of that once golden head, and which the arrival of Teddy had interrupted. Now she would not be denied. Finally she felt it coming out. Momentarily empowered, she turned on her home, on the cottage in whose confines she had felt her life destroyed, and just as she seemed about to tell it what she really thought of it, she stopped. Looking back at her own house, she could see her neighbour's beside it. Through the open kitchen window Emma could see Harriet and her husband somehow stuck together; and he seemed to have his hand over her breast. The pair had looked up, surprised at the commotion, but had not sprung apart. Emma's pretty bobbed hair and open face just cleared the garden fence. The couple stood there, as if they were rather surprised to see anyone in the green wilderness.

Emma did not want to see the expression on Martin's face, and as if to accommodate this he looked away. So the two women looked at one another. The expression on Harriet's face seemed to dare the young woman to supply subtitles to it, and Emma met this creative challenge unflinchingly, even with relief. 'Man for man, darling, love for love. Martin for Teddy.'

Martin did not appear that night. No sounds came from Harriet's house, and it may be that he did, indeed, help the Hendersons with their pool. Hot as it was, Emma did not join them for a swim. She went to bed and tried to sleep, but it was unbearably close. The little old-fashioned cottage baked under the sun, stored up the heat during the day, and it was now impossible to get cool. Towards midnight she got up, as if in a dream, and went from room to room opening all the windows in an attempt to let in some air; anything to be cooler. She went downstairs, poured herself a glass of iced water, and lit a cigarette. The smoke rose steadily, untroubled by any breeze. It hung above her in the soft lamplight. A quarter of an hour passed.

There was a double thump upstairs.

Between the familiar sound that she had not heard for so long, and the appearance of his inquisitive head around the kitchen door, Emma had found her purse, her credit cards, the car keys, her mobile phone and a bottle of milk; she had written a brief, courteous, explanatory note and propped it against the pepper-pot. As he appeared she forwent the usual formalities of a reunion, but took clean clothes from the washer-dryer, dressed, filled a plastic bag with the surplus and knocked back her iced water. Then with one, sublime and graceful movement, the more so in that she was normally physically so awkward, she swept Teddy up in one arm, holding her clothes with the other, and moving like a spirit through the old-fashioned cottage, was gone. The slam of the front door echoed briefly in the moonlit shadows of the Close until all was still once more.

She took the motorway. She was unsure how far she drove, Teddy asleep on the passenger seat. In the constant motorway twilight she lost all sense of time; only the brief, absurd Las Vegas glamour of service stations that passed distantly, like oases of neon in the night, gave her a feeling of distance. She wouldn't stop at them. There were too many people there and there were no shadows.

Then, for a short period, she was driving through a true dark. Only the soft psychedelic glow of the dashboard, the green and red numbers and dials that showed the details of their progress, shone up at her. Teddy was almost indistinct.

Slowly, the sky began to round with light and deepen like a bowl, like mother-of-pearl. They drove through reams of forest, piled row on row with pine trees, their spiky tops like sentinels outlined against the growing brightness of the dawn. For some reason they reminded her of the Black Forest, which was strange because she had never been there.

And always there is Teddy. Proprietorial of his passenger seat, occasionally watchful; mostly sleeping. Always self-contained. Still covetous of his separate heart.

He turns and shifts his head in dream. Emma sees, and turns away, moved, knowing her triumph is as yet only in the physical fact of his presence. Incomplete.

She has to stop for petrol. Stepping out of the car into the cool early morning, she breathes in the air. A cool breeze brings the sound of traffic to her as she fills the car with fuel; it's getting lighter all the time. Another brightness is competing with the sheltered haven of the forecourt lights. She pays. She walks back to her car, takes her place beside him and is about to start the car when she hesitates. How long is the endless brightening of the sky around the place where the sun will come up. But she turns to look at Teddy at the moment that the sun breaks over the dashboard and catches his waking ginger face with gold.

The Observatory by Daylight

1

Raafi held court at Mario's.

Strictly speaking, the town was out of bounds to pupils during the week. But Raafi had groomed the eponymous manager of the café into a state of complete submission. Mario was a thug; a tough Milanese, whose conception of our public school was along the lines of a maximum-security prison. An opinion probably founded on first-hand experience. He recognised in Raafi a fellow fugitive and Raafi did nothing to dispel this myth. It may also be that Mario suspected of the boy some Latin brotherhood. He would have been wrong, however, for Raafi was half Iranian and half Irish, but he was dark and exceptionally good-looking, and Mario got easily sentimental. Raafi became the café owner's sometime son and in return Mario gave him, Marcel and Trixy a table away from the window. There were masters everywhere, so he also kept his eyes skinned for tweed jackets and woollen ties. So far he had never been raided.

Raafi gave a lot of girls a lot of grief, whilst never overstepping a single boundary or wavering from the line of true friendship. Never once did he express an opinion – and opinions were to Raafi like cigarettes: no sooner had he dispensed with one than he had another – about a girl's appearance. He was, as far as anyone could gather, entirely chaste. His looks were remarkable. He looked like the love-child of Maud Gonne and Omar Sharif. His dark Adonis curls and his heavy-lidded eyes, his white teeth and helplessly good-natured smile, the way he tipped his head back and laughed at delights of which only he seemed aware, worked on girls as first drinks and first cigarettes work on the young, as melancholy portents that this may be as good as it gets. For however happy girls may have been, either alone or with a first-flush boyfriend, when Raafi appeared he smiled, they saw and they doubted. But of all the girls, only Trixy was admitted into the small, exclusive circle of Raafi's associates.

Trixy was seventeen, like the rest of us, and worked on the sweet counter in Woolworth's. She had spiky hair which was dyed many different colours; in fact she looked like a piece of confectionery. She had a pierced nose and a strange husky voice and had a pretty face like an Arthur Rackham fairy. She and Raafi roamed the streets together. In some indefinable way she seemed a match for him. She was a smart girl, Trixy. She'd read all Raafi's textbooks and would argue with him about whatever he was studying at the time, whether it was the European Union, the novels of D. H. Lawrence or prime numbers. But what she did principally was steal sweets and CD covers from Woolworth's to fund Raafi's black-market activities. It didn't matter that the covers were empty. Raafi just downloaded the tracks from the internet and burned his own CDs. Then he'd sell them on to the boys in the Remove for a massive profit. They even got a little bag of cough candy thrown in, to keep them sweet.

I knew about Raafi's illicit café life because the school caretaker, Phil, used to wheel me past Mario's on the way up to the Observatory. I've been in a wheelchair since I was seven when I had an accident and lost the use of my legs. I spent a few years at specialist schools, but since my father was the headmaster here, when I was thirteen, in a move the exact reversal of most boys' experience, I came home to go to school. Apart from the fact that I lived in the Master's Lodge and had Phil to take care of me, I was just an ordinary pupil.

My big hobby was Astronomy. Every Wednesday, when everybody else was playing games, Phil would wheel me up to the Observatory. There was, of course, a limit to how much you could do there during the day, especially if you were paraplegic, but I could polish a few lenses or read a book. I just liked to be there. It was funny seeing it all in the daylight. Like seeing school in the holidays, empty of boys – a place with its *raison d'être* removed. It was hard to really feel they were the same place. The Observatory by daylight was dusty and full of dead flies; at night you didn't notice that, you were always looking high up, looking out; the answers all seemed elsewhere. But by daylight it was nice to see all the old Victorian machinery and the antiquated maps of the heavens. There was an old record player up there and lots of Mozart. Phil would pop out to have a smoke on the grass in the sunshine, and I would put Mozart on. It was nice.

As I say, the Observatory was high on the Common, so we had to pass Mario's, and more often than not Raafi would be there, smoking his Camel cigarettes and flicking the ash with casual aplomb, as if he were cracking a little whip. He was full of restless energy. Marcel would be there, reading the *Sporting Life* with great seriousness, and Trixy would be doing her nails. And Raafi would be analysing.

Raafi, you see, was a conspiracy theorist. In spite of the fact that he seemed to have everything – looks, money, an iron grip on the listening habits of half the school, a café society – what mattered to him was working out what was really going on. Nothing, to Raafi, was what it seemed. His was a siege mentality. The world out there, outwardly conquer it as he might, was in the grip of forces determined to obscure, confuse, obfuscate and deny the truths of life. Raafi lived to be one step ahead. And that was the secret of his charisma. Within seconds of being in his company your life, whose choices and chances seemed no more than a game of patience, became, reshuffled and re-dealt by Raafi, seven-card-stud-no-limit poker. He raised the stakes. People ceased to be chance encounters. Everybody became a surname. His world was peopled by a potent dramatis personae of surnames whose names signified qualities greater than the person who bore them.

One day we stopped outside Mario's while Phil got himself some more cigarettes. I could hear Raafi's voice inside.

'Now, here's the thing. Dawson's a hunted man and, deny it as he might, he knows it. Why? Because to all intents and purposes, on this issue he's damned if he does and damned if he doesn't. How easily does the crown sit? He's being forced into a choice of either accepting the reluctant role of *Übermeister* over his peers, or taking the full brunt of the fallout from a compromise decision, which could prove ultimately fatal. Those who are against him must divide and rule. An administration brought down by fatal internal fracturing will render him no more than a paper tiger. It just won't wash. I believe Dawson will fall on his own sword rather than let Xavier carry the day.'

I listened at the door, hoping Phil wouldn't come back and wheel me away. Raafi's voice had the urgency of a front-line war correspondent; every moment seemed galvanised by a sense of choice, of life happening here and now, plural and fascinating, every choice laden with possibility. We were in the thick of it. Life was drama.

Who were these people of whom he spoke so knowingly?

Whose administration was full of such Shakespearian drama, so under threat, so riven with political schism? I thought the name Dawson a coincidence, for it was my own. Then I realised he was talking about my father. Xavier was the school librarian. And the subject of my father's alleged deliberations? The abolition of compulsory games on Wednesday afternoons.

My life was full of split loyalties. I went to normal classes like other boys, went to the Observatory instead of the rugby pitch and ate dinner with my parents. I was privileged. But in common with many people caught between two cultures I felt I belonged truly to neither. There were compensations. I had a unique perspective. I observed school life through many lenses. Some of the insights I was offered were telescopic, allowing me to see things denied other boys, details too far away from their dormitory lives to be discernible: I saw timetables constructed and syllabuses implemented, teachers sacked and teachers drunk. Others, by contrast were microscopic, visions deep into the forbidden minutiae of the other boys' lives: a parent's suicide, the police investigation into the ill-gotten gains that paid for one boy's schooling and the self-imposed privations that led to the bankruptcy of the parents of another. I had a kind of omniscience. My parents took my circumspection for granted. Perhaps they felt my intimacy with the private life of the school was small consolation for my legs. My mind ventured where my body could not.

It was the end of the summer term. Our final, A-level term. Boys no longer threw themselves with muddy abandon into rugby with no thought for tomorrow; they stood, fielding

41

the distant, introspective no man's land of the cricket boundary and wondered where they would be in six months' time.

Phil was wheeling me up the hill towards the Common. He had his tracksuit on. Phil always put this blue tracksuit on whenever he wheeled me up there, as if I was taking some kind of exercise by proxy. He was puffing away, it was hot and he was making heavy weather of it. We passed Mario's and, as I always did, I peered inside to see if Raafi was there. I could just make him out. He was alone, smoking a cigarette with even more than his usual suave expansiveness. I felt sorry for him, sitting there. It was unusual. The school without children, the Observatory by daylight – Raafi without an audience. For a moment I even thought he had seen me. But as Phil pushed on I just heard him say 'Un altero, signore,' and Mario went to work, thumping the old coffee machine, stoking up his surrogate cellmate with cappuccinos on the house.

The Observatory in summer was peaceful and cool. Phil got the old machinery turning, and we opened the roof; a perfect rectangle of blue sky looked down on us.

'Why ain't you revisin'?' said Phil.

He made these little half-hearted attempts to keep me on the straight and narrow.

'Phil, it's Wednesday afternoon. Everyone's playing cricket. I'm here. That's fair, isn't it?'

'You gotta keep your dad 'appy.'

'He is happy, Phil.'

'Shall I put a record on?'

'Yes. You could put one on.'

'Whatcha want? The usual?'

'All right.'

Phil put on the Mozart Horn Concertos. We listened to it for a moment. Then there was a knock at the door.

'Who zat?' called Phil, suspiciously. Then, to my amazement, Raafi walked in.

'Whatchoo want?' demanded Phil. He was rather officious with the boys sometimes, and I was worried it gave me a bad name.

'Hello, Raafi,' I said.

Raafi nodded at me and sized up Phil.

'Here's how it is, fella,' he said, and took an unopened packet of Benson and Hedges cigarettes – Phil's brand – and tucked them into the top pocket of the caretaker's tracksuit. 'I want to talk to the kid. Give us half an hour.'

Phil looked at me, and in my new role, for all the world like some schoolboy godfather, I nodded. Phil shrugged his shoulders and left.

'I saw you in Mario's,' I said.

'Timothy,' said Raafi, 'you have a hard life.'

'Thanks.'

'And Dawson is a good man.'

'I'll tell him.'

'He's your father, you should. But don't tell him I said so. One is apt to be misrepresented.'

'It's all right, I happen to think he's a good man, too. What do you want, Raafi?'

Raafi picked up the record sleeve and looked at the picture on the front, carefully.

'What's this?' he said.

'It's a French horn.'

As far as Raafi was concerned, nothing was what it seemed.

'Mmm . . .' he said, distrustfully.

'It's a record of the Mozart Horn Concertos.'

I don't know why I told him that; it was written in big letters on the sleeve.

'Is that what's playing?' he said, over the sound of the French horn coming from the record player.

'Yes.'

But he wasn't having it.

'Of course, you know this is not authentic. The French horn as we know it was invented many years after Mozart.'

'I did know that.'

'You're being slipped a mickey. I can get you period instruments. You want the Academy of Ancient Music?'

'I'm happy with this. And anyway, I don't have a CD player up here.'

'I could remedy that. On the other hand, what is authentic? Only experience, man. Only ... experiences. The past finds a place in the present only if the present can accommodate it. Only if there is room at the inn. Otherwise it takes its place in the stable.'

He took a seat beside the telescope and lit a cigarette. A thread of smoke wound its way upwards to the rectangle of perfect sky like a snake charmed out of its basket. Raafi tapped the brass tube, as if to make sure it was real. Then he looked down at my wheelchair and my legs.

'Man ...' he said. 'Oh man.' He paused. 'How is it, Timothy, we never speak?'

'Because I'm in a wheelchair and my dad's the headmaster.'

'Lenoir says you're cool.' This was Marcel.

'Thanks. Where is he? He's normally with you.'

'Here's the thing. Lenoir's heading the pace attack this afternoon, first eleven. He'll take wickets; he'll bounce those boys.

What nobody knows, because he won't tell them, is he's really a leg spinner. I've seen him bowl spin. They call him a useful paceman, he's a *devastating* spinner. He keeps it quiet because he thinks spinning is effeminate. Something to do with the wrist. Yes, sir. Lenoir is a fully paid-up closet spinner, living the lie that he is a happy, rounded paceman. Sometimes it's better to bowl slow.' He looked down at my legs, again. 'Or not bowl at all.'

'Raafi . . .'

'Yes, man?'

'This is kind of quality time for me and Mozart. It's obvious you want something. What is it?'

He looked up at the telescope, again.

'This is a hell of a place to smoke. Where do I put my ash?'

I gave him a Victorian lens cap.

'Timothy,' he said, tapping the cap with his cigarette like Morse code, 'I have a problem. I need something, and the answer does not lie within me, but in the world. And I am humbled by the fact that it is to you I have to come for assistance. Yes, I have a problem. Smith says she's never seen me so low.'

'Who's Smith?'

'Trixy.'

'OK.'

'It's almost a spiritual thing. Here I am, coming to you in your wheelchair . . . it's beautiful.'

'You always get what you want, Raafi, and so do the music lovers in the Remove.'

'Stealing music is playing Robin Hood. Hood happens to be a hero of mine. But what I need you can't get at Woolworth's.'

There was a pause.

'True pride, Timothy, is a Persian concept. An Eastern concept. And I am about to bring shame on my mother. And it will be ineradicable. I am spoken about in villages from Donegal to Tehran, I carry a unique set of hopes on my shoulders. What has not been done to one half of my ancestors has been done to the other. My mother is going to bow her head in shame.'

'Why, what are you going to do?'

'Fail my maths A level. And here's the thing. No maths A level, no university. They won't take me back for a retake – Dawson, Fielding and Xavier will kick me into the long grass. I will have to take my chances with the boys of St Thomas' Emmanuel Church Day School, Kentish Town. This cannot be.'

I had a hunch where he was going with this. As the exams got closer I felt more and more caught between Master's Lodge and Examination Halls. I was too close to the enemy to be trusted by the boys and my parents had become distant with me, as if they had no choice but to stand by while I was the subject of a ghastly experiment. I realised it was going to take Raafi, a boy as marginalised as I, to fully put me on the spot about which side I was on. But I hadn't expected this.

'No, Raafi.'

'Let me finish.'

'On your camel.'

'I come from Persian aristocracy, man. I'll be disgracing my family.'

'What, and if I steal the exam paper from my father's study and get caught I won't be disgracing mine?'

'White Anglo-Saxon disgrace is different. I'm just asking you to bowl a googly, a wrong'un. Here's what it is. I just need to know in what form and to what extent the general quadratic function is going to raise its beautiful but ultimately unforgiving head. It's a damage-limitation exercise, nothing more. Mere flood defences. I don't even need to see the paper. I don't want to see it! I want there to be some element of surprise. Just square me on the old quadratics and a touch of the complex numbers, the techniques of differentiation and I'm quids in. Those quadratics, man . . .'

I could feel some Eastern spell beginning to work on me; I didn't feel caught between school and Master's Lodge any more. I felt caught between T. E. Lawrence and Lawrence of Arabia.

'No,' I said.

'Man . . .'

'Don't "man" me, Raafi. They're my parents. I love them. And more than that, I like them. I won't do it.'

'No one will suspect you. You're in a wheelchair. Even if they did suspect you the climate of political correctness would make it impossible for them to say anything.'

'So me being in a wheelchair makes it safe to ask me, does it?'

'Timothy, on the souls of my grandchildren, you being in a wheelchair has nothing to do with this request.'

'It does for me! It's fucking difficult to go from filing cabinet to filing cabinet like a fucking cat burglar *in this*! What am I going to do? Ask Phil to help me?'

'It's an idea.'

'Raafi . . .'

'I feel for you, man. But you're safe *because* you got the chair.'

'What's that, realpolitik?'

'It's reality, man.'

He sighed like Kahlil Gibran after a long day and lit another cigarette.

'What's in it for me?' I said.

And he was up, pacing. We were in an instant council of war. Suddenly he was smoking his cigarette like a Churchillian cigar and I was his Western Front.

'Now here's the thing. Timothy, you got brains, you got music, you got money . . .'

'Who could ask for anything more?'

'What haven't you got?'

'Legs.'

'Oh man . . .' He paused. 'Here's the thing. Pornography.'

'The stuff you steal from Xavier's private collection behind the reference section?'

'Trust me, that stuff sells. And you know too much, Timothy.'

'I know how to do quadratic equations, too.'

'You could do it just for the thrill of it.'

'Too Eastern. I'll do it for a girl.'

'Whoah . . .'

'I'll do it . . . for a blow-job.'

'*That* could be hard to fix.'

'It's that or back to Kentish Town.'

'Man, *that's* realpolitik.'

'No, Raafi, *that's* reality.'

'I can do you cocaine and the best pornography money can buy. Trust me, the difference between that and the real thing is negligible. Negligible.'

'How will I know unless I try both?'

'What if I can't get a girl?'

'There's always Trixy.'

'Smith. There *is* Smith. Smith might. I'll have to have a serious chat with her. Hmm . . . but you *are* treating her like a tart.'

'You're treating me like a cripple.'

'You are a cripple.'

'That's the price, Raafi. If Trixy's no go then you'll have to find someone else.'

Raafi stopped pacing and looked up. He seemed happy to be asked the impossible. It seemed to have reinvigorated him. The sky looked down on him and his great beauty. It was a sight.

"'Look on my works ye mighty and despair . . .'" he intoned. 'Tell me,' he went on, 'is it true the Big Bang theory has been discredited but the authorities won't let on because it would mean all the government research grants would be cut?'

'No.'

'Is it true there's life on other planets?'

'Probably.'

'Hmm. Can you give me odds?'

'No.'

'You must see some great stuff through this,' he said, looking up at the telescope.

'Some,' I said. 'Do you want to read a poem, Raafi?'

'Shoot.'

I took my ledger from my bag, took out a sheet of paper and handed it to him.

'Man . . . poetry.'

He took a drag on his cigarette and put his hand to his head as if he were a folk singer. Then he started to read out loud:

Required Reading

When I was little I remember reading
How the sun it will embrace the earth;
There, the sun it will embrace the earth.

Astronomy. That was my required reading;
I had all the books. Supernovae, galaxies;
Of how the sun it will embrace the earth.

'Cos small stars grow big, and what was white and hot,
Or yellow like our star the sun will swell
Until our sun it will embrace us, destroy us.

Of course by then, who knows? The books were full
Of years measured to the power of ten or twenty,
And I was little when I heard the news, and innocent;
But my sense of wrongness in the world has multiplied
By ten to the power of ten or twenty, so now I think

How great, how marvellous, how humanely warm
The embrace that's still to come.
For the sun it will embrace the earth.

'Man,' said Raafi, when he got to the end, 'do you need a
blow-job.'

'Absolutely.'

'Leave it with me.' He looked up at the telescope again. I was
pleased he was interested.

'It's true, though,' I said. 'The sun is spectral type G, and over
its full life-cycle will end up a red giant, massively larger, and will
swallow up the earth.'

He looked at me, as if he was worried for a moment that this
distant apocalypse might prevent him from achieving all he had
to achieve.

'If you like I could show you sunspots,' I said. 'But I'll have to
let Phil go.'

'How will you get back to school?'

'You'll have to push me.'

'No, man. I can't be seen with the chair.'

'Why not?'

'I just can't. Don't take it personally. It's not a prejudice thing.'

'Just realpolitik.'

'How about a hand job?'

'Thanks, I had one earlier.'

'Not from me, legless one. From Smith.'

I shook my head.

'I like this music,' said Raafi. 'Is it true Mozart has been proved to improve intelligence and is piped into American classrooms in an attempt to boost IQ scores?'

'I don't know, Raafi. Was there anyone on the Grassy Knoll?'

'Timothy, there is a theory that the Grassy Knoll was itself a conspiracy. It may never have existed as we know it. You know, there are mushrooms out there. That Common is fertile territory. If the Woolie's CD market takes a slump I may have to dabble in a little psychedelia. A quick rifle through Xavier's *Natural History of Native Fungi* and a whole new market may open up. OK, kid, I gotta go and see if Lenoir is spinning or seaming. Poor Marcel, he's a troubled boy. End of last term he went home for Easter and got a touch of the tricky teens. Read some Nietzsche and Salinger and told his father he was going to run away to a monastery. They're standing in the kitchen of their three-million-pound house in Guildford and Marcel tells Lenoir senior he's a sell-out – he tells it to him straight – "You've wasted your life making money, you've no principles, no sense of Art, no sense of Spirituality, no meaning to your life. You're washed up!" So his dad takes this pretty bad and screams at him to show him some respect and lists all the sacrifices he's made. His mother's in tears. So they square up to one another and it's as much as the mother can do to prevent a punch-up. Anyway, the holiday passes and Marcel manages not to go to a monastery that particular vacation, comes back to school this term and rings up his mother after the first week. He asks how his dad is. Turns out he's converted to Buddhism and gone to Tibet. The poor guy's decided everything Marcel said was true. Now Marcel's set to become a merchant banker just like his pa, and his dad's wearing orange. Talk about role reversal.'

Phil came in out of the sun.

'You done?' he said.

'See ya, kid,' said Raafi. And he was gone.

'Funny he 'ad those Bensons on 'im like that,' said Phil. 'Shall I put the other side on?'

'Yes, why don't you do that,' I said.

We listened to the other side and then Phil pushed me home. The view from the Common was pretty nice, looking over the town and the school. The Downs looked like a great green wave about to break over the houses and the churches, the teachers' lodgings and Examination Halls. It was beautiful and I loved it; but it was a funny place to call home.

2

I didn't really expect to be able to pull off Raafi's *coup d'examen*. It seemed wildly unlikely that the opportunity would present itself to locate the exam papers, let alone read them and remain undetected. My mother was frequently absent on her voluntary work, but Dad worked from home. He was coming in and out all the time. Then help came from an unexpected quarter.

Just before the exam fortnight, on the Saturday, by long-standing tradition, we played another very important public school at cricket. It was a real grudge match and it was elevated into a test of nerve by how close it was to the exams. It was as if both schools were daring the other to cancel on academic grounds, but of course neither did. Now, Xavier was our pre-eminent cricket umpire. His efficient, librarian's touch was regarded as perfect for the job; he didn't so much give you out as file you under LBW or Caught and Bowled. Our team always played better under his merciless eye, for everyone had library books outstanding. It was a chance to redeem yourself.

Then, the day before the match, while trying to clean the weathercock on the cricket pavilion, Xavier fell (though Raafi could not help raising the spectre of his having been pushed) and broke his arm. Umpiring was out of the question since he couldn't raise his right arm to give anyone out. No one, it seemed, countenanced the possibility of him using his left arm, so strict was our school's observance of the Rules of Cricket. So, at the eleventh hour, only my father was regarded as having sufficient seniority and integrity to take his place. I would have the whole of the Saturday afternoon with the house to myself.

As soon as the distant trickle of applause began to filter through the leaded windows of the Master's Lodge from the far reaches of the playing field I set to work.

My hunch was that the papers were in one of the filing cabinets, the keys to which I knew Dad kept in his desk. The question, as I surveyed the study, was which filing cabinet, and, perhaps more crucially, which drawer, for the highest ones were well beyond my reach.

I wheeled myself over to the desk. And as I reached out towards the drawer which held the keys, I felt my hand plunge into that other world that shadows this one, sometimes closely, sometimes far removed – the land without licence, the land of Forbidden Trespass. I felt it, briefly, like another medium, as if I were snatching a jewel from icy waters, reclaiming and reigniting an ancient feud. I feared a paralysis – in my case, *another* one – but my hand did my bidding and the antique drawer gave way smoothly. There were the keys – one for the rest of the desk and another for the filing cabinets. For the sake of thoroughness I went through the rest of the desk but the other drawers yielded only cheque stubs and paperclips. I knew I was stalling. The three filing cabinets stood against the far wall, tall and cryptic. If the papers were anywhere, they were there.

I went over. Two of the cabinets were side by side; the third, alone. As I got closer they seemed so tall I expected their tops to be lost in faint cloud. I tried the lower drawers but there was nothing but old school reports. Resisting the temptation to rifle through this academic Book of Life I closed them and felt my stomach hollow out. There was no escaping it, I was going to have to get up there. Maybe apprentice bankers felt like this when they arrived for their first day in the City and looked up. High-rise anxiety. I backed off, took in the landscape and considered.

To one side of the cabinets was a beautiful Chippendale armchair with quite high sides. It was the chair my father read in. If I could manoeuvre it into the gap between the cabinets and get myself on to it, it was conceivable I could use the chair as a halfway house and from there clamber on to the top of the cabinets and, working on my side, open the upper drawers. In the absence of a small quantity of TNT to blow the lower drawers or a block and tackle it seemed to be the only hope.

I pushed the chair, which, thankfully, was on castors, into the gap. It fitted perfectly. Then, lifting myself up in my wheelchair, I transferred my weight to the arms of the Chippendale and swung myself into it. For one peculiar, fugitive moment of adolescent awakening I felt just like my father. But I had no time to reflect on this. Reaching up to the high back of the chair I lifted myself as best I could onto the antique arm and reached up again, to hook my hand over the top of the first filing cabinet. To my relief the top was within reach. So this was the moment. The chair creaked ominously. I put the keys into my mouth so as to have both hands free and took a grip. I felt the unforgiving edges of the sheer, steel sides, took a deep breath and pulled myself up. Almost instantly I fell back. It seemed hopeless. I heard distant applause from the cricket pitch. It sounded like an ironic commentary on my efforts. I tried again. Three times I managed to get my chin over the edge but failed to reach the far side of the top of the cabinet, therefore making it impossible to pull myself up fully. Each time I fell back, terrified I was going to swallow the keys in the process. Finally, with one monumental, breathless effort, I launched myself, oblivious to my own safety, got chin, then elbow, then torso over the edge and lay abreast the two filing cabinets, my useless legs hanging down like dead weights behind me. I surveyed the room. To my horror, the impetus of take-off – as Newton's Second Law of Motion might have told me – had pushed the castored Chippendale away from the cabinets, my body's action having had an equal and opposite *reaction* against the chair. In short, I had no return route. Base camp was effectively obliterated.

I went to work. I took the key out of my mouth and tried the cabinet nearest my head. As far as I could read, lying on my side, it was full of government reports. I closed it. Then I reached out to the one furthest from me, the one I had scaled first but which was now down by my knees. Every second I risked overbalancing and falling head first to the floor. With the utmost delicacy I turned the key in the lock and slid open the drawer. I could see a little row of manila envelopes stacked neatly on their side. What looked like the top of the letters of CONFIDENTIAL peeked over the top of them. They looked like a little magazine of ammunition. I had to take each one out carefully and replace it, like defusing a bomb. Luckily they had the relevant subjects written on the back and weren't glued down, but they were clipped together trickily and I was getting tired holding the same position. Eventually I found Mathematics, read the paper and put it back. I locked the drawer and put the key back in my mouth. The actual reading, the appreciation of the magical, sought-after text, was so brief. It seemed potent and quite inconsequential all at the same time.

I had no idea how to get down. The Chippendale was long gone, an antique memory of when crimes could be committed with the assistance of fine furniture. Now it was just me and the functional filing cabinet. In any case, to hold my position as I'd read the paper I'd let my legs shift a little and I couldn't get them back to their first position. That meant that I couldn't go back the way I had come even if I had wanted to. I was stuck. All I could do was drop off the sheer, front face of the cabinets and trust I could control my descent. But I couldn't. As my legs began to fall, gravity, now with the sure beauty of Newton's *First* Law of Motion, took my legs spinning round, pulling the rest of me with them. I hit the floor, and my upper body was thrown back. I cracked my head full on the floor and for a moment knew nothing. When I came round I felt the most excruciating pain in my arm.

I lay there for a few seconds wondering what to do. Another ripple of distant applause reassured me that the alarm was not about to be raised. To my relief there was no blood on the floor. I crawled back to my wheelchair and clambered on to it. The pain in my arm was making me sweat. I put the keys back in my father's desk – having miraculously failed to swallow them in my fall – and left the scene.

Back in the living room I found my Norton's *Star Atlas*, threw it on to the mantelpiece out of reach, stood up as if in an attempt to retrieve it, threw myself against the brass fender, crawled to the telephone and rang the Sanatorium to say that I had had a fall at home. Then I lay back and waited for them to come and get me.

My principal fear was that the blow on the head would have made me forget the contents of the maths paper.

3

Xavier was making considerably more fuss about his broken arm than I was about mine. We were both in the Sanatorium waiting for the results of our X-rays when Raafi came to see me. As ever, he took the librarian's presence in his stride, giving him a cursory nod as he passed; he was on the next bed to mine.

'Xavier . . .'

'Try "sir", Raafi,' said Xavier.

'Try Amir-Ansari-Cheybani, sir.'

The librarian scowled and winced. Marcel had switched to leg spin and taken seven wickets, and he'd missed it.

Through his spies Raafi knew what had happened to me and had guessed some degree of subterfuge had been involved. I could tell he was dying to know if I had been successful and that to have the discussion with Xavier in the next bed was giving him an unexpected but delicious boost of adrenalin. But to his eternal credit my well-being evidently came first. He looked at the plaster cast on my arm. I envied the girl who won that compassionate glance, for it was true gentleness.

Then I whispered, 'There's only one extended question on the quadratic function. The rest is complex numbers.'

He looked up at me.

'Dawson. Ah, *Dawson!*'

And that was it. I was a surname. I had been promoted from the ranks of the merely Christian-named to that great cast list of surnames from the centuries that peopled Raafi's universe, adding epic grandeur to the simplest of references. Homer, Shelley, Sinatra, Borg . . . You were classicised by Raafi; your every deed, your every thought bore your eternal name, bore the signature of your spirit. All you needed to get on the score sheet was a surname. Then your place in the team was unquestioned, play you well or play you badly. Never was the world so equal as in the mind of the school's most unequal boy. In that sense, for all his exoticism, Raafi was a great Englishman. For he appropriated the English spirit because it suited him to, rather than taking it as his arrogant destiny. And this was becoming. It was a language, like any other, to be translated and redefined. He didn't have the inarticulacy of patriotism.

'Man,' he said, under his breath, 'only one quadratics. With algebraic solutions, of course?'

'No. Graphical.'

'*Graphical?*'

He shook his head and sighed.

'It's sad,' he said, genuinely cast down. 'They had the opportunity for an interesting double bluff there, but they're playing to everybody's strength. It'll raise the benchmark. Tell me more.'

'The connection between Polar and Cartesian coordinates.'

'The Polar versus Cartesian gambit. Interesting. You have my interest.'

'Multiple angles.'

'Superposition of waves?'

'Some.'

'Compulsory?'

'One of three.'

'Dawson. Dawson. Great man.'

'Plotting points on an Argand diagram.'

Raafi smiled, as if he were remembering an ancient betrayal; an old, difficult wound, only just healed.

'Sketching an Archimedean spiral.'

'Enough,' he said. 'Let's leave something to the inspiration of the moment.'

Raafi got up and went over to the nurse and said something to her. She smiled and nodded. He conferred on her a moment of exquisite conspiracy and she walked away, happy, probably, for the rest of the day. He came back to me.

'Dawson, I need to smoke and we need to talk. I have secured your temporary release.'

We passed Xavier on our way out.

'Sir,' said Raafi, 'can we get you anything? A book, perhaps?'

Raafi himself pushed me through the town and up towards the Common and safety. Ensconced there, as if it were his tent and he was suing for peace on Persia's terms, as the cigarette smoke wound its way reluctantly to the open sky, as though sorry to leave our thieves' hideaway, and as the dying sun figured the hours on the whitewashed walls of the old Observatory, we surveyed the territory we had won.

'Dawson,' he said, 'Smith will oblige.'

'No, no.'

'The sheer improbability of my suggestion was to her the height of suggestiveness: it won her heart. She has seen your sensitive face, she has been moved by the tragedy of your situation, and feels the reflected glory of the great service you have done both me and my family. She will see you here, tomorrow night at ten. You must show her some stars and planets, too. She is an inquisitive girl, Smith.'

'What do I do with Phil?'

'We have business in the woods. Fungi.'

'OK.'

'Play her Mozart. But no poetry.'

'Sure.'

'One last thing,' he said, taking a last, deep draught of his cigarette and looking up at the darkening sky. 'Did we, Dawson – and I want the truth – did we really go to the moon?'

It all happened as Raafi said it would. He came early and took Phil away with him, armed with plastic bags to hunt for magic mushrooms, and fifteen minutes later Trixy came. She brought me presents – one from Raafi, a CD of the Mozart Horn Concertos on period instruments; she'd ordered it especially from Woolworth's and stolen the cover the day it had arrived – and one from herself, a bag of cough candy. I was really touched. We got on like a house on fire. I played her the old Mozart and didn't show her any of my poetry. She signed my plaster cast, adding her name to those of my parents, Phil, Amir-Ansari-Cheybani and Xavier. Xavier couldn't actually write his name because of *his* broken arm so he'd just stamped it with PLEASE RETURN TO THE LIBRARY. He wasn't so bad.

And in the end there I was, in my wheelchair, looking up at the open rectangle of sky, this time glowing with the fire of a thousand distant suns, all shifting and spinning to the laws of mathematics, of quadratic equations and Cartesian coordinates. And for one moment of my youth, for one moment of geocentric indulgence, I threw all that knowledge to the winds, and felt the heavens turn around me, felt myself the axis, felt this earth the one authentic centre, the rest mere satellites to me, my wheelchair, and the pretty, multicoloured head of Trixy.

The Chariot Race

1

Ben was nearly sixty-one, and had worked for the same engineering company for over thirty years. He often thought to himself that he was probably one of the last of that generation who could be said to have had a job for life. He thought it when he played squash with young John, who was barely thirty and had had several jobs, had worked abroad and would doubtless soon move on, leaving Ben to find another squash partner. Ben thought this was sad. Not least because John was not a bad squash player and took it seriously in the right way, and there were few such young men to be found. It was something of a reversal of expectations, therefore, when Ben was gently but forcibly pushed into early retirement.

It all happened in the New Year. A European competitor had shown an interest in the company, an aggressive takeover had been mounted, and just as everybody returned from the Christmas break the offices were suddenly full of healthy-looking European men and attractive but unapproachable European women all speaking English too well, with that accent that is the accent of the language school rather than a broad education. Very soon it was clear that there was no place for Ben in the ambitious future being planned for the company. To their credit, his redundancy was effected immaculately. He was given a handsome pay-off and, more importantly, a long explanation of why it was to the advantage of everybody that he should go. Ben had admired the process of the takeover – admired its efficiency and speed; now he watched his own dismissal with a not dissimilar appreciation. He felt as though he were the trial patient for a new drug; he would watch the effect it had both on him and on the company with a valiant attempt at objectivity. He knew, in spite of his being the last of the job-for-life generation, that he was not to take the loss of his occupation personally. His youthfulness depended on it. He let John know, both on and off the squash court, that he was not to be pitied. He let his colleagues know that he wished the company well.

When he came home from work for the last time he was a little flushed, both from the wine that had been circulated in his honour, and from the praise that had been spoken by those of his colleagues who chose to speak. Ben had been pleased by what had been said, but as he had stood there listening he had been painfully aware – and a little surprised – how deeply he needed it to be said. Had it fallen short of what he himself knew to be his due he was aware he might have slipped into something like bitterness. As it was, people said enough; just enough. The only thing that had slightly spoilt his enjoyment of it had been the fact that he had had to stand. Everybody had stood, and Ben hated to stand. He never knew what to do with his hands. He was not naturally self-contained so far as his body was concerned; he was angular and awkward and believed his arms and hands made him still more so. Only on the squash court, only when his honour or physical ability was under direct scrutiny did he forget this feeling and act without thinking; then he was fast and cunning. But standing and listening to praise which might prove unsatisfactory made him uncomfortable.

His wife, Elizabeth, stood in the alcove of their kitchen, waiting to welcome her husband. She knew in one way or another he would have had a difficult time of it. She knew that he would be home earlier than his usual time because they would have stopped at lunchtime to say goodbye to him. This early arrival home was an invasion of what had been, for all their married life, her time of day; her territory. Now that time – the coffee in the morning and the tea in the afternoon, the unfussy hours spent in their unfussy house – would no longer be hers alone. So this last day was a crisis for her, too; but a crisis which, for the time being, must go unexamined.

She listened very carefully to everything that he told her, smoothing her skirt.

'And, naturally, people spoke.'

'Did they?' she said.

'Of course. There were speeches.'

'Speeches? Goodness.'

Ben's arm twitched and threatened to spill the cup of tea his wife had handed him, and then he said, with a laugh that sounded a little like someone crying, 'Really, Elizabeth,' he said, 'why shouldn't there be speeches? Tell me why there wouldn't be speeches.'

She knew what to do.

'I don't know what I was thinking of,' she said. 'Of course there would be speeches. I expect John spoke.'

'Oh yes.'

'And I have no doubt he was the nicest.'

'What did I expect? A word or two. But John took the bull

by the horns. John spoke for twelve minutes. Happened to see the clock. I was proud of him.'

'I expect he was proud of you.'

'John ...' Ben steadied himself, as if recalling the experience had made him momentarily seasick. 'He spoke of squash. He nearly ... *nearly* went too far.'

'Eat your cake, Ben,' she said softly. 'I baked it to celebrate.'

'I *am* eating it.' And to illustrate the fact he took the untouched triangle of sponge and ate, mechanically.

'Nearly went too far. I didn't mind. Who was I to mind?'

His mouth was full, and he stopped, to steady himself.

'Did he?' said Elizabeth, helping him out, punctuating his eating and speaking for him.

'Nearly went too far,' he said again when he'd swallowed his cake.

Ben looked out of the window. He seemed to be slowing down, like a machine running on dry. His wife watched him, the tiny lines around her eyes tightened slightly with a gentle, worried smile; she might have been staring at a long-loved hieroglyph, still mysterious to her, no nearer to being understood for being loved. It was not the person himself she had never grasped, it was his manner, his energy, his picking up and running with ideas and sudden enthusiasms. It was a manner with the world that seemed unconnected with the man within, and it made her doubt sometimes that she truly knew her husband. Was it possible to know the content but not the form? Perhaps it was only that husband and wife were different. She was considered and patient; he bruised himself with his own harried energy.

Ben and Elizabeth had no children. In this, too, they differed in outlook. Ben had taken on young John in unashamed surrogacy. More than thirty years his junior, a well-meaning, uncomplicated family man, from the moment John joined the company Ben had very obviously and energetically championed him. His protégé was well regarded, and with the arrival of the European consortium, his career looked set to take off. This, Ben watched with something of a father's pride. Whatever may have been the conversation amongst the incoming executives over the boardroom table as to the relative merits of Ben and John, Ben felt that he could leave the company knowing he had left an inheritance of advice and good business sense to the younger man. Of course on the squash court none of that mattered. There they were fierce rivals, and the fact that Ben was so much the senior gave savour to their friendship. They were also fond of John's wife, Debbie, and their toddler, Tom. Debbie was expecting another baby in the spring.

'He only goes too far with you,' said Elizabeth, 'because he is so fond of you.'

She paused, and glanced at him again, and said rather fearfully, 'You won't stop playing squash now you're retired, will you?'

'What? Of course not. Playing Wednesday.'

Elizabeth smiled reassuringly.

He went on: 'You think I'll be lost without an occupation. I shan't. John will keep me up to date.'

'Perhaps we won't see so much of John and Debbie, now,' said Elizabeth. She was always slightly fearful that her husband's friendship with John was one-sided and that the younger man simply liked to play squash. She had a fear of Ben being humoured.

'He'll need an objective eye. He said as much this afternoon. Someone to put things into perspective.'

'As long as we don't interfere.'

'What? Interfere? As long as "we" . . . you mean me. Oh come now, Liz. Now come. Don't say that.'

'He likes you too much to tell you to mind your own business.'

'Mind my own ... What is this, Liz? What? Why would he want to do that?'

'He might,' she dared, not looking at her husband's face.

She felt her touch had failed her.

'John is a grown-up, mature, independent businessman and a great friend, who values my advice. Values it, I say. Spent twelve minutes this afternoon telling anyone who cared to listen how much he values it. I don't know why you'd want to undermine our friendship. I don't, Liz. I really don't.'

'All right, Ben,' she said, very softly.

It was critically important to Elizabeth that her husband not be disappointed. She would watch over him, over his enthusiasms, his refusal to age or to concede to younger men simply because they were young. She encouraged his appropriation of causes and of young people like John and Debbie. But all the while she was suspicious of herself; she feared that she might be contributing to some sort of ultimate downfall, some coming up against a hard fact of life that Ben was due, and to which she, albeit passively, was party. She knew, without vanity, that he was not disappointed with her. But that was not because of any remarkable quality in herself, but because he never measured her against himself. She was not the world, she was on his side of the fence. But whenever he looked over, to the other side, at the world, at the things that were very much *not* him, she felt his outrage herself, as if it were a physical hurt. Elizabeth was honest. She admitted to herself that her husband was trying, sometimes. He had a surfeit of energy, and she also knew that having children would in some measure have used up the surplus. It would have quieted him, dulled him, even; it would have made him easier to live with. He was popular, both at work and amongst their friends, but she feared not so popular as he would have liked. In spite of her fears of the one-sided nature of his and John's friendship, she guessed that John liked him, and guessed right. But Ben's fatherly attentions had no natural restraint to them. And John, being a thoroughly decent fellow, could never have told Ben to bugger off, as he would have done a real father. In this regard, whatever relief and gladness accompanies the achieving of a satisfying surrogate relationship, the danger of such a relationship is in its very success – for surrogate fatherhood is unalloyed by the dullness of day-to-day routine; it is fatherhood in essence, and if it disappoints it disappoints perhaps more potently than the real thing. John guessed this, and to his credit handled the older man with care, occasionally at no little cost to himself. His only recourse after one too many words of wisdom from Ben was to the squash court, and an unusually hard game. Ben would still win, applaud John's never-say-die spirit, and the latter would be left to bite his lip, and complain to his pretty wife of the old man's 'priceless' stubbornness.

Elizabeth's disappointment at having had no children was very different to her husband's. It was silent; it had no appetite for substitutes or surrogates. These, she felt, would have been tantamount to tinkering with her feelings; active unhappiness – the sort to look around for a remedy – would have spoilt the true nature of her disappointment, as if within it there were the germ, the kernel of what she might have had, which, once disturbed and open to comparison with what she did have, might have made her bitter. And she would not indulge in that. So when Ben encouraged her to take an active interest in Debbie, to go shopping for clothes or meet for coffee, she went quiet. She would cook Sunday lunch with her, smile conspiratorially with her as

Ben and John argued over politics or sport; but she held off from any contact with the young woman's inner life. She would not cross that invisible line between friend and parent, nor, as Ben did, accept one as a clever alias for the other.

One evening, a few weeks after Ben's arrival home from his leaving party – it was April, now – he returned home from the voluntary work he had since taken on and found Elizabeth standing by the open window of their living room, staring out at the garden, and the spring evening. It had become her custom on these evenings to go to bed early with her book, but this evening, though she was in her dressing gown, it greatly surprised Ben to see her up; surprised and alarmed him, he could not have said why. He had been out delivering pensioners to Rotary meetings and bridge drives; his sense of usefulness was high, and the sight of Elizabeth breaking their new routine with what looked like worship of the spring evening almost made him angry. Nor did she turn around when he came into the room but paused – he felt provocatively – in a manner designed, it seemed to him, to accentuate the fact that she knew it was him, and that she needn't turn round to say hello to an arrival so wholly predictable.

'Still up?' he said. 'I've deposited all my folks to their respective homes. Don't *think* I got any mixed up.'

Ben had taken up this new, charitable project with great energy. Despite the fact that many of those he was helping were barely older than himself, he regarded them as a different species; they contributed to this by deferring to his enthusiasm, by calling him 'young Ben' and being led by him. He brought business organisation to what had previously been an informal self-help group.

'It's spring,' he said, trying to anticipate and disarm her druidical pose in front of the apple blossom by the window. 'Getting warmer. Soon it will be summer. Wimbledon, soon, Liz, too.'

'I want to go away,' she said. 'I want to go away, Ben.'

'What's this, now?' he said, taking off his coat and not looking at her. 'What's this? You can't go making huge announcements like that out of the blue. Not announcements that don't mean anything. You can't. What do you mean by it?'

'By the big announcement?' she said, frowning very slightly. 'What?'

'What do I mean by announcing something?'

'No. What do you mean by suddenly . . .'

'By breaking it suddenly?'

'Yes,' said Ben. 'What does it all mean?'

He folded up his coat, automatically, as if he were about to hand it in to a cloakroom. Then he stood there, awkwardly, just as he had stood when they had made speeches about him and he hadn't known what to do with his hands.

'Do you mean America?' he said.

For a long time, many years before, Elizabeth and Ben had talked about driving across America. Neither could ever remember whose idea it had been first. Those to whom they confided their plan always commented, in private, that they couldn't imagine either of them first thinking of it. Even Ben and Elizabeth humoured each other, as if it were the other's idea, and then each found themselves secretly excited by what they had suggested. So it took root, this allowed, shared fantasy; and it grew. Like a constant work-in-progress, new details were added and old plans amended. In times of high optimism it was adorned with luxurious additions to the itinerary; in times of hardship

– when the house roof leaked, for example, and fixing it cost twice the builder's estimate – the expedition grew more modest. One year they would travel in an open-top Cadillac, the next it would be a station wagon or mobile home. There were itineraries that took in the Grand Canyon and others that went via Niagara Falls. All the details of their trip, how they ate, slept and drove, everything was negotiable, and they filled the darkness above them, as they lay side by side in their bed, late at night, with the promise of the trip. All this had taken place half a dozen years ago and had lasted a couple of years. In the end, all of a sudden, it had stopped. It was never mentioned again. And just as neither of them could remember who first had suggested it, so neither could have said who had spoken of it last, or why it was never alluded to again. But when Elizabeth had said she wanted to go away, Ben knew as surely as he knew anything that she meant America. They might have spoken of it only yesterday, so freshly did the word 'America' come to him. And when Elizabeth nodded almost imperceptibly, closed the window and went up to bed, leaving Ben to hang up his coat and follow – when they lay together, once again, in the darkness and the idea that had ruled their leisure time years before once again filled the darkness above them – when they lay in silence, they did so in complete knowledge of what each was thinking, and of what they would now set about to do.

Over lunch the following Sunday, John and Debbie were extremely supportive of the idea. And not only because it gave John an opportunity to talk about something other than the state of the company since Ben had left – the latter had rather hounded the young man with questions in recent weeks. Now it was John's turn to be enthusiastic and full of advice. He himself had spent his gap year in California and Debbie had cousins in Canada. As well as warnings and recommendations they promised a guidebook and the contents of an old whisky bottle full of American dollars and small change left over from ancient trips. Ben looked at his wife after he had thanked them and pointed out that such change would be invaluable for the purposes of tipping and paying for taxis when they first arrived. So it was, barely a month later, that early one morning John picked the couple up, leaving his own wife heavily pregnant at home, and drove them, in his new car (the European consortium having valued his services highly enough to warrant a substantial pay rise) and drove them to the airport. Ben and Elizabeth were dispatched, wallets and purses decently organised with dollars and pounds of all denominations, driving licences and insurance documents that covered them for every conceivable Act of God, John's borrowed guidebooks and even one of Ben's, ten years out of date, survivor of their original plans so long before. Finally, like errant teenagers they were provided by John and Debbie with a list of emergency telephone numbers. By the same token, John was under strict instructions to inform them, if possible, of the arrival of any baby.

2

As the sun was setting on the evening of the third day, still forty miles short of their intended destination, Ben turned the wheel of their hired station wagon, and they turned off the highway. Up till now their itinerary had been both immaculately planned and immaculately adhered to. This was their first deviation. Ahead of them lay a massive, archetypal Western silhouette cut out of the sky, of pillars of rock, of shapes as abstract as clouds and as easily conjured with; this extension of darkness might have been a distant shore, this pink or orange light a flooded estuary; this they turned from, and took instruction from a neon sign that promised that two miles to the left down a winding dirt track they would find Dan's Diner.

Ben and Elizabeth had been married for nearly forty years, and though the definition of such things is necessarily subjective, had never had a serious argument. There had been silences, there had been irritations, there had been mock disputes which bordered on the real and which, in their ersatz seriousness, had passed for the real thing and done the work of a real row just as well. But always they had held off from a truly threatening seriousness, and, in the absence of children, had not been made to feel that their silences or their forced politeness were ciphers for a more violent subtext. It would have taken a child to decode their true intentions, and this they were spared. So they got on very well. But now, forty miles short of their intended destination, they had an argument.

The first three days had gone very smoothly. So smoothly, in fact, that neither Ben nor Elizabeth had felt that the trip were really happening. Their experiences were so dovetailed to the dream they had concocted together all those years ago that they had taken on an almost posthumous feeling. Nothing remarkable or unplanned had happened; the first two hotels, which John had been so kind as to book for them on the internet, were clean and comfortable, and Ben had been impressed by the level of politeness. Elizabeth watched Ben and hoped that he was pleased with what he saw and Ben watched Elizabeth and hoped the same for her. Nothing novel interposed itself between them; only their being there at all, only Ben having retired, their having left their little childless home for three weeks was marvellous to both of them; but it was an abstract amazement, a thought indeed like that of a coming child, a loved idea, still half fearful until the Word is made Flesh.

Then, as the third day ended, Ben, in what Elizabeth daringly referred to as 'a moment of overconfidence', attempted a short cut through the penultimate town before the one which was their destination for the day and in which their hotel for the night was to be found. They had driven in circles through dim suburbs for over an hour, Ben having refused to retrace their steps. Now it was beginning to get dark.

'I only thought it might be easier,' said Elizabeth, trying, herself, to retrace the twists and turns of their disagreement, 'to go back to where we stayed last night.'

'Do you have *no* sense of how far we have travelled, Elizabeth? I don't understand you. What? Go back? Go back, *now*? At this stage? Do I speak a foreign language? I have explained in detail and at length the short cut I was attempting. I have told you several times how far from our original destination we are. What? Go back? And waste a day? Are you seriously suggesting this is a wasted day? Are you?'

'I'm not saying it's wasted,' she said, quietly.

'Is the holiday a disaster *already*? How dare you? How can you dare? You resented the organisation. You wanted it all done oh so casually. You resented John, now you resent me.'

'John?'

'Yes, John. You would have brought us here and cut us loose. You would have done that. You resented John's assistance in the matter of the internet.'

'Not at all.'

'You were rude not to thank him. I saw you not thank him.'

'I was talking to Debbie.' She paused. 'I don't really understand the internet, Ben.'

'You don't have to understand it to be grateful. You resent my bond with John. Had you made a similar effort with Debbie you too would feel useful.'

'I don't want to feel useful,' she said quietly, looking out of the window. She felt a lump in her throat. She glanced at the silhouette beside her, blocking out the desert sunset behind, of her husband hunched over the wheel, his lean frame peering theatrically at the road markings. He did it instinctively, even though in the big American car, with its generous windscreen, there was no need.

'Well,' he said, trying to maintain the momentum of the argument, but feeling his focus split unhelpfully between arguing and navigating, 'If you want to go home . . .'

'How could I go home?' she said practically.

'Thousands of miles of roads,' he said, 'and they illuminate them in Stygian gloom.'

'You heard that expression in the documentary last night. On the cable.'

'It struck me,' he said. 'Stygian struck me.' They had watched a documentary on bats.

Elizabeth smiled, and because Ben was concentrating on the road and the car had grown too dark for him to see her clearly, she laughed very slightly so that he should know she was smiling. He straightened himself behind the wheel and sighed. She grasped the moment.

'It's got so dark, Ben. Why don't we stop?'

'Stop? What? Where?'

'Before wherever it is we were going tonight.'

'There is *nowhere*. You don't understand the basics, Liz. This is a new country. Between towns there is nothing. Just a void. Desert. When you're not in the town you're in the desert. We have to press on.'

'I don't want to press on,' said Elizabeth, almost inaudibly. He raised his voice, sensing her own voice's submission.

'Well, I *do*. I have the responsibility of driving, and I *can* see,' he said, refuting an accusation she had not made. She looked out of the window; the suburbs were thinning and the desert, people-less and pure, stretched out ahead of them, as her husband had said it would. She looked down at the tin of car sweets by the gear change and wished she could have one, but was afraid of inciting Ben.

'You're frightened,' he said, as if he were a lawyer summing up at the end of a long trial, 'frightened we are going to be stranded – like *Psycho*.'

'Pardon?'

'Like Alfred Hitchcock's film, *Psycho*. Stuck in the middle of nowhere, and *victims*.'

'No,' she said, simply, 'I'm frightened of crashing the car. I'm not frightened of *Psycho*. I don't think I've ever seen it.'

'Everyone has seen *Psycho*!' he almost screamed, his whole body twitching with unnatural emphasis; he put his foot down harder on the accelerator.

'I haven't,' she said. 'Too fast, Ben.'

She herself felt oblivious to what she might say; drunk on her fear of his sudden temper.

'Not even fifty-five. It's all relative. You only think I'm going too fast because I am going *faster* . . .'

He shouted on, inwardly despairing. So novel was this currency

76

of anger to him that he seemed to want to spend all of it at once. He was angry with the car, angry at the darkness, angry with the childless woman by his side and with her silent, patient support of him, and he was angry with the man he could hear shouting at her, the man who listened to his own voice and marvelled at it. He shouted at her that he wasn't blind, that he wasn't one of the pensioners he himself took to the supermarket *yet*, that the holiday was a disaster and how would they ever tell John and Debbie they had hated it. But when the motel sign beside the road lit up their faces and filled the entire car with its hopeful neon, without a word he pulled off the highway and they bumped down the rough dirt track.

It seemed to both Ben and Elizabeth that it was further than two miles to Dan's Diner; it may have been because they had no choice but to drive very slowly, there being no light now save the car headlights and the very last of the sunset. But the establishment itself, when they found it, was substantial. True, it had none of the hopeful, modern clarity that the neon sign had had, and no trees or contours to the land around it gave any relief from the desert. But it was large and extensive – ambitious, even. Mostly of wooden construction, the motel spread, one storey high, in wings, away from the small, neat body of the diner. Evidently it had been extended in times of prosperity and optimism and, when times had got harder, other wings had been closed down; it resembled a tree, some of whose dead branches remained intact, their hollow limbs, at least in winter, indistinguishable from the living.

Ben switched off the engine with a sigh, and each sat for a moment and tried to take in the unaccustomed silence. They were too far from the main highway now to hear passing traffic. As they climbed out, their feet made neat scraping noises on the grit. There was no sound of a jukebox or of drinking coming from inside. Ben was relieved, for Elizabeth's sake. There was a veranda, well swept, a little old fashioned; two crates of beer bottles, one full and one empty, were propped against the steps that led up to the door.

'You'll be thinking it's threatening,' said Ben. But it was he who hesitated and she, who, unusually active and forthright, went forwards and up the steps to the swing door and peered inside. She seemed to have shaken off the lethargy of the planned holiday; this unscheduled stop, not accounted for in John and Ben's itinerary, had roused her, awoken in her a real curiosity.

'Come back, Elizabeth,' said Ben unconvincingly.

But she took no heed. Ben could tell, with a tiny shudder of annoyance, that she was about her business – her true business. As someone who is following some creative vocation – the thing they know, whether to play the violin or polish their car – who knows, whatever their timidity in every other walk of life, that they do this one thing well, perhaps uniquely so – so Elizabeth, her small, slightly greying head and un-made-up face barely lined with any unhappiness, peered and tapped at the doors and windows for signs of life within; she moved with a gentle, womanly confidence that the spirit of this novel building would awaken and spring to do her bidding. Ben stood, envious and fearful, his feet twisting in the dust, making the rasping sound for the sake of it. He felt his accustomed feeling of uncomfortableness standing and wished he could simply get back in the car just to sit down. Instead he stood with his hands on his hips and looked from his wife to the sky, as if for her to behave as she did beneath such a sky were insane, as one looks up when someone goes out to garden in the rain. But all he saw up there were the first stars struggling through. When he looked back down again, Elizabeth had gone.

He found his wife inside, in conversation with a woman in a pink dress. The woman was in her late thirties, was made up as if to go to a party, and was smiling with Elizabeth as if they had known one another since school. Ben felt instantly excluded.

'They have a room,' said Elizabeth quietly, almost to herself, just loud enough for Ben to hear. 'A nice room, this kind lady says. For sixty dollars.'

'Reasonable,' said Ben, at the same time leaning his whole upper body towards the lady in the pink dress in token of a bow. 'Have to have a look at it.'

'We'll take it,' said his wife.

In Ben's mind the two women winked at each other.

'Liz . . .'

'Where else are we going to stay?' said Liz, mostly to the lady.

'That's ra-aght,' drawled the other, 'Nearest motel going west is near fo-orty miles.'

'Yes,' said Ben. 'And we have a reservation there.'

He saw his wife attempt to telegraph an apology to the lady and shame gripped him, followed quickly by fury. He felt the full force of an executive, feminine decision go over his head, and for the first time in his married life – or so he felt – he knew what it was to be a cipher, male and superfluous. The shadow of something almost suicidal hung over his observation of his wife talking to this blowsy receptionist. It was unlike Elizabeth to seek solace or solidarity with any third party, let alone a stranger. She had no circle of like-minded women, no confidante, and it suddenly occurred to Ben, with a dawning of such force that he might have discovered the presence of a lover rather than the absence of a friend, that this might, over the years, have involved something of a sacrifice on Elizabeth's part. She had kept away from friends so that she could look after her husband better. The thought of this martyrdom began to eat through him, as if it were hollowing him out. He had been deceived. What he had assumed was a dovetailing of desires – a distrust of unnecessary socialising – had in fact been his wife's great, cruel sacrifice on his behalf.

The pink lady led them along one of the corridors to their room. Ben followed, his hands locked behind his back, as if he were being taken somewhere to be punished. She let them in, put their case on the bed and Elizabeth gave the woman a five-dollar note. Ben waited, tall and mute, for the lady to leave. As soon as they were alone Elizabeth went into the bathroom. Ben could hear her washing her face. He began to speak, unsure even whether she could hear him over the running water.

'Always check the room. Always. As a matter of course and a matter of safety. It is quite clear that they are desperate for trade here and will tell the unsuspecting traveller anything to get their fee. And I couldn't help but see that was a five-dollar bill you gave her. She, a receptionist. I have seen no porters, perhaps there are none. But whether or not there are, I would be fearful of offending such a lady as that by mixing up her duties.'

Elizabeth came through from the bathroom with a wet face, undid their case, took out a towel and dried herself.

'I'm going for a walk,' she said.

'What? A walk? Where?'

'Perhaps to the car. I left my book there.'

'I'll get it for you.'

'No. I want to go, Ben. I noticed there was a bar area behind the reception desk.'

'A bar area?'

'Yes,' she said gently, as if she were kindly and patiently coaxing a recalcitrant child. 'You could get yourself a drink.'

'What? You know I never drink in bars.'

'I don't think it was really a bar.'

'A *bar area*, Liz, is a bar.' She looked at him and smiled, non-plussed by her own grammar, and the sight of her like that gave him, for a moment, a fugitive memory of her as a young woman.

Then he said, 'I've drunk in too many bars.' He said it like a gangster. They both knew it wasn't true and he did not know why he said it.

'Go on,' she said, picking up her cardigan from the case and folding it over her arm.

'You can't go walking alone. Not here.'

'Why not?'

He paused.

'Coyotes,' he said, and she turned to the door to hide her smile.

'Just five minutes' air. To clear my head,' she said. Then she said, as much to herself as her husband, 'It's all right, Ben.'

And she went.

Ben stood, still awkward, still wishing he could sit down, though there was no one else in the room. He could see her hand-towel on the bed, stained with water from her face and hands. And beside it was their suitcase, open on the bed, as if it had been rifled by thieves.

3

The bar area was indeed behind the reception desk. It was not only impressive enough to count as a bar, but seemed disproportionately large for the rest of the motel. A vast open space, now filled with chairs, could once have taken half a dozen pool tables or a dance floor. The ceiling was low and the walls were painted yellow and hung with old black and white photographs; there were two lengthy newspaper articles cut out and framed, too faded now to be deciphered. A door gave way from the reception desk straight in to the bar, which was well stocked and tidily kept. The room was quite empty.

Ben stood, like a swimmer unsure of the depth of the water, on the edge of the room, and evaluated the scene. He was relieved there were no staring locals, but even the scale of its emptiness was in itself intimidating. As he had passed through the lobby he had seen, through the screen on the door, the silhouette of Elizabeth standing, looking out at the sandy car park. She might have been staring at the sea, so still and pensive she was. Something of that stillness made it impossible for him to go to her, and he had turned away and gone to the bar door aggressively, like a gunfighter. He went in.

The woman in pink soon appeared as barmaid. She smiled at him more broadly than when he had been with his wife and Ben felt she was now on his side.

'Perhaps you'd care to have a drink?' she said, slightly formally, as if she were reading from a bad script. Ben guessed that his formality made her attempt the same and he said, as casually as he could, 'Sure.'

He looked at the woman and reflected on the fact that after this evening he would never see her again. It made her suddenly seem more attractive. Her make-up and bright dress seemed purposefully designed to fulfil the job of a moment's attraction. Her femininity required no longevity.

'I mean, "quite",' he said.

He looked around at the room again. It didn't seem so vast now. And he was glad it was empty. He suddenly wanted it all to happen. To drink alone in an American bar, to be as alone as it was possible to be in the world. He wanted it terribly badly, and he wanted it to happen to him without having to do anything about it. It was delicious, this sense of foreignness. Then he realised he would have to choose something. Panic gripped him. The pink lady rescued him.

'Sir . . . would you care for a beer?'

'How terribly kind.'

She poured him the beer and placed it on a napkin in front of him. As she did so a door at the back of the long room opened. In the very act of serving Ben, and without interrupting herself, she looked quickly at the door. Ben's heart sank, as if he had walked into a trap deliberately laid for him. He, too, looked round, and saw a tall, angular man come in. He was in his forties, had a long, pale face, closely shaved, and black hair. He wore black Levis and a clean blue shirt. He seemed somehow very well dressed in a casual sort of way, and exuded quiet authority. He took a table some distance from the bar. The pink lady nodded respectfully at him.

'Candy,' he said, in acknowledgement. Then nodded very slightly to Ben.

Without being asked, Candy very carefully poured another beer and took it to the man. Ben took a sip of his own beer and waited for the stranger to do the same, but he only took out a newspaper and started to read the sports pages. Candy took up a position at the other end of the bar, and Ben felt caught in a triangle. Then the man, as if he had had a sudden thought, looked up from his paper and said, 'Candy . . . Marshall's coming.'

Candy wiped the bar, as if she was unimpressed.

'You seen him?' she said.

'He was buying water.'

Candy smiled at Ben, as if to apologise for the private, parochial nature of the conversation. Then she glanced at his half-empty beer glass to show that she was taking care of him.

But Ben was thinking of Elizabeth. Had they always been separate? Was this trip an acknowledgement of that? And yet once upon a time they planned it together. For years it had been their great, shared fantasy. But they hadn't done it then. They had waited, and when he had come home that evening he had known that she was going to say America. Known it before she had said it, it seemed to him, now. And they had lain in bed that night and each conjured the adventure anew. And this was what the darkness had bequeathed them: the argument in the car, the neon sign, the separateness in the bedroom, her on the veranda and his beer in the bar. He thought of their life together. Ben had always considered his wife a passive person; sometimes it frustrated him. Where he would make something happen because he wanted it, he felt she would wait. She was waiting out there now, he said to himself. Yet how relaxed she had seemed, in silhouette; how outrageous to be so calm in a stranger's place, in a motel; to appropriate a veranda like that, as if it were one's own.

He took another sip of beer and thought how clean a taste it had, this American beer; how impersonal.

'Which way was he headed?' said Candy.

But the tall man at the table didn't answer, and Candy didn't seem surprised; she carried on wiping and he carried on reading. Then, neatly and on time, at the back of the room the door opened again, and a small, slight man, at least seventy, with a round face, closely cropped grey hair and white stubble like snow that has only just settled, entered. Everything about him was neat

– he seemed cut to an economy size, with no extraneous detail, lest in his constant movement something snagged. For even in his pause, as he looked at the assembled company in the bar, there was readiness to move off again. His small, bright eyes might have been those of a seaman, used to scaling rigging, for they scanned both up and down, side to side, with amused alertness. His clothes were old but clean, and he wore them well, but they looked like a costume rather than his clothes; he seemed unproprietorial of them.

He came up to the bar.

'Candy, girl,' he said, and for some reason he laughed, 'I'm back.'

'Yep,' she said with a display of theatrical tolerance.

'Don't be that way. I'm back.'

'So you say.'

Marshall – for Ben was in no doubt that it was he – giggled and looked at the bottles of beer and at the beer taps and back to Candy, as if he and she had stumbled on treasure and the cache of booze were theirs to share. But Ben realised this was a form of appeal.

'Ryan missed you,' said the man at the table, before the effectiveness of the appeal could be ascertained. Marshall only creased up his eyes a little and stared at Candy. She stared back.

'Ryan missed you,' said the man again, still not looking up from his paper. It was melodramatic. Ben fancied Marshall was embarrassed.

'How so?' said Marshall, glancing at Ben like an errant schoolboy.

'The job at Aaron's Forge.'

'The Forge?'

'Ryan said he offered you the work and you never showed.'

'I told him I was going away.'

'That's not what he says.'

Marshall ducked his head slightly, each time the stranger spoke, as if the words were a troublesome swarm of bees; he laughed and ducked with mock terror at them when it seemed they came too close to danger. Then, as if only now becoming fully aware of Ben's presence he turned to him, and with one hand on the bar, like a ballet dancer doing exercises, he gave Ben what could only be described as a full bow. In contrast to the stranger with the sports pages it seemed an appeal to fading manners, a self-conscious theatricality that was curiously unembarrassing. Candy placed a beer for him by the hand that rested on the bar, but Marshall ignored it, apparently finding Ben more interesting. He took the stool beside him; or rather climbed on to it and into position; as if he had scaled the crow's nest. Every movement had a smooth, slightly exaggerated athleticism. Once up there, with impulsive sociability he turned to Ben with as sudden and direct a movement as if he were pulling a gun on him. But he smiled beautifully, showing his still youthful, even, white teeth and his face creased effortlessly with weathered familiarity.

'Sir,' he said, solemnly. 'An Englishman?'

Ben, without getting up, instinctively tried to return the little man's greeting and bowed his head till it nearly touched the bar. Marshall laughed, as if the conversation already delighted him, as if he had had an inkling that it would, and looked to Candy as much as to say, 'You see, this man is a delight!'

'A forgiving people,' said Marshall. 'Your Englishman exudes forgiveness as a horse exudes fine breeding.'

Ben fancied this was meant for the man at the table, who took such an interest in Ryan's affairs. Marshall looked at Candy as if seeking to be forgiven for an outrageous simile. Candy only stared at the man at the table.

'That's generous,' said Ben. He had a secret love of Americans' easy manners; they made his heart beat faster with a kind of intoxicated gratitude. Sometimes they made his throat contract, as if he might cry. They seemed suggestive of what Ben had always harboured as his notion of America – that everything was in abundance there, and that though it was fashionable to find this contemptible, or politically incorrect, it was monstrous ingratitude and immaturity to shun it; that only the old, only Ben knew how important it was for there to be things in abundance in the world. That the rest could wait till later. Now, after four days of the trip, Ben had realised something else – that he did not need to reciprocate these easy manners for them to be sustained. Quite the contrary, in fact. The more he kept his natural reticence, the more these generous people pursued him. It was bliss to him. Of course he would have enjoyed Marshall's company more if the stranger and Candy had not been there, but he had only to remind himself that he would never see these people again and all was well.

'You,' said Ben, 'are not Dan?'

Marshall looked up at Ben's face and stared at the Englishman, completely nonplussed. There was a pause in which Marshall looked as though he had been seriously outwitted for the first time in his life. He seemed actually amazed, as though the question were of a subtlety or subterfuge the likes of which he had never encountered; that he had heard of such conundrums being set well-meaning people but never been faced with one till now. Whatever her attitude to him may have been, Candy it seemed could not bear to see the man in such distress, so she turned to Ben.

'No, sir. Dan's Diner is only a name. I believe Dan's dead long since.'

The little man turned to her.

'Candy,' he said. 'This place called Dan's Diner?'

'Yes, Marshall,' she said. 'You not seen the neon sign on the highway?'

Marshall ran his hand over his cropped hair and whistled softly to himself.

'Sir,' he said, 'I defer to your observation. I came across the fields out yonder. I am the proprietor of the garage over there, and I walk here when I come. Had that garage over twenty years. Never saw no sign on the highway.' He whistled again and sighed; it seemed a great relief to him that the amazing question he had been unwittingly posed by Ben was not meant to make a fool of him. 'Yes, sir,' he went on, 'I have the garage. Marshall's.'

'Perhaps,' said Ben, 'you would permit me to buy you a beer.'

They ordered two and drank in silence.

'I can say that having spoken to you,' said Marshall, his face once again divided up into its constituent parts by a smile, 'I now know where I am.'

'It's a pleasure,' said Ben, assuming he was being complimented.

'Maybe Aaron was presumin' you'd come along,' said the man at the table. 'Maybe the work's still to do there.'

Marshall smiled stoically, as if it were now inevitable that one of the bees would sting; he seemed to be bracing himself.

'Maybe he's there right now. At the Forge.'

Marshall looked at Ben and smiled. Ben fancied, with a thrill of exclusivity, that he was being appealed to to come to the little man's rescue.

'Have you always mended motor cars for a living, sir?' he said, unconsciously slipping into the other man's slightly theatrical manner.

'No, sir,' said Marshall, an auspicious breeze taking the bees off elsewhere. 'No, sir,' he said again, as bright as a button, arranging his half-full glass of beer on the side of the bar with care, as though he might be about to paint it as a still life. 'Once I was an actor. Out in Hollywood, Los Angeles.'

Now it was Ben's turn to feel a crisis of security as far as this fact, this *assertion*, was concerned. His first, self-protective instinct was that he had been humoured by the entire situation, by Candy, Marshall, the whole American set-up, and that he was about to be fleeced; a sort of moral fleecing of a European whose dilettante aspirations had brought him to gawp at America. He feared this revenge, this ridicule; behind his ecstasy at American manners was terror, as perhaps there is terror behind every ecstasy, if only because in ecstasy are we revealed.

'That's extremely interesting,' said Ben, determined not to show his hand, and to play a double game, if game it was. 'What films did you make?'

'Sir,' said Marshall, 'I have embarrassed you by making a claim you have every reason to disbelieve. But the English love the truth, and I will pay you in your own currency.'

He stopped, as if his very theatrical manner were an annoyance to him, as if he struggled for a more plain-speaking persona. It became him, this instinctive modesty, and Ben sensed he had been wrong to doubt him.

'I won't lie,' he went on, 'I won't build up my life to make more of what I am to entertain you or these good people here, who know me and know what I am. I won't do it, I say. I know what I did.'

He ran his hand over his short-cropped hair once again, as though the wind had dislodged it, and stopped. Pride in his once fabulous profession and pride in keeping his own counsel seemed at odds with each other and it appeared uncertain which would prevail. Then he looked up at Ben, as if to say 'I shall be punished for it, you know,' looked back at his glass, adjusted it once more, steadied himself, as if some physical effort were now required of him, and said, 'I drove lead chariot in the chariot race in *Ben Hur*.'

The long room, already silent, could not have been quieter, but to Ben, after he said this, the room seemed like a church. And, though Candy cleared her throat, and the sports pages of the paper flickered a little, the silence, like that in church, after listening to the account of a miracle, seemed to highlight, to make space around the very notion of belief; of credence; of faith.

'Extraordinary,' said Ben.

'Yes, sir,' said Marshall.

'Well,' said Ben.

'Sir.'

'How,' said Ben, feeling a sort of hysterical ache at the thought of something so wholly unlikely: 'How does a man come to do such a thing? If you don't mind me asking?'

'Sir, how could you not ask? And how could I not tell you? It will be my pleasure. Once,' said Marshall, 'I was a young man.'

At this he paused, and again Ben felt a lump in his throat, felt ready to cry and at the same time felt a pleasurable paralysis of all his limbs, a passive ecstasy in the knowledge that all he had to do was stay still and this tale would unfold.

'I had no ties, and I found myself doing any work that came my way. And it always seemed to, especially in that part of the world. Well, I knew cars, and I knew a man who had a garage who occasionally would call on me when he was short on staff or he needed someone to fix a car that had broken down out of town somewhere. It happened one day I was called out to fix the car of a famous man, a Hollywood studio executive of some sort. Now, he had broken down out in the hills. Would I go and get him? He had a European car, and the parts for such cars were hard to come by and you must be a good mechanic who could improvise if you were to fix it. So I went out to fix his European car and it so happened that he had a European lady in the back of his car, as well, who maybe ought not to have been there. Well, sir, I fixed his car, and he seemed very satisfied and perhaps something of my discretion appealed to him. He was a very well-dressed man and had excellent manners and we took to each other. So he asked me if I would be his driver. Not his chauffeur – the studios provided those – but an unofficial driver who would be available for more particular assignments. Perhaps late at night, perhaps trips which I would forget had ever happened. In this unofficial capacity we were equal. I took to him and he took to me. I would drive and he would talk. He liked to talk a lot and he liked my driving. He liked it in a way a man who does not do a thing or does not do it well may appreciate another man who does it very well, or who is accomplished. I was a young man and I had no ties and I drove very well. This was in the nineteen-fifties, you understand. I was only in my twenties. Well, he would tell me all the gossip and the problems they were having with this or that actor and this or that actress. Any one of the stories I heard could have made me a very rich man if I had spoken to the movie papers, but he trusted me. Often I would recognise women I picked up and think I had seen them before. But I would never betray this man who trusted me. Well, one day my friend told me they were making a film. A big, big film, and they had to have men who knew horses. I told him I knew horses. I grew up with horses. He said the stunt men were all good at falling off buildings and being shot, but they were uneasy around horses. Then he said that he knew I could drive a car, but could I drive a chariot? I said if it was something between a car and horse I could drive it. He said it was more like driving a women, and we laughed. He had a lot of women. So he told me where to go, and the following morning I reported to the studio lot and I was met by the technical director and taken out to test these chariots. There were many changes to be made. Alterations to the balance, to the necessary points of safety. At first I was very polite with my suggestions but soon it became clear that no one really knew what they were doing and that it was up to me. That's not pride, only the truth. There were no experts because no one had driven a chariot for thousands of years. So they listened to me and we all learned together how to drive a chariot. I was the fastest. The race is run so fast because that is the pace I set. Yes, sir. Some people have called into question my part in the final race because they do not see me clearly in the finished article. Much had to be cut out of such an ambitious sequence, and besides, the race could not last an hour or the film would have been ruined. But those are my chariots. And that is my pace.'

He smiled as he finished his tale, as if the story had been about someone else. Just as he had looked at Candy and at the liquor behind the bar as though they had just discovered it together, so he looked now at Ben and seemed to marvel at the very fact that he, Marshall, had ever been young. He took a modest sip of beer.

'Did you ever know Charlton Heston?' said Ben in spite of himself.

'I kept myself to myself.'

'Of course.'

Ben looked up at the rest of the room. The man at the table was still reading his paper. Candy was folding a napkin at the other end of the bar and did not catch Ben's eye.

'Sir,' said Ben, 'would you permit me to buy you another beer?'

Marshall bowed his head gravely and gently. Candy, to signify that she had heard this offer, and perhaps to indicate that she had heard all the rest besides, poured two glasses. As she passed Marshall his glass Ben noticed the expression on her face. She looked at the little adventurer with a mixture of fury and pity; but also a kind of fear. Whether it was fear of him or for him, he could not tell. It was as if Marshall might have had a loaded gun and been a danger both to himself and to others, and Candy seemed even-handed as to which she feared most.

The two men drank their beers together, and now Ben was encouraged to speak. In spite of his recent realisation that he needn't talk himself to fully enjoy the charm of American hospitality, he held back in no way. He spoke of his work, of pride in work, of his feelings about retirement. And as he told Marshall all of this, of course he was telling Candy, too, with her napkins, and even the stranger at the table with his sports pages. But he didn't mind. He told them about John, and his pride in the young man, about his favourite films and his views on the depiction of America in them. He even attempted to describe to them life in the English suburbs. It was late when he made his way back to the little chalet-like room where Elizabeth already lay asleep. As he climbed into bed beside her and she turned, instinctively, to make room for him, it occurred to him that he had forgotten her existence that evening for the first time in forty years. Her presence in the bed actually surprised him.

'Did you have a nice time?' she murmured, waking.

'Yes,' he said.

'Oh good.'

'Absolutely extraordinary. I'll tell you about it in the morning. I met the man who rode lead chariot in the race in *Ben Hur*.'

They went to sleep.

4

They sat in the breakfast room that had once been a bedroom in more prosperous days, and Candy served them breakfast. She was dressed in a polka-dot apron and looked altogether more businesslike than the night before. They sat in silence, and were served hot coffee and pancakes. They had slept late and had hardly spoken a word to each other since they had woken. Candy assumed they had had an argument over Ben being so late to bed. In fact they had both slept better than they could remember.

'You're enraged with me,' said Ben.

'What's that?'

'Cross. With me. I was late.'

'Oh no,' she said peacefully.

Ben looked out of the window at the car park and at their station wagon, patiently waiting for them. It had become the constant reference point of their trip, as cars must always do when one is driving vast distances. The argument they had had while he was driving seemed like a dream.

'I swear to you I was delayed with good reason.' He looked at her to be sure she was aware of what he was saying. 'I looked for you, but . . . I couldn't find you.' He didn't know why he lied; he had seen her on the veranda. 'I didn't know where you were. But, Liz . . . I was delayed. Delayed by something remarkable.'

'Yes, Ben,' she said, softly.

But it wasn't enough. He felt weak. In the same way that he

had needed them to say certain things at his leaving party; in the same way that he must cling ignobly to being a 'good chap' and a 'fine squash player', so he needed Elizabeth to listen to what he was about to say just as he himself had listened to Marshall. He needed to be as good a storyteller as Marshall; for her to have the same experience. He smiled a hard smile.

'Of course you are under no obligation to believe me.'

'Of course.' She smiled at him gently. And he was instantly won over; he could not have said why.

'He took *pride*, Liz. That man. He took pride in what he had done. And it didn't matter that it was years ago. And it's so *rare*. So rare. I'll tell you about him. I will. Not now, but . . . He was so modest, too. But a sort of aristocrat. Americans are a great people, and this is a great country, whatever they may say at home. How dare they. And they do it so eloquently. Oh-so-eloquently.'

'It's all right, Ben.'

They ate their pancakes.

'And the food is so nourishing,' he said. His wife smiled and watched him while he ate. He ate fast and impatiently, removing the food as if it were an obstacle, as if he wanted to move on to the next thing. He was pouring maple syrup on to the pancakes. It was a new thing, this sweet maple syrup at breakfast.

'What were you doing out there?'

'Where?'

'Out there. On the veranda. Last night.'

Suddenly he was blind to his previous lie.

'Come on,' he said.

'On the veranda?'

'Yes.'

She paused.

'Thinking.'

The void in his knowledge of her, the separateness that had worked on him when he had seen her behind the screen the night before was like an ache again.

'What about?' he said, his voice a little thicker.

'The fact that we never had children.'

He was about to say something when she put her hand on his knee. He stopped, and put his knife and fork together and looked out of the window. He remembered again how he had known she was going to say America that night months before; and he had known just that moment that she would say about the children; and the ache that had grown out of his imagined separateness seemed to blend effortlessly into the ache of complete knowledge, the one keeping company with the other.

'Ben?' she said.

'Better get on.'

'Yes,' she said. 'I'm glad we came here.'

There was a pause.

She looked at him.

'It's all right, Ben'

'Must phone that boy. John will expect it. Meant to last night, but forgot. Meeting of the board yesterday. Baby on the way. Come on, Elizabeth.'

He got up, and passed her, and draped his hand across her shoulder as he passed; she cradled her coffee in her hands and smiled. A few moments later she heard Ben out in the reception asking Candy directions to the freeway.

As they drove out on to the main road, Ben unaccountably set off on the wrong side of the road. They met no traffic for several hundred yards, till the road turned and cut through a sheer rock-face. There they met a large truck carrying industrial material. In spite of the efforts of the truck driver to avoid them, they hit the truck head on. Ben and Elizabeth were killed instantly. The truck driver, fortunately set up high in his cabin, suffered only minor cuts and bruises.

So mangled was the wreckage, and so difficult to access, that the local police were forced to enlist the assistance of the nearest garage to cut the bodies out. The nearest garage was Marshall's, and he came himself to superintend the cutting and welding, since some of his boys were barely out of school and not used to seeing such a thing. He stood and watched the painstaking business and chatted to whoever came to stand with him. It took some time. As soon as the bodies were out, wholly unrecognisable, the removal of the wreckage began in earnest. Marshall busied himself at once, and he made a pleasant sight, instantly active and agile, moving amongst the wreckage, wholly at work, absorbed by the job in hand.

An Early Start

'You can't trust anyone any more,' said Josh, 'least of all a narrator.'

Having delivered this verdict – which was also, I suppose, a warning – he sat back, and the pub settle which he completely occupied with his massive form creaked under the weight. Josh didn't look like a student of English Literature. He looked like a prop-forward who had got on to the wrong coach after the game.

He wasn't done, either. With his eyes half closed, blithe as a Buddha, he intoned the rest:

'Why? Because the single voice is dead. The omnipotent observer of the novel . . . just *passé*. Shafted. Neither politically acceptable nor desirable. We are no longer watchers. We are left to be curators. Brilliant perhaps, but curators none the less. That's how it is, fucker.'

This last was said as gently as the word would allow.

I'd been at university a week and Josh was my tutorial partner. We'd just had our first, preliminary chat with our tutor. As we'd emerged from the darkness of the stairwell I'd tentatively suggested we have a drink. Josh had looked up at the sky as if I'd suggested croquet and it was about to rain; he obviously didn't want to.

He'd looked down at me, shrugged his shoulders and nodded. He was at least twice my size; as we set off across the courtyard I felt like a jockey leading a shire horse.

We went to the Eagle and sat ourselves in one of the little, old-fashioned booths.

I could think of nothing to say. He'd been frighteningly confident with our tutor. That sort of confidence some people have with policemen; as if they know it's a level playing field and that policemen break speed limits, too. That we're all in it together.

Josh was certainly impressive, sitting there with his straight-glassed pint in his huge fist like a medieval burgomaster. I noticed that he never troubled to frown – except at things that amused him. Then his black brows gathered over his Celtic forehead in hairy conference. On issues about which the rest of us frowned he smoothed his forehead, swore, and passed gentle, absolute judgment. Now his head caught the rainy light that shone through the stained-glass advertisement for Flower's Ales and its halo gave an unexpectedly ecclesiastical tone to his broad-boned profanities. He leaned forward and took a huge swig of beer and his thick throat swelled like a bullfrog's to accommodate it.

'As for the so called *fucking fine arts* – to use a phrase you used to our seedy little tutor just now ...' I had no recollection of having used the phrase and was as taken aback by this evidence as I might have been by a report from a private detective. 'As far as modernity is concerned, we shall never have innocence again. We shall never have peace.'

He belched, sat back comfortably and half closed his eyes again, as if in dismissing these two abstract states he had momentarily released them from captivity and was sampling for the last time their fugitive pleasures. The old settle creaked once more under his weight; I feared for the pub wall behind it.

The barmaid drifted towards our end of the bar and began to wipe the surface. Josh surveyed her indolently, swept with his analytical eye her too-tight T-shirt and the clichéd half-moons of her breasts; a brief confusion of desire flickered over his face and was effortlessly replaced by one of calm lust; he finished off his pint as if he were putting it out of its misery.

'As for you,' he said, as if he were about to do the same to me, 'your problem, obvious from even an hour of your intellectual company, is that you refuse to *unlearn*. English faculties would do better not to open their doors to every tyke who just preferred reading books to having a life. University is not a middle-class book club. And adolescent fondness for seeing yourself in the guise of your favourite Tolstoy heroes is not ... I repeat *not* a matter for intellectual enquiry. They are books, not holiday brochures for other lives. Your life is not theirs; their lives are not anybody's. Understand that and you won't make a tit of yourself.'

With this final dismissal of my sensibility he gave himself up to the unhindered appreciation of the barmaid, whose efforts to liberate a piece of grease from the part of the bar furthest from her and nearest to us threatened to liberate her liberal bosom all in one movement.

'Poetry in cunting motion,' he said, solemnly.

'But surely,' I said, pleased for a moment not to be the centre of attention and hoping to slip into the conversation unobserved, 'surely there is always personal testimony. That has power. Aside from all the politics and the social theory ... there is experience. There is experience before intelligence ... as it were ... still ... I mean ... that can be conveyed with a narrator ... There is ... testimony ... it's old fashioned, perhaps ... Testimony,' I said again, helplessly drawn to the word, but aware of how earnest it sounded.

Josh raised an eyebrow.

'Have an interesting childhood, did you?' he said.

I blushed.

'Everybody's childhood is interesting.'

'Nice try at democratising your sense of self-importance. Want to hear about mine?'

'Of course.'

Josh only smiled.

'Your round, isn't it?' he said, slipping the smile from me to the barmaid as she leaned down and began to rearrange things beneath the bar.

Josh was set to become the college's most brilliant student. Our tutor had seen many come and go; many promised and all disappointed. But Josh had an impervious resilience to outside influences that gave him staying power. Josh was a success because as far as an education was concerned to all intents and purposes he didn't need to be there. The pecking order in tutorials was Josh, our tutor and me as interested spectator. He was completely unemotional in his approach to literature, wholly unpretentious and merciless in his destruction of any emotion and pretension in others. His reading and recall of what he read was encyclopaedic. It was this quality (which in fact I was unmoved by – it was his cruelty that fascinated me) that cowed our tutor and reduced him to the likeness of a stammering undergraduate. Only slowly did it dawn on the poor man that Josh had bigger fish to fry than exposing the gaps in a mere Deputy Director of Studies' reading. So he gave up demanding textual references for Josh's more outlandish assertions and instead poured himself a large Scotch at the beginning of the tutorial and stared into it for the hour like a gypsy into her crystal ball, seeing no future for himself but recalling his own intellectual ambitions of twenty years ago, long dead, rekindled by this six-foot-six mountain of muscle, academic *esprit* and casual profanity.

Josh became a college hero, and in a sense he was a complex one. For he was not directly liked; his absence of manners and easy dismissal of all friendship made people frightened of him. But he was such a consummate reversal of the old-fashioned notion of the undergraduate aesthete that it was hard for people not to see him as a kind of modern avenging angel. Whatever his tracks were, he had covered them. He hadn't the aura of social entitlement of a public school boy, nor had he the defensiveness of the state school *arriviste*. Finals students bandied French philosophers with him and the porters bandied football scores; his mastery of both was such that either party might have been pleased to hear the other's exchange.

All I could confidently deduce about his real personality was that he was a man composed exclusively of appetites. Intellectual enquiry was, for him, a genuine appetite that had to be satisfied. In that sense, although cruel, he was positive. Everything was hunger; he seemed without aversions. The only thing he seemed to actively dislike was me. He gorged himself on everything, cerebral or physical; only friendship with me did he spit out. He would discourse on anything cheerfully and candidly, from masturbation to his toilet life; between these two he touched on almost anything. But nothing, I realised, that could be – for him, at least – embarrassing. Nothing, that is, that might have made him blush.

I was a blusher. Always had been. The moment between the thing that is said or seen and the burning of my face, I have often tried to analyse. As a teenager I rather romantically, and I suppose rather pathetically, thought that perhaps blushing was a creative thing, since in that moment in which the blush is born, there is a stringing together of associations, a piercing to the heart of some issue in which one feels dreadfully implicated. It seemed to me that, if not poetic itself, a blush at least ought to have the same origin as poetic feeling. But no doubt there is a simple and very unromantic psychological reason for it. I even blushed when I read books.

And I read a lot of books.

One morning I woke early. All through the first weeks of term I had slept late. I felt as if it was essential. But this one morning I woke before it was light, got up to drink a glass of water and pulled aside the thick curtains to inspect the morning world that till now had got along so well without me. I do not know why I had suddenly woken early. Perhaps the human constitution is incapable of always sleeping late. Perhaps like lost relatives determined to fill in the gaps in their family trees, lost parts of the day, ignored, or regarded as unsavoury by more respectable hours, come looking for the missing links. I was a stranger to the morning and the morning to me; as we eyed one another through the leaded windows of my room we saw no reason to extend the hand of friendship, let alone of family. It was now early November, and days started both slowly and stubbornly, and what seemed like the constant rain made for a very wet inventory of the night's work when the day finally broke.

I watched as the courtyard outside brightened by degrees. First only the pale stone stained brown along its upper edges by the rain but dry beneath showed a provisional, ghostly outline to the college buildings. Slowly, like a photograph developing itself, the vast slate roofs reluctantly distinguished themselves from the vaster sky. Slowest of all, the close-cropped square of lawn, devoid of detail, ungreen, seemed to recede, giving the centre of the court-yard the architecture of a Roman bath – the edges given to order and aristocracy and the centre to the indulgence of the flesh.

As the scene presented itself out of the darkness, for what seemed to me to be my sole appreciation, I felt my heart beat faster; I felt I was a voyeur. I forgot myself, and was taken up by what, I now realised, was a scene in constant movement. The fine rain turned and twisted, making every object seem temporary, as if it could not settle; as if it were only a reflection in another medium that one could not trust to last lest it shift and betray its accidental origin. It was fascinating. And yet I knew, the longer I stared, that there was within its temporary nature a tacit reassurance to me that I had been better off asleep; that my vocation as student sleeper was a true calling. I should wake to a more sensible, drier scene towards midday.

A lamp snapped on above the porter's lodge, short-cutting the painstaking business of the morning's brightening. With it another layer of movement was revealed, for the misty raindrops seemed to gather around the light like flies, implying that the very texture of the daylight was infused with rain, with dancing, fickle move-ment, and that this chance lamp held out with lighthouse-like security over the treacherous movement below.

The untidy wind ruffled the puddles on the flagstones like litter; untidiness was everywhere; the unnatural luminescence of the palest leaves on the trees seemed an accident, an experiment in yellow whose fellow disciples in that artistic school lay on the floor, trodden on the flags to a dull, uniform brown. Only the incremental brightening of the morning sky gave to the muddled scene a constant element, a will, though the morning, having revealed the picture beneath, its chaos and its incoherence, might have repented for all the sense it made, and turned the lights back out on such untidiness, as a parent faced with their child's shambolic bedroom might turn and shut the door on such an abuse of living space.

With similar disdain, but some of the voyeur's guilty pleasure, I was about to turn from the window and go back to bed when another light, and one that did not coincide with the arrival of the porter for his morning shift, came on in a room directly opposite mine. The curtains were drawn, but the room, occupied, as it were, with a sudden thought, was obviously home to some lunatic. Who could be getting up so early? I had been standing there as a spectator, in passing, but something told me that the mirror room to mine was home to someone in earnest. Where I had stood in darkness, happily incognito, this opposite presence, this competitor, had thrown the switch of their living-room light with abandon. So, at least, my imagination told me. Only minutes later, however, when the same light was switched off, I had to substitute 'abandon' with 'shallow bravura'. They had clearly gone back to bed, and my status as the most impetuous observer of the early morning was again indisputable. I had felt some competitive companionship in the appearance of the light. But now it had gone I felt, with calm authority, still master of the scene below.

But before I had a chance to enjoy my triumph for long, I saw the staircase light switch on, indicating that whoever it was had not gone back to bed, that they were up, presumably dressed, out of their room, and about to go out in the dark rain, and that I had better substitute 'shallow bravura' with 'religious zeal'. Into this swirling scene, this shipwreck of a morning, was coming someone with a purpose. There they were – moving as the clouds moved, constantly – there she was – for despite the dark hood and the undefined winter-coat silhouette, the stranger's quiet determination was weirdly feminine. In what seemed like an accustomed movement (or was it only natural elegance?) she looked up lightly and forgivingly at the sky above, pulled her collar up and walked swiftly out through the porter's lodge. She might have been a great actress, who, in the wings, looks up before her entrance only to see the wrong scenery in place, and yet, confident that the truth of her performance lies in the inner rather than the outer manifestation of her art, walks confidently on to the stage.

What the morning might make of the rest of its work no longer interested me. I turned sulkily from the window and went back to bed. I felt I'd been presented with a thought, a fact I did not want to examine. Like a dictator who clings to the artistic forms that were in vogue at the time of his *coup d'état* and accession to power, repressing new innovations, I turned back to sleep almost aggressively. Within seconds I was unconscious.

When I woke, I recalled this episode as one might a passage from a bedtime book read the night before. Remembered in repose it took on the quality of a fine deed from fiction or from history. Whereas I had gone to sleep aggressively I recalled it forgivingly. This person was up with a purpose; someone like me but who was not me was up, had an appointment with the abstract, hours before lectures, before tutorials, was out in the rainy streets and market-places, all as empty as if it were Christmas morning. It seemed delightful, disquieting, quaint; comic, somehow. There seemed a special sort of comedy in it; but if, as they say, all comedy needs a straight man, who the straight man was, I could not tell.

Me, for my bedridden, lazy appreciation of her, or her for her early-morning, meaningless impetuosity? I had decided it *must* be meaningless; the alternatives were too worrying. It would mean that there were parts of human life, experiences, realms of sensuous, religious or geographical identity that had their origin in the early morning and from which I was excluded. Just because I slept late. The fact that all I had to do was set my alarm clock was not the issue. I would have had not to be me, to have forgone an identity, to will my own dissolution to have done as she did. I would have had to have been like those figures in the Underworld who cross that river – I forget the name of it – and emerge on the other side transformed; to become a different *presence* in the world.

That said, I knew all this; I wasn't unaware that I *made* this mystery figure what she was – a reflection on what I was not. And yet alongside this self-knowledge was the simple fact (which made the self-knowledge of limited use) that she was nevertheless demonstrably different from me. I knew from her elegant and unruffled glance up at the rain that she was in her element; that she had limited patience with unnecessary comforts like sleep and warmth. Perhaps she had grown up in Wales or some rainy cathedral town in Devon or the Pennines. I struggled for excuses. Whatever she was I was amazed; I was *silenced* by her.

Over the next few days the sighting was repeated more than once. As observer, I joined the ritual excursion at various stages: sometimes I would catch the staircase light coming on, sometimes see only the fugitive hem of her coat nearly caught in the door of the porter's lodge as she deserted the scene.

In spite of all I have said, I did not romanticise her. I did not expect or seek redemption at her hands, either as an image or as a friend; I did not attempt to fill in details of her biography to satisfy a fantasy. But I was curious. She became fixed in my mind like those figures in Dutch painting, caught in a doorway, framed by expectation on their way to an anonymous appointment. And I envied her her walk in the town so early, whose old streets, I thought, empty but for her, might give up their true history to her, unembarrassed by cars. But this sentimentality made me think of Josh, and I saw him, in my mind's eye, raise a triumphant eyebrow.

I tried to sleep late, to carry on as I had done before. But it was no good. However hard I worked in the afternoons and stayed up late thinking, by turns manic and unconscious, I could not escape the fact that sleeping late had begun to make me feel unworthy.

Every morning I lay awake interrogating myself. Were my feelings of unworthiness dependent on where she was going? How would I feel, for example, if she were going to early-morning Mass? It was already a given that she was a better person than me on the strength of the hours she kept. Would I feel even more unworthy if she were training to become a nun, or would I feel the relief of a subtle superiority over her because at least I didn't trouble to set my alarm to get up to worship a non-existent God? It was very tricky.

At the other end of the – albeit somewhat old-fashioned – scale there was the possibility that she was having a passionate affair with a married man who could only escape his wife on the pretext of an early-morning business meeting; she might be having her heart broken over a full English breakfast at the Red Lion Hotel. Or he might be having *his* broken. Did it matter whose heart was being broken? Perhaps neither was. What if they were triumphant immoralists, happy in their early-morning vocation?

Not knowing the truth became something like a curse, an unresolved judgment. I had to know, and then regroup. I had to be released from the poetic trial, even for a prosaic verdict.

But when I finally made the decision to find out who she was I had a feeling that I was killing something in myself. Her independence from me – the secret of her excursion – defined my independence from her. So in finding out the truth – her destination – I was about to violate myself, lose the very identity that her strangeness had conferred on me. And what's more, without even becoming as good as her, or getting up as early as her. I was paying with my soul the price of not being able to sleep any more.

It was easy enough to find out her name. The light that came on every morning was on D staircase, on the third floor. The names inside the porch of D read, for the third floor, S. E. Fenwick and D. L. Bowen. From the team lists in the porter's lodge I noticed that S. E. Fenwick regularly turned out for the college first fifteen. So it was D. L. Bowen.

A more provocative and yet unsought insight into the girl I discovered the following week.

In the college library there was a large ledger, placed rather portentously in the centre of a table in the centre of the panelled room, into which you were required to write your name, the faculty to which you belonged, and the title of the book you wished to borrow. It was therefore possible to know what your colleagues were reading. Or what they wanted you to think they were reading. Unsophisticated attempts to impress usually involved Proust or Nietzsche; subtler strategies leaned towards foreign languages (untranslated), obscure nineteenth-century erotica or deep texts wholly unconnected with your degree course. (Once an unfortunate first-year Philosophy undergraduate took out a particularly advanced medical textbook and this was hailed as clever tactics indeed, until the poor boy died in the long vacation; it seems he was looking up symptoms.) Josh's entries were very provocative, partly because he would never have been so vulgar as to play such a snobbish game, so we knew they were genuine. He would take out nothing for weeks, which implied a prior mastery of any faculty reading list, and then we would see he had borrowed an H. E. Bates novel. We never knew whether this was part of his eclectic mission to bring every cultural item within the scope of his frightening intelligence, or whether, like everyone, he simply needed a break. In what I saw as his clinical foreknowledge of our pretentious games it was my belief it was an advanced ruse to wrong-foot us. Whatever it was, I read his entries as one might the diary of a murderer.

But that week I went to write my name in this academic Book of Life and found in the space above the name D. L. Bowen. Five nineteenth-century novels, all my favourites, were beside it. Or I should say, beside her faculty: Theology.

She *was* on her way to morning Mass.

I had flirted with the idea that she was on her way to church, it was true, but only self-provocatively, outlandishly. I suppose a piece of me must have wanted her to be, for it would finally have confirmed once and for all my feeling of personal unworthiness and put the issue beyond question. After all, the existence of God was not the issue – whether or not He existed did not take away from the heresy of my long lie-ins. And did not this sense of being a heretic establish my inability to be truly atheist anyway?

For if I was, I ought to be able to sleep all day without the fear of damnation. No, the truth was that if an interested observer were to ask me whether or not I believed in God, I might answer 'No', but if asked themselves, privately, by another third party whether or not I was a believer, they would reply, giving an analytical twist to their answer, 'Effectively.'

Perhaps further confirmation of my spiritual confusion came from the fact that I never really believed anyone actually *did* Theology at university. That a subject whose theme was the redemption of mankind could cheerfully find itself studied along-side Land Management or Mechanical Engineering seemed to reflect either poorly on Theology's confidence in finding the true God, or rather too exaltedly on the other subjects' pretensions to be found interesting. I left the library reeling.

I vowed to meet her and find out what on earth she was about. And I would do it on her own territory.

I set my alarm.

It was completely dark when I woke, washed and dressed. I took up what seemed now my habitual position at the window and watched. I had never seen the morning start from nothing; I felt as if I had gone from poet to scientist, in pursuit of comprehensive rather than subjective knowledge. I heard, without seeing, the same thin curtain of rain blow against the window; I knew the same suspension of wind and water outside held the court-yard in a murky solution. Then, as usual, as a faint blue-grey square of sky showed above the porter's lodge, the latter's porch-light came on in tireless competition with the dawn.

As with friends we think have changed towards us following a crisis in our lives, on whose behalf we must remind ourselves it is we who have changed, not they, so the once friendly architecture of the courtyard seemed to brighten accusingly. I had to remind myself this was no ordinary morning, but that I was like a habitual theatregoer who, owing to some personal drama or sudden insanity, takes his usual seat in the stalls, all the time knowing that at some point during the performance he is going to give up his delicious anonymity and climb on to the stage himself, interrupting the drama irrevocably.

The rain grew stronger with the light, seeming briefly complicit in my growing desire that she might, for once, stay indoors this morning. I tried to impress upon my imaginative picture of her the good sense in staying out of the torrential downpour. But even in my imagination she was not like me; I felt her refuse, and as I saw her bedroom light and then the staircase light switch on, I knew she refused not only in my imagination, but also in the real world. Without waiting to see who emerged, I ran out of my room and down my staircase, my own light illuminating the courtyard in guilty reciprocity.

As I felt the early-morning rain on my face I thought how weak it was. For a moment, the waking in darkness, the insubstantial rain all seemed so tame that I nearly turned back, ashamed, retrospectively, of how weak I had been; how I had inflated the understanding of the otherness of another's life into an insurmountable act of vision; I was doing as she did, and it was easy. But, I realised now, I did not want that. My hesitation to 'cross to the other side' of experience was not laziness, or fear. I wanted to be defined by what I could not do, not what I could; by what I wasn't, not what I was. After all, what if this disparity between the anticipation of doing something and the doing of it were to be replicated through the whole of life? One could do anything – like Josh, one would be made of appetites, all assuageable and none of them *charmed*. Was that all I wanted, a charmed life? And could one die easily, too, if the coming of death were as unimpressive as this autumn rain on my face, when from my window it had seemed so impossibly chill and malign? In that regard the warmth of my room, the denial of the experience of walking in the rain, felt, paradoxically, a wiser path, more loaded with human wisdom than this active adventure. I suddenly felt that to have gone back upstairs would have returned to me the invaluable experience of watching life happen to others rather than to oneself, reinvesting it with a sense of awe and terror, which, after all, if we *were* speaking of death, one would feel for the loss of someone one loved, over and above the fear one felt for one's own death. And is there not in that paradox a hint that a life exists in which one might free oneself from *all* egoism, even if only at the moment of the death of a loved one?

I reached the porter's lodge before her. Forced to wait, I could not but feel I was blocking her path. I took a step back to seem less aggressive and then realised, as she approached quickly, that to stop her I would have to take another step forward, and very quickly, too; I felt myself move forward, like an assassin.

She approached with head down, obviously not expecting to meet anyone else. The differences in our height meant that without looking up at all her gaze met mine in the natural course of her walk, which lessened the surprise; even so, she stopped suddenly; long enough for me to realise that I was not alone in regarding this early hour of the morning as her private domain.

'I hope you will forgive me,' I said, guessing that formality was the only way of surviving the absurdity of what I was about to do, 'but I live *there*.' I pointed up to my window. I was grateful to her for looking where I indicated: it seemed to *place* me; I had a geographical identity, if no other. 'And I have happened to see you ... to catch sight of you ... leaving the college at this ... extraordinarily early hour. Of course I am insane ... it goes without saying ... but I'm not mad. I just ...'

I looked at her, and realised she was looking at me very intently, and for some reason I wanted to laugh.

'Tell me where you're going,' I said. 'It's nothing. Goodness, you're getting wet.'

She pulled her hood down, showing her face, and I saw it properly for the first time. It was pale, very slightly rosy in the cold; her hair was fair and flecked with rain. She smiled and the wind pulled at her hair; she seemed to keep her head very still, as though she were enduring it. She wore no make-up; only a very fine silver necklace that disappeared behind her neck into the darkness of her hood.

'My name is Dinah Bowen. Would you like to come up for a cup of tea?'

'Oh God,' I said, 'I couldn't impose. I really am not a lunatic.'

'That's good,' she said.

'On the other hand,' I said, suddenly struck by a new idea, 'perhaps you'll miss your boat. Perhaps you're going rowing,' I added, more to myself than to her, and ready to be completely wrong-footed by stumbling on the true reason for her early mornings; somehow being presented with the simplicity of her presence made any outlandish reason seem out of the question.

She only smiled. 'No. Come on,' she said with a more reproachful glance at the rain than usual – no doubt on my behalf. 'We shall get soaked. I've got nothing to eat.'

A sudden sense of luxury seemed to surround us. I couldn't help looking at the rain and the lights of the old buildings starting to come on and feeling that I was terribly lucky to be not twenty yet, and able to read and think and study. I felt confident, but I knew I was blushing; I could feel the rain doubly cold on my hot face. We went inside.

Her room was unpretentious and rather bare. I spotted a well-made bed in the bedroom and on the desk was a fine china cup and saucer still half full with amber tea; a pot of honey stood beside it, as if she had left in a hurry. No food.

Dinah was also unpretentious. She had invited me up, which was socially bold, and she chatted away politely, asking me questions about myself in the manner of an old-fashioned society hostess. But her confidence had a carelessness that seemed to suggest that it was the minimum she expected of herself, that she had nothing to lose by being relaxed; that she might have been quite pleased if she could be allowed to be anxious. She made one think that both anxiety and calm can disappoint as conduits through which to experience the world, and when both have failed perhaps there is nothing left but to be sociable.

Or perhaps there was a third way, for as I watched her make our tea there was a quality about her that did transcend the management of the moment. She seemed to be *waiting*. She seemed – and I thought it was more than simply the fact that I had interrupted her morning excursion – to be about to go somewhere special, the specialness of which it was beholden upon her to downplay to strangers lest they be jealous, and she be suspected of flaunting. For a moment I felt again the shadow of some religious issue over the whole business and tried to dismiss it.

'What a pretty room,' I said, though it was exactly the twin of mine opposite, which I thought ugly.

'I haven't milk, either. Will honey be all right?'

I laughed a little, for some reason. She was beginning her day all over again, for my sake. Ordinarily I was appalled at the prospect of putting people out, but something made me bold. I looked out at the rain and my room opposite, like an old friend I had lost interest in; it looked back at me, dumbfounded perhaps by my rejection.

'I've gatecrashed both your room and your morning. I ought to be ashamed of myself. I'm an impostor. I sleep so late. And you are so brilliant to get up. I'm in awe. What's your secret?'

'If you don't get up it's because you don't want to,' she said.

'Yes, that'll be it,' I said, wrong-footed by her simplicity. 'But I like the fact that you do.'

We both laughed, I think for the same reason. Then there was a pause.

Then she said, 'How do you find your first term?' like a doctor.

'I'm not sure.'

'Me neither.'

'I don't really know anybody,' I said.

'You're my first visitor,' she said. 'Apart from the chaplain.'

'Yes, I saw him, too. Do you believe in God?'

'Isn't it a bit early in the morning for a theological discussion?'

'A bit early for any conversation, I should say.'

She sipped her tea and smiled at me through the steam. Behind her head I noticed two of the novels whose names were written in the library ledger; I took them in as mutual friends.

'Don't you cover the existence of God in the theology degree?'

She paused for a second.

'Not in the first term.'

'It's probably third-year course work.'

'Doctorate,' she said. Neither of us smiled, I think for the same reason. There was a pause as the joke ran out and I struggled to find another so as not to lose the intimate thread.

'How do you know I do theology?'

'I saw your name in the library.'

The next question was, of course, how did I know her name? I saw her think the thought and hold off from putting the question; she left the conjecture to hang in the air, purposefully, I thought; and in not addressing it established both for herself and for me a reassurance that full as the world may be of peculiar motives, inappropriate enquiries or gauche fantasies, she would not pass judgment on them, least of all when they might be about her, and when – to extend the metaphor I had found so apt to describe her – she was waiting to go somewhere so special. A place whose specialness gave her a sort of diplomatic immunity from having to judge people.

'I had it in my head,' I said, 'that you might be going to church at such an early hour.'

She laughed and shook her head very slightly and quickly, as if the question were a troublesome fly.

'I don't even know your name,' she said.

I told her.

'I know *your* name,' I said, 'because I checked in the porch of your staircase downstairs. I'm so sorry I've interrupted your morning. I shall learn to be more polite. I must go.'

'But you're my first visitor,' she said. 'Isn't it nice to drink tea with the rain outside?'

For some reason I wanted to cry. I had a terrible conviction that it would all end badly. I blushed and she saw.

'You came to find out why I get up so early. When you know you'll be off. Perhaps I should refuse to tell you and then we might have tea again, one day.'

But she got up and went to the mantelpiece and took something down. She came towards me and in her hand I could see a little black and white photograph she seemed half reluctant to hand over.

'My mother died just before I came up. Look . . . I found this . . .' She said it as if I hadn't seen her take it from the mantelpiece, as if she were conjuring it, like a magic trick – 'It's a photograph of her when she was at this college. They say we look alike – do you think we do?'

I took the photograph and looked at it. A rather plain young woman looked back, not at all like Dinah Bowen.

'Yes,' I said.

She took the photograph back and I saw her struggle with her desire to look at it herself, wanting to, but wary of her own emotion. She took a brief glace at it, smiled hesitantly and replaced it on the mantelpiece. Then she turned and smiled more confidently at me.

'I don't sleep. So I have to wait . . . wait, wait, wait . . . till it begins to get light before I can get up. I hate being up in the darkness. And with the rain, of course, it gets light even later. Then I walk along the river. It's beautiful in the morning.'

She said it dully, as if it were a second-hand recommendation that at first hand had been a disappointment.

'How did she die?' I said.

'Cancer,' she said, informatively, as if she meant the star sign. 'I was always going to read theology, even before she got ill. Now I have the whole faculty thinking I'm looking to save her soul.'

She paused. I guessed she was standing back from this last remark, taking in the irreverence of it and wondering if she had got away with it, whether she herself found it acceptable to have spoken like that. I smiled and she seemed reassured.

Then she said, 'Next week's the last week of term. I've kept myself so apart all term . . . I only know a couple of people here. Perhaps I'll have a tea party. Will you come?'

'Of course.'

'Will you?' she said, challengingly, as if I might be fibbing.

'As long as it's not too early in the day.'

'Four o'clock Thursday?'

'I'll set my alarm,' I said, and got up. I felt exhausted.

'Thank you for coming to see me.'

I was struck again by her self-possession. Her emotions seemed to confer great confidence on her, and on those to whom she spoke.

'Will you still go for your walk?' I said, then felt the question was a little impertinent.

'The morning is the best time,' she said; I couldn't be sure if she'd answered my question or not.

'Well, goodbye.'

'Goodbye,' she said.

On the Thursday of the following week, the last week of term, two hours before my appointment with Dinah, I had my last tutorial. This final meeting with our tutor was to be a review of our progress; the hour was split in half, and Josh and I would get thirty minutes each. I met him on the stairs, looking like an Olympic shot-putter fresh from the medal ceremony.

'He's all yours. He's had a big Scotch.'

I bet he has, I thought. Poor bastard. I couldn't deny I'd watched Josh's careful dismantling of our tutor's intellectual pretensions with pleasure; it was like a blood sport: fast-food academic fare that left one feeling a little sick afterwards, and a little ashamed. It didn't reflect well on me, for I knew it was just a relief that if I could be humbled in my talents so could my Director of Studies. This fighting for premiership academic form was something new to me. I half expected to turn up one day to find Josh sold to another, richer faculty for a vast transfer fee. Or find myself on loan to a desperate one facing relegation.

Josh passed me on the stairs; I had to press myself against the wall to let him go by.

'Listen,' I said, with the sudden confidence of the condemned man, 'let's have a drink when I'm done here.'

'Can't,' he said, his great form blocking out the daylight from the stairwell.

'I can't stay long, either. Just one. Meet me in the Eagle in half an hour.'

'What he's got to say to you won't take half an hour.'

'Then go and get a head start. You usually do.'

I *would* make him acknowledge me. He shrugged his huge shoulders, as if dealing with me only made him wish for more challenging reasons to go to the pub.

'On you,' he said.

'You bastard,' I said.

He raised an eyebrow and, turning, went out into the daylight.

For once he was wrong. Our tutor, perhaps in an attempt to justify his existence, brought the full, pedantic weight of his profession to bear on me. I felt sorry for him as he trawled through my essays for the term. The thirty minutes began to draw to their close, and if I was to meet Josh and not be late for Dinah I would have to get out.

'You see, you puzzle me. You work hard, of that there is no doubt. It's almost that which concerns me. If you were a loafer this would be easier . . .' He paused, sighed, and a faint Highland haze drifted towards me. 'Oh Christ,' he said, 'let's not beat about the bush – your work is dull. It's wholly lacking in ambition. When it's not detailed to the point of tedium it's vague to the point of total meaninglessness.' He stumbled over this last word, and I could see his disappointment that the put-down had not come off better. I stole a glance at my watch. 'Do you think . . . and I don't want you to take this the wrong way . . . that you might have been happier at a slightly less . . . high-powered university?' He didn't wait for an answer; the self-confidence of my college made the question rhetorical. A suicide here was to be preferred to mild depression anywhere else. 'It's not that you have to want to be a don – God knows there are enough of us – but some intellectual curiosity, at least . . . would be a great start. Become a banker, become a stockbroker afterwards, by all means, but while you're here . . . *engage*. Do you understand me? There are things to be learned here. After all –' he stumbled up and filled his tumbler – 'you have the best tutorial partner a man could hope for. One might have hoped a little of his *esprit* might have rubbed off on you. If he can't provoke you, no one can.'

'But I don't want to be provoked,' I started to say, but stopped. It was no good. There was, I realised, between Josh and our tutor something almost akin to a shared sexual predilection. In their pursuit of academic rigour they were bound by a private language that superseded any morals or manners that might bind the rest of us together. I was an interloper, a tiresome heretic without true heresy's vigour, unglamorous and cowardly.

'What you say is all true,' I said. 'What can I say to put your mind at rest? What indeed? Over the vacation I shall do some serious soul-searching. I *can* do better. I *will* do better. It only remains for me to thank you for your patience. I look forward to the challenges ahead. No, no ... I'll see myself out. Happy Christmas!'

And I was gone, unashamed. I hadn't blushed once.

Josh was cradling his second pint in his huge arm like a baby when I made it to the Eagle. He was someone who never looked up when another person came into the room; I stood a moment looking at him. No one could have arrived with any information that could interest him. I thought he must have parents and wondered if the news of a bereavement or a tragic accident could have broken his calm. It seemed unlikely. His broad jaw and arms and legs that swung on such huge hinges had no tension in them. He was a hero, it was true; his ego had no commerce with his talent – not in the vain sense. He was a triumphalist, admittedly, but one felt that if he were raised on others' shoulders in triumph it was only because he found the air there easier to breathe; other people's mediocrity suffocated him; or perhaps he just liked the view. If I hadn't known him I would have liked him. Then I remembered I was going to see Dinah; I remembered affections, and, trying to hold off from the hubris of the reflection, considered how wholly lacking in affection Josh was. I knew the thought ought to have empowered me, and knew too that had I not sought affection from him myself, it would have done. But I was alienated from him as one might be from a celebrity one meets accidentally and whom one has only seen and known in the public arena and from whom one requires, in private, endorsements they are wholly unqualified to give.

'Do you know,' I said, as I presented him with his pint, 'he called me by my surname. Like being back at school. Funny, really.'

'Did he cane you, too?'

'No. No, he didn't cane me. It just reminded me of school . . . my surname.'

'It's your name, isn't it?'

There was a pause.

'You probably don't remember our first conversation,' I said, 'if your monologues can be called conversations. But it was in here, after our first tutorial, you told me the authorial voice was dead. Well, shall I tell you the problem? Your modern literary theory manages to make of every text some hidden message, a meta-language or whatever you call it, revealing the true intent behind cultural activity – the imperialism of omniscient conventions, the activity of elite modes of thought . . . capitalism working invisibly in modern media . . . whatever. And eventually you're going to be left with nothing that your cleverness has not left tainted. Tainted! With sin! Yes, that's it. Your cleverness actually makes things sinful because you always add sin to the equation! We are all guilty, eventually, of having blithely engaged in any cultural activity . . . in reading a story, or listening to a piano concerto . . . anything that makes us *think about ourselves*. Eventually the motive for entertainment, or poetry, or bloody basket-weaving, will be shown to be savage, or selfish, or societal, or stupid.'

At each word Josh's eyebrows arched a little.

'We have to risk the sin,' I said, 'we have to risk doing what, of course, is ridiculous. Fiction is ridiculous, but it's no more ridiculous than life, and for as long as the two go hand in hand we shall at least be entertained. We have to reclaim fiction from self-consciousness, from the fatal step of seeing it in terms of other disciplines like psychotherapy and sociology. It's you, Josh, who should *unlearn*. What's wrong with the discredited narrator – me, I'm a reader, and I'm there in good faith – if he's not, if the narrator's not, just because your theory says he's not, well . . . render unto Caesar that which is Caesar's. I just want something of life, something to make me smile . . . something . . . to get me up in the morning.'

I saw him wince, as though he'd smelt something unpleasant or swallowed his own sick, but I carried on:

'Life has got to be got through. And I won't have the "study of English literature" destroy one of its few pleasures.'

'With the grades you get,' he effortlessly interpolated, 'I should say there was little danger of that. Or is your failure a subtle form of fifth columnist activity? If it is, I salute you.' He belched loudly and looked at his pint. 'Either this beer's off or the conversation is. Get another, will you?'

'Why do you devour everything?' I said. 'Look at you – Haven't you had your fill of life yet?'

He looked at me, for all the world like an elder brother.

'It is my intention,' he said, 'to leave nothing left over. No false reverence. I love my knees too much to dirty them by kneeling before anyone or anything.'

'Why, you pompous fool.'

'Perhaps,' he said. 'You see, we don't kneel down before that which is worthy – to think that is to make a mistake in psychology. We kneel to make *ourselves* worthy. We kneel as a means of generating the true spirit of submission. Not the other way around. So it is that the weak kneel, for it empowers them. It is the slave's religion. If Narcissus kneels, Narcissus is worthy. That is the Western deal. So he kneels wherever he can. And you, you are the greatest kneeler I have ever met. You would even kneel to me. You are a born slave – yes, born to it – for you have not even the primitive republican's desire to question your captivity. You see yourself in the heroes of books and you feel emancipated from the tyranny of living only one life. But heroes in novels are slaves, too – which is why you identify with them; they are trapped in their fictional worlds and you are trapped in the real one. If someone gave you the key to liberate yourself from your prison you wouldn't know what to do with it.'

'What is the key?' I said, in spite of myself.

He paused, and gently pushed his empty glass towards me. 'Brilliance.'

At that moment I despised him.

Perhaps I fail in my role as narrator when I tell you that I don't remember what happened next. I don't think it was as dramatic as it might have been; it probably wasn't dramatic at all, in fact. I wanted to dismiss our friendship but there was none to dismiss; I wanted to answer his criticism with a devastating reversal of his logic and throw it back on him, but I couldn't think of one. If I'd wanted to punch him, I couldn't have reached. I think I picked up his empty glass and made as if to go, wearily, to the bar and get him another, but went through the public bar, out through the lounge bar and out into the street, realised I still had the glass in my hand, went back in, left it on the bar, was seen by Josh, who was going to the Gents, and just turned and walked out again, banging my shoulder on the frame of the door. I remember all of that, so why do I say then that I do not remember? I suppose because something abstract in my head must have made sense, which I am not recalling along with the concrete facts. I went out into the rain, and I walked up the high street, away from my college. I had to be on some sort of neutral ground, in a field somewhere, or in the back streets. I hadn't forgotten Dinah, quite the opposite; to see her was now of the utmost importance. What Josh had said must be true. It must. It made sense, he had watched me, he knew me. To take criticism was essential; if I couldn't take it from him I couldn't take it from anyone. And I *would* take it, if it was true.

I realised I was in a part of town I had never been in before. There was a college whose name I did not even know, but which bore the same, generic look of cool stone and dark windows. The suburbs, if they existed, must be miles away. I stopped at a cheap shop and bought an umbrella; I thought I would be more efficient with my life and not so passive. I put it up and began to retrace my steps; I'd walked further than I had meant to and it was an hour into Dinah's tea party. She had implied I would not be the only guest, but even so, I ran the last two hundred yards to our college gates.

Our courtyard was empty. All the students were packing or in the pubs and college bars. Warm rain fell on the flagstones, clear now of leaves.

I walked to D staircase, caught between the novelty of willing my own journey there and the familiarity of having been there before. I had barely looked out of the window during the last week; I wanted the watcher in me to be wholly dismissed by the time this formal, allowed invitation took place. But the other, early-morning trip still hung round me, like a social carapace, easily filled again; easily delightful a second time. I climbed the stairs. I remember they were incredibly chilly and I could hear my steps on them, as if they were somebody else's.

Dinah's door was open and I heard voices, which reassured me about being late. As I got closer I realised that it was not so much a voice as the sound of someone laughing. It was an extraordinary laugh, complete, ecstatic, uncompromising; like a gift laid at the feet of that which was being laughed at; generous, establishing that the person laughing thought not of themselves, but of the genius within, like a muse, that gave them the wit to see the humour; irreverent, in that the humour wasn't conditional on the propriety of the joke, but complete and healthy: no scruple had to be set aside or repressed to share the ecstasy. I didn't envy whoever laughed, I felt no pang that I had missed the joke, I was only glad that *someone* could laugh like that.

I turned the corner of the stairwell and looked inside Dinah's room. There she was, sitting beside her desk, a cup of tea to her lips, smiling through the social situation, and at her feet, or, to be strictly honest, a few feet from her feet, on the rug, was Josh, lying on his back like a St Bernard puppy, his feet in the air, laughing. There was no one else there. On the small table beside Josh was a cup of tea and four biscuits, piled neatly on top of one another, and a book of poetry, open. They hadn't seen me; Dinah looked down at him, unfazed but wonderingly.

This man of no affections, no friendships, suddenly broken open, blissful, lying basking in the attention of my early-morning friend. I blushed, turned and walked back down the stairs.

My room was now as empty as the day I had arrived. I drew the curtains and opened a bottle of wine, something I hardly ever did, drank three glasses in quick succession, and though it was barely six o'clock, I went to bed. I went to sleep very quickly, and when I woke four hours later I lay and wondered how he could have known Dinah. Perhaps they were cousins. As I went back to sleep I decided I would wake early and go and apologise to Dinah and we would have a cup of tea before we both left to go to our homes for Christmas. We would arrange to be friends next term. I went to sleep.

Perhaps it was having had three glasses of wine but I didn't wake up till past nine o'clock the following morning. I knew, partly because I suddenly remembered, having inexplicably forgotten the night before, something she had said to me about leaving *very* early to catch the correct train home. So I knew I had missed her. And I knew, in a not dissimilar way to the way Dinah had pointed out to me that morning, that I must have wanted to sleep late, that also I must have wanted to miss her.

Eventually I got up and went to the window, pulled the curtains and looked outside.

At first I thought there must have been a mistake – a mistake in the way sometimes one imagines the world may have slipped up in its presentation of itself: the window was white and completely opaque. I wondered if I had gone blind. Then I noticed that the edges of the glass were marbled with ice, and that the white was mist in the courtyard. I pushed the window and there was the sound of cracking as the hinges worked. I baulked somewhat at the beauty of the scene outside. Everything had stopped, arrested as by a new thought and frozen in the night. Each detail had become itself – each window frosted uniquely, every branch still with cold, each channel or fall of water turned into a monument or decoration. The endless movement of the wind and rain, the puddles in the interstics of the flags, once blown this way and that, the pale stone stained dark with dripping water from the roofs above – everything, it seemed to me, had been redeemed by this moment of fixedness, this sudden, insistent refusal to carry on, this freezing hesitation from further movement, this holding off.

I took a deep breath of the cold air. Somewhere, in a distant street or courtyard someone began to hammer something, and the regular noise seemed transmitted carefully and slowly on the freezing air, echo-less and pure, and died quickly, and the still-ness afterwards was as if it had never been disturbed.

Dinah never came back. I heard her once spoken of briefly; the impression she had left behind was of someone whom outside, family influences had claimed, and that following some tragedy in her life she had tried too soon to continue her education.

At his own request Josh found both another tutor and another tutorial partner; I thrived with his old one and got a first-class degree – he even shared his Scotch with me occasionally.

A couple of years ago I met a woman at a party who, after ten minutes' conversation, I realised was Dinah. She had known me straight away. She told me that I was the only person she had liked in her one term at college. When I asked her about Josh she didn't seem to remember him. Perhaps she was being tactful. As I was coming back from getting her a glass of wine I stopped and looked at her. She still had the quality of waiting that had struck me so when I first met her. So many years having passed I thought perhaps it was my imagination or a mere habit of her features – it seemed disproportionate to be still waiting to go somewhere and not having gone there yet. On the other hand, perhaps she was only waiting for her wine.

We were joined soon after by her tall husband.

The Fat Girl

Not so long ago, I went down to the river, again. It must have been twenty years since I had been there last. It has to be said that the river in my old town is not impressive. Most of it snakes through ugly modern developments and concrete precincts where you can't actually get down to the water. Only for a brief stretch between the supermarket car park and the weir is there a real riverbank and a towpath, kept up by the town's angling society. They keep the cow parsley and wild blackberries in check so that you can walk unhindered. It's where I used to fish.

My memory of it was of a peaceful, though not particularly attractive, place. However, small boys have no eye for beauty, so on revisiting it I was prepared to be surprised. I remembered that the water was slow moving and that on the far side of the river were tall, flat-looking buildings that backed directly on to the water, so there was no riverbank at all opposite. They were all built in an old, uniform industrial brick. Dark compared to the Cotswold stone of the rest of the town. These buildings cast long shadows over the water so that at the height of summer when elsewhere it was hot, there it was cool. We always hoped the fish would go there to keep cool and we could catch them.

The supermarket was a short walk from the railway station and I arrived about eleven o'clock. It wasn't raining or sunny. It was a normal day. Some of the shops in the high street had changed but the charity shops were still there, though they seemed to serve different charities. There was a McDonald's. Even a modest antique shop.

When I got to the supermarket I remembered there was a short cut to the river through the car park. You had to get through some particularly dense undergrowth, but it was still there. The ground dropped away steeply. You had to be careful. I rather hoped I wouldn't be seen making my way through the hawthorn. It was very much as I remembered it; there were still Coke cans and plastic bags littering the inside of the hedge. Even a supermarket trolley. Once, my friend Joe and I had seen a dead cat down there. Joe had said it had gone there to die. I said that I believed it had been thrown there, as a corpse. Joe said it had looked for a private place to die and I said it wasn't *that* private, since every boy from the school took that short cut once in a while. We'd agreed to differ.

As I slipped down the bank I could see through the trees the bend in the river and the pub by the weir some four hundred yards away. There, the river dropped some distance and continued, winding its way through the agricultural land beyond. The pub, the Kingfisher, marked the end of the towpath. You couldn't walk any further. It surprised me to see it in the near distance. I remembered it as being miles downstream: as a boy I had certainly never seen it through the trees like that. Perhaps that is the difference, being a child. You don't look up so much and see things in the distance.

When I reached the edge of the water the river, though, was just the same. There were still the little fishing stations along the bank where the grass had been cut to give access to the water. Worn patches of earth showed where the anglers put their chairs and umbrellas. It all looked neat and well cared for; the Angling Society must have gone from strength to strength. A smart blue sign had been put up on the brick wall opposite informing passers-by that fishing was for members only.

Joe had been my fishing friend. We had been friends since we were three or four, so that the fact that he was what my mother would have called a rough lad, and I was not, had not prevented us being friends. He lived on a council estate and his father hit him; I lived in a big house. No one even hit the dog.

Joe being a rough boy and me being a swot we did not acknow-ledge each other at school. This was easy, since I was in the top classes and Joe was in the bottom. Occasionally I would see him fighting in a distant corner of the playground, and sometimes I found myself sitting next to a fellow swot next lesson who was having trouble seeing out of one of his eyes, having had it panned against the playground tarmac by Joe half an hour before. I enjoyed Joe's violent school career vicariously. If we had talked at school we would have had nothing to say to one another. What we did together was fish.

Each Saturday morning we met in the supermarket car park at seven o'clock and, without a word, went down to the river. For a while I was fearful that if any of his other rough friends saw us together Joe would disown me. This thought haunted me for a while. It was resolved one Friday afternoon after school when, as we left the school gates, we were planning the next morning's fishing and were overheard. Someone asked why he was bother-ing to talk to the posh git. Joe turned to the boy and punched his face, very casually, almost friendlily, for although it was done with great force, it was graceful. As if the boy weren't to take it too seriously or be too surprised. Joe and I were best friends, and we lived for Saturday mornings. And no one ever came with us.

Then, one Friday night, I got home and my mother announced, outrageously, that she wanted me to take someone along with us the next morning. As tactfully as I could I let her know that she had taken leave of her senses. She plainly had no notion of the ridiculousness of the suggestion. She said it so matter-of-factly, too. I said it was impossible. The rules of the Angling Society forbade it. I said that Joe would never agree. But she smiled a horrible, comprehending smile and went to make supper. I followed, whimpering.

Apparently there was this child. His name was Adrian and he was about our age. He went to a different school to me and Joe. Or rather, had done. He had been removed the week before because of, to use my mother's phrase, 'unhappiness at home'. He was now school-less. The idea of a boy without a school was as peculiar to me as the idea of a vicar without a God or a soldier without a gun. I hated school, but I knew it had to be there. I would have been nothing without the loathing I had for school; it defined my existence. But here was a boy who had been set free and who, somehow, still existed. He had cut loose to float freely, fishing and muscling in on other people's ordered lives. As adults did. And he had come to flaunt his early promotion before us.

This was bad enough, but there was more. I asked my mother what this 'unhappiness at home' meant, thinking I could probably muster a little unhappiness myself if pushed. It was the first time in my life that suffering seemed to count as a kind of qualification; an achievement that might count towards early release. She told me. This Adrian's parents had put him up for adoption when he was four years old. It seems they hadn't wanted him and were violent. Social Services had put him into care for a while. In the end a childless couple had adopted him. They had looked after him for the last seven years but were now divorcing. Neither the adoptive mother nor father wanted to keep him. He was at present being looked after by a friend of my mother's.

I felt a mixture of feelings when she told me this. Firstly, I was tempted not to believe it. So many dreadful things happening to one boy seemed disproportionate. I felt as if I had just eaten a meal that was too rich; I felt sick. I had to grapple with the outlandishness of such a story as with a mathematical conundrum of great complexity. A conundrum to which I instinctively doubted there was a solution. Also I felt rage. Two rages, to be precise. I was enraged that there could be a world – not to mention the same world as the one in which I lived and in which I was allegedly secure – where such combinations of tragedy were possible. And I was enraged that Joe and I were expected to take this boy, who was evidently marked out for some serious grief and rotten luck, *fishing* with us. I mean, surely he had better and more pressing things to do, given the precarious nature of his future, than to stand on the riverbank with a couple of boys he didn't know and who were hardly qualified to add to the sum of his happiness. How happy was it going to make him? What difference could it possibly make? It was barely going to scratch the surface.

Needless to say, I did not adequately articulate these arguments to my mother and I agreed I would meet Adrian at seven o'clock, in the supermarket car park, the following morning. I rang Joe and told him, speaking to him as I would later learn to speak to my bank manager when I had gone unexpectedly overdrawn.

I was under instructions to, as my mother put it, 'take Adrian out of himself' – that curious adult expression which is such a mystery to the child, whose self seems a perfectly acceptable place of residence. How I would accomplish this geographical and physiological impossibility, I had no idea; nor, as a recreational pastime, what it really entailed. On the whole I had no great hopes for the following day.

When I woke the next morning, however, I found myself very curious to meet this child, and as I got closer to the car park I was almost excited. I wanted to see what a tragic boy looked like. I could not get it out of my head that he was bound to have some evidence of his misfortunes about him. I thought he might be dressed in black, or carry a Bible, or have a little grey, cumulus cloud over his head raining on him lightly. If he were to look like an ordinary child I thought it would alarm me. It would make me think he was in disguise; like a spy.

As it happened, he was, for all his extravagant woes, extravagantly ordinary. One might almost have suspected a double bluff, he seemed so unconcerned with life. He was standing alone in the car park. Desertion number three, I automatically reckoned in my head. Perhaps his present minders were just punctual. He was slightly smaller than me, unathletic-looking, squinted when he looked up at you, had little foolish eyes set too close together and he smiled, showing slightly goofish teeth, almost constantly. His face seemed caught in a rictus of good-natured optimism; one was anxious that his teeth might actually dry out, so infrequently did he close his mouth.

We chatted while we waited for Joe. I omitted asking him who had dropped him off, in case we got on to parent talk. I was left gesturing vaguely at the odd car in the car park, half implying that perhaps he had driven himself. But he was oblivious. And he seemed totally lacking in gratitude for the chance to crash our fishing trip. I suspected it had not been his idea, but that fact did not make me better disposed towards him. He quizzed me on the river, the town, the supermarket. For all his childish gaucherie, he asked questions with the confidence of an adult. Perhaps talking childishly had shown itself, in the face of stubborn, adult will, to be a useless medium, and only direct questions gave him the information he required – where he was to live, who he was to live with. It was, as far as I could see, the only extraordinary fact about him – he looked like a cartoon character, and spoke, for all his high voice, like a political reporter. It was an unnerving and unattractive combination. And he knew absolutely nothing about fishing.

Joe made no bones, when he finally arrived, about his feelings for our guest. He walked past both of us without a word, his head down, and made for the gap in the hedge. We followed, dutifully.

At the riverbank, as Joe and I unpacked our fishing things, Adrian unpacked his lunch. There was a lot of it. Egg sandwiches, three bags of crisps – breakfast, lunch and tea, presumably – cupcakes, two Mars bars, some wholemeal muck dressed up as scones, two cans of Coke and a flask of tea. Whichever people didn't love him enough in the world certainly kept him well fed. Perhaps one was meant to pass for the other. Joe had set himself up and cast out into the deep water before Adrian had finished wiping the egg sandwich off his hands and mouth. I knew there would be bits of sandwich in his teeth and I didn't want to look. He asked which rod was his. Joe looked away. I gave him the beginners' rod I'd got out of the attic at home and brought for him to use.

I didn't want him there. It was a perfect morning. There was a light mist on the river, the sun had barely broken through. The water on the far side was as dark as a bruise and still as a millpond. If you put your hand on the grass you thrilled to the coldness of the dew. Out in the gaps in the reeds the fish were feeding; there were bubbles breaking on the surface making faint concentric circles in the water, each one like a bull's-eye, waiting to be hit. My heart was beating faster and faster at the promise of the morning. And I had this boy by my side, this cross between Daffy Duck and Hamlet, loitering and talking too loud, asking questions and handing sweets around like it was someone's twelfth birthday. I ask you. I swear Joe would happily have watched him drown.

I would have liked to talk to him. In my heart I would have liked to have been armed, as I supposed all adults were armed, with the magic formula, the perfect and mature phrase of condolence, as rare and heartfelt as poetry, that would work on him, move him with useful emotion, strengthen where strength was wanted and, above all, soothe. I fancied the expression of true sympathy must exist, and it would be as precise and directed as a painkilling needle or an aspirin. I swear I wanted to relieve him of the suffering in his life more than I even wanted to fish. And I didn't only want it for him. I wanted it for the world. For as surely as I knew that if I were an adult I would know the magic formula, so I believed that once in receipt of it, there would be nothing to stop me applying it to all suffering. As a general principle. What was local would become universal. Not only did I want him not to suffer, but I was ambitious. Individual consolation was not enough. In fact something more universal was probably to be preferred, in case the one-to-one expression of feeling was mawkish and embarrassing. Far better to manage it on a grander scale. Nothing less than the wholesale realignment of love, duty and consolation was required. Those parents, so cavalier with their child's future would find my arguments irrefutable. I looked at him, standing on the riverbank staring at his fishing rod on the grass in front of him as if it were a gun that might go off. I would have made him the fulcrum upon which to turn the world upside down and make me Lord of consolation. If only I were an adult. And if only the fish were not feeding so enthusiastically.

I went over to him and started to get him set up. He was amazingly clumsy. He wasn't like other boys. He made no pretence that he knew anything about fishing at all. At our age any admission of ignorance about anything was simply out of the question. Silence or a forceful expression of your expertise were the only two courses acceptable. But Adrian revelled in his ignorance. It was a terrifying humility. He looked down at the tackle box as at a casket of treasure from Aladdin's cave. And he looked at me as if I were Aladdin. Was this the badge of suffering that I had looked for? This putting yourself in other people's hands and trusting them to help you out and advise you well? It seemed perverse and misguided if it was. I could have told him to bait his hook with a five-pound note and he would have done it. I wanted to say to him, 'Look, you idiot – we don't want you here. Don't be a mug and put your trust in us. You've got a bad enough track record with your various parents, don't expect better from a couple of kids.' He put the hook through his finger, he put his float on upside down; I suspected that he pitied the maggots. Eventually I had him all set.

Joe and I fished two places, which we called the Far Reaches: two breaks in the reeds out on the other side of the water. To be honest, they were the only two places worth fishing on that particular stretch. Elsewhere you got snagged in weeds or old bicycles just below the surface or the current carried you away. I'd been thinking about it all morning, how the three of us were going to fish those two spots. I couldn't ask Joe to share. This Adrian was my business. Joe knew that and I knew that. There wasn't room in the reeds for both of us, and if he fished the centre of the river, where the current was stronger, he'd have to re-cast every three minutes and it was odds on he'd have one of our eyes out by lunchtime.

So I made a deal with myself. I would fish the Far Reaches until I caught a fish and then I would let Adrian go there. We would take it in turns. In the meantime he could just fish off the bank and get used to the feel of the rod and the sight of the float. It involved a certain economy with the truth, but he wasn't to know. I explained that just four feet off the bank was a surprisingly good spot. You had a good view of your float and landing fish from such a place was a piece of cake. He seemed grateful not to have to squint over at the far bank. He just held his rod out at arm's length and let the float dangle foolishly in the water. He seemed in ecstasies. Joe, who had already caught two fish, was smiling wryly to himself. Adrian's total trust in my guidance did not weaken me in my resolve to make him fish this hopeless spot. If anything, it strengthened it. Joe was reeling in another fish as I was casting out for the first time. I felt a sudden agony of competitiveness which I had never felt with Joe before.

An hour went by. Adrian proved a ridiculously patient case, sitting on the edge of the riverbank, the emerging sun glinting on his teeth, smiling at his unknowingly hopeless situation. He was happy enough. Meanwhile I was getting nowhere and the sun was beginning to warm the water. Soon the fish would stop feeding. Joe had eight fish in his keep-net. The expression on his face was one I had seen before, when he was fighting, pale and unmoving.

I caught a fish, a small thing. I didn't even want to put it in my keep-net but Joe said I was an idiot not to. I hated him for that. I knew he knew my desperation. I remembered the deal I had made with myself about swapping places with Adrian. I told myself the fish was so small that it didn't count. But I obeyed Joe and put it in my keep-net. I knew that with the sun on the water if I didn't let Adrian fish the Far Reaches soon he'd have little chance of catching anything. I knew what the right thing to do was and I knew I had to do it. I really wanted him to have a good time. I wanted him to love fishing as much as I did and for that love to go some way towards consoling him for the dreadful time he was having in his life. But I couldn't do it. I was paralysed. I couldn't stop looking at his little hunched figure fishing a yard from the riverbank, staring at the water as if it were a book, but I couldn't swap places with him. I caught another fish, a bigger one this time. Then another. And another. They were feeding my stretch now, sun or no sun, and I kept catching them. Hours went by. Each time I caught one, Adrian congratulated me. Each time he asked me a different question. Occasionally he asked me if he was doing it right. He just made a careful enquiry. I told him he was. He asked about different species of fish. At lunchtime he got out the remains of his lunch and offered us his crisps.

I might as well have been fishing the river that leads to Hell for all the pleasure I took in it. Once I was guilty, once I had held on to my spot for one second longer than was charitable I had to stay there. I had to do wrong where wrong had been done already. Where I could not save – since salvation for me, a mere child, seemed beyond me – I would condemn; where I could not relieve suffering I would increase it. Even – or was it *especially?* – when Adrian did not even feel the pain, or know it *as* suffering.

I remembered my mother's injunction. I had not, according to any calculation, 'taken him out of himself'.

Some time in the mid-afternoon the fish stopped biting. Joe had finished before me, guessing things were over. He had caught twenty-seven fish. He sat on the bank quietly eating his lunch. I had caught eighteen. It was far too late to do the right thing. I wanted to cry. For the thousandth time that day I looked at Adrian, sitting there. I knew him. I knew his fate, even though I pretended not to. Life had done to him what the playground does to some bullied boys and girls. In his case circumstance and bad luck had gone about it in advance of any injury another child might have done him. And for this reason he was safe from the bully's interest. School was probably easy for him. Bullies pass over such easy prey in favour of the protesters, the children who still have a sense of outrage and justice in their hearts. These the bully loves. Not the already broken, the smiling, the freshly bruised. No. These, the Adrians, are left to my sort, the passive wounders, the negligent, the lazy and the ungenerous; those for whom active charity is a terrifying call to arms which they feel incapable and unworthy of answering. I thought what a thrill it would have been for him to have fished the Far Reaches and pulled in a good fish and gone home and told his tragic parents about it. How it might have made them realise they loved their little adopted boy; it might have woken them up, they might have been galvanised to see Adrian's appetite for life suddenly rekindled, to see him active and adventurous; to see that there was more to him than a mere receptacle for adult grief.

But I was already damned, and to have offered him this gift now would have revealed my earlier selfishness. I had to maintain the fiction that he was fishing a promising spot, express dismay that he had not yet 'got lucky', and that his patience did him credit. I even felt a terrible, absurd envy that that he was at least happily fishing a spot he believed to be the best, whilst I had wretchedly fished a spot that *was* the best. I was aware of the gruesome comedy of the situation, aware of him as a comic figure. He was my comic creation, and it was the comedy, not the tragedy, that truly damned me. Because I had made it, and he could not see it.

'It's gone,' he said.

'Eh?'

'It's gone.'

I sighed.

'What has?'

'My float,' he said.

'Lost it?' I asked. Patiently.

'It was there. Then it just wasn't.'

'Well, strike, then.'

He lashed upwards with his rod as if he had been electrocuted. This is when someone gets hurt, I thought. Expecting to get at least his line round my neck, I ducked. Joe had dropped his sandwich in the water taking evasive action. But Adrian's line held.

'You're snagged,' said Joe, fishing for another sandwich in his bag. My heart sank – we were going to have to wade in to get it out. But when we looked down at the line, it was moving out into the river. It was a fish. I suppose I ought to have been relieved. I expected to be. But I just felt a kind of resignation.

Adrian, with impressive theatricality, was making great and absurd pantomime out of fighting his fish. He strained and puffed and cried out that he wasn't sure if he could 'hold on'. Joe and I looked at one another and then down at the water with embarrassment. The etiquette was simple; if you had Moby Dick himself on the end of your line the most you were permitted to say was 'He had quite a pull on him.' You just didn't milk it. Ever. But I knew I must endure my penance. If this was the memory he wanted to take home with him, so be it. It was out of my hands.

Only after ten minutes did the joke begin to wear a bit thin. I actually wondered if there was a fish at all. This damaged boy might be deeper than I had thought. There might be no fish, and this might be an elaborate ploy to punish me for my self-ishness. A practical joke. Or, if he really had a screw loose, he might be pretending for his own benefit, playing out a fantasy to convince himself the whole fishing trip had been worthwhile. Joe had finished his lunch and was packing up his things. He said quite loudly that he was getting fed up and would 'pull the bloody thing in himself' if it carried on for much longer. It was definitely becoming embarrassing.

Eventually, once he had allowed the fish to take nearly all his line, and had painstakingly reeled in every last inch ever more dramatically, Adrian's float showed above the water, and, in spite of ourselves, Joe and I craned our heads over the bank to see. We were staring right into the very spot Adrian had fished for the whole day.

Did I cry out? I don't know. I know that something gave way in me, something cried within so loudly that it drowned out any sound in the world outside. Up through the dark water, its face fixed in a medieval cast of outrage and violence, came the head of a massive pike. It rested there, the boy who had caught it not strong enough to drag it up the bank. It stared at us, old and gnarled, hooked neatly in its upper lip. Joe, with sudden, graceful efficiency, found his landing net and slipped it gently under the fish and, together, he and Adrian dragged the huge green body up the bank. It took both their strengths. Only I stood back. Joe was beaming. And I envied Joe his joy. Neither of us had ever seen a pike caught on the river, let alone caught one ourselves. It was something we spoke of as belonging to that distant land of adult accomplishments and qualifications we could only imagine. They were grown-up fish, to be caught by grown-ups. We didn't suppose they took small boys' bait.

'What is it?' said Adrian.

'It's a pike,' I said, my voice unsteady, as if I had swallowed a sweet and it had gone down the wrong way. I thought if I had to speak again something terrible might happen.

'Well, that's pretty good,' said Adrian.

Joe just laughed and took the hook out. He was careful. I remember how careful he was, for a pike will bite you. His hands didn't shake. He was doing it all as if he had rehearsed it in his head a thousand times. As if he knew that one day he would be called upon to do it. Then he looked serious and started to weigh the fish, but it was too heavy for his scales. Joe started to make preparations to throw it back. I'd forgotten that you did that with fish. I felt sorry. I think, absurdly, that I wanted it to stay with us. Perhaps for ever.

'Can't put it in the keep-net,' said Joe. 'It'll eat the other fish.'

We all stood round one last time and looked at it.

'A pike,' said Adrian, to no one in particular, as if he were remembering it so that next time he caught one he would be in the know.

I don't know if he knew, or was even interested in the fact that this was the most precious catch Joe and I would probably ever witness. Probably not. I envied Joe because I could see that in spite of his prior loathing of him he embraced what Adrian took for granted: that we had all caught that fish. Only I, in my secret heart, was on the outside looking in; and no one need know that. I was left to ask of life whether Adrian's effortless embracing of that ethic was an embrace whose sweetness was born out of suffering and adversity, or whether he was just a simple boy less covetous and less competitive than I. I had had a chance to do a small, good deed and failed, had turned from it, been turned to stone by it, paralysed by its very image. And I had been rewarded with the greatest moment of my childhood. Not only the fish, and our excitement, but I had been let off the hook on an epic scale. I had been redeemed.

I looked at him. He was smaller than the fish he had pulled out of the water. He was all wonder, as he had been all day. As he had been while staring at the little patch of water just off the bank as if it was his happy destiny. If ever I prayed in my life I prayed that I need never apologise to him, that he need never know how mean I had been. And I wanted that, not because I was ashamed or did not want to lose face, but because I wanted him, with all my heart, not to have another disappointment, another observed selfishness to add to the catalogue of betrayal and negligence that had marked his life to date. I wanted to protect him from myself.

The fish was thrown back.

We deserted the scene like mutual friends of a person we had just buried. And we were strangers still, the only thing that might have brought us together gone, now, for ever.

Joe and I continued to fish, though neither of us ever caught a pike or saw one caught on the river. I never saw the boy again, so do not know whether his fortunes improved. At some point

Joe and I no longer fished together. He left before the sixth form. I think his appetite for adventure took on a more challenging and probably illegal aspect. He got a motorbike, and there were girls.

I walked on. A couple of swans made their way smoothly against the flow of the river. I didn't remember ever having seen swans there, before. The wind ruffled the water.

The Kingfisher nestled in a prime spot, where the town became the country and the river dropped and joined the green plane of hedges and fields below. The pub itself had come up in the world. The dirty Cotswold stone had been sandblasted and had a beige respectability more in keeping with a brand new building. There were neat window boxes and hanging baskets with purple petunias cascading down their sides and someone had trained the beginning of a wisteria on the front of the building. I went inside. The lounge bar was empty and smelt of polish. I tried the public bar and found it empty, too. I realised I had thought it would take an hour to reach the pub and that I would arrive at lunchtime. I looked at my watch. It was only half past eleven. I could see, out the back, through an open door, the edge of the weir and I could hear the rush of the water. The place seemed to be deserted. The smell of the polish made me want to cough but I didn't want the management to think I was an impatient customer. Then I noticed a bell on the counter for service. I coughed and rang the bell at the same time.

A beautiful woman came out from the kitchens.

'What can I get you, sir?'

She was polite.

'Could I have a coffee, please?'

'Certainly, sir.'

She smiled at me, as if she knew me, and I thought of the clichéd stereotype male response that confident men have of assuming pretty girls are chatting them up. I looked down while I found the money to pay for the coffee. I felt tired and wanted to sit down. I didn't have any change. I looked at her. She didn't look like a barmaid. She was dressed in a business suit and had put a file on the bar when she came in. She was carefully and well made up. Her dark hair was gathered neatly on the top of her head and she had cheekbones.

'I don't know,' I said. 'Perhaps I'll have a pint of Best.'

I sort of wanted her to make the decision for me. She smiled.

'Where are you sitting?'

'I don't know.'

'I'll find you,' she said, and took down a glass.

I looked through the door at the edge of the weir; I could just see a little white ribbon of water where the river broke over the edge. I chose a dark corner, away from the open door.

It was nice that she was there, but I didn't want to have to think too much about how attractive she was, or how friendly. I felt she would expect me to behave like a confident man, and I suppose she made me feel like one. But I had other things to think about. I felt that after my loitering by the riverbank I had some catching up to do. Like someone with a lot of outstanding bills. For some strange reason I considered doing a runner. I would run back down the towpath and perhaps, I don't know, throw myself in the water at the other end. I felt all worked up.

There she was, putting my pint on the table.

'Thanks.'

But she didn't go away. She had her file under her arm.

'You don't recognise me, do you?' she said.

I looked at her. It seemed unlikely that I would forget a face like that, but I spared her the cliché and said simply that I did not.

'Are you sure?' she said, and she smiled. She seemed to be enjoying something, something that I did not understand. She made you want to enjoy it, too.

'I . . . don't,' I said, and smiled back. If only all of life were like this, I thought. I felt happy. She was carrying that silly file, and I had been walking and there was a pint in front of me; it seemed silly and like a game, compared to this unknown but shared joke. I shrugged my shoulders and laughed. She sat down opposite me.

'Were you at St Edward's?' I said.

'Yes.'

'Oh.' I had only said school because I had been thinking of Joe.

'With me?' I said.

She nodded. I frowned.

'In the sixth form?'

'In the sixth form.'

I wanted to laugh, again.

'You're not going to tell me your name, are you?'

She shook her head. She was watching me so closely. As if she wanted to see the very moment when I worked it out. I had never felt, within five minutes, so close to the quick of someone's inner world, to their sensibility. I felt, in this suspended moment of playing cat and mouse with memory, that I could have told her anything. I would have had to slip it into the conversation, in parentheses, as it were, but I could have told her my life's story and then, ideally, recognised her. But there was no time.

'I'm really sorry,' I said, the moment already beginning to fade, 'but I don't recognise you.'

She looked a little disappointed, but she still smiled.

'I'm Abigail Phillips.'

I knew the name; and with the name came a sensation of something unattractive, of bad jokes and barely disguised revulsion. Abigail Phillips was the fat girl.

'It's all right,' she said, 'you were never horrible to me.'

'I don't know if we ever spoke to one another, did we?'

'No,' she said. 'But I wasn't very sure of myself then.'

I suddenly remembered boys saying things about her. Dreadful things. I think someone dared a boy to send her a Valentine's card, and I think they sent it and watched her open it. I think I may have witnessed it, too. She was extremely fat and had bad skin.

'You look sure of yourself now,' I said.

She smiled, modestly. She'd had a nickname which wasn't very nice, but I couldn't remember what it was.

'You . . . you went out with that girl who killed herself, didn't you?' she said.

'Yes.'

'I remember that. That was terrible. What was her name?'

I told her. I must have looked strange, because she put her hand on my arm.

'Sorry,' she said. 'I shouldn't just have brought it up like that.'

'It's all right,' I said.

'Things don't go away that easily, do they?'

She looked at me kindly.

'You just passing through?' she asked.

'Yes. I live in London, now. What do you do?'

'I manage this chain of pubs. We have seven.'

'You're in charge.'

'Oh yes.'

She smiled. She looked so dignified. For all her business clothes and jewellery and make-up and beauty, she looked dignified. And as soon as I saw this dignity I could picture her exactly as she had been at school, because I realised she had looked pretty dignified then, opening that card.

'You're so beautiful,' I said. No doubt it was too much, just to have said it like that. I got up and went out before she had time to be embarrassed. I went through the open door and stood on the weir looking at the water. I thought of the fishing trip, and for some reason tried to put the two experiences, the past and the present, together. All those years ago I had been let off the hook. I had been both punished and rewarded. At the moment of greatest selfishness circumstance had saved me.

I thought of the girl who was dead all those years before, and of the girl inside, Abigail Phillips, who had been the fat girl, still seated at my table, looking at me out on the weir. I thought of the daft memory I had had earlier. Catching that miraculous fish. But that girl's beauty which life had drawn out of unhappiness, unlike the fish, could not be thrown back. It was not a brief visitor. It must be loved, and then it would be known, captured in the moment. If not me, it would be someone else.

The swans had caught up with me, and interested themselves about the water's edge. I looked down at the water, at the transcript of sky streamed with weed rushing to the place beneath where the water fell like a white apron. And felt, as I had years before, something break in me, give way, and I would have cried out. Instead I looked back at the still water above, where I had come from, and imagined myself broken, and reconstituted somewhere in the green, anonymous fields below.

I felt taken out of myself.

Mountains

Now, in the eightieth year of her life, Eleanor realised that she no longer took pleasure from her body. No food tasted nice enough, no wine rich enough; no long hot bath soothed her aches and pains sufficiently and no fine, silk nightgown was quite fine enough to make a long, sleepless night bearable. Even the new spring sunshine on the delicate lines of her face seemed weaker than she remembered it and did not warm her. All these things of pleasure she continued to administer to herself, like medicines, but it was out of habit, not conviction, and the habit of pleasure yielded no pleasure itself.

She expected to be disappointed, but to her relief was not. She had always suspected that she was a puritan at heart, and a long life full of genuine pleasure, of love, of privilege and good health had not shaken her in that conviction. It was just that the puritan had never had to show herself. She had been able to enjoy her good fortune and she was grateful. And now so many of those pleasurable things were in the past she hoped that her retrospective gratitude went to show that she had not taken them for granted, and she felt the puritan in her say 'and a good job, too'.

Emmanuel, who more than anyone witnessed this change in

Eleanor's attitude to luxury, automatically attributed it to the death of her husband. But then as manager and keeper of No. 14 Brockenbury Mansions, Eleanor's home, he tended, either consciously or unconsciously, to attribute every failure, whether of pleasure, health or the plumbing, to the absence of the governing influence of his sometime master. Eleanor sensed this, and though her husband had been dead for ten years, she did not correct Emmanuel. It irritated her, it was true, the fact that the old servant did not understand the core of her personality, but she could hardly hold it against him. Instead she was pleased that his appreciation of her husband had lost none of its unquestioning devotion. Besides, for some reason she felt that to have said, No, I have always had a spartan approach to life, *really*, would have sounded like a confession; she herself regarded it as something she had to admit to. And Emmanuel's English was stubbornly poor. Confessions made in a foreign language, stripped of nuance and subordinate clauses, seemed to her more damning.

Dead ten years. He had been prone to depressions, fiercely private miseries that ran contrary to his brilliant public appeal. She had been bright and energetic, perhaps necessarily so, cultivating his indulgences to divert him from his black moods. She became an expert in pleasure, and so knew exactly what she was losing when she began to take less of it in life. He had been ten years older than she and he had died ten years ago; she was herself the age her husband had been when he died. That pleasure should die for her now seemed apt. She had adored him.

Philippe de Neves, Portuguese Ambassador to the Court of St James had been enough like a figure from romantic fiction for her to feel a slight embarrassment at her life's good fortune. At times she felt her memories were unreal, as if they were bound in leather and to be read by lamplight. So unreal that they might not even be hers. It was all so perfect. But the moment she began to lose faith in the reality of her memories, she had only to remember the early years of their marriage, her love, his body in bed, recall the rough perfection of his love, and it was arresting and real for her again.

They had met in the months following the end of the war, at an embassy party, in the afterglow of peace. She was barely out of school and he was twenty-eight, handsome, educated at Oxford, drove a fast car and was forecast to have a brilliant career. Someone even said he had played cards with the Prince of Wales. They had danced, danced again, and he had taken her for a walk through Green Park in the moonlight. He had kissed her and told her she was the most beautiful girl he had ever seen and that London was the most beautiful city, after Lisbon. To the dismay of his family and the incredulity of hers, in three months they were married. After fifty years of happy marriage, a knighthood, four children, a faultless career, prudent financial investment and a stroke, he was dead, mourned by family, friends and all who knew him. With only his old manservant, Emmanuel, Eleanor now lived alone in the vast house they had shared all their married life, a stone's throw from the very Green Park under whose boughs, in the moonlight, he had kissed her all those years before.

'Time,' said the servant, as the massive bedroom door swung silently on its hinges.

'Thank you, 'Nuel,' said Eleanor from the bed. She did not move her head, but stared up from the white linen sarcophagus at the vast bedhead above her. 'Time' was Emmanuel's daily morning greeting when he brought her tea, and was the result of a gradual erosion of 'It's time, my lady.'

The old man – for he too was old now – moved silently across the carpet. He was slow and graceful, like a retired bullfighter. He made as little concession to being old as he did to speaking a foreign language – plainly enjoying neither but never showing it. He was dark, with a hook nose and heavy eyes that seemed to have left their enthusiasm in Portugal; they were beautiful, nevertheless. He had elegant hands and wrists, disproportionately long fingers and had a gold ring on the middle finger of his right hand.

He placed the tea on the dressing table furthest from the bed and drew one, huge, tapestried curtain aside to admit the daylight. Then, his duty as doorman to the morning done, he left, silently, for her to enjoy the company of the new day.

And for her, it was a longed-for encounter. She could no longer sleep for more than an hour at a time. All she could do was watch the vast architecture of her bedroom emerge from the darkness. Everything in the house was made on such a large scale that the two old people living there, bowed now in their spines, seemed to be shrinking, and the already huge bed, the massive armoires and gilt dressing tables seemed to grow in size and opulence. Eleanor and Emmanuel were coming to resemble those useless, ill-made figures that architects place beside the models of their latest projects to establish the scale of the buildings, but which, inevitably and unwittingly, suggest the dispensability of real people in their great, abstract creations.

As she felt herself shrinking, so she, with a kind of reciprocal compassion, found herself concentrating on the smallest, most insignificant objects around her. From the first glimmer of light in the room she watched the tiny, beaded details emerge out of the mahogany edifice above her and reveal the cheeks and nose of the particular climbing cupid she had adopted from the sculptor's overcrowded celestial kindergarten above her. The little constellation of lights that the convex wood presented always dumbfounded her – it seemed to her that each morning she assembled the features of the baby's face differently, mistaking nose for forehead and forehead for cheeks. Every morning it distressed her that the child might be gone, swallowed up by the swirls and ornament of the creator's artistry. But slowly, the morning would brighten, and just when there was sufficient light to bring a glow to the grain of the wood itself the cupid's face would suddenly smile down on her, and her amazed relief was as great as if the carving itself had come to life and laughed.

These details, and there were many of them – cupids above her head, clambering out of foliage in search of grapes or a better vantage point from which to shoot their arrows; gilt birds around the glass of her dressing table and Nereids and dolphins around the huge, defunct washstand – gave her an intense childlike pleasure, a world away from the cultured, masculine sensibility which had acquired them years before, at immense cost.

Once awake, and her menagerie of carved playthings reanimated by the morning light, she lay for some time quite still in her bed. She liked to lie there, motionless, so that before she tried the muscles in her wasted legs, or lifted a frail finger to brush the sleep from her eyes, she could just imagine that when she did move, when she did attempt to rise up, it would be with the ease and enthusiasm of the young girl she once had been. She had always woken with such readiness and thrown herself into the morning with such abandon – it was her gift, and she knew her husband found it very attractive. Her ten years of extra youth were to him a special, vicarious dispensation from his own consciousness of decay, of introspective middle age. And she marvelled at the good fortune that had given her a gift in his eyes which she had done nothing to acquire but which came from her mere existence. It made her extra appreciative of her own energy; it made her feel she had enough to go round. And the notion that she was so rich in youth, that she had a surplus of life in her, that she was the means of warding off mortality, became so fixed in both their minds that when Philippe lay on his deathbed, she thought she saw in his pleading face a last request – a last assumption, even – that she must have some days or weeks of life to offer him on account.

This morning magic, achieved by a temporary triumph of imagination over her body, always brought the memory of her husband back to her. The feeling that she was young again allowed the instant assumption that she was desired again. She had been so desired, and had met his desire, and matched it. She remembered how surprised he had been by her passion; he had seemed to expect indifference. They fell into bed as if by doing so they were surrounding themselves with riches.

Of course they argued. He was impatient of stupidity; never of hers and rarely of women; mostly of men. She learned quickly to allow him this and maintain her distance from his work. She still remembered the time, early in their marriage, when a very junior member of the Consulate appealed to her to intercede with Philippe on his behalf following a shaming error on his part. Thrilled to involve herself in her husband's world she had gone straight to Philippe and pleaded the poor boy's case, arguing with increasing eloquence for his youth and inexperience and begging for his pardon. She had seen her husband's face grow pale, and something almost like hatred seemed to possess him. She was devastated. He told her she was not to concern herself with such things. And they had argued. But afterwards she knew quite well that it was no old-fashioned chauvinism that motivated him, but a simple self-preservation. He loathed stupidity and incompetence, and it threatened to make him loathe the world. She was not these things, she gave him hope. She was to remain evidence of a better world. She couldn't argue with that. And looking back over the fifty years they had spent together she could not have asked for more love, either given or received. It had all been love. Now Emmanuel was keeping her company to the end. Keeping that love alive.

Eventually the fiction must end. Limbs infinitesimally stiffer than yesterday, bones brittler and muscles weaker must accept movement, and through movement regain their use. The magic charm dispelled, the darkening of her body's well-being by arthritis must be endured. She sat up and swung her legs over the side of the bed. Like a sailing ship leaning into the wind, each sinew and each joint took the strain and the structure beneath accommodated the movement up and forward. She lifted a finger to her lips as if silencing a thought, and she felt like an old woman again. She stood up.

It was not only the love of the past that had kept her so still for so long. Something opposite to indulgence always made her hold off from movement. Eleanor hated the pantomime of pretending all was well. The geriatric obsession with 'soldiering on' she thought dishonest and vulgar. She felt that she had been so lucky in her long life that to artificially prolong a youthful attitude was to her ungrateful. She felt that when she could no longer walk she would sit, when no longer sit she would lie, and when no longer lie, she would, well, die. She wanted no Zimmer-frame heroics.

What she feared was not death but a hollowness: a fear that she hadn't the means or sufficient opportunity to express her gratitude for her life. And there had been so much of it. Who was there to thank? Sometimes she watched Emmanuel's growing incapacity with the hope that one day she would come to be his nurse and somehow thank *him*.

She walked, at first unsteadily, to the bathroom. After this trip of maybe twenty paces, she felt the worst of the day was over. The last rite in the initiation into a new day was to look in the mirror. The suspension of years that her stillness in the bed had achieved was usually just fresh enough in her mind for her to feel some disappointment, if not dismay, at the sight of an old lady in the bathroom mirror. And, of course, she saw that dismay in the face that looked back at her, but Eleanor had retained her sense of irony and saw the look with amused contempt. 'Will she never learn?' she seemed to say of her own reflection, and doused her old face with cold water.

She dressed slowly and carefully, taking items of clothing one by one from the vast armoire; taking and replacing those that did not please her. A considerable proportion of her income went on her wardrobe. She dressed well, not ostentatiously. But there was not one thing that was not beautifully made or beautifully worn. Her touch rarely failed her. It was not vanity or even particular pleasure that motivated her, but a kind of duty. Philippe would never have her make do. He was impatient of the casual. She felt she would have held his very love itself casually if she had dressed down. And this fear remained. Her wealth, which was considerable, had come from Philippe. It had to be spent, so she would do as he would have wanted. And as she took the silks and linens from the callow shop assistants, unappreciative of an eighty-year-old woman's sure touch, she would find in both the quality of the fabrics and in the vast prices they commanded the whispered insignature of her husband's pleasure, as vivid to her now as on her wedding night, when he had slipped the fine white silk gown off her shoulder and kissed the finer white, youthful skin beneath.

In the first years following the death of her husband Eleanor and Emmanuel saw comparatively little of one another. Without the centre of gravity which Philippe had occupied they were as two satellites wandering aimlessly in the dark. That they should stay together at all seemed questionable; that they should part, unthinkable. This contradiction neither seemed ready to examine, so they took themselves apart, wary of one another's territory and nursed in secret their respective griefs. The man brought Eleanor her meals in her room with the official detachment of a prison warder. The fact that they remained largely uneaten seemed to have left him unmoved; perhaps he attributed it to grief's temporary hunger strike. He himself grew thinner.

Then, after perhaps a year of this, as he was climbing the stairs one morning with the breakfast tray he found his way blocked. She was up and dressed and he had no choice but to turn and retrace his steps. Eleanor followed both him and the tray downstairs. Henceforth they would take their meals together in the vast basement kitchen which was as much Emmanuel's domain as the bedroom was hers. At first, sitting at either end of the long refectory table together, sharing the food, felt as shocking as sharing a bed; but to each of them it was as comforting. The man whose gravity had held them together existed, in the wake of their great deprivation, as a kind of photographic negative, whose dark absence now held them together as surely as his bright presence had done.

There were concessions to be made. In defiance of her choice over a lifetime of tea for breakfast, the Portuguese man presented her with coffee which she was too timid to refuse. He seemed to have his own particular method of making it, and at first she found it pungent and unpleasant, but gradually she began to enjoy the way it gave her old body a *frisson* of nervous energy, like being late for an exam or being in love. It was heady, and its richness, combined with the old servant's language, which in the kitchen he seemed unable or unwilling to translate, reminded her of her husband and the trips to Portugal they had made together in the early years of their marriage. Then they had drunk coffee in bars and cafés up and down the Avenida dos Aliados in Oporto, fresh from their latest attempts to placate Philippe's family, who had disapproved so strongly of his marrying an *Estrangeiro*.

For his part, Emmanuel sat and watched her eat, and refrained from lighting his heavy, Portuguese cigarettes until she had finished her toast. Then she would read the newspaper and he would smoke and at the end of the cigarette she would tell him of any engagements she had that day and suggest things he might like to buy from the market.

This particular morning Eleanor took her place at the table, and as she sat she was aware that Emmanuel did not look at her, but at the table in front of her. She even detected a tension in his look, normally so languid. Following his gaze she saw that propped up against the toast rack were three letters.

She frowned. Letters came occasionally. She almost assumed that Emmanuel would never allow her to be *assaulted* by them. At least, not three. His look almost seemed to say, 'It'll never happen again.' She didn't want messages from the outside world. There could be no news, at her age, that could give her pleasure.

The apportioning of pain and pleasure, at eighty years old, was a ministry out of human hands. No unexpected inheritance, no new honour for him or billet-doux for her which she must repel in her husband's name – nothing could be welcome. If there were cheques to be written, Emmanuel would do it. The dead sent no letters, and it was with the dead that she was billeted for the duration.

Eleanor had thought about it all. She was not indulgent of the past; she was not sentimental. But nor would she entertain the prejudice against nostalgia that was so neatly summed up by the phrase 'moving on'. She and Emmanual lived alongside the past, they accommodated it into their lives, and they refused it nothing, showed it due deference, but like all good hosts intimated that normal life must continue alongside their guest. In this way good relations would be maintained. And there simply didn't seem room for three letters at the breakfast table. Emmanuel was turning his packet of cigarettes in his elegant fingers, looking at the envelopes as if they might be little bombs, waiting to go off.

One bore a Portuguese stamp portraying the Castle of São Jorge and the typically anarchic European handwriting that still made her heart beat faster in memory of Philippe's letters. This was probably a letter from a distant relative asking for money. The next was marked Inland Revenue. These two letters she pushed a few inches towards Emmanuel, who took them in with disdain and lowered his heavy-lidded eyes; 'Small fry,' his look seemed to say. It was the third he was interested in. He turned the packet of cigarettes once more, and though Eleanor had not even buttered her toast, he took a cigarette out and held it, unlit, in his fingers.

Eleanor sipped her coffee, and, thrilled by the caffeine and inured to his heavy sigh at her prevarication, looked at the third. Innocuous as it seemed, it was just the sort of letter to dismay. It showed a woman's frail but distinct handwriting and bore a Godalming postmark. It was addressed to Eleanor de Neves. No title and her name spelt out. That was intimate for a woman who was no longer familiar with being called by her first name and had almost forgotten what it was. Emmanuel pursed his lips as if preparing a berth for the approaching cigarette and watched her as she troubled the seal of the envelope as clumsily as a schoolgirl with a first valentine.

She withdrew the letter and read it, silently.

> Godalming,
> Tuesday,
> (The 3rd I think)

My dearest Eleanor,

I do hope you are well and are not too amazed at me writing to you. How long is it? Sixty yrs? It honestly seems only yesterday that I saw you last, but [a sentence heavily blotted out] never mind. I am *en route* to Switzerland from South America and am flying out on Friday and am in London on Thursday. I thought we might meet for an early dinner.

I have sent this letter so late, and I only have this old address . . . Can you still be there? It is one in a million, I suppose.

Are we friends? Are we?

I can be reached on the number below till early afternoon on Thursday.

What say you?

> Celia

There was a telephone number at the bottom.

It was the sort of letter they had been made to write to their parents every week. 'What say you?' She'd said that then, too.

Eleanor dropped the letter. Or did she throw it? A tiny adjustment of her fingers caused it to travel through the air in such a way as to fall unceremoniously on the table before her. She knew, as she did even the subtlest thing, that Emmanuel would have seen. There was no disguising it. Yes, she threw it from her. Cast it down. And if she had been on stage she would have spat on it and turned from it full of righteous fury and thrown the toast rack after it for good measure.

After the absurdity of this act – for she had done it with the spirit of 'about time, too' – 'sixty yrs' – could she not spell 'years'? – she braved Emmanuel's dark, ironic face and gave him a look that might have been most accurately translated as 'What do you think you are looking at?' This so amazed him that, like an automaton suddenly switched on, he lifted the cigarette to his lips and, in helpless defiance of breakfast protocol began to smoke, though her toast had not yet been touched.

'A . . . friend?' he said, as if the English word were a particularly exotic one. And he raised an eyebrow.

'Yes. No.'

'I see.'

She wanted, for a second, to give him his notice. Her hatred of him was so intense. In a flash she decided she hated the peculiar effeminate masculinity Emmanuel had. He went about the housekeeping, the shopping, the ironing with the graceful tenacity of a woman. But his core was so male, so iron in its will. And this acceptance of her 'Yes. No' – his relaxed concession to feminine contradiction made her weak with rage. Philippe had been far simpler – feminine contradiction had simply given him a migraine.

'What do you see?' she said, braving him.

He said something in Portuguese.

'What? How dare you? How dare you speak to me in a foreign language! In my house . . . in my country, I must . . . I must understand everything!'

The man took a deep drag of his cigarette and looked out of the little basement window. There was silence but for the hum of distant traffic.

'I . . . am . . . sorry,' he enunciated carefully.

Tears welled up in her eyes and through her blurred vision she realised she was trying to put the letter back in the envelope, but it wouldn't go. When she blinked, her eyes cleared and she saw that the man had stood up and was standing in front of her. She looked at his face without recognising it. Whether the tears had momentarily cleared her eyes, or whether their sudden absence offered something like a clarification, the vividness of what she saw amazed her. She felt assailed by almost unseemly detail. She saw the closely shaved chin of the old man, the blue tint of the stubble beneath like a soon-to-be-reckoned-with bruise. She saw the fleck of cigarette ash on his carefully ironed apron. She was frightened. Suddenly the fact that she had lived alongside this male creature for so many years filled her with retrospective alarm. The smell of his cigarette, so insistently male, seemed horribly novel to her, like the kiss of a man who had not shaved; it was totally other, a missive from a world of masculine expectation. It felt like her oldest fear, that Philippe had so expertly kept from her – the feeling that something was required of her, that something rough would hold her softness to account, that she would be required to act according to a man's independent demands of her. She felt she could be annihilated by the servant. He was a stranger.

He stared at her for a moment and left the room. And, in his absence, she realised that the smell of the tobacco, the smell she had known for fifty years, felt new and temporary, in the same way as, when she read the letter, she had felt herself to be something she had been accustomed to think of as long dead – a self, a very young self, that predated both Emmanual and her husband. Something that existed before the whole mass of her long and happy life.

Celia and Eleanor had been best friends. Between the ages of twelve and seventeen, at their boarding-school in the Sussex Downs, they had been inseparable. Their friendship was famous; a template to teachers, parents and girls of what true companionship could achieve. Everybody knew and took for granted that what one did, the other did, too; where one was invited, the other came; where one went, the other followed. To their credit, and perhaps unusually, their friendship caused no jealousy. In the hothouse of girls' alliances, competitiveness and general backbiting, they were regarded as exempt from ridicule. Perhaps it was because they never showed off their intimacy, never flaunted their good fortune. They could not have been driven apart, so no one attempted it.

Adults saw the friendship and were powerless to restrain it. The two girls studied together and got better marks for doing so; they holidayed together and returned to school steadier, wiser and more loyal every year. They seemed beyond criticism. If you had to find fault with them, all you could have said was that they had not had to fight for their friendship: their love had come unopposed, and, to some people's tastes, with no Montagues and no Capulets there's no drama. In that sense they were unromantic and untortured, so those usual currencies of adolescent emotion went unspent. But they didn't care. Their love seemed no less sweet for that.

It was 1945 and the end of their schooldays, as well as the end of the war. However inappropriate it might have been to compare the two, it was inevitably the case that one came to be identified with the other. Those girls who were leaving school were going to join a world where to have a good time was legitimate. London waited, free of bombs and free of housemistresses; no one knew quite what awaited them, but whatever it was would be unchaperoned and free. Those from richer families spoke of visits to a peacetime Continent; the rest would be content with a day return on the Up train and Knightsbridge shops.

On the last day of school, as cases were packed and taxis ordered, Eleanor and Celia watched the frantic arrangements of their contemporaries with detached wonder. The two girls had made no plans. It seemed part of their particular friendship never to look beyond the present. The huge, imminent rift in their lives had gone unexamined. As Eleanor watched the exchanges of addresses, the professions of undying love, she was sure she saw in operation a law of life that the greater the expression of love, the less likely it was the two people concerned were ever to see each other again. She was pleased she and Celia had made no arrangements, had made no professions of eternal devotion. They were built to last.

But of course some parting was required.

Between the school and the Downs, reclaimed from the provisional, slight slopes of the latter, were the playing fields, a lush bowl of green, never level in any one place and therefore treacherous for hockey but perfect for a summer stroll. It was four o'clock, the sun was dropping slowly towards the smooth contours of the fields above, which cast an equally smooth shadow over the green depression and over the two girls as they walked arm in arm. In the distance the echo of their newly confident school-mates, hours from release, drifted over the grass; teachers were shaking hands with them like equals and the younger girls looked at those about to leave as if they were visiting royalty. Eleanor and Celia were glad to keep themselves apart.

They had walked some distance in silence.

'So,' said Eleanor, 'where will you go?'

She was the darker of the two, the more serious in outlook; Celia was fairer and taller; the recent hot weather had brought out the freckles around her nose.

'Home, of course,' said Celia.

'Yes,' said Eleanor, smiling, 'but after?'

She felt a surge of love for her friend, the likes of which she had been wary of in view of the other girls' excessive displays of affection. But she couldn't help it.

'That is,' went on Celia, 'if there are any taxis left.'

'We'll share,' said Eleanor, and pursed her rather thin lips. When people pondered who was the prettier of the two Eleanor was always defeated by her mouth, which seemed lacking in sensuality.

'There goes Milly Thomas,' said Celia, nodding her head towards a distant girl who was running with great purpose with her head down. 'She'll always run like a hockey girl.'

But Eleanor didn't smile. She felt the approach of a crisis. They were walking in the cool shadow and looking at the distant school, bright with sunlight, like another land they had already left. She needed confirmation of something.

'When will our dinner be?' she said.

Celia smiled.

It was their fantasy, to meet in London and blow all the money they had on dinner at a real restaurant. They had gone over it many times.

But Celia didn't say anything. Instead, she walked a little faster, turned and blocked Eleanor's path. They never surprised one another. Nothing ever came out of the blue. But Eleanor knew something was coming. For a strange moment she thought perhaps Celia was going to kiss her.

'Nell,' said Celia, 'I have the most wonderful news. I can't wait any longer. I will tell!'

Perhaps it was all all right. Celia was the more impulsive of the two of them. Perhaps it was that she had already booked the restaurant.

But Eleanor did not want a surprise. Not today. They just didn't do surprises. Their friendship was inclusive of all things.

'Why, what is it?' said Eleanor, rather weakly.

'I'm going to become a nun.'

Eleanor had laughed. Laughed because it was a good joke, and laughed out of relief; for a moment it had looked as though there was going to be a crisis but it had passed. Then she'd looked at Celia's face.

'You're not,' said Eleanor, part query, part instruction.

'You don't seem pleased for me.'

'How long's this been going on for, then?'

She said it with a hard edge, like a wife's early, businesslike take on the revelation of her husband's affair; there would be time to throw china later.

'Is that all you can say?' said Celia.

Eleanor looked at her. It wasn't an affair. It was supposed to be good news. Good, grown-up news. And she must be good and grown-up, and do what she had never had to do with her friend – find the right thing to say, fit the word to the world properly and generously. Like sending a thank-you card for a birthday present.

'I am, of course, thrilled for you. Forgive me, it's a surprise.'

'I suppose so.'

'Wonderful for you,' she said, lifelessly.

Because Celia had withheld something, because so much information to do with God and life and the future had been withheld from her, Eleanor, in a peculiar reversal of justice, now poured out a stream of recommendations to Celia as to why it was the very thing to do. She was full of congratulations, and so fulsome in her praise that Celia looked dumbfounded. It was as if Eleanor thought to poison her friend with sweetness. And every second she wanted to cry and hug her and beg her to tell her it wasn't true. It was ridiculous and absurd and totally unbelievable.

Never once in all their years of shared schooldays had they ever mentioned God or religion. They had stood side by side in chapel, sung the same hymns and stifled giggles in their handkerchiefs over the same, dreary sermons. And as they lay side by side after lights out they had stared up at the same, shared darkness and jointly peopled it with lovers and husbands and children, and played provisional godmothers to their respective futures. When they'd done with their futures they'd slipped effortlessly back to the internecine politics of the Upper Fourth. It was all equally real. No shadow of anxiety about death, or sin, or anything that within the daily inventory of their lives might be filed under the broad if rather vague category of 'Religious' had ever come up. The present was so satisfactory, and the future the darkness bequeathed them so promising. It was incomprehensible.

Eleanor had had great faith in that shared darkness above their heads. A *frisson* of almost supernatural togetherness had exercised her. They had lain there, sometimes in the same bed, their teeming minds working just inches from each other, and to Eleanor they seemed to take leave of their bodies, their thoughts twisting and turning in a sort of grand release from the tyranny of their girlish bodies. The subject of their talk was trivial. But the form it took, the dovetailing of thoughts, the game of intellectual tag, the sentences begun by one and finished by the other was so satisfying, so far-reaching in its associations – all the more so in that the substance was so slight – that the *display*, almost, was joy itself. To Eleanor it was like a magnificent maze into which one threw oneself with abandon, sure that one could be lost within it, but always contained *by* it. She was confident the ecstasy of the adventure had its own, sure navigation.

But something, some overlooked signpost, some kink in the narrative must have been there, to which Celia was wise and she ignorant. And no trivial detail. But grown-upness itself – God. How could she have missed it in her friend? For a start, all their games and all their gossip were, by definition, thrown into dreadful, adult relief by this revelation. Celia could not have talked as she had about love, of boys and men, without casting an eye upwards. After all, so much of their talk had been full of inevitable, ignorant suppositions about sex and the mechanics of love – how could Celia have pondered with such ignorance knowing that He Who Knew All Things would claim her in the end? Why mess with the Profane when the Sacred had you marked out as His? Why dance at all when your card was marked not only till the end of the evening but until the end of time? Why? Why? Why? It was a complete betrayal. She hated her.

As they walked, and the beauty of the evening deepened, and girls streamed around them, marvelling at the weather, grateful as if for some kind, extracurricular bonus their school had stage-managed for the sake of the longevity of their memories of their last day there, Eleanor continued to praise her friend and congratulate her. Celia looked like an actress who desperately needed reassurance that you had liked her performance, but who is, instead, congratulated on having managed to learn so many lines; so Eleanor killed her friend with praise for the form and not the content of what she was doing. They had played a game and Celia had taken a trump card from her hand that Eleanor had not even known existed. It was unforgivable.

Eleanor had no memory of what happened next. She saw the beautiful evening in her head, remembered the distant chatter of girls, the taxis and the tears. But after her friend's betrayal and her congratulations she remembered nothing.

Six months later she was married.

They did meet once more, however, a year or so later, in Switzerland. For their honeymoon, Philippe had wanted to drive through Europe. The autumn of 1945 – the time of their marriage – was neither the year nor the season to do so, so they delayed till the following spring. They drove through France, which, despite having suffered occupation, seemed a brighter, more plentiful country than post-war England. Their destination was Rome, and Eleanor, having heard from a mutual friend that Celia was in Geneva, had contrived to make their route through Switzerland. The mutual friend had provided an address but had been wide-eyed with wonder, not only that Eleanor did not have it herself, but at the suggestion that Celia might have taken Holy Orders.

Somehow they managed to meet up. Eleanor remembered

meeting a girl whom she had struggled to recognise as her old friend. Celia was not yet a nun but was studying; exactly what was not clear. They had piled into Philippe's little two-seater and driven along the coast road, along Lake Geneva, through Vevey and Montreux.

It had been terrible. Philippe, in a misguided attempt to get on with the first and only friend of his wife's that he had met, attempted to charm, even to flirt with Celia. Eleanor saw that he meant no harm. She saw that he was full of the self-confidence, the surprise of having found love, in her, Eleanor; that his life had opened like a flower. She knew him well enough to guess that it gave him a rare feeling of invincibility. Her own heart swelled with joy that she had been the instrument of that. He was able to be the charming man he was because he was taken, spoken for. He seemed to her more beautiful than ever, for he was confident, without needing to achieve any object with his confidence. She knew she had been the making of him.

Her penance, however, for this pride, was to see him fail with her old friend. Celia sat squashed in the back of the car in stubborn silence and responded to his charm as if he were a cheap, serial seducer.

Eleanor died within as she watched this. The beautiful blue of the lake, the lush green slopes above and the Alps above them – the sheer *inclusive* landscape, that seemed to contain everything, seemed to taunt her. However luxurious the shoreline, the pleasure boats that dawdled from jetty to jetty, the expensive, cosmopolitan restaurants with their lawns wet from sprinklers in the heat of the day, the unhurried lapping of the tideless water against the moorings – everything tended, in the end, to draw one's gaze to the mountains. She resented them, distantly towering, like severe relations come to witness the two friends' disastrous, self-conscious reunion. They seemed to imply that the blissfully happy Eleanor had failed to incorporate the truly monumental in her life. That a more honest, severe beauty existed, cold and pure as new snow, that *would* be acknowledged – such as perhaps Celia had acknowledged – and superior to the warm, sunny complacency of Montreux and the cocktail bar of the Palace Hotel. At night, in Philippe's arms again, she wished Celia might be abandoned on the north face of some accommodating alp, with just her faith to keep her warm. In the morning, when they met for breakfast, she thought she saw in Celia's face the triumph of abstention. Her look seemed to imply that it might have been she, Celia, who might have been lying beside the warm, animal beauty of her husband, but that instead she had selflessly given way to her friend.

After two days the married couple moved on. When they returned to England some months later Eleanor heard from their mutual friend that Celia had, indeed, taken vows. The friend could not help remarking how extraordinary it was that Eleanor's joke about Celia becoming a nun had come true.

And that was that. Eleanor heard neither from nor of Celia again. She was left to run the gauntlet of the profane, worldly world alone. And she ran it very well. Her happiness was total, and what's more she had the imagination and natural humility not to take that happiness for granted. She regarded any sense of entitlement as unforgivable indulgence. If she had a faith, it might have been characterised by an almost obsessive gratitude for what she had. In her travels with Philippe she had seen the world, she had seen poverty and looked it in the eye. She was not of a generation to fetishise guilt; where she could not alleviate suffering she did not linger. But where she could help, she stopped. And then she moved on, always grateful.

And yet.

When that evening by the Downs, in the evening sunlight, came back to her, it was not the beauty of the setting or even the sadness of the rift between the two friends that was most vivid to her. It was the memory of an ineradicable sense of competition. She felt it then, and she felt it when she came down to breakfast on the arm of her handsome husband and Celia had looked as though she had awarded Philippe to Eleanor as a consoling second prize.

Nor was this sense of competition eased by sixty years of great happiness. Paradoxically, the very success of her worldly life seemed to imply that a worldly life was what she was cut out for; *all* that she was cut out for. All that she was good for. Had her husband beaten her, had she had affairs and wrung her hands she could at least have imagined jumping over the convent wall into the arms of Jesus and Celia.

Even the sense of betrayal at her friend's secrecy just looked callow. How gauche to value a schoolgirl's candour above God and a true vocation. 'Bless you, my child,' Eleanor imagined some well-scrubbed, habited Celia saying: 'there are schoolchildren and children of God; don't mistake the two . . .' And at this thought Eleanor remembered school, remembered the rare times they had encountered men at close hand; any men: young men, married men, porters. Celia had had a manner of speaking to all of them as if they might already have heard of her. As if she possessed something about which they must, inevitably, have an opinion. Something they must want. At the time, Eleanor had been unable to recognise or articulate exactly what that thing must be. But now that she was married, there came from the half-light of her unconscious the reproach, clear to her now, though too late, 'You're not pure! You wanted a lover when the most I wanted was a new ribbon for my doll!'

So it was with frustration and still a whisper of that competitiveness with which she threw the letter down. It rested there, now, a few inches from her hand. She looked at the prominent veins standing proud of the skin around them and the arch of her hand like a broken swan's neck, turned back on itself; that cruel but expressive contortion that arthritis had made. The present wasn't like the past. She of all people should know that, because she had so much past with which to compare it.

Celia must want something. She couldn't be coming for anything of the world, which was all Eleanor had. Perhaps she wanted forgiveness. Perhaps you were told that when you got old you had to go round to all the people you had known in *this* world and make your peace in readiness for *the next*.

Strangely, it never occurred to Eleanor that Celia might no longer be a nun. The thought never crossed her mind.

She feared for herself. Could someone come and reveal to you that when you thought you had been happy, you had, in fact, been mistaken? Could Celia reveal to her that her life had been an error, and that the bliss had really been bitter and it was too late? Eleanor felt the same dread she had felt on the shores of Lake Geneva, looking up at the dark architecture of the mountains, lit by snow and sunlight. Her friend could come back, and just as Eleanor had once feared that Philippe might have been Celia's had Celia only chosen him, so it seemed she might come now and seduce the memory of him. Just because someone was dead didn't mean you couldn't lose them twice. And then she would have nothing.

'Emmanuel?' she said, her voice unexpectedly firm and far-reaching. The man came from wherever it was he had gone and stood before her. 'You are to forgive me. For being cross. You are to phone this number –' she copied it from the letter on to the back of the letter from the Inland Revenue – 'and tell the lady, Miss Celia Woods, if she has not left for London already, that I will meet her this evening. She must choose the place. That is all.'

She got up, without looking at the man's face, walked upstairs to her room and lay down.

She waited, sure that the man was taking his time, purposefully, over the telephone call. It had felt grand and novel, talking to him as if he were an old-fashioned servant. It wasn't like Eleanor at all, to behave like that. But she had to be grand. It was the only way through this. It was the only way to compete with her friend the nun. If friend she was. If she couldn't open her heart she would retreat into the aristocratic hauteur she was sure Celia expected of her.

But the price she paid for this retreat was isolation. She didn't want to be in her bedroom. It didn't seem to want her at this time of day. The instruments of the early morning were all around her, hairbrushes and hairpins, a hand-towel fallen from its rail. It had the otherness of events that precede a trauma or personal catastrophe, perceived now from across the divide, from a present wholly altered and vital, to a past sleepy and unknowing.

Eleanor watched her own impatience, appalled that it mattered to her so much. And Time, as if to punish her, stopped. Though the months and years had made her old, she was accustomed to think of herself as a governing mistress over Time. She felt they had settled their differences. She knew that if she was tired, sleep would come, eventually. If she needed Emmanuel, it was only a matter of time and he would come. But now she felt ashamed to have prided herself on her command of such a shallow medium. Like someone in a hospital waiting-room, who awaits news of a sick loved one, and for whom the abstract hours marked by the communal clock on the wall are as bleak and functional as the disinfected walls and trolleys – Time was a useless medium. Only what it might bring, the message, the hopeful prognosis, the professionally administered breaking of news – only this was valuable. And this sudden valuing of the message over the messenger began to remind her of something else, very different to the anticipation of good or bad news. So different in fact that she realised it was ecstasy. It was just being young. Having days and hours to burn.

There was a knock at the bedroom door. Before she could say anything it opened. It was like a replay of the morning ritual. She half expected Emmanuel to say 'It's time', if only for a joke and show there were no hard feelings. But he didn't. Nor did he enter, but stood, the door just six inches ajar, and spoke to the wall.

'The lady . . . she say . . .' He was enunciating every word very clearly, rather theatrically; he might have been trying to be accurate, to be loyal and make up for his insolence earlier, or he might have been in a hysteria of loathing for her; she could not tell. She felt she didn't know him. She didn't know how she came to be living with him at all. 'She say . . . *says* . . .' he went on, 'she will meet you at . . . at seven o'clock at the restaurant Le Louis Quinze.'

It was all so neat.

'Is that all?' she said.

'That is all the lady says. What else could she say?'

It was clear to Eleanor now that Emmanuel was proud of having accomplished his task.

She relaxed her head into the pillow. She looked up at the cupids and the mahogany undergrowth above her. She wasn't used to seeing it in the bright morning light. The bloom of the dark wood was unresponsive to the sunlight, stopped it in its tracks, and the little boys that scaled the heights of the bed looked less expertly realised than they had at dawn, struggling out of the half-light. It was still all there, the same dark architecture, like mountains, above her. Then she remembered the man was waiting.

'You've done very well, 'Nuel.'

'You would like me to reserve you a table?'

'No. She can do it. It's her job.'

'Taxi?'

He hated driving her. She knew that. He would do anything, however menial, but driving was beneath him.

'I would like for you to take me,' she said.

She could hear the man shift his weight from foot to foot.

'The clutch is bad,' he said, unconvincingly.

'That is all, 'Nuel.'

'Is it?'

'Yes. That is everything.'

The door closed.

Celia had been the spendthrift at school. She was always borrowing money from Eleanor. She constantly overspent. She had extravagant tastes and would happily spend her friend's allowance for her. Eleanor, on the other hand, was careful and wrote down everything she herself spent in a little book. She didn't disapprove of this aspect of Celia's personality, but it interested her. She could see that her friend tried to lose herself in extravagant things, in gestures of luxury and fine living. Celia wanted the trappings of the adult world: to drink cocktails, to smoke expensive cigarettes. She wanted to be contained, as in a film, by objectively glamorous moments; she liked to take a gramophone into the fields and play it, looking up out of the grass at the blue sky. She liked to lose herself in carefully stage-managed perfect moments. Eleanor never quite understood it; she just wanted to be with her friend.

So the choice of the Louis Quinze was typical, in so far as anything could be said to be typical after sixty years in a convent. It was vastly expensive. At first Eleanor felt reassured by the reversion to form, but then it occurred to her that choosing such a place might be a form of condescension. A concession to Eleanor's worldly entrapment.

But it was too late. She could hardly ask Emmanuel to ring back and change the rendezvous to Westminster Cathedral.

Eventually the time came for Eleanor to dress. She hadn't dressed for dinner in a very long time. Thanks to the consideration of those who invited her, if she went out these days it was to lunch, not dinner. Dinner, such as it was, was bread and cheese at the refectory table with Emmanuel.

She dressed very carefully. She took the clothes down slowly, feeling their weight. She never prevaricated over her choices and she was determined that this evening would be no different. Even so, she could not help but feel the alien formality of the fashionable things she tried against herself; she felt something wanting, and feared that it was to be found nowhere in the dark armoire. Then, for a moment, it occurred to her that what she sought was to dress herself as a young girl, to pick up the thread dropped so long ago.

She scowled and put on the first thing that came to hand. And some diamonds.

'Nuel was waiting in the hall when she came down. The car was parked outside. She walked past him. She could not afford to look at him, or try to work out whether his mood was angry or submissive. He was staring at the floor. She could smell the tobacco on his clothes. He had been smoking.

In the car he was unhappy. He sighed at the traffic and at the clutch when he changed gear.

'You wish for me to pick you up?' he said.

'No.'

'Then may I ask how will you get home?'

'Taxi.'

'You wish for me to book a taxi?'

'No.'

He started to drive very slowly. Another car honked its horn and Emmanuel said something under his breath in Portuguese, very softly. Eleanor knew he was swearing. He did it very gently and almost languidly, as if he was singing a little song. There was something very confident about Emmanuel. His confidence reminded her for a moment of her father and of his driving her to a piano exam when she was a little girl. He had left her there. The idea of being examined in the piano had seemed strange to her. Being tested in something that was supposed to be beautiful. Her teacher always grew impatient when she took criticism personally and shouted at her that it was about the music, not her. But when her father had taken her to the exam and left her there, she was sure that it was about her. And she was sure that her father thought it was about her, too. And now Emmanuel was driving her to a sort of examination or test, and she felt it was all about *her*, again.

The restaurant was an immaculate place. They had placed standard box trees in a row in front of it, along the pavement. So even if you were just walking along the road you had to walk between the little trees and the windows with the menus and the gilt lettering. It was like running the gauntlet of privilege. It made you scared you might be asked for your order even if you were only popping down the road for a pint of milk. On the other hand the windows had blinds halfway up which gave a feeling of secrecy about the place; it was like some blacked-out limousine.

The car pulled up outside and 'Nuel opened her door, stood back, and her frail hand reached out for the support of the door as for a loved one. Finding only vacant air, she groped for a moment, and the old servant took her hand, and she lowered herself on to the pavement outside the Louis Quinze.

In seconds he had got back in the car and gone.

She was alone.

When Eleanor arrived it was still very early for dinner and the napkins and tablecloths were very starched and neatly folded. A man was putting candles out on the tables as she presented herself to the *maître d'*. He was new and did not recognise her from the old days. As she said her name it occurred to her that she was meeting a nun for dinner. The sudden thought that she might find herself sitting in the vast open spaces of the Louis

Quinze with a nun in full habit was so appalling that she nearly lost consciousness. But as this fear worked on her, so too her peripheral vision had presented to her mind the presence of a lady sitting in a far corner. Eleanor did not look directly at this figure; she did not admit her presence to be of interest to her. She just waited for the *maître d'* to look up the reservation. As he did so, Eleanor took the time to think how apt it was that for so many years as girls they had fantasised about meeting in London and having dinner together. And now they were. However one looked at it – even if she had only come to tell Celia she hated her – it was astonishingly apt, like a story. And all the time she had these thoughts she was perfectly aware that there was a lady seated in the corner, in a cheap print dress, drinking a glass of white wine in a balloon-like glass such as they used in the Louis Quinze, and somewhere in her mind she knew, of course, that this was Celia. But she did not look at her or prepare herself to meet *that* particular woman, because it wasn't time. The new present was terrifying to join; the bureaucracy of the restaurant's reservation book was so attractive. If there was no immediate record of a reservation she would just go home and have a sandwich with Emmanuel. Peripheral vision or no peripheral vision.

The waiter took her to the table.

'Look at your hair,' said Celia as they met: 'just the same.'

'Grey.'

'No. Well, yes. But it still has that little wave in it.'

'Some things you have for ever.'

'I was always envious of that little wave,' said Celia.

Perhaps in all their respective years of growing old, no moment in the mirror or new decade negotiated ever presented to them the vividness of their body's decay as clearly as seeing what time had done to the girl that each had loved above herself. As once they must have shared a uniform, a new fashion or a new style of hair, in an ecstasy of keeping pace with one another, so they did still. They were two old women.

They sat.

'And yours,' said Eleanor, 'is still straight. Not as grey as mine, though.'

'Easily as grey.'

'No.'

'Quite as grey as yours.'

Eleanor shook her head.

'We'll ask somebody,' said Celia.

'Who? You're still so bold with people.'

'Am I?'

Eleanor found herself unfolding the thick, immaculate linen napkin and gathering it round her knees like a travelling rug.

'What a choice,' she said, 'the Louis Quinze. Well.'

'Are you still so thrifty?' said Celia, looking at Eleanor's beautiful clothes and the diamonds around her neck.

'Me? I'm happy with a sandwich.'

Eleanor said it with some conviction. When Celia laughed she frowned and looked around her as if already dissatisfied with the service, 'You needn't laugh. It's quite true.'

It was in no way going as Eleanor had thought it would. She didn't want chat. She wanted a full and unreserved apology. She wanted shame. Celia laughed a little more. Like an afterthought.

'You've no shame,' added Eleanor, hoping that the accusation might be taken in the more general sense.

'No,' said Celia.

'Hmm . . .' said Eleanor, and looked at her friend closely for the first time.

She was not as thin as Eleanor and so probably did not look

as old. She wore little make-up and her cheap clothes made her look very ordinary. She seemed complacent and happy. Unworried. Only her inquisitive glances around the room and at Eleanor gave her an unusual quality. A touch of girlishness, perhaps. The world was still novel to her; Eleanor couldn't decide whether this was a product of the convent or her enduring personality.

'What a surprise to hear from you,' she said.

'Was it?' said Celia.

'Of course it was. Why wouldn't it be? How could it not be?'

'To me it seemed the most natural thing in the world.'

'Then why didn't you do it before?'

'I was waiting.'

'For what? Just water, thank you.'

The waiter filled up Eleanor's glass.

'Have wine, Nell. Have red. You like red. Rioja,' she said to the waiter.

'For what?'

'Pardon?'

'Waiting. For what were you . . .'

'I don't know,' said Celia, looking at her friend quickly and then away. Then she looked at the waiter who was leaving. She looked at him as if he were one of the party who had got up to leave. Eleanor saw the momentary craving for reassurance. It may have echoed the time when Celia had sought reassurance from her at the moment of revelation years before. Eleanor remembered how she had congratulated Celia so effusively whilst meaning none of it. This time Eleanor just looked into her lap. She was beginning to get angry.

'I just don't know how . . .' she began. But the waiter had returned with a glass of red wine and a basket of bread. Then another appeared with matches for the candles and a jug of iced water. A match was struck, the candles lit and the match placed in the white ashtray where it made a little smudge; Celia took a bread roll and broke it as if she had not eaten for days. Crumbs spread around her, making the soft linen as rough as sandpaper. The place was getting roughed up.

'How,' went on Eleanor, trying to follow the contours of her anger and make the terms of the discussion larger, more devastating, 'you can just appear, write to me with a day's notice and then . . . I don't know . . . expect me to . . . fetch up at the Louis Quinze.'

'Don't you like this restaurant?'

'Don't be stupid, Celia. You know that's not what I mean.'

'Then you shouldn't have come.'

'I had to come. You gave me no choice.'

'Is it . . .' said Celia, rather slowly, 'that . . . it must be that you are still angry with me.'

'Still? What makes you think I was angry with you? What, angry *then*?'

'Yes.'

'That afternoon?'

'Yes.'

'I was nothing but supportive of your choice.' Pause. 'You abandoned me,' she added, helplessly melodramatic.

'Haven't you been happy?' said Celia.

'Of course. What makes you think I haven't been happy?'

'Nothing.'

'I have been blissfully happy.'

'Then what . . . I mean to say, Nell . . . if you've been that happy . . . I didn't really abandon you. Did I? Not to such a handsome husband and money and good health. You haven't suffered from being abandoned.'

'Is that what they taught you at the convent? How to get out of your responsibilities?'

But Celia laughed a little laugh. She just looked like a good-natured woman in a cheap dress, laughing with pleasure. She was relaxed and casual, as if she knew how to enjoy life. Like she had been at school. Eleanor saw it all.

'Is it funny to abandon your friend?'

'No,' said Celia, looking serious.

'And why are you dressed like that?'

'Like what?'

'Aren't you still a nun?'

'Yes.'

Eleanor knew she had to stop. She was getting so worked up she was running out of respectable options. At school Celia's casualness had been a source of excitement to her. Of relief. With Philippe she lost this. In his arms she always felt her femininity was a thing of gravity, which her husband approached with almost religious formality. Within seconds of seeing Celia again, this dissolved and she felt a girl again. Without being able to enjoy the pleasurable ramifications of this she felt herself slipping into bitchy, spoilt helplessness, and she was appalled. She wanted to pour the jug of iced water over her self-possessed friend. There was obviously no apology coming her way, so she wanted revenge. A schoolgirl's revenge, not an ambassador's wife's. She wanted to tell Celia her hair was wonky, that her make-up was amateurish and even – which shamed her the most – that her clothes were cheap.

Celia was scanning the menu with what Eleanor regarded as obscene interest. When the waiter came to take the order she called out her choices in a clear voice, as though, thought Eleanor, she were calling out the hymn numbers. Eleanor, with a perfect

French accent, ran through her order in a low, quick voice. The waiter took the menus.

'*Merci beaucoup*,' said Celia, brightly. The waiter winked at her.

'Your clothes, Celia.'

'Yes. They're not me, are they? I've escaped for the day.'

'Isn't that rather naughty?'

Eleanor took a sip of the Spanish wine. Celia had been plainly taunting her with it; if she'd known a Portuguese wine no doubt she would have ordered that.

'If,' said Eleanor, 'you expected me to be anything but furious you might as well leave. Please don't be so falsely bright. Anything but that. We're both too old for chat, Celia. For *chatting*.'

It was what they'd always said other girls did at school – girls who didn't have what they had: they were 'chatting'.

But by using the word she'd appealed to their old love; there was no way out of it.

'You *are* cross,' said Celia. She bit her lip and looked away, inadvertently catching a waiter's eye. He took a step towards them thinking he had been summoned; Celia shook her head at him.

'You needn't shake your head at me,' said Eleanor.

She picked up a bread roll and tore it open as if she were opening a letter.

'You always hated surprises, Nell. I should have known better. I was a bit blinded by it all, you know?'

Eleanor wondered how she, Eleanor, was *supposed to know*.

'Look at us, now, though. We were always going to do this, weren't we? Meet up for dinner. We were going to do it after the war.'

'And here we are,' said Eleanor, in a monotone. She'd heard it all before in her own head.

'Instead we met in Switzerland and I was horrible to you.'

Eleanor became attentive. Was this the apology she had been waiting for? She wanted an unreserved apology, which would be swiftly followed on her part by an unreserved forgiveness. Surely her friend could manage that.

'But I'm not going to apologise, Nell.'

'Oh.'

'I wasn't nice, it's true. But think how it was for me, you coming like that with your impossibly handsome husband. If you'd had a heart you would have come alone or at least stopped him from flirting with me. It was flaunting your happiness a bit, Nell, you know? When you choose God everybody treats you as if you are so sure, as if you're immune from everything. It's no easier than any other life and sometimes a great deal harder, if you ask me.' She laughed. 'Listen to me. I sound as if I were a schoolgirl still. But I've never forgotten that silly sports car of his, and me squeezed in the back. I remember his hands driving the car. He was so confident. I wanted to throw myself out of the speeding car.'

'Good job you didn't.'

'Yes.'

'I just hated those mountains in the distance.'

'Nell, you do say the most silly things.'

'Do I?'

Eleanor looked up at Celia for the first time with friendly curiosity. She looked wondering. Despite her age there was the attractiveness there. Celia saw it and smiled. Eleanor was remembering those mountains seen through the haze of iridescence that came off the lake, so their darkness was something you guessed at in spite of the pale cast the water gave the sky. She felt some relief that she could mention those mountains and that Celia should laugh. That anyone should laugh.

'You might tell me about it,' said Eleanor.

'About what?'

'Being a nun. Was it . . . is it . . . I don't know. Nice?'

'Nice?'

'Oh Celia, really . . . what word am I supposed to use? Which one is best? Nice? Meaningful? I have lived a shallow life, haven't I, so I don't know what word to use. You tell me.'

'Why has your life been shallow?'

'It hasn't. So what's wrong with nice?'

This was said loud enough for two waiters to look over at the two ladies.

'Yes, it was very nice. I don't suppose I would have done it otherwise.'

'Well, I don't understand that at all. If you have the thing with God going then surely you have to do it. Whether it's nice or not. Don't you? Whether it's nice or not oughtn't to come into it.'

'Then why did you ask me if it had been nice?'

'Please don't try and run rings around me. I was and am brighter than you. Isn't it obvious? I'm just trying to ask you if you've been happy in your life. Isn't that what friends wish for one another? Irrespective of God. Do you hear?'

'I don't think I've ever heard you so . . . strident.'

'What, not in all these years?'

'Then.'

'Well, here I am.'

'Have you been angry all of your life about this?'

Eleanor had a lump in her throat and in her arms she felt the mixture of arthritis and old, hopeless anger and sorrow for herself and her friend. A crisis was approaching.

'I don't know what a vocation, or whatever you call it, is,' she said. 'I don't know anything, so you'll just have to teach me. Presumably,' she said, not able to stop herself, the words coming – more words than she had said perhaps in the whole of the last year – 'it's about faith.'

'Sometimes.'

'So you have doubts?'

'Oh no. I've never had any doubts about *that*.'

Celia poured herself some iced water and Eleanor watched with disappointment the level in the jug go down. There'd be less to pour over Celia's head.

'I never even knew you had faith. I can tell you it came as quite a surprise.'

'I'm sure.'

'You might have let on. We giggled together in chapel.'

'And prayed together. You might have let on that you had *no* faith. As I recall, you said the Lord's Prayer with the best of them.'

'I had as much schoolgirl's faith as the rest of them.'

'Besides, everybody giggled in chapel. Let's not argue, Nell. What beautiful clothes you have.'

'Yes. I'm rich.'

And with that she took a sip of the wine and dabbed the corner of her mouth; when Celia looked the other way she dabbed the corner of her eye, too. There was a long pause.

'Nell,' said Celia, gently, 'is Philippe dead?'

Eleanor looked at her and wondered who Philippe was. Then she remembered, and thought, 'I haven't even met Philippe yet.' Then she nearly cried out when she realised she had met him, loved him and watched him die. It had taken sixty years.

'Yes,' she said, 'he died ten years ago.'

'I'm sorry.'

'It's all right.'

'And . . . I do hope you don't mind me asking . . . Do you have another husband?'

'Another?'

'The man who phoned.'

'Oh . . . that's 'Nuel. Emmanuel. He makes my breakfast.'

The thought of the Portuguese man was, at that moment, enormously pleasurable to Eleanor. She imagined herself sitting at the refectory table, pouring out her thoughts to him as he smoked his cigarettes in his elegant hands.

'She is as I always feared,' she would be saying to him, 'a madam, a vain and silly girl!' She would laugh. 'And the funny thing is that she has given herself to God but it doesn't make any difference. She's just a silly girl! How ridiculous of me to think it makes any difference, the fact that she is a nun. You can be a nun and be a silly girl! The vanity! Don't you think, 'Nuel?'

And behind this gossip, she knew she would be appealing to the little servant who had been with her for all the long progress of her wordly life: 'I did all right, didn't I? It wasn't terrible of me *to have been happy all my life?*' And 'Nuel would just smoke and say something in her husband's language and Eleanor would nod and say, as if she were saying it behind her hand like a snitch in the back row of the classroom, 'Well, yes, of course . . . it's common knowledge, that Celia W . . . such an angel on the one hand, but *such* a madam . . . so vain!'

'I've told you my half,' said Celia. 'You might tell yours.'

Eleanor forgot Emmanuel and looked at her friend.

'You've told me nothing.'

'Tell anyway.'

Celia was looking kindly at her, expectantly. Eleanor could see over her friend's shoulder the restaurant slowly filling up, the ranks of tables and chairs lining the route back outside to the street where Emmanuel had dropped her. What was 'her half'? Just that? Half a life? When you looked back over where you had been, even if it was only across the restaurant to the street, what you saw wasn't what you'd known at the time. The look back wasn't at a journey – it was just at a place; a location. They were completely different things. It was horrible.

And to counteract this horror, she began to talk. She said anything that came into her mind. Then, almost instantly, found herself in the past. At first she did not trust to the substance of what she had to relate, nor to her expertise in telling it. She had always been a painstaking but lacklustre raconteur at school. She would get bogged down in detail and in the truthfulness of what she was relating. If the two of them were called upon to tell the story of something they had done jointly, it was always Celia who took it on. She told a real tale. She knew when to exaggerate a little, how to time the denouements; Eleanor had been proud of her friend's facility. Suddenly it felt strange to be taking Celia's role and telling her information. She began with her early married life, her children, Philippe's career. At first she did it badly, and almost expected Celia to take over, to pick up the thread and tell it how it really was. But Celia, of course, had not been there. So Eleanor struggled on, and slowly, as she dealt with those she had loved, and more particularly those who were dead, who, perhaps, in common with all their kind, have received inadequate inter-ment at the hands of those who loved them – she relaxed. She relaxed for the sake of those she had loved, including the young Celia, whose peculiar incarnation she was speaking to. And as she had gossiped in her imagination with Emmanuel, now she gossiped for real. She was powerless to stop it. All its charm, the forbidden exclusivity of their friendship, was so desirable; for it seemed to her now that it could not really have been all so easy – its essence *must* have been forbidden, and if it wasn't it ought to have been. She made Celia laugh. Her thumbnail portraits of the figures from her life and even of her husband became more and more irreverent. She began to sketch previously sacred moments with careless bravura. It was obscenely liberating. She seemed almost to be tearing up the past before her eyes – before forgiving eyes – smashing the mirror of the past in a great tempting of fate, a great exhortation against superstition. Philippe became the Diplomat and Emmanuel Sancho Panza. She, Eleanor, began as the Abandoned Friend and later was the Empress Josephine.

She remembered the incident when she had tried to stand up for the young man at the Consulate and had appealed to her husband on his behalf. From this true memory she suddenly found herself fabricating an entire fiction, in which the young man, whom she christened Barnaby, had been madly in love with her, and she, her heart beating faster with unrequited affection, had braved the Diplomat, risking everything for the poor boy. Philippe became cast as a slightly unhinged, jealous Latin lover, and she as a prisoner of Affairs of State, misunderstood but dizzy from the attention of a beautiful boy.

Eleanor did not know why she did it. But she did it brilliantly. Celia laughed when she should and raised her eyes to heaven – in the secular sense – when the story called for it. It was strange. Eleanor had never considered being unfaithful to her husband. She felt she had never done a remarkable thing in her life. Certainly nothing as radical as be a nun and book a table at the Louis Quinze. Perhaps she did it out of the old sense of competition.

But there was modesty, too. She did not want to relate to Celia pure happiness. Eleanor couldn't really compete with Celia on a profound level because complete happiness did not seem to

Eleanor to be profound. So she laced her tale with sin. And more than that, she enjoyed doing it. As if it might have been true.

As she neared the end of her story, Eleanor realised that she had come to the restaurant thinking she was owed something. But when pressed to tell the story of her life she found it was quite the opposite. She owed Celia a kind of absolution. To meet her friend properly she had to get the past off her hands, as if it were stolen booty, which so long as she carried it around would oppress her with its worth; arrest seemed imminent. She had to devalue it slightly; it was the only way to shift it. So in a great, profane, naughty, schoolgirl way, she gossiped it out of her. It was ecstasy.

A moment's hesitation would have been fatal. She must make it to the end. She had to trust to her gratitude for her life, trust that it was secure, and that out of extravagant disloyalty her loyalty, by default, could be taken for granted. The profane, taken to its ultimate limit, would be the proving of the sacred.

When she had finished the two women shared a glass of thick, sweet, dessert wine.

'What an eventful life you've had,' said Celia.

'I loved him,' said Eleanor, out of the blue. Celia smiled and put her hand on Eleanor's arm.

'Look at the mess,' said Celia after a while.

It was true. The table looked as if it had been the victim of an enthusiastic adolescent tantrum. There were waves of candle wax fixed like marble around the bases of the candlesticks and bread sticks broken around them; it looked as if someone had been shot, for rings of red wine covered the white cloth; there were olive stones and fish bones propped up against pepper-pots, terrines of butter upturned or smudged with food. There were napkins on the floor and the tablecloth was buckled like an unmade bed.

Celia tried to insist she paid her half of the bill but Eleanor was imperious. The two old ladies threaded their way through the now crowded restaurant and fled the scene.

Outside it was dark. In the distance a thread of lights showed where the cars passed down Piccadilly and the smaller, Christmas tree lights of the Ritz rose above the street's movement in static luxury. Beyond that, to their left were the dark, billowy shadows of the trees of Green Park.

'I left my case at Victoria,' said Celia.

'Never mind. We'll pick it up in the morning.'

They walked slowly on.

Eleanor led Celia up the wide marble steps of Brockenbury Mansions and used her own key to let them in. She did not want to disturb Emmanuel unnecessarily. Inside the vast, porticoed hall she saw his basket on wheels which he took to market for their provisions. He had left it there for tomorrow, propped against the hat-stand.

Eleanor and Celia lay on the huge mahogany bed and stared up at the darkness above them.

'I thought,' said Celia eventually, 'that if I told you, you would try to dissuade me.'

'Told me what?'

'That I wanted to be a nun.'

'Could I have dissuaded you?'

'Perhaps.'

'Then I wish I'd tried.'

'You shouldn't say that, Nell. Really you shouldn't.'

'All right.'

'And anyway . . . I didn't tell you because I didn't want to spoil our last weeks. I kept putting it off and putting it off. I still thought you'd be thrilled for me. I thought anything I did would be all right.'

'And what about love?' said Eleanor.

'There's no lack of love in doing what I do.'

'You know what I'm talking about.'

There was a pause. Then Eleanor went on:

'I might have died and we would never have made up. I might never have seen you, again. You left it rather late.'

'Not too late, though.'

'Mad girl,' said Eleanor.

Celia laughed.

'And where,' said Eleanor, 'did you buy those terrible clothes?'

'Primark.'

'What's Primark?'

'It's a kind of shop. You see . . . I know more than you. It's very cheap.'

'Do you need money?'

'No.'

'And the Louis Quinze. Mad, mad girl.'

'Don't pretend you don't like expensive things,' said Celia.

'Rubbish. I was the thrifty one, remember.'

'It's the thrifty ones that like luxury.'

'Hark at you, wisdom.'

Celia pressed her head back into the pillow and Eleanor did the same. The little cupid which began Eleanor's day was lost in the shadows.

'Nell,' said Celia, 'I can't tell you my life because there's no story to it. It's not like for you. We wake very early, you know. To pray.

No . . . it's not a story because we do the same things over and over. So much of it stays the same and we change, but . . . it's sort of invisible. There are no events, landmarks. I can't tell you how wonderful that is. There's something wonderful in repetition . . . repetition of prayers, of work, of . . . service. I think that in the world one tends to do things only once, and then move on.'

'Yes. Like friendship.'

'I know you, now. You don't mean that cruelly. You're not cross still. Are you? I know you.'

There was silence. It was now nearly completely dark. From where they lay they could just make out the vast wooden canopy above them. They lay beneath the elaborate, baroque indulgence of the bed like two figures from a Renaissance frieze, two shepherdesses or peasant women, thrown into the great divine organisation just to give scale to the magnificent creation – not in themselves significant. But as the darkness deepened, the room began to shrink and give up the vast carved spaces above them, as night draws the curtain over the mountains and gives, for a night's respite, the local, lamplit world of human interaction its rightful place at the heart of human affairs.

And looking up together they found their place together, the shared darkness, as they had looked up sixty years before, in the forbidden, shared bed of the dormitory. Once again they looked up with parallel hopes; and as two lines of constant distance apart are said to meet, eventually, at that mythic point infinity, so they felt that untouching they touched, that leaving everything unsaid they spoke and that the wide expanse that separated them from their girlish incarnations was only the operation of a peculiar equation that allowed them to return to bed, to peace from the classroom, from the timetabled daylight to the extracurricular darkness of their shared imagination. All those years before they had figured a future for each other, full of husbands and families, and, in truth, though Eleanor's future had held all these and Celia's none of them, though one had outwardly realised these girlish ambitions and the other so radically departed from them – it seemed to both the old women that the potency of the shared fantasy remained. They were back there. Life remained there to be lived and was marvellous.

'What time is your flight tomorrow?' said Eleanor.

'Not till teatime.'

'You must have a good lunch, then. They won't feed you on the plane.'

'That's good advice.'

''Nuel will cook you breakfast.'

'Who?'

'Don't you remember? Philippe's man.'

'Oh yes.'

'He will cook you bacon and eggs. You are not to mind him.'

It was now completely dark. Eleanor felt she had entered a room, suddenly, with her friend. She felt her hand in hers at their sides. That was her only sensation and the pure dark. She had entered a room in which all would be revealed, where her mind would at last be with her love, where the secrets of all their long absence would be disclosed, where a most miraculous catching up would be accomplished. She felt the dearest wish of all her life had finally been granted.

'Nell,' said Celia, 'you don't know why I'm going to Switzerland.'

'Don't I?'

'No,' whispered Celia, and her hushed voice wrapped them closer still. 'Because I'm ill.'

'Oh. I see.'

And in that confession Eleanor saw, once again, the sunlit field, the distant girls walking arm in arm, the Downs – all the things that had accompanied Celia's last revelation. But this time, as she clung to her friend, and as the darkness stole the last shadowy architecture from the room, leaving the two women with only their bodies and the ache of physical incompleteness on them, Eleanor blessed her friend as she had failed to do before. She went to meet the imminent departure, the incomprehensible farewell, equipped. Equipped with love, armed with the articulacy the darkness had taught her, that they had learned together, and which they had found together, again. And just as, years before, the walk on the playing field had been an end when it should have been a beginning, so the two women, in whose lives a glorious friendship had been salvaged, clung together in the dark, and slipped, gratefully, in each other's arms, into sleep.

A Critical Moment

Jonathan Rabinsky was happy and comfortable on the apricot-coloured sofa. The standard lamp cast a pool of light in which he was included, and also included his end of the sofa and half the coffee table. I say his end of the sofa, even though he was alone.

From where he sat the street outside seemed windswept and intense. It was the middle of October. Between the house which he and Juliet shared, and the road, was a large lime tree. Jonathan had never managed to rid himself of the expectation and the hope that one day it would produce limes, though he knew perfectly well that the lime tree, as such, is not the tree that produces them. It is a different tree in the tropics.

This particular tree outside was large and rather melodramatically forbidding. Its arms seemed flung up in larger-than-life dismay. One moment it would bow its dark head towards the window, then a few moments later Jonathan would look up and it would be leaning back, as if recoiling from something. Alongside the tree was a streetlamp, and the dark branches of the tree cast disproportionately large shadows on the wall of the drawing room. Had he not been so happy and comfortable in the safety of the sofa, with its remarkable apricot fabric, he would undoubtedly have gone and shut the curtains.

Juliet, for reasons her husband had never investigated, called this room the drawing room. For his part he would never have called a room a drawing room unless it were found in a house of vast proportions. He didn't think it merited it, in spite of the mighty rise in the value of the house over recent years. But he didn't mind. She had decorated it, or rather *had* it decorated, in pastels and ancient shades. He didn't mind that, either. He didn't really think of the house as his house, or the room as his room. Everything was theirs, and this pleased him. And the design of it all was hers, and this pleased him, too.

Juliet had gone to Shropshire. To visit her sick father. She and her husband had reasoned that it was far more sensible for Jonathan to remain in London while she dealt with the extremely personal ordeal of witnessing her father's illness, than for him to clutter up her mother's eleven-bedroom manor house. And her father really was very poorly. Jonathan had acquiesced, in truth feeling a little disappointed that neither his bedside manner nor his shoulder to cry on were required.

In the end, though, he had embraced his solitude. He had had an early bath, which had made him feel like a child, and poured himself a very large glass of Sancerre – which made him feel like a grown-up.

And then he had sat on the apricot sofa.

His glass of white wine was on the table in front of him. Jonathan still remembers, as he remembers all of this very clearly now, that there was a bloom of condensation on the outside. One could tell, just looking at the glass of wine, how cold its contents were. He liked that, the fact that it *looked* how it would feel; there was a straightforward honesty about a set-up in which one medium, touch, was corroborated by another, sight. He tried to remember whatever Physics class it had been at school when they had all learned about condensation and dew. He knew it had something to do with different surface temperatures and humidity. But he couldn't remember the exact formula. It didn't matter. The fact that there was an explanation, either in his past or in a textbook somewhere, he found reassuring and pleasing. He wasn't upset by his ignorance.

He left the wine untouched. He didn't want to spoil it. And also he thought Juliet might phone, and he wanted to remain as sober as possible. In case it was bad news.

The telephone rang. He went into the hall.

'Hello,' he said, but not too brightly, just in case it *was* bad news.

'Jonathan?'

'Yes?'

'It's Mary.'

'Mary . . . goodness me.'

'You know why I'm ringing.'

'No.'

'I think you do. I'd like to see you.'

'I'd like to see you, too.'

Which was true. He did want to see her again, one day. He hadn't seen her for ages.

'Then I'll come round.'

'What? But Mary . . .' he said, his voice strained with the outlandishness of this statement, and the fact that he had expected her at the funeral and been upset that she hadn't come, 'why didn't you come to the funeral?'

But there was silence. It was very soon to have asked her that, out of the blue.

'Look,' he said, pressing home his advantage, 'let's fix a time and meet relatively soon.'

'No. I'm at the end of your street. I'm coming over, now.'

'What's that you say? At the corner of—'

But she had hung up, like they do in the films.

He replaced the handset and went back into the drawing room. He looked at his drink sitting on the table, still untouched. It was at room temperature now and the dew on the outside of the glass had disappeared. It didn't have its frosted coat on. The glass sat there like a guest at a party that was over, but who would not leave.

He lifted a big pile of newspapers off the floor and put them out of sight. He plumped a crushed cushion, went into the kitchen and poured his glass of wine down the sink. Then he put the kettle on.

Soon Jonathan was mentally calculating whether the kettle would boil before Mary made it from the end of the street. It was a little competition. The kettle hissed, cheerfully. It depended which end she was. He stared at the headline of the local paper that lay on the side. He stared without reading the words. The evening had been so empty, he thought. Why were voids always filled?

The doorbell went and he realised he had missed the kettle boiling. He wasn't sure by how much the kettle had beaten his old friend Mary to the door.

Of course he was very cross that Mary should be turning up in this cliff-hangerish manner. He took exception to her style. After all, today we have telephones, we have e-mail, we have family meals; in diverse ways we can present our grievances to those with whom we share our lives. She could have come and sat down with them and talked, and eaten. If she had grievances. He assumed she did have. They had all passed forty.

But someone had died, and it is true that after a death anything is meant to be allowable. She had not gone to the funeral, he assumed also, because she must have had grievances. He had gone; he had read a poem. Perhaps this visit was making up for it. For his part, he believed she should have gone. That's why we have funerals after all, isn't it? So that we don't always have to be making up for it.

And there she was. Quite small. He thought, suspiciously so. He had remembered her as taller. He kissed her on both cheeks and took her coat. She was like a bird – a black-coloured bird, for her coat was black and underneath she had a black pullover. Jonathan felt, if one lifted her, that, like a bird, she might be surprisingly light. She had very straight, uniform hair, like an advert for conditioner, of uniform sheen and softness. Large eyes. She looked businesslike, was businesslike in her movements; nothing wasted. She carried, as she had when he had first seen her twenty years before, a black, neat, rectangular handbag, that was just a little more like a student bag for carrying essays than a fashion accessory. Of course, twenty years ago, it *had* carried essays. As she was released from her coat, so with her came the scent of perfume. Jonathan was shocked. Coming as she did from the corner of the street he had expected nothing so calculatedly feminine. The coat was heavy. Perhaps even heavier than she was. As he was hanging it up she burst into tears.

'Don't mind me. Don't. Ignore it.' It was like an instruction. So much so that he found himself obeying and asking cheerily if she would like a cup of tea. He steered her into the drawing room, and fighting the impulse to cry himself, sat her on the apricot sofa. Her large eyes held a lot of water and seemed provocative in their readiness to well up. He left her to mop up and went off to make the tea. When she came back she was looking at the colour of the sofa wonderingly. Her face was brighter and she took the hot mug in both hands, like a chalice.

'Do you remember when we first met?' she said, and sniffed.

'We?' he said.

'The three of us.'

They sat for a few moments in silence. They were both remembering.

'It's funny, isn't it,' he said, 'but the thing is, I only went there to get a free drink. It was what you did during the first week. Do you remember?'

'*You* didn't. You weren't like that.'

'That's the funny thing. I was.'

'You were there for the music.'

He looked out of the window. What was the point of being disbelieved? The lime tree that produced no limes had got stiller.

'I didn't want to sing,' he said. 'Not at all. Just a drink was all I wanted.'

There was another pause.

'I was only there,' joined in Mary, 'because Miriam made me go with her.' Miriam was the girl who was dead. 'Because,' she went on, 'we lived on the same staircase. We lived opposite one another.'

'I know you lived opposite one another.'

These were all things they knew. They were going over them, seeing what they felt like now that one third of them was dead.

'I know all these things,' said Jonathan. 'I was there. Remember?'

'I know,' she said.

'I am thinking of something that cannot have been the case,' he said.

'What?'

'That it was only you, me and Miriam who auditioned. That we were the only ones.'

'Yes. I've though about that. It's because you were late and we were early. For the allocated slots. So we were in a way separated from everybody else.'

'That's clever of you.'

It's true, that was the sort of thing Mary was good at working out and always had been. Jonathan found it invaluable and infuriating all at the same time.

She went on:

'There were sixty people in the choir, so they took twenty from each year. Fifteen minutes per person means it must have taken them five hours.'

'I was never in there for fifteen minutes.'

'With coffee breaks.'

'It's clever of you. You know all the figures. I only auditioned,' he went on, 'because in the foyer, on that big noticeboard was a poster. And on it was a list of all the places the choir had toured that summer: Belgrade, Prague, Helsinki, Siena, Rome. It was like a young man's Grand Tour. Where they used to go to be educated. That's the only reason I agreed to sing. I would have run a mile, otherwise.'

'You loved the music,' she said, again. Then she gave a little cough, politely, and sipped her tea. She looked like a bird taking water from a dispenser. He knew, as she tucked one leg under the other and looked with the vague distracted gaze of the amateur storyteller, that she was now going to tell him things that he did not know, or else things he did know but in a new, upsetting way. He knew when she started to speak it would be with a slightly different tone to her voice. She was administering memories to him like a doctor with a prescription.

'She came to me,' said Mary, 'at five o'clock. I was drinking a cup of tea, just as I am now. She stood in my doorway and she said to me, had I ever, ever, sung in a choir. And I said yes, but only at school. She said, very authoritatively, "We're going to a party." I just nodded. I didn't even really know her. She said there was only one thing, and that was that you had to sing to get into the party. It was a condition. I remember a sort of fear gripped me, though it was only when we started to get near the concert halls I realised what was really going on. But even in my room I had been terrified. And she must have noticed because she looked very gently at me – you remember how impulsively gentle she could be – she said, "Don't worry, there is nothing more satisfactory than singing for your supper." I know that if you had told me there and then that it was an audition for the University Choir, I wouldn't have gone. But she was in charge. If she said it was just a party you had to sing to get into, then that's what it was. And for us that is what it was. Not for her. But for us. Yes. She stood in my doorway, smoking a cigarette. She had long, smart clothes that no undergraduate would have worn, designery but all her own. I'd never had a glamorous friend before. Within five minutes of meeting her I would have thrown myself out of the window if she had told me to.'

Mary stopped and looked as if she was remembering a time when she nearly had thrown herself out of a window.

'Since she died I have thought a lot about that evening. I was wondering why she chose me. Was it because I lived opposite her and she was too lazy to go and knock on anybody else's door? She was very lazy, wasn't she, sometimes? She wouldn't have wanted to be seen to be desperate for company. Maybe because actually she wasn't desperate for company. She might just have liked the look of me. But most of all – and I can say this knowing that it doesn't compromise how much I loved her, or how much I think she loved me – I think she picked me because I wasn't a threat. Not in any way. I was never going to compete with her. And that's not because she wanted to be the undisputed queen. It's because she never wanted anyone to be in competition. She didn't want there to be losers. No. I wasn't competition.'

This last remark Jonathan didn't like. The repetition of 'competition' made him look at Mary quickly. What was she implying? That he was?

He sat back in his chair and looked at Mary and wished she would bloody go away. He'd gone to the funeral. He had held himself together, and seen poor Miriam's parents in tears, in the dreadful, wordless agony of seeing their child die before them. He had read a poem in the pulpit, he had marshalled mourners and shaken bleak undertakers' hands and chatted with aunties who'd chalked one up for longevity by surviving a youngster. He'd not drunk wine so he could drive a half-comatose grandmother with a hip flask back to the nursing home, who'd thought he was Miriam's husband, though she had never married. And he had come home and drunk half a bottle of Scotch and thrown up in the downstairs bathroom while Juliet shouted at him through the door. He'd done it.

'Do you know,' he said, trying to relax into easygoing anecdotal mode, 'how striking the two of you looked in that empty foyer?'

'Did we?' She smiled.

'Oh yes. I remember walking in and some officious man with a clipboard came up to me – do you know who it was? Miles. I was expecting a drink to be put in my hand, and he put a piece of fucking music in it. I remember looking at the highly polished floor and wondering how I was going to get out of it. And I looked up and there were two girls coming towards me. One of them was smoking. I have to say you both looked proprietorial of the place.'

'So did you.'

'You looked potentially disapproving.'

'Well, I wasn't,' said Mary, severely.

'I felt you were.'

'We were early. You were late for your slot.'

'I didn't *have* a slot. How could I have been late for it?' he said, his voice tightening.

'You were late without knowing.'

'*Contradiction.*'

'You were there—'

'I was there to get *drunk*,' said Jonathan, finally.

Mary put a hand to her a brow for a moment and then took it away. There was silence. Stalemate.

'So,' she said, eventually, 'you sang first.' She was articulating each word, as if for the benefit of a child. Jonathan felt as if she were going through the whole thing in case they had to do it all again, and get it *right* this time. 'And Miriam smoked and talked right through your song. I remember listening through the smoke and the chatter to your voice and thinking that you had a nice voice. Miriam said that they'd have you however bad you were because choirs always needed tenors.'

He ignored the implication that he had been lucky to get in.

'They were so smug, weren't they?' he said, with a forced laugh. 'The judges.'

'They weren't judges, Jonathan,' she said softly. 'It was a selection panel to fill places in the University Choir. It wasn't a competition. It was a necessary process. It was a very renowned choir.'

The humourless bitch.

'I know it was a very renowned choir. All I meant was that

they *felt* like judges. I meant that that was how they felt. Of course I know they weren't actually judges. I'm not stupid. I was there. We were both there.'

He felt like someone with a temperature who knows the fever has yet to break; that things were going to get worse before they got better.

'Then *you* sang,' he said.

'Yes,' she said, and over the new, confident Mary's face flickered the late-adolescent terror of that remembered moment. 'I was appalling,' she said.

'You should have been more confident,' he said, keeping the focus on her.

'I was relieved when I came out that the two of you were so deep in conversation. That you hadn't been listening.'

'Oh, we'd listened.'

'You mean you started talking when I came out to make it look as if you hadn't? Because you were embarrassed?'

There was silence. An impressive silence, like the silence of an auditorium rather than a drawing room, and he made no attempt to break it. What Mary said was true, and Jonathan thought that in that silence was his cruelty.

'I can tell you now what I could not have told you then,' he said. 'You weren't confident. And not just in your singing.'

'No,' she said, 'I wasn't confident. You're right. What a waste of time not to be confident.'

She smiled. She was only just forty but she smiled a wistful smile like an old lady or a wise old aunt. From the memory of the immaturity of twenty years ago she distilled a maturity that aged her beyond her years. Jonathan was not sure where the person was in between.

And she looked at him, intently, and suddenly he felt like a pupil up before their tutor for an end of term report. A pupil who had been read the riot act the previous term and given the chance to redeem himself and who had not. A pupil who lives the disappointment of that teacher, and who, ironically, achieves in that look across the desk the second time around an intimacy of adult contact not granted the dutiful child. The intimacy of failure. For all adults have failed, and in the failure of the young they meet themselves.

'I stood there,' she went on, 'with my hands down by my sides, and I started to sing and my throat just shut like a trap right in the middle of the piece.'

'It was quite near the end.'

'You see, I had a record of Allegri's *Miserere* that the choir had made the year before. I'd bought it when I'd applied. I'd listened to it in my bedroom at home for weeks and weeks and worn it out. And right in the middle of singing I'd thought of it, and my throat just shut. Shut like a door. You see I was trying to put myself into the thing I had listened to and loved. And I couldn't do it. I had listened to the choir and loved it and here I was about to be in the thing I had loved ... the two were about to be joined and I thought I might just pass out, or something. But do you know, now ... now I think that is how it should be. It's dangerous if the dream and the reality join like that ... one becomes ... *famous*. Do you understand me? Famous to one's self. I couldn't become the experience of *listening* to that choir, even if I became a *part* of that choir. It would have been too much. And fame is the only word I can think of. A sort of universality ...'

'Right ...'

'The danger of ecstasy, I suppose. There would have been nowhere left for us to go. So my throat closed and said "too much". So I had to start from scratch, build up my sense of belonging and learn to be confident. Learn that it's all right to be in a choir and sing, and that singing is not the same as listening. I think that's a good lesson.'

'Sure.'

'No,' she said again, 'I wasn't confident, then.'

She looked out of the window.

The tree was swaying in the sickly lamplight. Jonathan wished with all his heart that she'd stop talking. He wished he could have stopped her as one stops a radio. He wished he knew the formula for switching her off.

'And then Miriam went in,' said Mary.

'Would you like another cup of tea?' he said. But, inevitably paralysed, neither of them moved.

'She made a point, didn't she,' said the girl, 'of finishing her cigarette. They called for her, and she finished her cigarette, so they had to come and get her a second time. They were so cross.'

'No,' he said, for some reason suddenly strident with the truth, 'she didn't want to finish her cigarette. That's what she said to them, but actually that is not true. I may be a terrible person guilty of crimes I am as yet unaware of, but you must not level that at Miriam. She paused before she went in because you were in tears when you came out. She went to you and kissed you and stroked your face.'

There was more silence. The effect of this information on Mary's face was that it seemed illuminated from within by a new ecstasy, quite different from the one she had taken upon herself to describe with reference to Allegri's *Miserere*. Jonathan had surprised her with a fact; he had joined the conspiracy of memory. He could not quite shake off the suspicion that she had purpose-fully forgotten this detail of Miriam's behaviour in order to drag him into the memory-fest. But her joy at the memory, whether this was true or not, was obviously intense. He got up and went to the windows and drew the curtains. He waited there. He didn't want to go and sit down, again, but he had burned his bridges by closing the curtains. He felt foolish. He opened one a little and stared out. Quite a lot of time seemed to have gone by.

'There was a long pause then, too,' said Mary, 'when Miriam had gone in.'

A car hissed by on the wet tarmac. He closed the curtain and sat down.

'Yes,' he said.

'Wasn't there?'

'As you say.'

Mary had stopped smiling.

'I thought,' he said, 'that they were reading her the riot act. You know, for keeping them waiting.'

'It was keys.'

'As you say. We know that now. That it was keys.'

Mary laughed. Jonathan allowed himself a smile. They were in tandem, now.

'Then what did you think had happened?' he said.

'That they had put on a record.'

'Did we both say that that's what we thought had happened? Then?'

'Not at the time.'

'No,' he said, decisively.

Jonathan thought to himself that he knew their memories differed. But that particular moment, of Miriam singing, they knew was a common one. It was so specific, so surprising, so local to the time and place, the memory had a style you could not have differed over. It would suit a sentimental reading of the situation – or at least of Miriam's life ahead of her – to say that her voice was astonishingly brilliant. And it may have been. But what Mary and he remembered was their being nineteen and a trick being played on them. It wasn't complicated. Miriam was a singer and neither Jonathan nor Mary had ever heard someone sing like a real singer. At least not someone they had just been talking to and watching smoke. She put their youth and inexperience in a sort of grand relief. She placed them. And in placing them she had given them a moment they would always be able to refer back to. Even as she started singing they probably had a glimpse of themselves outclassed by the moment. And they were gratefully outclassed. Already, after the brief conspiracy of sitting together in the foyer they were a three, a gang, a conjunction of personalities bound together, and she, Miriam, was already their heart, their mascot, their adored, vicarious star.

So as they sat there, sharing a memory, listening together, as it were, to their dead friend, they knew, too, that a thought was shared, shading dangerously towards sentimentality but with its foundation in truth – they both thought that they had sat and listened to Miriam through closed doors, separated from their friend, not able to see her. And they sat together now, Miriam dead, listening to her sing in their heads, separated once again, this time irrevocably.

'I felt,' said Jonathan, 'as though I would never have to be a student again. Never be disadvantaged by an institution.'

'That's right.'

'She made you feel as though she was bigger than a group of young people. She made you ashamed of all that teenage aspiration.'

'Yes,' said Mary, 'but perhaps, you know, she wanted that. If she'd done the obvious thing and gone to music college she would have had to compete. She would have had to use the whole experience of being with other singers as a way of proving herself. And I think she thought that was vulgar. Far better in her eyes to go to university and be the undisputed star. Some people thought her too starry, but now I realise it was a kind of modesty.'

'And what? Fear?' he said, riled. 'Isn't that your implication? She was scared of testing herself against the competition?'

'No,' said Mary. Then she plainly and publicly contradicted herself, but she did it confidently, as if she need not be ashamed of contradicting herself in front of Jonathan. 'Yes. She *was* afraid. I see that now. She was. But it wasn't a fear of failure. It was a fear of undisputed success. And it was a grown-up fear. A fear of putting other people down with her talent.' Then, after a pause, 'She *was* afraid.' And she said it again very softly, very gently, as if she were consoling Miriam twenty years on. Something in her tone, something in the whispered echo of her teenage voice, fervent and satisfied with the quality of love she offered her friend and confident in its being reciprocated, made Jonathan almost insane with hatred. He didn't know why.

'You forget how tough she was,' he said. 'I don't think she had any fear of being brilliant.'

Mary turned and looked at him, Jonathan thought, oh, so very composedly.

'No,' she said, 'she was tough on you. She was tough on men. But she wasn't tough on music, or *with* music. She was simply more at home with music and with singing than ...'

'Than what?' he said, then, instantly regretting not letting her finish and finding out the truth, 'Than what other things? Sex?'

She paused. Jonathan felt she was letting him destroy himself. It was genius and creative brilliance on her part to allow him to annihilate himself. He wanted to congratulate her.

'Well, anyway,' he said, with fake brightness and trying to move on, trying to shake off the memory's embrace, 'we all got our places in the choir. She even got a solo. Do you remember? It had never happened before, a solo in the first concert of the term for a first-year student. Imagine. She got it. It was as if all three of us had triumphed.'

He smiled, but Mary looked serious.

'Jonathan,' she said, 'don't be angry. Don't be angry, still.'

'I'm not angry, Mary. I'm remembering. Like you. We're both doing the same thing.'

'Yes,' she said, tentatively.

She looked at him and smiled slightly, as if there were still hope. She put her thin little hand to her lips as if she were quieting a child. She was silencing a thought within, Jonathan knew the signs. But it would come out. The torture was not over.

'I have a picture of her,' the torturess said, 'of her at the Ambassador's lunch in Rome. Easter of our last year. Do you remember? She had been such a star the night before. And she stood there with a glass of champagne in one hand and a cigarette in the other, chatting to the Ambassador and the Ambassador's wife, and you and I were sitting in the corner like naughty children eating canapés and she looked over their shoulders and winked at the two of us.'

'Why did she wink?' he said.

Mary sighed, as if he had deliberately spoilt her story.

'It's obvious,' she said. And for the first time since she arrived he thought she might burst into tears, again. 'We'd got so drunk the night before in that smart hotel and made those paper aeroplanes ... and stood on the balcony ... there had been those complaints ... she winked at us and ... and ... I felt ... don't know ... I felt ...'

'You felt?'

'Yes. I felt something I think I must always have wanted to feel. Something I had always wanted from family and never found. A feeling of childhood conspiracy. As if everybody else was grown-up and we three were children. And it was all right to be a child, so long as you had other children to play with. And the things you said and the people you laughed at and the judgments you passed didn't matter, because they were childish ones. A sort of diplomatic immunity.'

She said this last very neatly.

'I don't remember that,' Jonathan lied.

'In Rome. At the Ambassador's,' she said, lifelessly.

'I remember we always used to say, "at the Ambassador's." Like that. The Ambassador's.'

He said it a couple more times until Mary smiled. Then he stopped. He was worried that a bit of him wanted to keep on saying it. Perhaps until Mary cried.

'But it was around then,' she said, with a new, subtle urgency to her voice, 'strangeness of strangenesses, that the two of you got together and I never knew, or at least never knew the exact moment when you two were . . . an item. Strange you kept it *so* secret. One minute it was equal and democratic and we were friends together, and the next, like some invisible shift in international relations . . . the two of you were sleeping in the same bed. You both seemed so intent on keeping the actual moment a blur.'

'Do you count it as a betrayal?' he said, feeling matters speeding up and wanting to be dead.

'What if I did? I'm here to talk about betrayal, after all.'

'Are you?'

'Yes.' She looked away, scanned the room, as if she were looking for a friend. 'Oh Jonathan,' she added, sadly.

'Shall I tell you, then? I kissed her first by the Colosseum. You were off buying ice-creams. I'm sure you remember.'

'When I came back with them you'd gone.'

'I'd gone for a walk.'

'Why?'

'I'd kissed her and gone for a walk.'

'I see.'

'She didn't want to be kissed.'

Mary started thinking. You could sort of see her thinking. She made no effort to hide it. He felt he was watching someone retarded – like seeing someone read silently but who cannot help but make the words with their mouths; an imbecile.

'The Colosseum,' she said, like a tour guide, 'was the day before the Ambassador's lunch.'

'So?'

'And you say she didn't want to be kissed.'

'No.'

'So you weren't together?'

'No. But that night . . .'

'The night we stayed up late and got drunk and made the aeroplanes . . .'

'Yes,' he said.

'That was the night you first were together.'

'Eventually you went off to bed.'

There was a pause.

Mary said, 'Even though she hadn't wanted to be kissed.'

Jonathan sighed.

'So that wink,' went on the great interrogator, 'at the lunch, to us in the corner . . . may well have been . . . wasn't . . . was perhaps not for me, or *us* at all . . . but because . . . but for *you* . . . because you had fucked her.'

She used the word fuck and he hated her for it. He thought fuck you and your fucking past-orgy, your historic hard-on of finding moments to crucify him with. Fuck her.

'I don't like talking about the past,' he said.

'No,' she said. Jonathan felt the way she said it implied that he was one of those people who never did anything they did not like doing. But he did hate it. And not only was their conversation making the past alive again, but the evening itself was, as it happened, as Mary moved her hands to express something, the cut of her dress, the way she reached for her black handbag every few minutes as if she were going to get something from it or about to up and leave – all this was becoming the past so quickly that he felt, as each fugitive moment came and went, a dreadful, galvanising sense of nostalgia for it.

But he wanted her dead, too. He wanted both those women dead.

'I did want to say,' she said, 'I'm sorry I didn't come to the funeral. It was wrong of me and I am sorry. As much for your sake as Miriam's. I think she would have understood. I'm not sure you do.'

'Do I have it in me to understand?'

'I wanted to be alone.'

'Right, Greta.'

'Yes,' she said.

'I have to say I missed you being there.'

'I'm sorry.'

'It was dreadful. *Dreadful*. Imagine.'

'I did.'

'Did you, though?' he said.

'Yes.'

'Hmm.'

'But you know, don't you, Jonathan, what I'm going to ask you, now? What I'm going to put to you. What I'm going to ask you to explain.' Jonathan felt sick. He suddenly felt a great abstract guilt for all the unacknowledged crimes in the world he might have committed, and even for some he had not. 'Oh dear,' she said. 'Now I sound like an examiner or a judge. And I didn't want to sound like that. That's not my reason for being here. I just have to know certain things. You may feel that I'm already against you, and if you do I don't know what to say to convince you I'm not. If I was against you I would never have come. I would have left it all to the past. But I had to know one thing ... perhaps ...' and she smiled, 'the only thing I really do need to understand since she died. Why ... why you wrote that article.'

'Article? What article?'

'Pardon?'

'What article?'

'You *know*, Jonathan,' she said, softly and urgently. 'You *know* ...'

'It,' said Jonathan, for a moment holding his breath like a child, willing a sort of tantrum, 'it was an *obituary*.'

'OK,' said Mary, 'her obituary. Why did you write it?'

'I wrote it, Mary, because someone had to, and the girl we both loved was dead.'

He was pleased with the line, because he sensed his defence had to be a good one. But as he said it he had the dreadful feeling of wanting to cry and of having been tripped up by his own sentence.

'Look,' he said, trying to sound like a casual hack, 'newspapers are dreadfully political. Everyone does things for different reasons. One thing was certain – if anyone else had written it, they wouldn't have been doing it out of affection for Miriam. You could be sure of that. In this case there were two candidates apart from me. One of them was an old stick who'd given her a couple of rough reviews over the years, and I didn't trust him not to dust them off and quote from them. And the other was some Young Pretender to the old stick's throne who has a prose style so rich you wouldn't believe it. I didn't want Miriam submerged in purple prose, I wanted her to be properly represented. And as it was my paper I thought it my duty to protect her. So I lobbied pretty hard to get the job, even though I found it an upsetting thing to do. Mary, I was the most qualified person to do it – not only on my paper but on any paper. They couldn't refuse me, and in some ways I couldn't refuse to do it. I wanted to protect her, but I also knew I had seen her develop from a student singer to one of the finest sopranos of her generation. It was a story that needed to be told, for Miriam's sake. I have to say I find it hard to understand why you find it so hard to understand. As it were.'

He smiled at his bad phrases. Mary was frowning.

'I didn't say I found it strange. At first, when I saw it was you, and not another critic, I was glad. Until I got to the end.'

'The end?'

'Yes. I have it here.'

And at last the little unfulfilled action of her arm reaching to her bag was finally accomplished, and she leaned down and took a small piece of folded newspaper out. It was very neatly folded, and as she opened it she looked like someone at an awards ceremony, about to announce a winner. She laid it out on the coffee table.

'There was a sentence,' she said. 'I just want to understand. I want to understand *you*, more than anything. Here it is.' And she read, without expression, like a bad actor: '"Audiences were always moved by the deep spiritual longing of her Leonora and the emotional depth of her Violetta. If her Valencienne lacked a sure comic touch, she always made amends with her vocal brilliance and intuitive sense of theatre."'

When she had finished she put the paper down and looked at him.

'What don't you understand about that, Mary? Which bit?'

'It's an obituary. And you told us she wasn't very funny.'

'What?'

'"Lacked a sure comic touch" means not very funny, doesn't it?'

'It can do. Hang on a second. Only as Valencienne. She sang it brilliantly. I said so. But she wasn't funny. She always said so, herself. Don't you remember? We met her that time in Paris, and we went out to dinner. She'd just had the dress rehearsal and she wouldn't eat anything. She just kept saying "I'm not funny. I know I'm not funny." But she always laughed about it, afterwards. She was honest about her failings. It was a great quality of hers.'

'You could have put that in your piece, too. As well as being not very funny in that part, you could have talked about her great qualities and her emotional vulnerability. I'm going to be hard on you, Jonathan. Why not really humiliate her?'

'Humiliate her? But . . .' Jonathan could feel his neck and throat contract, as if he was slightly choking; he felt like a fish hooked at the bottom of a river, being pulled up towards the light, his head bent back with a drowning emotion. 'But the whole piece was a like a hymn . . . a hymn to her special qualities, to her beauty, to her talent.'

'Except her comic talent.'

'I wasn't reviewing her comic talent. I was writing her obituary.'

'Exactly. So why mention it?'

'I was being balanced. Hang on a second. *Hang on a second*. I had a job to do, Mary. It's a national newspaper, not a sixth-form circular. I have to fulfil a number of things. One of them is to present to the readers an objective account of Miriam's career. It's like an archive. I can't just write a rave piece about my dead friend.'

'Right. So in actual fact, you did the very thing you told me a moment ago you were protecting her from. You wrote a critique. Which anyone could have done.'

He started to speak.

'No, Jonathan, I know what you're going to say. Whether or not another critic would have been harsher on her than you is not the point. You were either being a critic or not. It's not a question of degree. And you were.'

'I'm a professional person. Miriam was a professional person. There's nothing pure in this world, Mary, and Miriam knew that. You have a choice whether you take the spirit in which this piece is written, or not. It's not bitchy, it's not opinionated. It's a celebration of her career. People took Miriam to their hearts. Do you really think they care about one sentence? They probably loved her more for the fact that she *couldn't* do comedy! That's how much she was loved. Are you really going to crucify me over five words?'

'Yes.'

It was strange that just before she had started talking specifics he had thought that he must have done something wrong, too. But as her accusations started tumbling out, he felt, he *knew* that he was unjustly accused. He had tried to be fair.

'Look,' she said, 'I can see this offends you. I can see you're incredulous and a little upset. How much of that incredulity is an act, either for my benefit or your own, I can't tell. I'm really not here to beat you up about it, though I'm aware that that is how it must seem.'

She sighed and looked around the room.

'We don't see much of one another any more, do we? I ... I read that piece, and I thought ... I thought, "He's got something wrong in his life. That's not Jonathan. He's taken a wrong turning." It made me angry, your article, yes. But most of all it made me sad. Now, you think that insufferably pious of me, no doubt. From the look on your face I can see you do. There's nothing I can do about that. But think about it, just for a second. Think about life from the point of view of death, of total, absolute loss. The end. However much you may justify what you do in worldly terms, think about what art and music and your job must mean to you, such that your great friend, who was a million other things than just a singer – one of which, incidentally, was once being your lover – dies. And you, by virtue of what happens to be your job, your role in the world, in the national press, find yourself writing about this *one* thing that she did publicly – singing – and mentioning – not even highlighting – it's true you didn't highlight it that much, but mentioning it is surreal enough – her shortcomings. *What she had trouble with.* Jonathan? Can't you hear the angels laugh? It's a sort of madness. Brilliantly but tragically absurd. To think that in the face of death ... in the face,' here her voice nearly broke, 'of a death so young ... in the face of her mother's grief and her friends' dreadful sorrow, that performance means *anything*! That being funny fifteen years ago means anything. Well, perhaps you will say if it means nothing then you can mention it; that we can take it as read that it is a mere detail. But here's the crux. It wasn't nothing to her. If she could have read that so-called obituary, she would have remembered all the shame and embarrassment of Paris. It would have brought it all back. And surely, if a person has been a good person, and by God she was a good person, you have to write an obituary that salutes that person's spirit and which they could have read and thought "I did all right!" Because if you don't, you're no friend. And she deserved friendship, to the last. It was her gift, to be a friend. Think what Valencienne meant to her. You were there. You saw what she went through, what went on in her head – the fear that she was wrong for the part, the self-consciousness, that dreadful costume they put her in, the things that conductor said to her after the dress rehearsal, the sudden loss of confidence, the tears. You knew her inner world, and at the time you honoured it by saying what she needed to hear. We both did. And she bloody pulled it off. And I don't think it's too terrible to say that she partly pulled it off because we were there for her. I truly believe that. So what's changed? It's true, she wasn't that funny. She knew that. But you? You want to be honest at all costs? To whom? Strangers? She was a professional, yes, and so are you. But no one's going to judge you harshly if you fail to mention the fact that she wasn't funny as Valencienne. There's no judge of judges, is there? No critic of critics. No teacher from whom you must get top marks for covering all the relevant mistakes in someone's life.'

Jonathan stared at her while she spoke. He wanted to suffocate her with a cushion and dismember the body, but the carpet was too pale, the blood would have stained permanently. Besides, murder would lead to misunderstandings. It would have to be suicide. Thank God he didn't have children whose lives he would be blighting. Juliet wouldn't mind.

'And think,' she went on, careless of her own safety, 'for whom was that little remark, that unnecessary aside written? God? Yourself? Was it for the Miriam of twenty years ago, because you hadn't been honest then? Or is it for the Miriam, dead two weeks. *Two weeks.* No . . . no, I *won't* cry! Jonathan, it has to be aggression. Against what, I don't know. But I have to say . . . there are two dreadful scenarios, here. One is that, as a critic, because you're a critic and not an artist, you are, I don't know, envious of Miriam, of her talent and her spirit, and can't help – perhaps without even being aware of it – diminishing, reducing what the free artist does. Perhaps you're in competition with it, and all you can use is your intelligence . . . Your intelligence has to be triumphant in the end. And you are an intelligent man, Jonathan. You are. I always thought that. But you can't compete with creativity. Not because you'll lose, but because it's not a competition. You should have let Miriam be Miriam and mourned her, and . . . and passed by on the other side. The other scenario . . . the other scenario is that you always loved her, and that you never forgave her for leaving you. I'm sorry to have to suggest that. But in the circumstances it's the only explanation I can think of for writing as you did. If it's not true, I suppose you have every right to be very, very angry.'

'Really, Mary, my dear friend . . . Really, really, really. Oh dear. Shall I tell you? Fuck. How fucking dare you? Can you really do no better than the hackneyed old "those who do, do and those who can't, criticise"? The very idea that such an obvious criticism might be true is in itself an insult. Mary, you think I haven't worked all that out? You think I haven't gone through it all in my head a hundred, a thousand times? Quite honestly, I'm not even going to grace it with a defence. I'll just say this. There's nothing Darwinian about being a critic. We're not evolutionary failures. We're not further down the food chain, not hyenas that failed to evolve into beautiful lions. My love, for want of a better word, my *enjoyment* of music is just that, enjoyment. It's not a bitter, unrequited passion that means I must shit on what I love to give my emotions some spurious legitimacy. But leaving that aside. Your second accusation is deeper than that. You're suggesting that I must shit not on the music but on the musician who I happen once to have been in love with.'

'*Happen* once to be in love with . . . happen? Is love something that happens, as some kind of side dish to the artistic main course?'

'Mary, Mary, your view of the world is a sort of monomania. Do you want only personal love, loyalty and the three of us sitting in the corner of the embassy eating canapés, and absolutely nothing else?'

'Yes.'

'What, no society, no music-making with or for strangers, no good and bad, no objective criteria, no cultural community of shared goals, no conservatoire standards, no colleges promoting excellence, no publicly funded elite institutions, no artistic forum in which we write and talk and discuss what we are about in the modern world, about finding a role for the arts, about what we aspire to, about what gifted children should be able to do, about promoting brilliant teachers, about having some art and beauty in the face of consumerism and multi-corporations and funda-mentalism, in the face of death, even in the face of dreadful cancer and AIDS and bereavement? Miriam believed in all of those things, Mary. And in the midst of those things sits the good critic, believing those things, too. And do you know what he does? He salutes the real thing when he sees it, because the real thing is what all of those efforts and dreams aspire to. The best. Because without the best there's no second-best, there's no amateur music, there's nothing. And egos in the music business, in any business that matters, actually know that. There have to be critics. They may not like it, but the truly brilliant know that we need it all – including the dreadful moments of loss of confidence, the taking-criticism-personally, the whole diva thing. It's necessary.

Artists know that. Why don't you? Miriam was good at some things and bad at others. We all are. The fact that I'm able to talk about that objectively in an obituary is evidence of the fact, actually, that I *am* able to separate the public from the personal. My readers aren't interested in her cooking, though I know all about that, too. According to your analysis, to be balanced, I should have reviewed our sex life, as well. What I did was to exercise a public duty as well as I could and keep the private private. Balancing those two seems to me to be not just good, humane journalism, but the challenge of adulthood. And if that doesn't dovetail with your ... your neo-adolescent craving for unconditional acceptance, I'm sorry.'

Jonathan felt buoyed up by the unexpectedly articulate defence he had mounted. He no longer felt doomed. He couldn't understand why he had been so passively accepting Mary's criticism of him. The grown-up world was here at hand, and he was the articulate maker of it. Of course she had a point. That was why he wanted to kill her. Best to accept that and balance the impulse to kill her against the fact that he had a point, too. He even had a reputation among critics for not being hard enough on inferior work. The truth was, he hated to criticise.

From the moment he sensed Mary was there to condemn him he had expected that the condemnation would be something more devastating. With this eloquent rush of feeling, of passionate self-justification, he felt out of the woods. And, perhaps inevitably, he could not stop himself from instinctively running on with the underlying logic of his argument. And that involved becoming more personal.

'However, Mary, tell me ... why it is so important that I honour the private ... *in this instance.*'

'Pardon?'

And suddenly a voice, distant and sorry, told him he had gone too far.

'Why is it important? Because Miriam and I were lovers?'

Pause.

'Because, Mary, *she and I were lovers?*' he said, stressing the words as though trying to disown them.

Slight pause.

'Perhaps,' she said, quietly.

'Why is it so important to *you?*'

To Jonathan, this last word was like a casual murder.

'Why is it so important to you that I don't betray a lover?'

She stared at him. The advantage he had over her was awful to him. He pressed on. But they were back in the past, and he had taken them there.

'Everybody makes judgments, Mary. We judge a good dinner and we judge a good friend. If you are determined to make my one, small, critical aside the foundation of accusing me of monstrous crimes then it is you – you! – who seek to judge adversely, not me. This is not about judging Miriam at all. It's about you judging me! Why is that?'

He wanted to say it was she who had brought him to this place; she had made it impossible for him not to say these things. She had driven him to the scene of her heartbreak and said 'break it again'.

'You also,' he went on, 'have to come to terms with two unpleasant scenarios. One is that you quite simply haven't got over Miriam's death, which is quite understandable. And the other . . .'

But his nerve failed.

'What's the other, Jonathan?'

'Never mind.'

'No. Not never mind. Damn you and your lies and your public versus private!'

'The other,' he said, wearily, wishing he was dead, for her sake, 'is that you were in love with me. And you resent me, and the *private* way in which Miriam and I got together, and your *public* humiliation. You see yourself in that obituary and it enrages you. You think I betrayed my lover, and you think that had you been my lover I would have betrayed you. That I betrayed you. You are angry by proxy. Perhaps not even by proxy – I betrayed you. It all comes down to the Bateau Mouche.'

'Why the Bateau Mouche?'

'Because that's where I kissed you.'

'You're determined to make this all about you, aren't you?' said Mary. 'Absolutely determined. You're going to fight with every memory, every psychological strategy you can come up with to try to convince me that you weren't wrong to write that piece. But I believe you know you were wrong, or you wouldn't be defending yourself so vehemently. You'd just say, each to his own. And you'd have the confidence, the moral confidence, to let it go.'

'Bateau Mouche! Bateau Mouche!'

'What, Jonathan, because you kissed me, and led me to believe you liked me and then had misgivings and went and told Miriam that I was desperately in love with you?'

'Mary, you'd already told her that yourself! Listen to me. My God, you're a confident woman now, but trust me, *you weren't then*. All right? I didn't know what I'd let myself in for. I did something impulsive. It was a mistake. It obviously meant a lot to you and I felt dreadfully guilty. I was confused. You didn't exactly hold back from criticising me at the time yourself, as I remember.'

'I wouldn't mention it in your obituary.'

'You were so gauche! I mean we were friends, and you go to Miriam, my girlfriend, and you tell her that you are desperately in love with me. Not that I'm nice, or that you'd like to meet someone like me, but that you are *desperately* in love with me. We were pretty amazed, Mary. I can tell you. Pretty amazed.'

'We always said the three of us would come first. That there would be no secrets.'

'We weren't a bloody *ménage à trois*, for God's sake! How long was the three-way friendship going to last with you going round wanting honest conversations with everyone? It was exhausting. I thought if I kissed you you might just stop, or go away, or realise I wasn't the answer. It was a misjudgment, I admit. I just wanted you to forgive me for being the person you'd decided you loved.'

'Forgive you?'

'Yes. You were so moral. Miriam and I were so scared of your judgments. Always. We had betrayed you by becoming lovers, and you loving me felt like a sort of moral revenge. To make me feel dreadful. This whole visit this evening is moral revenge! You are the critic, you are the judge, and you will do anything to justify yourself! Bateau Mouche! Bateau Mouche!'

Mary put her head between her hands and screamed.

The phone rang, like an alarm going off. Jonathan got up and went into the hall.

'Hello?'

It was Juliet. She seemed to be shouting at him, and for a moment he felt as if she had just joined in the argument. Then he realised it was a very bad line. It was a pay-phone. Mobiles were banned from the hospital. Her father had been moved into intensive care. Through the shouting she sounded very tired. She said it was the waiting that was the worst thing. That and the absence of drinkable coffee. And the helplessness. The shortage of doctors was a crime. There must be a remedy. Either through taxation or central reform. They would speak very early the next morning. No, no one had called. The nurses were saints. Saints.

Jonathan put down the phone. He stood and stared for a moment. Mostly at the stairs. NEW BYPASS PLANNED FOR CIVIC CENTRE the headline had said that he had stared at while he waited for Mary. It seemed like a long time ago. Without turning round, as if fearful of the sight of the woman on the sofa, he went to the kitchen to make more tea.

He had written Miriam's obituary on the floor of the drawing room, surrounded by CDs, her recordings, by gifts she had given him, by diaries and by photographs. And the thing that he had written had brought him to the Bateau Mouche, with a different girl and a different memory. It seemed inconsistent. Was it possible to look back and trace a different route out of the past? And, more importantly, would that mean a different present?

He noticed that now, curiously, when he thought of Mary and the moment in Paris, attendant on the guilt which accompanied the memory was, in fact, a deep pleasure, a remembered aching pleasure that might have been recalled as pain. He remembered the circumstances, the big vulgar boat, the French commentary and the throng of tourists, the sense of killing time before the concert in the evening, the intimacy of the water with the city which, for anyone used to the chaste and formal distance between the Thames and the city it dissects, is like an instantly accessible, urban *frisson*. Had he kissed her really as a means of getting rid of her unwelcome professions of love? Just to get rid of her? Perhaps all desire is founded on the desire to annihilate, even if the foremost object of annihilation is desire itself. He had leaned down and kissed her, swooped, almost perfunctorily, and yet he had not expected her response. She had seemed unsurprised, had shifted her head slightly, accommodated her mouth to his with confidence, her kiss assured, easily feminine, as if she had to hand at all times, if required, a blithe, knowing, abandoned sense of the moment. Normally so considered and unspontaneous, this easy commerce with the sensual had surprised him. He had known, instantly, that his idea of dispelling her infatuation by kissing her was ridiculous and counterproductive. He felt guilty. They were there for Miriam. She was the star and she was his girlfriend. Mary and Jonathan were hangers-on, and therefore equal in a way that Jonathan secretly loathed. Mary was untalented and gauche and did nothing in the world. She made no mark. Her very acceptance of his kiss was masterfully passive. Only now, twenty years later, now that a new guilt had been presented to him – the obituary – would he admit that he had found this passivity – now raised to new moral heights by Mary's confrontation with him – devastatingly attractive. That kiss, twenty years later, returned to him now as a moment of such total pleasure, such sheer beauty. Such pleasure that it had in fact warned *him* off. And the realisation that it might have been Mary that he had desired, not her talented friend, was so dreadful, it filled him, firstly, with the most indescribable rage. He was in an agony of terrible, inarticulate loathing; he was unsure for whose thwarted desire he felt more cross – Mary's, ruined by his callowness, or his own, ruined by fear. Accustomed to thinking that sexual desire alone was a pretty poor foundation for any behaviour, he now looked back at that kiss and realised that having missed the *absolute* sexual moment he had missed the moment of his life. He should have been with Mary. Suddenly it seemed to him the dreadful, incalculable disaster of his youth, of his time in the choir. And now that the whole past had come to reproach him with his conduct, it was also clear that it was the disaster of his life.

He finished making the Earl Grey and carried it through to the drawing room. To his horror, Mary had stood up and seemed to be about to leave. She had found her coat herself; it seemed her autonomy extended to other people's closets.

'What would she say about it all, I wonder?' said Mary.

'Who?'

'Miriam.'

Jonathan had thought she meant Juliet.

'I don't know. Look,' he said, 'please don't go. We . . . we still have it, don't we?'

'Have what?'

'The thing that kept us together. That . . . that made me kiss you.'

'No, Jonathan. She's dead.'

'Was it just her?'

'Just?' She said it softly, so softly. 'I really must go.'

And her face came up to his with the sure gravity of gentleness and kissed his cheek. The disappointment of this single kiss lasted for only a fraction of a second, for her head had not been withdrawn but was still close; she moved across his face, and the very moment that he realised she was going to kiss his other cheek was the moment her mouth was directly in front of his. For one brief moment the past and present were conjoined; in mutual eclipse. He did nothing. She kissed his other cheek and stood back.

Jonathan felt he must do something or say something sudenly noble or absurd, or preferably both, since by doing one he would disable the humiliation of doing the other. So he said:

'I want to walk with you all the days of my life.'

'I beg your pardon?' said Mary, and took a step back and frowned. All evening she had been strict with her friend, had been firm and sometimes authoritative. But she had never frowned or looked cross as she did now. Jonathan was standing to one side of the door, and as he said it he moved very slightly to block her way and he saw her glance nervously at her exit. For an appalling moment he thought she looked upon him as a potential rapist. He wanted to say, 'I'm not a rapist,' but thought perhaps that was the sort of thing rapists said. But the immediate memory of her mouth passing so close to his, of the touch of her fine hair on his cheek and the scent of her neck was so vivid to him, his conscience immediately whispered to his heart, 'You *are* a rapist.'

The phone rang, again. He picked it up with the automatic reflex of a switchboard operator.

'Jonathan, it's Miles,' said Miles. 'I just wanted to say you are a wonderful man. I read your beautiful piece about Miriam last week. Truly beautiful. And so sensitively done. I thought you caught her quality perfectly. It can't have been an easy thing to do.'

'No.'

'She would have been so proud of you, darling man. I thought that when you read so beautifully at her funeral. Of course everybody said nice things about her, it was only to be expected. But only you captured her spirit. But then you really knew her. She always said it was only you who really knew her. Did you know that? I remember she said to me once, she said, "Miles . . ."'

'Miles, darling man, forgive me, but I've suddenly got a nosebleed, and before I know it I shall have blood on the proverbial carpet . . .'

'Say no more. Another time. God bless you, Jonathan, and well done . . .'

Jonathan put the phone down and looked at the girl in front of him. Mary still stood there. Everything that Miriam had been he wanted to put aside, for in his mind she had become the thing, in her every manifestation, that had kept him and the unbearably beautiful girl opposite him apart. Mary had been wrong – Jonathan wasn't envious of the singer's talent, he loathed it because it was adept at achieving dreadful divorces of style and substance, such that he had got the wrong girl. It was Miriam's talent that had been the gooseberry, preventing consummation. And now, with a great, dreadful, obscene thrill, he decided he was glad she was dead, thrilled with childish wonder, as if it were Christmas. The death of talent. So we could all be left in peace. He thought how he hated the high-flown poetry of their shared past, and how it was only prose that was sexual and redeeming. Only prose could cover confession and absolution, only prose could describe the moment-to-moment revelation of his love. And Miriam had been always turning life into fucking song and abandonment. It was to be regarded as a great benefit to his inner life, her being dead.

'Jonathan, are you all right? You look pale.'

Mary was a fact beyond argument. He had been wrong to write the article because Mary, the irrefutable principle, had said he was. And the proof of this, as if to facilitate the understanding of how wrong he had been, was the actual, physical fact of her, insisting on her rightness: her pretty hair, her small accommodating mouth whose softness he now remembered so clearly, the excruciating ecstasy of the Paris memory – the chill of the air in the boat on the Seine, the sense of undisclosed, feminine warmth beneath the heavy folds of her winter coat, the lightness and receptiveness of her body beneath, swamped in scarves and pullovers, his sudden curiosity to know more, to travel with newly won permission about her body; the impossibility of doing so. And now, years later, for him to possess the moral certainty she had brought to bear on his life, he must complete his partial intimacy with Mary which he had begun, clumsily, all those years before: to be the whole convert he must know the whole. With the desire to understand came the need to possess, to take her, know her, have her. That this path to goodness had begun twenty years before was irrelevant. He had not recognised it till now. The creative memory – or more accurately the recreative memory – and the truth contained within it had supplanted his occupation.

'I think I had better go,' she said. 'Now, listen to me. You'll miss her. Don't give yourself a hard time.'

'I love you, Mary.'

'Oh dear,' she said.

'It's true.'

She sighed.

'I don't know,' she said; 'for some reason I was frightened you might say that. Come on. Look, I came to reproach you. It was mean of me. The Jonathan that I . . .'

She stopped.

'What? The Jonathan you used to know would what? Understand? Is that what you're saying?'

But Mary just looked at him.

'Mary . . . I am the Jonathan you loved. Don't presume to . . .'

'I'm going,' she said, decisively, and moved to the door.

'No, you're not,' said Jonathan Rabinsky.

'*Christ* we can do better than this,' she said, and tossed her head. He thought she looked rather ugly being angry.

He took a step back and she walked to the door unhindered.

'Meet me tomorrow,' he said. He couldn't remember why he

needed to see her, and then remembered it was to elope with her. She turned and looked at him and opened the door and stood, caught between the hall and the outside world. Then, very gently, she laid her head against the door frame. This simple act undid him, because he stared at her and all sensations of his own ceased, he lived only through her. He felt the cool door against his head, the smooth white paint, the momentary peace of this simple place, as if the door offered momentary absolution, like the hand of a priest on her brow, or a hard compress of reality, insisting on facts that otherwise might go soft and ungraspable: all this he lived through her. Then he stared at the floor. There was complete silence.

At some point in the next few minutes Mary left unseen.

After a decent interval Jonathan Rabinsky picked up the phone.

And what of Mary?

She left, unobserved and in tears. Her dead friend seemed very close to her, more vivid than even the man she had just left. She made her way quickly through the October wind and rain, as if her speed would help her get through the emotion she was feeling more quickly, for she felt she needed a clear head. As she got closer to her bus stop, she slowed down. A taxi passed her and she watched it, black and anonymous, disappear into the neon streets. Taxis were something she never allowed herself, for she was not well-off. Another passed. To hail one would be a guilty act. More passed, like sins. Then, in an uncharacteristic act of indulgence she hailed the next one. She gave her address to the driver as one might to a policeman, seated herself in the hearse-like expansiveness of the broad-backed seat, and stretched out her legs in unaccustomed luxury.

As the cab slowed in the traffic over Waterloo bridge she looked from the lights of the City to the invisible water beneath, far beneath. She had gone to Jonathan's with her friend in mind, but had left, as the bereaved are perhaps always left, not with a diminished sense of self, but with a more intense one. As she plunged once more into the city beyond the bridge, and the streets became the streets closer to her flat – her exceptionally modest flat, as befitted a modest girl – she sensed, as she knew she must, the approach of more urgent questions.

One thing was clear to her. She had been wrong to go to Jonathan with her outrage at what he had written. It was a terrible mistake. A full and frank apology was required.

And yet. She examined her thoughts, and tried to understand the rush of feelings she felt, her flushed face, her nervous hailing of the cab. It all had something of the get-me-out-of-here feeling about it; it was melodramatic – the back of the taxi, sealed by the glass partition, the driver almost absent from the journey, the wide seats, the outrageous, almost immoral excess of space and the irresistible injunction to put your feet up. The masculine presence of the driver in the front of the cab was itself a dreadful provocation. He would take you wherever you wanted. Say a name, a train station, a posh address, a shop . . . he would take you there. Each place was equal, provided that you paid. Moral signposts were not included in the fare. She must understand her feelings. Things were about her, now.

First she realised her excitement. She had taken a taxi in an inexplicable rush of celebrity emotion. She was nervous – the trip across the river and the illuminated City made her feel rich, as if the lights of the banks and financial houses were a kind of convertible credit. How was she rich? What was it that burned a hole in her pocket? What did she have that she could not give away?

There would be a message from Jonathan waiting for her. The message so long looked forward to. And she knew, with horror, that for all the implications that would be contained within the message, and the pain and heartache – both to her and to those she cared about and those she would learn to care about – that the message would not disappoint. It was late coming, it was true; twenty years late. How was she at fault? She had done nothing so wicked as to pursue it, to bully it out of him. She had just *been there*. At the Ambassador's lunch, at the Colosseum and at the choir party. And now, tonight, Miriam dead, her great friend, she had gone and been Friendship's champion. That was all. She had argued for loyalty and indestructible closeness. And now Jonathan would leave her a message.

And she knew it thrilled her. She cried again for her friend. As she looked back and surveyed her own passivity she felt a new and unfamiliar longing to be more active, to affect people, not to stand mute. And when she thought of Miriam, and realised that Miriam would never see the fruits of this resolution, she cried over again.

The first thing she must do, clearly, was to rebuff Jonathan, to explain and point out to him the awfulness of what he was suggesting; to clearly portray to him the pain and the futility of infidelity and break-up. It was up to her. She would do anything to do this: construct barriers, issue proclamations of indifference, refuse to see him, argue that for the sake of his wife he should stay away, etcetera, etcetera. There would be time for all these things.

But in the meantime, thank God, there was this brief moment in the taxi, of anonymity, for she had not yet heard his message. She was not yet wholly answerable. She could take a moment. Shame was working on her, sick shame, burning her face, filling her with dread that she had been wrong to see the man she once had loved. She was terrified she was the thing she had always sought not to be. But alongside this feeling, in the expansiveness of the taxi, in the luxury of the moment, working like counterpoint with her dread, was her delight, doubly shameful, but undeniable. As a fugue juxtaposes forms of the same tune, separated only by time, and makes great play of similar ideas set against one another, so this dread and delight worked together, wrestled, conscious of their similar origins, working like a chorus, towards a grand 'Amen'. Mary's heart sang within with greater gusto, greater confidence than she ever had out in the world.

For Miriam was dead.

She savoured these last moments of anonymity and prepared to leave the taxi, to brave the metaphorical photographers of her conscience. As she did so she realised, retrospectively, the pleasure of being nobody – and she realised, now that her time of being nobody was coming to an end, that she had quite enjoyed it. But naturally, it was not enough. Passivity had its own dangers, she realised.

She instructed the taxi driver to drop her at the end of the street so she could run the last two hundred yards to her door. As she ran, years seem to fall off her as the leaves did from the trees around her. Faster she ran, more and more careless of what anyone might think. It was all right – she would do the right thing. But still. One had to run to meet great news, run because one was no longer led – not to parties, not to concerts, not up the garden path – run because it wasn't too late. If it was gauche she didn't care.

She was, after all, unaccustomed to the limelight.

In the Vestry

1

etween the street and the sky you might have traced a gradual progress from chaos to peace. Everything was on show, it seemed, for the first true days of spring. And it was a Friday evening. People were being released from offices and shops; building sites disgorged their muddy workers; banks threw their human resources back into circulation, as if glad to get them off their hands. At ground level everything was swimming with the atmosphere – as of a theatrical first night, or a general election – of a new urban spring evening, a city spring which knows, with almost adolescent self-consciousness, that it is really spring, but must, in the absence of birds, the absence of flowers, make itself felt with only urban materials. So the cars, running silently on roads newly dried by the warm day, seemed to leave a furrow of anticipation behind them; the bloom of a sun just set rested on plastic billboards and concrete façades like the polish of a master-craftsman, forced to accomplish his task with unpromising tools, the final product more basic, purer, closer to the work of his youth for being so worried over.

Built upon this busy foundation, a level higher, and nearer peace, were the mock-Georgian solicitors' offices and dental practices, seemingly still behind their lettered windows but for a glimpse of secretarial blouse or an imperative pinstripe arm caught mid-instruction. Now the occasional arm was raised as if in a cry for help or in exaggerated greeting. Only on closer inspection could the arm be seen to be plunging skywards through the sleeve of a jacket, unwittingly celebrating the end of the working day as excessively as a child at home time.

Above these white-collar ends to the day was, in this corner of London by the Thames, the old, rough front of St Mary's church, as high above the offices as the offices were above the street. Incongruously pastoral, its medieval stone coloured like oatmeal in the evening light, it echoed something of the shires rather than the city; it gathered the new warmth around it, garnered it, alone was worthy of it, its excess seemingly run off into the surrounding graveyard, where it rose up again in ripples of yellow daffodils.

And, last stop before the receding blue of the sky, a short step to heaven, the new riverside development rose without conscience; luxury flats in smooth and arching steel and glass, made out of the very materials of the sky, reconstituted for profit and ease of construction. This vast building seemed to have authority over the assembly of the spring beneath, almost to take credit for it, as if all great constructions must have as painstaking a history of profit and loss as it had itself. Where the sky failed, a faint rim of blue lights finished off the upper limit of the building, setting a temporary edge to the world till morning.

To drop back down again, to return to busy principles, far beneath, was a man, waiting. Although he was, as we have observed, in the midst of life below, he was standing to the side of the church, by a door, in what was a kind of backwater, an eddy in the tireless flow of people who passed the church as they crossed the river. Traffic lights winked red and green, and the people's progress stopped and started. But the man who waited by the door, a tramp, a down-and-out, was stubbornly still.

The door was open, and a tall, thin man was standing in the doorway talking to the old fellow. The tall man stooped so that his head was hooked over like a shepherd's crook. He was wearing jeans and had a kind, very clean-shaven face. The old man was looking up at him, not aggressively or pathetically, but stubbornly, immovably.

'I can't do it, Frank,' the tall man was saying.

'Man of God, man of mortal material rendered fantastical even in my agnosticism, man of blood and man of Jesus ...'

'Frank ...'

'Behold the man!'

'Who, Frank?'

'Me, vicar, or you. Or Jesus. Pilate meant Jesus. But if we are all made whole by Him, Pilate could have been talking about anyone, effectively ... don't get me wrong ... I mean don't get me wrong ... or Jesus ... or Pilate ... *I don't blaspheme!*'

'Gently, Frank ...'

'What?'

The dirty man – for he was dirty, his coat caked almost black and solid with grime, he looked like a moving lump of shiny coal – spoke theatrically, like a Victorian actor, or someone ridiculing the upper-class accent. He looked like an actor that had been poorly made up to look like a tramp and who was having trouble discarding his last role. It was clear the old man liked to show his learning.

'I'm sorry that I haven't more time,' said the kind-faced vicar, simply and sincerely. 'It's Wednesday and the parish council.'

'Damn bureaucracy!'

'I'm inclined to agree with you.'

'What is my soul to a filing cabinet?'

The vicar smiled.

'What indeed?'

'It's spring, Father! Oh my father. Tell me, Jim, do you object to the Roman salutation of Father? It ain't your dusty C of E, but it has a kind of spiritual cachet, would you not concur? Fuck my aunt! Father, Father. It gives a beautiful gloss to the idea of parents, it undoes the brassière of Anglicanism and releases the . . . What!? Eh? Ah! The English have barely one father, and yet the Catholics have thousands, for every priest is their father. Perhaps given the Boccaccio-esque predilection for Italian priests to engage in sex *in the margins* of their Holy Writ, "Father" was well said, since any priest might turn out to *be* your father. My giddy aunt the spring is here! We must have many fathers on earth to understand our *über-Fater in Himmel*.'

'Are you a father, Frank? I've never asked you.'

Frank looked at the vicar, steadily.

'Twice,' he said, and pulled his beard as if it were stuck on and he was trying to tear it off. 'Daughters!' he almost screamed.

'I never knew,' said the vicar, gently.

'One less than King Lear,' said Frank, evidently pleased with the parallel. 'I missed out on Cordelia. Shame. Where will I find her? Do you know King Lear, Jim?'

'Not very well.'

'Not a parishioner of yours?'

'No.'

'Shame. Can I come in?'

The vicar looked sad, for this had been the prevailing request for some time.

'We have a meeting, Frank. I'm sorry. The refuge is open.'

The old man took a step back and let out a long, inarticulate cry. The vicar had seen this before. At some point, if he was thwarted, the old man just put his head back like an old bloodhound and roared. When he had done, he would stamp his feet, turn around on the spot twice, clap his hands like an Eastern potentate and set off, joining the tide of people that parted as around a buoy, effortlessly holding off from the smell and the sight of the man who lived on the streets; a tide that washed nothing clean.

2

It was indicative of Robert's present crisis in his life – and to his mind a benign manifestation of it – that he should keep Emma, his young assistant, waiting for a few more minutes longer than strictly necessary. She would knock very quietly, enter his office and sit herself down silently and, as he finished whatever he was doing, he would analyse very closely what it was exactly that she had brought into the room, what it meant. How his universe, albeit infinitesimally, had changed. It was not that he was fixated on her – he felt at present so questioning of his life that he might have done the experiment on anyone, for he was, though now over forty, only just, he felt, waking up to the notion that there really was anyone else in the world but him. And not only that, he felt that the multiplicity of selves, the sheer, plural abundance of different personalities, religions, ethnicities should wake him up from his thirty-something stupor of comparative success, and *change* him. When he left university he had concerned himself with compassionate politics as passionately as he now worked in compassionate broadcasting. But only now did he feel he was understanding that other people really did have as vast and contradictory a palette of experiences as he had. Partly it came from the position of power he now found himself in. He was a boss, a leader. Someone who had other people less powerful beneath him. When he had been very young and inexperienced and had been at the beck and call of more powerful people he had not felt sorry for himself. He had worked. But now that he was in a position to help students and impoverished researchers he felt their disadvantages very keenly. He expected them to weep – the female ones at least – and for him to damn well help them.

Emma was a provocation because, not only did she not weep, but she rarely smiled. In these pauses, as he evaluated her presence, he sought a weakness he could help and counsel, but all he ever sensed in her arrival was determination. She was twenty-four and he was past forty; he was a success and one day she would be, too. He had no doubt of that. She was brilliantly organised, articulate, pretty and energetic. Rob just wished she could show a little humility and weakness, just for form's sake. She never even looked annoyed to be kept waiting. Her blonde hair was scraped back severely; she looked like a superb head-girl. He pitied this, her one, it seemed to him, clear gaucheness – she still dressed like a student, not an executive, or even a proto-executive.

Eventually he nodded for her to begin. She looked down at her notes.

'Jim, the vicar, was polite and helpful, but I'm not sure he's totally for the project.'

'I'll talk to him.'

Rob saw Emma move on to her next entry. Did she doubt he could win the vicar round?

'Of the six we met last week,' she went on, 'he vetoed us working with three of them.'

'Well, why did he let us meet th—'

'He wasn't aware of the long-term nature of the filming. Or that we would concentrate so much on one case. He said there were issues that he couldn't disclose. Speaking to him wouldn't help because he'll just refer you to Social Services. It is my opinion . . .'

Here, she stopped, as she often did when she was expressing a personal view. At such moments as this she and Rob would look at one another and each would be aware of her conundrum and both would feel implicated by it. She wanted to express her opinions, she wanted to take on her boss, if need be, but she wanted the man to whom she expressed them to be worthy of them and her. And it was not that she did not respect Rob, it was just that it was doubtful that the man existed, anywhere, to whom she would feel sufficiently in thrall to then feel any satisfaction in overthrowing.

'It's my opinion,' she said softly, 'that having gone to Jim in the first place . . .'

'We can hardly go against him, now.'

'Precisely.'

'I agree.'

'As it happens,' said Emma, visibly relieved not to have a disagreement – she was not by nature argumentative – 'the three we have to choose from are the three that were keenest to talk.'

'Keenness to talk isn't everything.'

Emma looked as if she wanted to kick herself. Only the week before she and Rob had discussed the readiness of the homeless people to talk and he had said he wanted someone with the will to communicate, and Emma herself had said she thought that silence was eloquence enough if the filming was handled sensitively. Now she knew that she could not say to Rob, 'I said that to you last week.' She must suffer having her own arguments put to her as if they were his own.

But this one time she did him an injustice.

'As you said yourself, last week,' he said.

For Rob's part, he found Emma's longing to put him right both flattering and alarming. He wasn't sure if he was up to it. He took on Emma's disappointment with executive father-figures, lived it vicariously, till he was as disappointed with himself as he imagined she was.

'Who have we got, then?' said Rob.

'Firstly, there's Fred.'

'I remember Fred,' said Rob, cheerfully.

'Yes, you met all of them last week. Fred was the one who'd spent a lot of time with the Salvation Army. He drinks. He fought in Korea.'

'Though presumably not with the Salvation Army.'

'I don't understand,' she said.

'His service – the Korean War – was not with the Salvation Ar—'

'I see.'

Emma smiled and frowned at the same time. Rob was unsure whether she did not get the joke or thought it in bad taste.

'He likes to speak about the war,' she went on. 'He was born in Canada but came to England with his parents. Went back there to get married and returned again when his wife died. Social Services are the first to admit they haven't always got it right with Fred. But they're happy for us to talk about that. Jim says Fred is very popular with the other homeless people. Jim warned us that when he's drinking we may lose him for a while. So we'd have to be flexible. He wants us to film Fred because losing a wife is often the reason men end up on the streets.'

'I liked Fred,' said Rob, decisively. Emma looked at him questioningly. She wasn't sure whether this was a provocation or just a quaint expression of personal preference. To Emma this choice of candidate for the documentary seemed clinical and objective. She turned over a leaf.

Rob looked at her closely. He did feel an almost forbidden sense of ease as she read to him. Then he realised it was because she looked like an undergraduate and he was sitting there as tutors had sat and listened to him at university. It was always said to be the great enduring tradition of Oxford that you still read your essay to your tutor. He had always liked the one-to-one, the complicity of speaker and listener. As you read your essay and your tutor sat in silence you were about to be either the powerful half of the couple or the complete victim, all according to how well you had written. And this absolute dichotomy, this absence of middle ground and the fact that your fate was deferred to the very end – so that even in the act of reading you were either a walking shadow or top of the class – was violent and thrilling. Sometimes he found his tutor's gaze like a camera, and he played to it, brazening out failure or modest in triumph.

Emma read on, her hair still pulled back, unrelievingly. Rob wondered if she had a boyfriend.

'Then there is Clarence. And here, I believe, we have the conundrum at the heart of this documentary.'

Rob looked at her in close-up. She stopped, for this was saying too much. Rob and Emma's working relationship had little real intimacy to it – as Rob's ignorance of whether or not she had a boyfriend testified. But it did extend as far as Emma's ambition. Both knew that Emma probably had very strong ideas about how they should go about making a documentary on the problem of homelessness in the capital. What they had tacitly agreed was that Emma would save direct expressions of her opinions for her private life, accompanied by boyfriend or not.

She blushed.

'When I say conundrum,' she carried on seamlessly, her calm voice at odds with her glowing face, 'I am put in mind of what you said to me at one of the very early briefing sessions – that we must be careful when filming people whose lives are in trouble, or who see a lot of tough things going on, not to anecdotalise, not to cherry-pick the remarkable, just to make entertaining television. It would be easy to pick Clarence because he's very funny. An hour of Clarence edited for laughs and remarkable stories would be great entertainment, but – as you yourself said – bad documentary.'

It was an impressive turn-around, flattering Rob and quoting him like that. Rob could not but acknowledge it. But it irritated him. He thought he would have preferred her just to laugh and apologise for being too forward. He was tiring of the head-girl performance, not least because for as long as she played head-girl he had no choice but to play forbidding tutor. He wanted something more. Rob did not want authority, he wanted influence. It had taken him a long time to realise that the first did not necessarily offer the second. He wanted Emma to tell him who she wanted to have as subject of the documentary. He wanted her to tell him in a glorious laying down of arms. He wanted all the world to just tell one another what all humankind wanted and for there to be a great sense of relief. He wanted her to release the band that held her hair up and for them to be just damn good friends. He wanted to feel as young as she did. He hoped she had a boyfriend just so she had at least some life going on.

'And then,' she said – and Rob knew instinctively that whoever was next on the list was not a serious contender in her mind – 'there is Franklin.'

To Rob it was clear Fred was her man.

'Yes,' said Rob, 'I remember Franklin.'

'I mean, personally . . . Well, I find . . . I think you will find him totally unreliable. He is from an upper-class background. He is different. But for all his talk he's not coherent. After five minutes you've seen all you're going to get.'

'Emma, it's not an audition.'

She sat back quickly, as if she had been burnt. It was an intimate reproach and they both knew it. Emma blushed again, then went pale.

'I am aware of that,' she said. 'You think I have a personal dislike of him. On the contrary, he is charming. It is not that I have a dislike of him, it is that . . .'

But before she had finished, the phone rang. Emma sighed very slightly when Rob took the call. Just enough to let him know that she thought he might have found what she was about to say next considerably more enlightening than anything the caller might have to say. It was Rob's wife. He had left undone that which he ought to have done. His wife gave a calm inventory of those things left undone and Rob promised they would be done by the weekend. When he hung up, Emma, with as much of a toss as her imprisoned hair could manage, began again.

'The principal objection to Franklin . . .'

'It's a strange name . . .'

'It is. The principal objection to Franklin is that he is atypical. He is the least representative of the three men. And that is serious. If we concentrate on a man from a privileged background we may be accused of a kind of social voyeurism. It will appeal to middle-class viewers—'

'Emma. Does it matter what class he is? If we do it well? In the particular lies the general. A down-and-out is a down-and-out. Besides—'

'No, Robert. He is a misleading subject. He sounds as if he is an intellectual but in fact he talks gibberish.'

'Are there,' said Rob, himself reeling slightly from having been interrupted, and trying to regain control, 'are there personal issues here? What is your objection to a middle-class subject? Don't the middle classes count?'

'Personal issues?'

'Are only those born with nothing to be pitied?'

'Of course not. That isn't my point.'

'No,' he said, understandingly. He knew it wasn't. Maybe she'd just split up from her boyfriend.

Rob was thinking of Franklin, of whom he had only a hazy memory. The *idea* of Franklin that Emma was describing, however, seemed vivid and interesting.

'We're all,' said Rob, 'struggling for legitimacy, aren't we? We all struggle with the weakness of the things we say and think. Perhaps Franklin's gibberish is just an attempt to give his life meaning. And maybe it's as good as the next man's. What I mean when I say personal issues is that perhaps you don't like the intellectual pretensions because he reminds us that all intellect is . . . a kind of pretension.'

'No, Robert. I simply think one should be careful about falling for the idiot-savant thing. I suspect the stakes aren't actually as high with him as he makes out. I don't think he's mentally ill. He is an act. A fraud.'

'And intelligence isn't?'

But she only looked at him.

'Well,' he said, 'you may be right, young Emma. You may be right.' The camera was pulling back, now. 'I'd like to take this opportunity to say what great work you've done on this project. I hope it will be the first of many. Not too many, of course, because I know you're ambitious and will be wanting to move on. But don't move on, yet.'

Rob talked on, unable to finish the conversation satisfactorily, unable to placate his young researcher, and unable to quite articulate to himself why he felt it so essential that the subject they should have for the coming documentary be Franklin. He could not have said whether it was because he had been crossed and wanted to assert his authority, whether he liked the sound of Franklin, or whether it was simply that Emma was prettier when she was being angry than when she was being polite. But one thing was for certain: Franklin was the man.

3

The old man had found himself talking to Emma on the night of the church interviews because it was in his nature to talk to the nearest person to hand. But he was now informed by his friend Jim that they would like to film him, Franklin, for one day a week for three months; follow his progress, learn about his life. The documentary would be a portrait of an individual life on the streets. Franklin guessed, and guessed right, that Jim disliked the whole enterprise. Jim could not understand why the normally so solitary Franklin would agree to do it. He thought it possible that it was to gently goad his friend, and possible that he did it because he thought the girl, Emma, rather good value. Or because he simply liked to talk. Whatever the reason, on the Monday of the following week Franklin arrived early for the first interview. He made his way to the small modern annex attached to the church and knocked. Jim let him in. They stood in the doorway of the vicar's office.

'Presenting myself for duty,' said the old man.

Jim looked at Franklin intently for a moment.

'Frank . . .'

'Vicar?'

'It's not your duty to do this, you know. You're under no obligation.'

But Franklin, after glancing quickly at the clergyman, just looked out of the window.

'Do you hear me, Frank?'

'Where would we be without the spirit of co-operation?'

'I don't know.'

'You bless the enterprise, don't you, Jim?'

'I don't know if you need to use the word bless. If you're asking me whether I think this sort of thing is part of my ministry, then no, I don't bless it.'

'Isn't everything part of your ministry? Even Satan's minions? Whoever they may be.'

'Frank you're argumentative. I think you're too intelligent to let them take advantage of you, but . . .'

'What, O man of God? Spit it out for fuck's sake.'

'Keep me posted, all right?'

'Yes. Yes! My blood's up.'

'I can see that. It doesn't need to be. Remember this is your place and they are visitors.'

'The Church always offered sanctuary, didn't it?' said Franklin. 'By which was meant, I suppose, that it is truly none of ours, but God's.'

'When you've finished preaching to me . . .'

But the old man went on –

'You might say the same of the streets. To live on the streets is to live somewhere possessed by no one and everyone. Are the streets God's, too?'

'Perhaps,' said the vicar, smiling in spite of himself.

'And what about television?'

'What about it?'

'Is it God's preferred medium do you think, democratic and vivid?' There was a pause. 'Oh my giddy aunt ... Jury's out, eh?'

The old man laughed his rich, theatrical laugh.

'He's here,' said Jim, looking out of the window.

Rob, carrying a camera and a black case, was walking up the church path, flanked by daffodils.

4

The following morning Emma found Rob in the editing suite.

'Interested?' said Rob.

'Of course.'

'I don't, as a rule, watch too much of the previous day's filming, I always fear I'll start making assumptions about the direction the piece will take. But in this instance ...'

'May I?'

Emma took a seat.

'Let's watch it together.'

With the advent of new technology Rob had dispensed with cameraman and sound man. He was able to operate the units himself and it gave him greater freedom. He had got into the office very early that morning and had let it be known he would be in the editing suite. He wanted her to hear that he was watching the previous evening's work; he wanted her to join him. And she did. Even as he had started filming Rob had been aware that she was his audience. The background of daffodils in the spot behind the church he had chosen to do the interview in; his feel for the pastoral within the urban; everything he looked at through the viewfinder of the camera he saw as a revealing signpost to his sensibility, to his self, which, when she saw it, would lead her to him. So that she would know him; so she would be forced to acknowledge him. He had no thought of seduction or sexual conquest; he had no appetite for the vulgarities of infidelity. Had he even found himself considering the appropriateness of his motives he would have distanced himself from the provoking girl. On the contrary, Emma was a provocation to be better, to be worthy of the position of authority he had found himself in when he had kept her waiting in his office the previous week. Rob had a horror of illegitimate authority; he had tolerated it in its traditional manifestations at Oxford by outwardly conquering it; success made you isolated from the corruption of snobbery because it freed you from envy; but success also, now, made the common touch elusive, made you lose the fresh honesty of youth. Emma, with her gauche ambition and her principled attitude, threw into relief Rob's life, made its successes seem like failures and its failures unforgivable. So now it was up to him to show her.

They looked at the screen. There was Franklin, sitting on a bench, not looking at the camera but seeming to take in the scene around him, as if he was seeing it all for the first time.

Rob's plan was to allow the subject to tell his own story with the minimum of interference. He wanted no fake spontaneity, no pretending that the camera wasn't there. He wanted to acknowledge that a real documentary traces not only the story of the person who is its subject, but the story of that persons' relationship with the documentary itself; with the camera. He believed that characters created their own stories and then enacted them, that life was largely that, but that life lived before a camera accentuated it. In this sense he wanted a collaboration; he wanted equality between the watcher and the watched.

Franklin asked Rob what he wanted to talk about. The tramp seemed depressed, as if the whole project was doomed from the start. He asked if Jim was around and seemed relieved that he wasn't. Then there was a long pause and he started to speak. Occasionally a car passed in the distance, the birds sang, but mostly, as the daffodils nodded in the breeze in the background, as if in solemn agreement with everything he said, Franklin told his life story.

He began dutifully, with none of the excess of language and abstract theorising that had put Emma off. Rob seemed totally vindicated in his choice. Franklin described how he had come from a well-off family in Kent. He had been charming, good-looking, wild and unlucky. Good at many things, he had dropped out of school and come to London. It was the sixties. He had been a drummer in a band, worked briefly as a photographer, a waiter, a chauffeur, a window dresser for Fortnum and Mason and had played cricket at the weekends. When a magazine printed one of his photographs poorly he had threatened the editor and thrown his camera through the window of their offices. He had written off a Bentley and there had been problems with the insurance. He had married a rich girl and quarrelled with her family. There were two children and then divorce. He'd got wilder; walked the King's Road and watched the sixties happen, as a party to which he was not invited, though he was far wilder than anything the official *Zeitgeist* had to offer. He came to loathe the pretensions and the self-congratulation of that decade as only a fallen apostle could. He attempted a legitimate enterprise in the form of a business deal with a friend on money borrowed from his parents, importing cultural artefacts from Africa to be sold at inflated prices in Chelsea art galleries. He was swindled and saw neither friend, money nor parents again. He was thrown out of his flat, declared bankrupt. As the seventies began he was on the streets. He was twenty-five.

Franklin related all of this as if it had happened to someone else. He told it well, but there was a sense almost of shame that he did so. He seemed uninterested in it; as if the past were shackles that he had spent years wearing and had only just got used to and did not want to draw too much attention to in case they became a novel nuisance again. When he had finished relating the events leading up to his going on to the streets he stopped, as if he were done. There was silence and again the birds could be heard singing; the daffodils bowed their heads.

Then, as if he realised that more was required, very slowly he began to talk about the people he had met as a homeless person, the characters who had shown him the ropes, the men who had hurt him, the illnesses, the charities. And a grand manner came over him again. The epic superiority. As a young man it was clear no one had listened to him or understood him. As a man on the streets, having set himself beyond any, as it were, social under-standing, he was free to be the man he wanted to be. And he had, over the years, played the role of dispossessed knight, of patrician grandee, of the disguised prince moving among his subjects to the hilt. He was ignored, as every prophet must be, and his being ignored was a blessing where it had been a curse before.

Rob and Emma watched in silence. When it was over Rob got up.

'Let's have a coffee together.'

He wanted to get out of the room; they both felt they had been a little too close to the man they had been watching.

In the cafeteria they sat for a while in silence.

'I want,' said Rob, 'to know what you really think. Forget our roles, forget the fact we work here. Tell me what you think.'

Emma's face softened. In fact she appeared quite different. She was looking down into her plastic cup. Rob could see the fine lines of her young frown. She looked up at him straight in the face.

'Well . . . it's not about homelessness. And won't ever be.'

'No,' said Rob, and smiled.

Emma smiled, too.

'I'm sure I was wrong,' she said.

'On the contrary, you were right. It isn't what we wanted. But as a portrait of a man, just as a piece of documentary . . .'

'Absolutely.'

'Fascinating.'

'Yes.'

'I think,' Rob went on, 'he is like all of us, but more so. He feels dispossessed of the things that everyone wants – comfort, recognition, admiration – but on some level or other he knew he was never going to get them. Not really. Because none of us ever really do. And instead of accepting the compromise he just cut free. But here's the crux, the human comedy – he cut loose without giving up any of the attitudes, the social habits, the class mannerisms that had been his life. He said "I will not change, so I shall just change the nature of the world in which I live." It's both totally conservative and totally revolutionary. He is a man of his class – he feels superior – but he also has the instinctive generosity of a philanthropic millionaire. He treats the rest of the homeless men like a lot of unruly boys he's forced to share a dormitory with. He is obedient but totally individual. In short – an Englishman.'

Emma watched him with shining eyes.

5

Several weeks went by and Jim had neither sight nor sound of Franklin. The vicar, fearing that something was wrong, phoned Rob. Rob informed him that, on the contrary, Franklin had been exemplary both in his attendance and in the enthusiasm of his contribution. He had taken Rob over the whole of his patch, filming his haunts, his days, his nights. Rob was very pleased.

But Jim was concerned. And, if truth be told, a little hurt. When he had asked Franklin to keep him posted it was out of genuine fondness for the man. He felt the two of them understood one another. Jim could not get it out of his head that if Franklin had given up coming to the vicar and arguing with him, pestering him and generally winding him up then all was not well. He made enquiries. Franklin, normally so solitary, had taken up with Fred, the man who had been Emma's choice for the subject of the documentary. Franklin was definitely of no fixed abode but Fred lived in a little construction of his own devising between the allotments and the railway track. One evening when he had finished at the church, Jim went in search of his old friend.

It was now late May and the sun was shining with intent upon the dirty brick walls beside the railway line and upon the allotments, beginning to overflow with new green. Jim, threading his way between the two could not help but feel he was playing truant. He was very aware what a novel spectacle he must make; he wished he'd taken off his clerical collar and found a pair of jeans. A man planting potatoes made him jump.

'Bit late getting these in, Vicar,' he said, like a confession.

'Yes. Good luck with them! Goodbye!'

'Nice evening for it, though.'

The shack was further than he thought. Eventually, beneath and surrounded by an almost impenetrable lot of hawthorn, he found the place.

Franklin was sitting on a tree stump and looked up with amazement at Jim. Jim saw a thought flicker across his face: the thought of making a run for it. The vicar wished he hadn't come. But he must see it through.

'Why do you look as though you'd like to run from me, Frank?'

'You're mistaken, my dear boy.' But he looked into the middle distance, as if he wished he were there and not here. 'If you want Fred he's gone to town.'

'No. It was you I was after.'

There was a pause that almost amounted to a stand-off.

'After me?' said Franklin, suspiciously.

'This is absurd,' said Jim. 'Frank, I will be honest with you. I was worried and . . . a little hurt. I hoped the filming was going well, but was alarmed . . .'

'What? Have I obligations? Have I!'

'Of course, you have none.'

Franklin put his head in his hands.

'Is it that you're ashamed, Frank?'

'Something like it, sir, something like it. I've taken up with Fred. You're thinking that's not Frank. What? Is it too late to be sociable! Hah! Too late to love my neighbour as myself? Will you tell me to go back to my old ways? What? Is something up if I am lonely? Fred's grateful. Let's all be grateful.'

'Gently.'

'No, Jim. I have responsibilities.'

'What responsibilities have you?'

'So the man of God asks. Isn't that evident to a Christian?'

'Frank, you're not a bloody Christian, so stop talking to me like a child. I know you. For the sake of our friendship . . .'

There was a rumbling that for a moment terrified the vicar with such a primal fear he thought he would lose his composure. It was a train. The side of the bank shook as it passed and the hawthorn dropped some remnants of May blossom along the track and on the clearing where they sat. The men waited till the noise had died.

'Well . . . never mind,' said Franklin, as if the chance for a real conversation had passed. But the vicar was stubborn. He brushed the blossom off his sleeve.

'What responsibilities?'

'To Rob.'

'I knew it. This filming is dreadful. I should never have agreed to it. Withdraw. It was a condition that we could pull out at any time. I will explain everything. Why should you be ashamed? Look at you. You've lost your fire.'

'No. I save it, dear boy. For the filming. Man cannot live by personality alone. I feel for him.'

'For who?'

'Rob.'

'He is a man from the media, that's all. You're not stupid enough to—'

'My dear chap, just because you're a man with a profession you must see everyone in terms of their occupation. Perhaps you only care for me because I have none.'

'I certainly don't relish seeing you become a celebrity tramp. If that's the profession you have in mind.'

'I feel for the man.'

'What do you feel?'

'Pity.'

'Oh Frank . . .'

'He's a lost soul, Midas. He is, truly.'

'Why do you call me Midas, Frank? They're out for recognition, for money, to salve their consciences. Damn it, Frank . . . you don't owe him anything.'

'Why not?' And Franklin turned with such fury on the vicar that he took a step back. 'Why not? Don't you know at school you shook the hand of the master who beat you?'

'What's that got to do with it? Talk sense, Frank . . .'

But Frank put his head back and roared, and, as if to give the old man unlooked-for support another train passed, and the two men were once again showered in blossom, like a fall of late-spring snow; the flakes picked out the sunlight in the shadow of the embankment.

The two men looked at one another as the silence regrouped around them and birds began again to sing.

'I suppose no harm will come of it,' said Jim, softly.

'I can't stop now, anyway,' said Franklin, 'or what would become of the contribution to the Church Restoration Fund?'

Jim shook his head.

'There's no contribution, Frank.'

'What?'

'Did they tell you there was?'

'No. I assumed.'

Jim shook his head, again.

'What, no tithe, no tax, no portion for the Lord? Ahh! No.

Nothing. My giddy aunt. No rendering unto Caesar that which is Caesar's . . . or not, as the case may be . . . an interesting reversal of the traditional order of things . . . I thought to have overturned the tables of the artists in the office instead of the money-lenders in the temple . . . shit! Shit my pants, where's Fred? Where is decent company on a spring evening?'

Jim turned, and with his arm held before his face to protect him from the thorns he plunged into the hawthorn to make his escape back down the bank. And the action, so like a man about to cry, made him think he was crying and his eyes filled with tears. He made his way, half blind, back along the allotments, careless of himself and full of rage. The mild-mannered vicar of St Mary's was decidedly not himself.

6

As this scene was finishing, high up in the offices of the television company Emma was finishing her day's work. As had been her habit for the last few weeks, she had stayed beyond normal office hours. Rob, too, found much to do at the end of the day; he was, after all, out of the office a lot these days, filming, so the evenings presented themselves as little oases of labour to both executive and assistant.

The offices faced west and the evening sun was sinking over the city.

Rob and Emma had not repeated their meeting in the editing suite when they watched the first day's filming together. But Rob knew that Emma took it upon herself to watch what was being done; as his researcher it was perfectly understandable. Occasionally they even passed one another – she having seen the previous week's filming, he on his way to watch the latest. They were civil to each other; the project had established an intimacy that did not require renewal.

'Still here?' he said, weaving his way through the empty desks to her lone, feminine outpost.

'Lot to do,' she said. She looked up. 'Going somewhere?'

Rob was smart. New shirt.

'National Theatre. In fact, I'm late.'

But he stood still, irresolute. He wanted to ask her if going to the National Theatre was a good idea. Everything had to go through Emma, these days.

'See you, then,' she said.

'If I wasn't late, I'd help you out.'

'Oh, it's definitely PA territory.'

'Don't do yourself down.'

'I wasn't.'

She was so tough. Rob looked out of the window where the absurdly huge and impressive sun steadied itself, seemingly thoughtful before its plunge into the cool, distant green of Berkshire and all routes west.

'Actually,' she said, 'I want to talk to you.'

He looked at her, but couldn't see her; the brightness of the sun had temporarily blinded him. So he just smiled foolishly; he could feel the smile on his face so he knew he must be smiling. But her tone didn't change. Whatever he did seemed not to placate her.

'About Franklin,' she said.

'Oh?'

'I'll find you. Tomorrow.'

He was still swimming in purple shadows, so he felt, rather than saw, himself take off his jacket and fling it at a chair.

'Talk,' he said, and felt the ridiculous thrill of executive melodrama.

'You'll miss your play.'

He sat down, and Emma was sitting on her desk, in front of him, like a pupil granted that concession after school hours. Suddenly she seemed, in her physical proximity to Rob, unknown to him. As if the sudden familiarity had rendered her strange. What had been distant had been knowable. He could generalise about her. Now she was close, and they weren't in the editing suite watching Franklin, who had, as an image on the screen, acted as a kind of chaperon. She was looking down at him, and Rob, in a moment of unpleasant novelty, found her very attractive.

'You'll think me stupid,' she said.

'Why?'

She sighed.

'I think you probably think I'm a bit of a cold person. A bit of a swot and bit of a pain.'

'Not at all.'

'I am concerned about Franklin. And about you.'

Rob had never felt so nonplussed in his life.

'Go on,' he just managed to say.

'Well . . . Look, just tell me to shut up if I'm out of order. I know I shoot my mouth off, sometimes. But this is different. I . . . I think Franklin is in danger. I think he is unstable. And I don't think this filming is doing him any good at all. I mean . . . it's compulsive viewing. You were right – he was the right choice. We've tried to help him, and he's gone along with it, and whether or not he changes his way of life, the documentary will be an extraordinary portrait of a man.'

'There's a "but" coming.'

'He's complicit.'

'Meaning?'

'He's using us. He's taking something from this that he's prob-ably always wanted. And we're going to take it away from him. We're going to get up and leave him. With no camera, no more interviews. No more audience. He's turning his life into a story. For you. He adores you. He'd do anything for you. I can tell from the way he speaks to you in the interviews. That's what makes it so moving. Because the audience will feel that he would do anything for them, too.'

'I don't think he adores me.'

'He does. He thinks you're like he used to be. Or something.' She shook her head, uncertainly.

'I think,' said Rob, 'he's stronger than you take him for. And more intelligent. He knows the score. And if he's using us he also realises we're using him. That was the whole point of doing this project. We talked about it in the editing suite that morning, remember? Yes, he tells us the story we want to hear. Because that's what we do in life! The interest is in how we tell it. Whether we signal that we are telling a story, whether we are born story-tellers – and Franklin is. At the risk of offending your right-on sensibilities, Franklin is a star.'

'And what does that tell us about documentaries?'

'That we want drama, not lectures. That life is in stories, not liberal, hand-wringing social-policy-driven broadcasting.'

The sunset was doing all sorts of extraordinary things outside.

'But,' said Emma, 'the remit of this documentary – even if not stated explicitly – is to see if someone in trouble can be helped. You can't just watch someone who is ill, or a victim of violence or mental illness, without implying that they need to be helped. Making the audience think about what can be done to help. And if we don't actually help him ... if we just tell his story ... and don't help him ... then we might as well just be voyeurs and accept that we are providing entertainment no more humane than seeing Christians thrown to the lions. I was wrong when I said he was a fraud. I think it's we that are the frauds. We're simply not helping him.'

'Radical thought ... Do any of us want to be helped?'

'Yes.'

'Does Franklin?'

Rob was going to add 'Do you?' but didn't. He felt a surge of pity for Emma. He wondered if she would have said yes, if he had asked her. She seemed to him suddenly rather plain, and he was amazed he had been so vividly attracted to her only minutes before. He had a clear picture of her life; of her going home to her first-time-buyer's studio flat or rented haven with a student boyfriend. He imagined he would be a Social Sciences under-graduate, or an actor. He wouldn't appreciate her, whatever he was; he would be jealous and not leave her be. Rob felt an irra-tional rage at the idea of her being the victim of some callow youth's uncertainties. It was really time she was appreciated more profoundly. She needed promotion. In every sense. He wanted to tell *her* story and have it come out well. What role he would play in that story was not clear; he certainly did not covet a leading one. Perhaps he really did just want to be the cameraman. She was, to him, his principled past; his only real fear was that there was an obviousness to a heterosexual forty-something finding that his past was ... blonde. But Emma wasn't done.

'I said it wasn't just Franklin I was concerned about. Again, forgive me if I speak out of turn ...'

'"Though I speak with the tongues of men and of angels,"' quipped Rob.

'Yes,' she said, smiled briefly and forgivingly and moved on. Now she looked more like a vicar's wife. 'I'm concerned about you.'

'That's kind of you.'

'No, listen.'

Rob would have liked to have broken her like a reed, like a precious vase, so pious did she seem. If Rob was expert in one area of management it was the appreciation of status. It fascinated him. Where other men might have sport or wildlife programmes or the study of warfare in which to observe the intricacies of power, of victims and predators, Rob watched the orbits of the ambitious and worthy, the talented and the bullshitters, all revolving under the solemn gravity of status. He told himself that only a committed mastery of it could keep a man safe from its attractions. He wanted a life whose value was beyond status. Perhaps that is why Franklin attracted him so much. But however much he might try, he could not bear the pressure Emma put him under, the challenge to his peace of mind, the challenge to his success. Her strident opinions were one thing, but this new tone, this piety, worked like a madness on his brain. He wanted to show her the door.

'You romanticise Franklin, Robert. He has taken a place in your life disproportionate to his real nature.'

'I see.'

'Oh . . . you are going to be offended. But I'm worried about you. You are such a brilliant putter-together of the raw materials of life. I admire you so much. But . . . I think you're unhappy. And I think you think of Franklin like a kind of saint. And he's not. Sometimes I see you a bit in awe of him when in fact he's actually just talked a lot of . . . well, gibberish. You're in love with him as if you had created him. As if he were a fictional character. You must take care. I don't want to pour cold water on your project, which is in many ways excellent . . .'

'I have come to think of it as our project.'

'Of course. I should like nothing better.'

They stared at each other. The garish slabs of orange light the sun had thrown on the walls of the offices had all gone; the walls were grey.

'The way you see it,' said Rob, giving in to the logic of her arguments, 'is that neither subject nor author is happy with the work we are doing.'

'Perhaps.'

'And what, young lady, would you do about it?'

But she just looked at him.

'We are friends, yes?' she said. For a dreadful moment Rob thought she was going to suggest they prayed together. But without waiting for an answer she went over to him and hugged him. The hug itself was a peculiar lean-to affair: the softness of the top half of her body at odds with the awkwardness of holding her bottom half well away from him; but Rob could feel the softness of her breasts and the tickle of a stray strand of hair against his cheek.

'I'm so relieved we are. I wasn't sure about you,' she said, 'but I realise now, you are lost, too.'

He just looked at her.

'Robert?'

'Oh call me Rob, for fuck's sake.'

But she just smiled. They left together.

Downstairs Rob hailed a cab. He'd given up the idea of the National Theatre.

In the taxi he said, 'Seriously . . . what do I do about Franklin? In practical terms.'

'Release him. It's the only charitable thing you can do. He's deteriorating. He admires you, but trying to please you is putting a strain on him. You are too close to him to see it. He means too much to you. I think you should stop.'

'That's an over-reaction.'

'It's not.'

'For Christ's sake will you cut out the lectures? Talk to me about it if you will, but stop treating me as if you were my boss!'

'I would speak to Jim.'

'Jim is a vicar, not a clinical psychologist.'

'Jim knows him'

'Really, Emma . . . how much does any of us know about anyone else?'

He said it savagely.

Then, like a schoolgirl, or a bashful undergraduate, she took his hand and held it between them on the taxi seat.

'I know you,' she said, when they had finished kissing. She put his head on her chest, and Rob looked out of the window at the end of the rush hour.

7

Rob phoned Jim the next day to tell him that at present the documentary would be put on hold. Rob explained that they had enough footage to make a very good portrait of life on the streets; he didn't know when it would be edited together. He thanked Jim for his help.

'I don't mind telling you that I am relieved you are finishing,' said Jim. 'Frank has not been himself.'

'I felt the same. I do feel that I should meet him one last time. To say thank you. Are you happy with that?'

'That would be handsome of you.'

'We'd also,' said Rob, 'like to give a little something to the Church Restoration Fund. As a way of showing our appreciation.'

Jim was pleased the other man could not see his smile, and thanked the television executive profusely. Rob agreed he would meet Franklin at the church at the usual time to explain that the filming was at an end.

8

It was not easy, given Rob's recent domestic upheavals, to get to the church on the night promised, but he managed to arrive early and was relieved to have the time alone. It was raining a fine, warm, misty June rain. Everything seemed soft and slightly out of focus. The trees, heavy with leaves, now, encroached upon the street and on the pale stone of the church; the countryside seemed to be making an advance upon the town. Rob wandered in and out of the church very much at home. He thought how much he would miss it. It struck him as ironic what pleasure he took in moving around such a holy place, how the moral certainty of the Church was so attractive and calming when he himself was launched on such a morally challenging course in his personal life. It had been hard to persuade his wife of his destination that evening. For a few minutes, as he walked up and down the quiet aisles and over the graves outside, he guessed that these were the last quiet moments he would be granted for some time. It made him nostalgic for a calm he had actually, probably, never felt. But he was grateful for it, now.

A middle-aged woman in a flowery dress was putting the

finishing touches to two great vases of roses on either side of the altar; there must be a wedding the next day. She smiled at him. Rob pondered the contrast between the flowers on her dress and the real ones she arranged in the vases. There seemed no connection between the two, and this disappointed him, perplexed him. All he could glean from the comparison was a vague criticism of the quality of the fabric whose design reproduced a flower's shape; Rob was definitely coming down on the side of the real flowers, and their beauty made him melancholy. As if they were a direct reproach to anyone who attempted *design*, at all.

He liked the fact that in church everything was done in silence. He wondered why that was. Was it that the inevitable echo encourages you to be quiet, to hold off from making a sound, just as the moral silence of the place encourages you to hold off from action, lest the repercussions echo unfavourably through the world? Rob hoped the noisy life he lived at present would soon give way to something like peace, if not necessarily a holy one. And that the louder the clamour of his misdeeds, the deeper the silence would be.

He was nervous about this meeting with Franklin, not only because he was there to tell the old man that filming was at an end, but because, as he suddenly realised, he was meeting him for the first time without a camera. The great enabling objectivity – the distancer of art made manifest in a machine you could switch on and off – he missed. For once he would have to have a conversation that was disposable; to be thrown away. Heard, seen, by no one. Unless you were someone who counted church as the one place you could guarantee at least one listener: God.

Jim had long ago set aside the vestry for Rob as a place he could go to work, or to meet Franklin if the weather were bad. The spring had been so fine it had so far been unnecessary; but this evening, as the rain grew a little stronger outside, Rob waited among the old hymn-books and strange clerical clothing. He disliked it. There was something weird about there being individual rooms in a church at all, so expansive and unspecific a building. He felt hemmed in. And the presence of so much text, and the pantomimic air of the robes and surplices seemed ridiculous. It seemed to imply that Rob had been about some religious business all along, rather than making a television programme. The dust and the smell reminded him of a second-hand bookshop full of queasy thrillers and cheap paperbacks; he felt a peculiar, abdominal dread.

There was a knock at the door and Franklin, in comic mode that night, poked his head round the door.

'Tory comforts and Anglican misdemeanours,' he chuckled, 'isn't that what this place reminds you of, dear boy? What the fuck are you skulking in here for?'

'It's raining.'

'On the living and the dead. It is.'

Franklin looked around.

'No camera?'

Rob just looked at him.

'Sit down, will you?'

Franklin sat.

'We have decided,' said Rob, 'to call a halt to the ... filming. The general consensus is that we have enough material to finish the documentary. So we have called a stop to things early. It is a testament to how well we have got on. I want to thank you, and tell you you have been wonderful: generous, honest and committed. Thank you.'

Franklin frowned.

'Stop?' he said.

'Yes,' said Rob.

'Hmm.'

There was a pause.

Franklin stared at the television man so intently that Rob looked down.

'My dear boy,' he said, again, but not indulgently – he might have been an earl about to tell his naïve son the facts of life – 'we was in it together.'

'Of course,' said Rob.

Franklin sighed and put his head in his hands.

'You're relieved?' offered Rob.

'We shared a cell these last weeks. I ain't a squealer and I ain't no patsy,' said the old man, in a New York accent, looking through the lattice of his fingers that covered his eyes.

'A patsy?'

'Don't you know what a patsy is?'

'No.'

'And you in show business? A patsy, dear boy – listen and learn – is a fellow from the criminal ranks what finds himself used and abused by his criminal brothers – used unknowingly. Low status. Used. There are many in the films of Jimmy Cagney. Fellows who take the rap. "I ain't no patsy,"' said Franklin, in a passable imitation of the film star.

Rob looked at the old man and felt a long, aching regret that he had not lived his life better after leaving university. He should have gone abroad, he should have read the novels of Victor Hugo and learned to farm. In the absence of the camera, this new, disposable interview now seemed about him, not Franklin; he felt on the spot.

'I suppose ... the problem is ...' murmured Rob, half to himself, 'is that ... that ...'

'What?'

'We don't really have an ending. But documentaries don't always . . .' he trailed off.

'What? This project's a failure? An ending?' Franklin looked around him melodramatically, as if somewhere in the broken books and dusty clothes there might be a recalcitrant ending ready to hand, skulking in the shadows. 'Yes! What is the end of your story – *my* story, you little turd?'

Franklin was grinning at Rob. Rob grinned back.

'*Our* story, isn't it?' said Rob.

'That is my hope!' cried the old man, ecstatically. 'I was an artist too, once.'

'I'm not sure I'm an artist,' said Rob.

'Well you should be!' roared Franklin and grabbed the young man's arm; Rob winced. Franklin said it savagely, for once, in all the times Rob had seen him, overcome by a feeling larger than himself. Then he was quiet and looked at Rob who was staring at the floor, seemingly defeated by an epic, general disappointment. His arm ached where the old man had gripped him with his powerful hands. Never had Rob felt so lost, so hopeless.

'I'm sorry,' said Rob.

'That there is no ending?' said Franklin.

'What? No, that . . .'

But he wasn't sure what he was sorry for. For the fact that he wasn't an artist, whatever Franklin meant by that word? For the fact that he had brought the old man this far but could take him no further? Suddenly the idea of representing life on film did seem to him dreadfully callow. Rob could not help but conjecture that the only truly valuable things in life must exist outside the lamplit circle of his study or the oasis of light around the television monitor of the editing suite. But how did one qualify for the better, more worthy experience? Tireless charity? Total self-abnegation? Christianity?

Suddenly the little, absurd room that he shared with the old man was horribly necessary to him. It felt like a beginning. Rob wondered whether Franklin might agree to meet him there out of hours, so to speak.

Franklin, for a moment so passionate, now looked lost. The self-consciousness that Jim had so accurately diagnosed as his doing what he regarded as his duty had now disappeared. He might have been about to slowly undress, take off his make-up and join his fellow actors in the bar. Instead, very slowly, he stretched out a dirty hand. Rob looked at the old man and paused. He baulked at the gesture, felt that it was insufficient, wanted to hug him, or help him; a handshake was too old school, too formal. But Franklin looked down at the hand he had offered and saw how dirty it was, and imagined Rob had baulked at the dirt. He wiped it, gently, on his even dirtier coat and looked away. When Rob realised the misunderstanding he wanted to cry. His mobile phone went. Franklin gestured that he would wait outside. He let himself out. It was Emma on the phone, to tell him she had slipped away from work and was waiting at the church gates. When Rob went outside, Franklin was gone.

9

A week later Rob received a phone call from Jim, and was summoned to visit him. Jim gave no reason and something in his tone prevented Rob asking for one.

Rob made his way through the hot afternoon traffic and slipped into the car park by the parish offices with a mixture of fear and familiarity. Jim showed him into his office. The vicar was dressed in jeans and a T-shirt, and looked hot. Rob could never shake off a certain disappointment whenever he saw him out of uniform, as it were.

'Forgive me asking you here without more explanation,' began Jim, softly, 'I . . . I want to understand something. I do not know if I have the right to do this, but I want to ask you a couple of questions. I have no intention of trifling with your feelings.'

Rob suddenly had the outlandish notion that his wife had asked the vicar to speak to him.

Jim went on:

'You met Frank a week ago, I think.'

Rob nodded. Jim went on, with the same, quiet voice, as if he was singing a song under his breath:

'As we had discussed, Robert, I was pleased you were bringing filming to an end . . .' He trailed off. 'I have to ask you,' he went on, abruptly, 'what was the substance of the conversation you had with him at that last meeting? Did you talk about the success or otherwise of your project?'

'Yes, I said I was pleased. I congratulated him on his contribution. He knows how much I like him. Is he upset?' asked Rob, remembering the moment with the handshake. Jim was about to speak, when Rob added, 'I did say . . . yes, I said I didn't think we had an ending. He seemed to think we needed an ending. He teased me about that.'

'Teased?' said Jim.

'Perhaps teased is the wrong word,' said Rob, and laughed slightly. He felt silly being interviewed by a vicar in a T-shirt. 'Perplexed,' he added, trying to help.

Jim looked at him and then looked down at the floor. Across

his face flickered something like the hint of a cruel smile, a smile that remembered a past happiness with reproach and regret. A disappointment untempered by the solace of religion – the private, too-late recognition of brotherhood with the man who was the subject of their conversation. But when he resumed the conversation it was with same singsong softness.

'I am doing a terrible thing,' he said. 'I am talking to you, and I know things you do not. I suppose someone who is a professional interviewer must take a dim view of that. Forgive me. I have to tell you that Frank is dead. I suspect it will be an open verdict, but it is fairly clear he committed suicide. He fell from the new riverside block just here by the church.'

Jim's voice was shaking very slightly with a soft, unregulated vibrato, and his hands on the desk seemed very still, as if he had lost the use of them. Then he stood up abruptly and went to the window.

'I should like, I suppose,' went on the vicar, 'to say that we, as a parish, do not agree to the transmission of the material you have filmed, as, under the terms of the original contract, we have the right to do. But if I were to bring that right to bear I fear that I would be satisfying myself, but not the person most intimately bound up with that material: Frank.'

The world was so against Robert at this particular time that he could not help staring at the vicar and saying, 'Are you suggesting that he killed himself to give me an ending?'

There was a pause.

'I suppose you are not to blame,' said Jim simply.

The brutality of this meagre absolution felt very un-clergyman-like to Jim, and it haunted him for a long time after. Something in the meeting of Franklin and Rob had stirred a competitiveness in him that he had thought long buried, and the former's death had reduced Jim to a hopelessness and a bitterness that he had felt previously many years before when he had nearly lost his faith.

Rob walked out into the sunlight. Through the gates of the church car park he could see the flow of people to and from the bridge. He went to join them.

In the wake of the emotion at hearing Jim's news, all Rob could think now was how he hated Franklin for saying, 'Be an artist!' It seemed a dreadful, absurd reproach given the rich, creative horror of Franklin's fate. And worse than that, it implied a foreknowledge of Rob's wishes and ambitions. Perhaps it was what he wanted – looking back at that last meeting, Rob had to confess that it had thrilled him, his arm taken in that vice-like grip, the sudden passion of the old man stealing the scene.

But it was all conjecture. For though Franklin had, indeed finished off the story, its final chapter existed only in Rob's head. Rob found himself clinging to its memory like a guilty secret, coveting the moment in the vestry, repeating it to himself like an obscene mantra.

The truth was that Rob felt powerless to finish anything. His marriage would not die. His brief, blonde audience, Emma, stood ready to turn on him with all the righteous fury of a spurned head-girl. They were all so pious. Franklin, too.

Rob elbowed his way into the throng of people and felt the populist comfort of the crowd.

It was another Friday night. The experimental warmth of the spring had been discarded like a first, unsatisfactory draft, replaced by a confident but formulaic heat. It seemed to Rob it went, creatively promiscuous, where he could not; the heat dried the banks of the river where they showed above the tide; the glossy leaves of the plane trees at the entrance of the graveyard shone sure and impermeable. And the Friday night finished off the week, exiling the leisured classes to country pubs and shady country lanes, choked with flowers like the thickened arteries round a sick man's heart. Those condemned to stay and see what the summer made of the city felt the heat extended, like an elaborate metaphor, through the bars and pubs along the river, between the impatient smiles and sighs of the city's flirtatious creatures, hours from the sweaty consummation of their desires, for the time being spilled out on to the pavements, leaving the dispossessed pedestrians to wander among the stalled cars in the road, like wandering shades from the Underworld.

Rob pulled at his tie and loosened his shirt. He'd been envious of the vicar's T-shirt; his effortless informality. But only one thought really gnawed at him – his dreadful, profane regret that he had not had his camera with him that night in the vestry. And he felt, very strongly, and perhaps for the first time – as he planned his excuses to Emma and calculated to just how expensive a restaurant he could dare take his wife that evening – what an awful lot of work he still had to do.

Children's Story

L ydia's mother was baking a cake.
     'School soon,' she said, from inside the fragrant cloud of icing sugar and hazy confection that surrounded her.
'Not for a week,' Lydia said, defensively, but meeting the suggestion as a welcome challenge that might enliven the quiet afternoon. And she could see unused cake mixture dwelling in the bottom of the bowl.

Her mother had on her gingham apron. The little girl had never seen one spot or stain of cake mixture, cooking oil or fat on it in all the years she had watched her cook. Only recently had she realised that the apron was an insurance policy against a clumsiness that would never happen. In fact the apron might have been a kind of gingham machine of which the woman behind it was merely the operator, so welded were the clothing and the function performed in it, and so unconnected as it was with protection from grease. This mechanical illusion was strengthened by the mother's stiff movements about the kitchen which years of repetition had failed to smooth. It was impossible to say whether, like a music box ballerina that must run through her dance once wound up, the mother's movements betrayed simple disinterested labour for her family that now was automatic, or whether, as one might suppose the ballerina to feel, some sorrow attended the mechanical movements that fell so far short of the elegant, feminine tune the box played when opened.

'Why aren't you playing in the garden?' said her mother.

'It's too hot.'

Both of them knew this was a poor answer, and both knew that they were fighting over possession of the kitchen. The little girl, Lydia, would have a tea party for her dolls if her mother gave an inch, and this could not be. A spoonful of the cake mixture might just buy her off. Lydia waited, her upper lip smothering her lower, watchful as a private detective. For some reason the gingham machine had come to an early stop, or had not been wound sufficiently, for the bowl still perched above the washing-up, next in line for clean and peremptory execution. The little girl awaited the reprieve and the sweet ransom.

But the mother's face just hung over the sink full of soap bubbles and stared down at it and the bubbles seemed to reach up to her, their surfaces running with the rainbow sheen that soap imparts to water. Nothing happened. The girl imagined a tear joining them. Then the cake bowl was pulled, like a stray log succumbing to Niagara Falls, towards the sink. As it was about to be lost Lydia reached out her hand to redeem a fingerful of the surplus mixture. The gingham machine, with sudden, smooth violence, picked up a wooden spoon beside the sink and like a conductor bringing in a recalcitrant woodwind section on the beat, rapped the girl's hand sharply. Then the mother turned away, to attend to other sections of the orchestra, no doubt, and when she returned to the woodwind they had gone. Looking up through the window above the sink she saw her little daughter's legs, thin and gauche, running from the house, running as only crying children run, as if carrying a message somewhere, spreading a little, momentary gospel of unhappiness to the agnostic wilderness of the garden. A gospel the mother could now, over the sink, uninhibited and alone, keep herself.

It was the last day in August. A slow, yearly evolution was nearing its close; from the novelty of the last days of the school term in July – when it was impossible to tell whether the run home from school was away from something dreadful or towards something desired – through the excited, first days of the holiday, in the garden, moving from special place to special place, as new householders will wander through the rooms of their new home and guess, wildly and creatively, how their lives will fill up the empty vessel of the future – reaching the end of August, exhausted by play, by adventures had or imagined, and emerging into temporary maturity at the month's end, tired, like a sort of libertine, for whom only some moral catastrophe will give renewed vigour to their sensual appetite: so at the end of this summer the girl knew that only the inhibition of the classroom would give the garden and the fields their *frisson* again. Nothing new ever happened in August.

This shadow that school cast over the last week was as impressive, and as inescapable, as that cast by that other weighty closure, death. The girl had no direct experience of death. But just as one might say of a dying man, 'He felt, as death approached, the same dread he remembered feeling as a boy when summoned back to school', can it not also be said that the girl felt in the approach of school a premonition, a childhood foretaste of death? Those who see knowledge as a cumulative acquisition, who are raised up in wisdom in direct proportion to the amount of experience they rest on, who throw themselves into life in such a way as to maximise their experience, will luxuriate in the old man's sensation, in his linking of the childhood memory with the later crisis. But perhaps there is an alternative consolation. Namely, that however much we dramatise the present with reference to the past, so the child's life is also dramatised by portents of the future. Perhaps our lives possess a unity which is invisible to us at the time, and the life of childhood, so brief, is, in fact, peopled by an invisible dramatis personae, whose roles we fill as we meet their grown-up incarnations. So we may be blessed, at the end of our lives, not with the wisdom of nostalgia, but by the pleasant surprise of casting the one unfilled role in our childhood's drama, and knowing the last days of the summer holidays for what they really were, the moment before death, acted now, definitively, by us, as we rehearsed it once before, unknowingly, fifty years ago.

Half an hour later, Lydia emerged from the hollow oak tree, whose dark and rainless reaches had been witness to more than one tearful tantrum and, more recently, given her advanced age of twelve, soulful exile. From behind the vegetable-garden hedge she could hear her grandfather digging. A rasping sound of spade in stony earth alternated with his cough; everywhere about the house there seemed to be such labouring. She went to inspect him.

'Why ain't you indoors?' he said. He was digging potatoes, bent over the earth bed like a gold prospector over a stream. The old man had lost a leg in the war and now had an ill-fitting tin replacement that creaked at its hinges. The whole man, from his cough to his creaks, seemed to need oiling. He smoked a pipe and then sucked peppermints which he had previously broken into small pieces, so any close encounter was always accompanied by one of two overpowering smells. This afternoon he did both simultaneously, something Lydia had never seen before and assumed was impossible.

'Those potatoes are too small, I think,' she said, seeing the pale, yellow things on the earth, no larger than thrush eggs.

'Is that so, miss?'

'Yes.'

'Well, I'll learn you to tell your elders their business.'

On the strength of expressions like 'I'll learn you' for 'I'll teach you', Lydia regarded her grandfather as her intellectual equal. She would never have told him it was incorrect, and by the same token he would never have told her she was naughty to have been cheeky to her mother. Altogether her friendship with the old man was a useful introduction to the idea of bartering concessions; both of them were aware of this and both of them liked it.

'Want one of these?' he said, fishing in his dirty pocket for an equally dirty segment of mint.

'No, thank you,' she said.

'Fussy minx,' he said, guessing her reason.

'It's not because it's dirty,' she said, superbly guessing *his* reason, 'but I recently had some cake mixture.'

Her grandfather, who was her father's father, did all the gardening. The greenhouse, the herbs and vegetables and fruit trees were all kept by him; only the lawn was the special province of the father and a point of pride with him. Lydia assumed that the cutting of the lawn, which involved the terrifying mower, was both a more dangerous job and also a more artistic one. Sometimes she would remark to the grandfather that 'Daddy was having particular trouble with the dryness of the season', when the lawn turned yellow in the drought, or 'No one knows how difficult it is to keep the lines straight' when she had noticed a kink in one of the usually perfect stripes. And her grandfather would look at her and smoke his pipe, and solemnly nod in agreement. Lydia assumed cutting lawns was a generational advance on vegetables. Not least since the grandfather's seed-boxes were labelled 'letis' and 'carot', and cutting the lawn, being a wordless job, could never be misspelt.

The old man put the mint in his mouth, momentarily mixing up mint and false teeth and for a while sucking both. Then he resumed his search for treasure. As his old hands sifted the soil between his fingers Lydia saw that they shook, and realised that she had mistaken their shaking for a method of potato detection. In fact they shook uncontrollably. As she looked up at his face she saw that he would not look at her, that he was smoking and sucking furiously and that he was swearing under his breath. She stared at him and seemed suddenly to see a picture of herself standing there, as if she were disembodied for a moment, so superfluous did she know herself to be, witnessing this incomprehensible crisis.

'If you have a mint,' she said, to break the spell, 'I wouldn't mind it, now.'

But the old man only looked into the earth, as if trying to bury his crisis in it or find it reflected there, or merely find solace in his labour; but his face suggested he found none of these and after a silence the little girl turned around and walked slowly back to the house.

One place where labour was impossible, and where Lydia felt sure to find stillness and adoration, was where her grandmother sat, in the alcove of the bay window, staring out at the lawn. This grandmother had been more or less crippled for twenty years

with an ill-defined malady of the lower spine which made it difficult to walk and caused her great pain. The granddaughter was
frequently deputed to fetch her pills, which always seemed to her
disproportionately small for the huge pain they were required to
relieve. If these miracles of medicine failed, as primitive as the
pills were advanced, an old, thick hot-water bottle was the next
remedy. Lydia liked especially to fetch the bottle when she had
been naughty. She was assured at such times by her grandmother
that she was the best and brightest of all her grandchildren. And
at such times the girl always felt the cruelness of a certain dilemma
– the fact that the impetus to relieve her grandmother's suffering
had exactly coincided with herself being naughty and in need of
assurances that she was a good girl. How could she relieve pain
without admitting to her own vanity? Every time she stood before
the old lady and received the sought-after benediction and the
hot-water bottle was placed between the back of the chair and
the old lady's pain, she vowed to make it her mission to provide
such relief every day. And every time, once she was a good girl
again, she forgot her grandmother's suffering.

This day, Lydia was more aware than she had ever been of
this inconsistency on her part. Everywhere something seemed
amiss, and although she was sure she had done nothing wrong,
she put on the kettle herself. The kitchen was now empty, like
an abandoned post deserted in the face of an approaching enemy.

'It's you,' said the old lady, barely opening her eyes as Lydia
crept round the door of the living room.

'I've brought you a bottle,' she said, holding it up to her grandmother like a proud spaniel with a rabbit in its mouth.

But her grandmother, without taking it from her as was usual,
simply leaned forward and Lydia realised, half horrified, that this
was a signal for her to put the bottle there herself, in the empty

place between her grandmother's spine and the back of the chair. Standing on tiptoe, she reached behind the frail body of the old lady and placed the water bottle where she had seen it placed before, in the very sanctum of the woman's pain, a sort of holy place, the place which seemed to her now the origin, the oracle, even, that administered the benediction she habitually sought: a dreadful glimpse of the sweetness gleaned from suffering.

The old woman leaned back into the heat and sighed, opened her eyes briefly and said again, 'It's you.' Lydia realised, with disappointment, that today the old woman's suffering rendered any relief anonymous. She was only staring at the expanse of uncut grass outside that stretched, vacantly, to the road, unrelieved by detail or design.

Then, for no apparent reason, Lydia began to sing a song. She felt in her meetings with her family so far that day as though she had become invisible, that there existed between herself and their thoughts and feelings a gap, a void, that she was at liberty to fill with whatever nonsense her fancy might conjure up. So she began to sing, and to walk in stately procession around the room, confident that however grand her misbehaviour, the focus could never be brought back to her, so bound up in other worlds were the rest of her family. Her stately walk turned into a skip, then a run, she barked like a dog and exited, and in the hall immediately ran into her father.

He was entering his study, and for a moment seemed taken by surprise to see his daughter. He greeted her as an old acquaintance, stiffly. As if they had not met since an unpleasant phone call, when they had said harsh things to one another. He seemed eager to placate her.

'Come in, come in,' he said, breezing into his room. Suddenly Lydia felt that, at last, someone would take notice of her. They went in, and her father instantly picked up a newspaper and sat with it like a travelling rug over his knees.

'Where's Mummy gone?' said Lydia, sure that an apology for the blow from the spoon was overdue.

'Eh? Lying down, I expect. Headache. I shouldn't trouble her. Emily will be home soon. Do you know where she's gone?'

'Why haven't you cut the grass?' said Lydia.

The man looked at his daughter as if she had spoken a foreign language; a language she had learned on the sly and in which she suddenly revealed herself to be fluent. He lifted up the newspaper and ballooned it out, snapped it into shape and let it settle back on his knees. He laughed, as though the operation amused him. When she asked the question again, he looked as though he'd hoped the question had been answered. Then he laughed again, with a little laugh that was like a sigh and nodded his head, twice. It might have been a ritual dance for all the sense it made to Lydia. Then he billowed out the paper once more, like a schooner in full sail, but instead of snapping it shut he embraced it, controlled it, folded it up, put it on a chair and walked to the window. He stood there for a while, staring at the lengthening shadows on the uncut lawn.

'I asked you where Emily was, missy.'

'She went to town. Shopping, she said,' said Lydia. 'Things for university,' she added in a singsong voice.

'You'll miss her when she goes back,' said her father.

'When's she going?' said Lydia, though she knew very well.

'Tomorrow. First thing.' The man stared out, perfectly still. 'She should be here,' he said, more to himself than his youngest daughter. This judgment on the absence of her sister felt to Lydia something like a reproach; and the memory of Emily, her older sister by nine years, stocking her handbag with cigarettes and a thick novel and muttering under her breath, in a rare unguarded moment, that 'she wasn't so stupid as to hang around the house, today of all days . . .' compounded this, as if, having overheard the remark, she, Lydia herself, had been party to her sister's desertion.

This remark – that Emily ought to have been there – for some reason depressed the little girl, and she felt all the wind gone from her sails. Her attempts to enliven the house with her finer qualities had all failed. She turned her back on her father, who seemed more interested in the lawn than her, and wended her way through the hall, the kitchen, down the garden path to the field. Soon it would be supper and bed, and one last trip seemed necessary, perhaps to establish the boundaries of her domain.

The edge of their garden gave way to a field, which was also theirs, but the field beyond that belonged to a vicious and unpredictable farmer. This walk, from garden through their field to the edge of the unknown had become over the summer a little, daily catechism of sensations for Lydia. An education. From the garden to their field was an obvious journey, as her grandfather's lines of vegetables and bean canes and paths gave way to long grass, stakes, occasional barbed wire, unkempt nettles and cow parsley that raised seedy heads in summer and obediently bowed them every autumn. This, up as far as the old stable, they owned; it could be brought within her instinctive control; the mistress of her room, sometime mistress of the kitchen and her dolls could *just* be mistress of the nettle patch, just manage to extend her rule so far.

But the field beyond, in every external regard identical to the one she saw as hers, was a different matter. Some deep prompting suggested that the grass that grew there was of a different species, the rabbits who popped their heads above the far side of the boundary were of a different breed, the electricity, even, that ran high over both fields on anonymous wires changed in power and provenance as it crossed the boundary. It was, and must be, a different world. Nothing could convince her that her self would subsist if she stepped from the field that she knew to the *terra incognita* she saw through the hedge. She was aware, with the certainty of the seasoned traveller, that to move within a new domain transformed the mover, that one did not remain unchanged like a catalyst in a chemical experiment; if she ventured there she would have to give up old knowledge to be replaced by new, and only then could the landscape be hers. So the only choice in the face of this alien land was aggrandisement, a frontier-minded foreign policy, that, irrespective of the threat of prosecution for trespassing, could imaginatively annex this field, then the next and the next. And the homicidal farmer must be annexed too, and brought, if not under the constraint of her benign constitution, at least within its observation.

She reached the stable, which lay on the boundary, and looked inside. The late afternoon sun broke up the recessed byres into light and dark; huge prism-shaped cuts of sunshine were set against deep shadows made mobile by the millions of golden motes that drifted from the hay. The whole architecture of the building seemed reduced to great building blocks of sun and shadow; shade was a sophistication not yet acquired. And the similarity between the dust motes and the flies that moved also in the stable suggested a prehistoric union of dust and life that made the girl think, half with horror and half with wonder, that one had sprung from the other.

Only after peering into the shadows for some time could Lydia see the horses: set back, like living sculptures, like watchful saints stationed in the transepts of the stable. And before she could make out their actual forms she sensed – as a quality so distinct that it seemed to possess the darkness like a thought – the presence of something *waiting*. Even when her eyes had got used to the dark, the two still, kind heads of the horses which she could just make out submitted to the quality of being horses, it seemed to her, as an ancillary quality to this prime one of patience. Their ancient, twin roles of noble animal and beast of burden were in thrall to this, and their submission to it was complete. For it seemed to Lydia, they bore selves distinct from their incarnations as horses, as the wolf is imagined evil prior to its appearing as a wolf, or the lamb in a medieval triptych benign, before the allegory reveals Our Saviour. From their quality of self they waited to be released, yet for all that Lydia stared, their big dark eyes, as still as their eyelids were busy warding off the flies, seemed to say they waited without expectation.

She actively sought bed that night, for the first time in her short life, and the discovery of bedtime as something to be sought rather than succumbed to was a revelation. She had looked for someone to say good-night to, spotted a thread of pipe-tobacco smoke drifting across the no man's land of the strawberry patch and heard the creak of her grandfather; made out the tall figure of her father still standing behind the reflections of the garden in the bay window; been surprised to see her grandmother dart with the swiftness of a girl into the living room, carrying a fresh water bottle, looking as if she hoped she'd not been seen. And Emily was still not back from town. She took herself to bed, perhaps unconsciously surmising that only sleep could replenish and refurnish her unsatisfactory waking life, pillaging the dream-world for reinforcements.

Faced, though, with the climb upstairs to the attic room, her nerve nearly failed her.

In the autumn of the previous year, a rook's nest had fallen from one of the tall trees in front of the house. Lydia had been the first to spot it and had run out to it. She had frequently tried to make friends with the rooks, whose high social life in the limits of the trees had seemed to her particularly attractive. They were always calling to one another in cross voices, flapping their big black wings in an attention-seeking way that made her laugh. And now, having imagined herself up there, her mind having assimilated with great effort the manners of the high trees, a miracle had occurred, and the high trees had come down to her. The nest was empty – there was no trauma of eggs or chicks – but was still perfect, despite the fall, and she had looked inside, and burst into tears.

The nest had the same quality as the distant field had, a sense that this foreign place must be constituted differently from her world. But whereas the field could be approached as adventure, as assimilation of mystery, this was an invasion. This thing she had held in awe and peopled with her fancy was at her feet, herself made into a giant by association, by a trick of relative distances that made her head spin: she towered over that which had towered over her. And she was powerless to put it back. To imagine that the beautiful smooth-sided nest, so painstakingly made to receive eggs and chicks, was now useless was dreadful; that she had this tragedy on her hands and had, literally, seen into it – was terrifying. And ever since that day she had felt her bedroom at the top of the house to be the same. The attic had taken on this high-up quality, this foreignness, and it was this that she had to walk into alone. No amount of staring at the walls or at the bedspread, of patiently living alongside the ubiquitous otherness of the high trees, that had come, Messiah-like, to speak the language of God in the words of men, would render the strange high place familiar. The otherness, which in the fall from the tree she associated with tragedy, and which had made her cry, was now around her; her imagination was on high, and she could not be talked down. It was as if she had been besieged in her tower; yet today, the only possible besiegers – the members of her family – seemed to be in the grip of some abstraction that rendered them apparently unthreatening. But like the naïve watcher from a castle who sees the besieging enemy going about its business of cooking, taking Communion, arguing amongst itself, and supposes that its appetite for the siege must be waning, and who begins to think of opening its gates to the heretics beneath, she had to remind herself that this high-up place was all she could call her own, and that this strange truce could only be illusory.

But that night, she had a visitor. It wasn't yet dark when she heard her sister climb the stairs, open the door without knocking and sit down on the bed. Emily looked towards the window almost before she had looked at Lydia's face on the pillow. Outside there was activity, though it was gone nine o'clock; sounds of the lawn-mower being dragged across the drive and on to the lawn; sounds Lydia tried to ignore lest the timetable of the day were to be so upset that sleep would prove impossible.

'Do you want a story?' said Emily. She had said nothing of shopping; there were no clothes to be shown and shared before sleep; no gossip.

'Isn't it too late?' said Lydia.

'No.'

'Past nine, though.'

'Not too late, tonight, my love,' she said, as if she enjoyed the special dispensation, but found the dispensation sad.

'All right,' said Lydia, hearing her own voice and being surprised herself that it sounded so indifferent.

Emily, dressed in black, thin, pale, with hair held down by modest grips and bands, got up and walked slowly to the bookshelf and instead of asking, as was customary, what her little sister wanted, took down the first book her fingers found. As she returned, her dark frame seemed even thinner as it briefly eclipsed the window, ablaze with evening sunlight, gilded at its edges with gold as though it were showing off its wealth.

The older girl settled herself beside her sister and began to read.

When Emily had first arrived in the room, Lydia had been struggling with the notion of sleep and had been attempting to understand the recurrent paradox of how it was possible to achieve the unconsciousness of sleep with a conscious thought, how the two did not nullify one another, and wondering whether she would ever sleep again; now Emily came, like a nurse with a medication Lydia had forgotten she had asked for.

At first her grown-up sister seemed to bring too much of the world beneath for the little girl to wholly trust her. The attic room had once been hers, but she had given it over to Lydia in some magical act of generosity that now seemed as legendary and indistinct as prehistory. But Emily came to the room no less frequently when she was home from university; she climbed the stairs as a fellow exile and sat in the window looking over the garden and smoked cigarettes. She came even when Lydia was not there and read her books. When her father had brought her home for the long vacation he had commented on the heaviness of the suitcases, and she had had to patiently explain that they were full of essential reading matter. This fact, she also explained at length, forbade her socialising with her old school friends or finding a fun part-time job. They were not to think her unpopular or without motivation if she read in solitude at the top of the house, or to think she was not studying if Lydia happened to join her there. So she smoked and read, and played with her sister, and grew as thin as the books she read were thick.

But today, with so much strangeness in the house, Lydia was slow to accept her visitor and felt the influence of the adult world on her. It irked her like the suggestion of an infidelity. Looking at her face she seemed to trace the working of thoughts that had their origin in habits and customs from a foreign land, recalcitrant tricks of language and manner that betray the foreigner abroad. And it seemed to Lydia that her sister made insufficient attempts to disguise her foray into these adult dominions; and just as the jealous lover feels, or at least imagines, a change in the style of her lover's kiss and stubbornly sets out to trace the change's origin to its source, even if that source is shown to be the mouth of a rival, so Lydia tormented herself with her adored sister's otherness.

'Where have you been?' she demanded, over the sound of Emily's reading. But Emily did not stop, only negotiated the interruption, accommodated the sound, gently highlighted the words around it so that the narrative thread should not be lost; only as the story steadied itself afterwards did her voice quiver and nearly break, as though her mind found some corresponding, inner obstacle to be negotiated, perhaps more difficult than Lydia's interruption. Lydia noticed this, and suddenly she knew, nightmare-sure, that some terror lay in store; it waited at the door, a terrible messenger from the world beneath, a dreadful intruder who waited there and seemed, as she listened, to listen with her.

And yet, slowly, the story worked on her. Just as sleep, once it is ignored, grants us its concession, so her fears, assuming the story to be superfluous and so ignoring it, granted the narrative admission to her imagination. Or as a famously tyrannical schoolteacher will, to the classroom's astonishment, end one particular day by letting the children sit on their desks and sing songs instead of doing arithmetic, only for the school to be told in assembly the next day that the teacher's husband was killed in a car accident the morning before and she had been granted compassionate leave, so explaining the miracle of generosity with the tragedy of loss – so *not willing* the story, Lydia felt, in her sister's low voice, the world, and her fears, taken out of her hands and an unexpected paradise set up in its place. It was a story she knew well, and concerned the exploits of Kitty, her favourite heroine, but the words themselves seemed not to matter, their explicit meaning being nothing compared to the implicit intimacy of their being offered now. There was set up, between the three of them – the book, Emily and Lydia – an unwritten constitution, as finely balanced as that between monarch, parliament and subject, and just as in the great world, there was, between these three, no one, single authority.

She read on for some time and then stopped. Lydia did not register at first the silence; the narrative adventure she had been following in her head maintained its own momentum, Kitty and her friends still had choices to be made and crises to avoid, and only slowly did the silence begin to rob them of energy, like a slow poison, and leave them, as equally astonished as Lydia that they had no immediate future. Lying with her head pressed deep into the pillow, not looking at Emily, Lydia was aware of the sound of crying in the room. And it was as if at first, in the brief moment between the ending of the fiction and the beginning of fact, in her imagination Emily's tears became part of the story and Lydia found herself trying desperately to assimilate these tears into the daring exploits of Kitty, and, realising that this was an unlikely transposition and artistically beyond her, she, as it were, came to, disentangled the two narrative impulses from one another and turned to see the crying young woman beside her.

'What is it?' she said.

'Mum and Dad are getting divorced,' Emily said.

'I see,' said Lydia.

There was a pause. Then Emily looked at her sister and said, as if this were as important a piece of information, 'I'm not supposed to tell you.'

A sweet silence of conspiracy settled on the two girls. Lydia stroked the black velvet sleeve of her sister's dress for a moment and coveted the dark softness of the material.

Then, after a longer pause, she carried on.

'Dad's met someone else. It's been going on for months . . .'

She trailed off, as if she had lost faith in the narrative and wanted it off her hands.

'When?' said Lydia.

'Soon. He'll leave soon,' she added, to make sure they were talking about the same thing. 'And we have to leave this house. Grandma and Grandpa, too.'

Lydia wanted more forbidden information; she was terrified of the prosaic at that moment. But, in fact, she found she need not be terrified, for she could not shake off the story her sister had been reading to her, and the effect of the lingering suspension of reality gave to this dreadful moment, by the story's insistent logic, a quality that was itself fictional. The moment of revelation was irrevocably connected to adventure, to invention, to drama, and also connected to the medium of being expressed in the measured, soft and gentle voice of her sister; it was a created thing, and from this creative union of tale and teller there seemed, for the moment, no escape. There, high up in the attic, their father walking across the lawn beneath them, about to cut the grass, the shadows of both he and the trees lengthening into infinity, there his two daughters were witness to the remorseless and promiscuous unfolding of narrative; the sometime desperate reflex of observing oneself conjured by circumstance into feeling this and that, and then feeling it related, by the operation of one's secret soul, as a story – in which joy and despair appear as mere contingencies, from whose pain one is immune only in so far as they can be related *as stories*; and to which one stands one place removed, divorced, absolved. The presentation of a story one loved, like the story of Kitty's adventures, in which one cared for Kitty's fate almost as much as one cared for one's own, introduced to Lydia the idea of living within love. Kitty was watched by Lydia, and loved by Lydia, though Kitty knew nothing of Lydia. Similarly, when she conjured for herself the idea of the house which she loved so much, and which surrounded her like a universe, she felt, under its broad eaves, that it loved her, too. Her narrative seemed contained within the fictional boundaries of her private domain.

And also, by extension, narrative forgave. Though the idea of blame – this mysterious woman her father had found, for example, who must have set in motion the strange phenomenon of her family's behaviour that day – though this blame, this adult sophistication Lydia knew differentiated between what was naughty and what was *wrong* – though this was as yet indistinct to her, she knew instinctively that forgiveness would be required, and the soft voice of her sister seemed to make, for the time being, all things possible. Emily offered, by love, the passing of fact into fiction, and in doing so, ratified both.

The older girl dried her eyes. A moth had come through the open window and began to circle the central light above them. Emily got up and turned the switch off at the wall, leaving only the glow of the bedside light, in itself too weak to read by and therefore signalling the end of the story for the night. The moth gave up its fruitless vigil and disappeared into the darkness of the eaves. Emily sat back down again.

'I have to go, my love.'

Outside an engine started up, and Lydia could just see from her bed the figure of her father, in the fading light, begin to cut the lawn. At the sight of him, the little revelation she felt concerning stories was thrown into confusion; the conjunction of the news of the divorce and this absurd detail presented itself to her as something almost like an insult. All Lydia could think of was why her father, knowing they were going to leave the house and garden, continued to go about his business so conscientiously, so undramatically. This final detail of the evening became fixed in her mind, and as someone unused to looking at an abstract painting might cling to one small segment of the canvas which to her fancy reminds her of a little dog, and therefore grants her at least one literal reference point in her attempt to enjoy the picture – though she knows full well that the painter had no intention of putting a little dog into his abstract creation – so, in a reversal of this phenomenon, Lydia came to cling to that one abstract, absurd detail of the day: her father cutting the lawn; and she clung to this image in the face of the over-literal presentation of family catastrophe which otherwise threatened to overwhelm her. The father set about his task, outwardly at odds with the great machine, his thin, tall frame steering and shepherding his labour over the grass, finishing off his tasks for the day, seeing them through, finally, against what he himself might have recognised as his will. So we finish off the story of our lives, attending, as we think to meaningless details, but giving, as we do, the final gloss, perceptible only to others, to the peculiar, unmeant reality of our lives.

Emily turned to her little sister, turning as if from conjecture to certainty, weary of the demands the former made on her, and kissed her as she had used to do when Lydia was poorly. Only at this point did something like a trauma begin to work on the little girl, and the speechless terror that had seemed to wait at the door and listen to her sister's story with her seemed now admitted. Just as a longing to love will eventually result in love finding an object, so terror, no less promiscuous, was already settling on the night ahead. Both the sisters knew this, but neither waited unnecessarily to say good-night; they parted like business partners.

Lydia lay very still as it grew dark. The stiller she lay, her arms like dead weights beside her, the more her mind filled up the high attic room, and the freer from the imprisonment of her body she felt. She lay as still as those figures of crusading knights that lie above their bodies in church, staring with cold eyes at the vaulted ceiling above them, around whose bodies are the records of all their travels, whose labours in hot countries and against inhospitable enemies are so various it is impossible not to think that as well as being dead, they must also be *resting*.

Soon Emily went to bed herself, the machine stopped outside as the light died and the garden exhaled the last of the day's heat to that other, roofless, vault, the evening sky. Apart from the occasional drone of voices from the rooms below, everything was silent. Lydia finished off the work of storytelling in her head, in which she was both subject and worker after the event, reconciling impossible opposites, filling out the biographies of those people she had dealt with during the day, and making of their abstract actions a map whose key, whose buried treasure lay in sadness, not unfriendliness. And for a while everything made sense, whilst still within the echo of her sister's quiet voice, as it gave continuance, gave timelessness to the presentation of the world, all presented for no reason but that in her sadness it gave her pleasure to read to Lydia, her gift no more than sadness' reflex, the stubborn operation of gentleness, but gloriously illuminated, like a window catching the last evening sunlight, by love.

The Last Word

Once upon a time, the cunt who passes for my publisher phoned me up with a request. I had sent him the manuscript of my latest collection of short stories some time around the extinction of the dinosaurs and he was just now getting back to me. By the time the call came through I had gone from assuming he had died to hoping he had. But he had at least read them, and began his customary summing up of his feelings about each one. He weighed each of them up, fondling their themes like a pederastic form master with a small boy's bollocks. Finally, the dreadful little poof came to the point.

'The fact is, darling man, that the collection is light.'

My mind scrambled to make sense of this new adjective. Patrick's adjectives came in eras. Some lasted years. 'Visceral' lasted three years. What did he mean by 'light'? As in 'soufflé-light'? Or as in 'Light Opera' – 'Light Short Stories' being presumably more hummable and more amenable to Amateur Groups than, by extension, 'Grand Short Stories'.

When I had, as gently and penetratingly as I could, enquired of him What in the Name of Sweet Fucking Jesus he was talking about, it became clear that by 'light' he meant 'short'.

I was, according to the heady homosexual heights of his judgment, short of a short story.

'Because,' he went on, 'we must cut "At the Zoo"'.

'Why?'

'It's too . . . *femme*.'

'Patrick, have you been drinking? What the fuck does *femme* mean?'

'As in French for woman.'

'I didn't think you even knew the English for woman.'

'Now, now. Don't be naughty. It's too soft. We need an edge. You have to cover all the angles. I need masculine definition.' I started to speak. 'And before you weigh in with one of your cheerful homophobic ripostes . . .'

'There's nothing cheerful about them. They depress me. But you like them.'

'As I do your stories. Look at Chekhov, look at *Raymond Carver* . . .'

Whenever these names came up I always imagined Patrick's face. I knew only too well that when he mentioned Raymond Carver he assumed an expression not unlike the one that passes over small boys when they have wet themselves, or have an unwanted erection in the showers after football; a look of embarrassed, fecund presence. I always nod sagely and wait for him to metaphorically clean himself up.

'I want,' said Patrick, and I knew he was trying to think of something clever to say, something that he could preferably relate later on at an awards ceremony, so as to take the credit, 'a last, casual fuck.' Maybe not an awards ceremony. 'Something,' he went on, 'to show you don't take yourself too seriously.'

'You could print my bank statements.'

'Now, now, we'll get you a decent advance this time. Be a good boy and please Patrick. Your stories are charming. Charming. The one about the cat – what's his name? Freddy? *Beautiful*. Title story.' There was a pause. 'The cat's not meant to be God, is it?'

'No, Patrick.'

'No, I didn't think it was. But you do have a religious thing going on, dear boy. You do. Your stories are religious.' I thought fucking hell, I preferred 'visceral'. He went on. 'Did you have a religious upbringing?'

'Patrick, I don't have another story. We're going to Norton for the Bank Holiday weekend. Let's talk next week.'

'The one about the small student. Does he have a name?'

'I don't know. To be honest, Patrick, I don't remember.'

'That's not a good sign. When was the last time you read it?'

'I'm not sure I've ever read it. I *wrote* it.'

'The student boy – he's short. You're not tall. Is it . . . *very* true? But then,' he went on, 'as Jesus said, "What is truth?"'

He was elated to have picked up the religious thread.

'Patrick, when do you want the new story?'

'And the one about the critic . . .'

'Yes?'

'Mmm . . .'

'What does that mean?'

'Careful, careful . . . Darling, be careful.'

'It's not anti-critic.'

'I didn't say it was.'

'Then why do I have to be careful?'

'Because it's dangerous territory.'

'What, critics' territory, you mean? Off limits? They should be bloody flattered . . . if anything, it's anti-anti-critics. If anything it's about the dangers of doing nothing, of passivity, it's about love, not criticism . . .'

'You say all this, but is that clear just from reading the story?'

'Patrick, what do you want me to do? Put a disclaimer at the end of the collection saying I'm not against the critical process?'

'It wouldn't be a bad idea.'

'Some of my best friends are critics. Shall I put that in as well?'

'Don't sulk. One more story and Patrick will be happy.'

'When do you want it by?'

'My dear boy, a watched pot never boils. Never force it . . . The muse must never be taken for granted . . .'

'When do you want it by?'

'Next Wednesday would catch me before my little holiday. How is Julia?'

'About to be told her Bank Holiday break is ruined.'

'*Such* domesticity. You are like a character from one of your own stories.'

'So are you, Patrick. And for the record, it was Pontius Pilate who said "What is truth?" before he crucified your friend and mine.'

'You did have a religious upbringing!'

I hung up.

Norton, the house with a ridiculous name, was our country retreat. I couldn't tell you where it got the name, nor why Julia's right-on Old-Labour-voting parents had a house in the country, anyway. When Julia was a child they had lived there, briefly; when they had divorced they had let it, and in the following years, when it transpired neither of them would marry again, they had drifted back together and spent their summers there. Just when they might have moved there for good, they both died, in quick succession. The house was left to Julia and her older sister. It was a retreat – that word that is such a comic mixture of monastic denial of the world and upper-middle-class enjoyment of it. Julia says she spent the happiest days of her childhood there, so she is attached to it, and values her visits there extremely highly. Extremely highly.

When we were first married, and I was getting nowhere as a writer, Julia was obsessed with the notion that it would be a wonderful place to write. She seemed to think that if I looked like a writer, with a desk at the window and ivy round it and the scent of jasmine on a summer's evening, I would write about the beauties of Nature and be a success. That the place would do the work for me. Instead, I would sit in our tiny kitchen in our first, cramped flat and all I would say was, 'I don't want to write *there*. I want you to leave the room so I can write *here*.' I was bored by the beauties of Nature, and my suspicion was that all Julia really wanted was to revisit the scenes of her childhood happiness, which bored me nearly as much.

So we just went away for the weekends. You get the idea. Just long enough to fix the disproportionately large number of things that had gone wrong with it in our absence and then come home again. On a really classic weekend we'd get back to find out we'd been playing hosts to burglars in our London flat. Then, all I wanted, like a painkiller, was the blank page of my brain back on Monday morning. Anything that didn't feel like chasing a lifestyle; chasing a portrait of the past; chasing Nature.

People who live in the past, as Julia did, have no notion quite how selfish that whole deal is. Because it is, by definition unshareable. Don't get me wrong. Artists and writers are a selfish bunch. But it's at least tempered by the fact that they produce something. And that something, made up of their egoism or not, is up for grabs. But Julia's silent meditations on the richness of her childhood rather got my goat. She'd talk about it, of course. Sometimes for quite some time. And I would just end up saying, 'I think, darling, you had to be there. You just had to be there.' And then she'd go *really* quiet.

Arriving there was the worst; on a Friday night, after cutting a swathe through the rush-hour, motorway cannon fodder, me exhausted at the wheel. She'd go Laura Ashley, and drift through the garden, remembering being in love with some tree, some book, some *ballet*. There were hundreds of old vinyl records there she wouldn't throw out. The paraphernalia of other people's pasts seems to me tainted with obscenity. The portentousness of other people's old, passive, objects. To their owners they are as rich as fine loam and as fertile; to strangers, manure. Shit. Keep away.

And it was so bloody expensive. I thought Nature was supposed to be free, unconditional, like the love of parents we'd never had. Bollocks. We were paying a tax just to look at trees and grass.

And do you know what? I never had any good ideas there. Lying in bed the morning of a trip to Norton, in the hospice-like hopelessness of a hangover (I always got drunk the night before a long drive, just to feel extra sorry for myself), I might dream up a whole novel. In the chilly agnosticism of the garage forecourt, filling up before joining the motorway, in the walk from the pumps to the cashier I might dream up three plays and a fucking novella. But in the daffodil-nodding-ivy-clad-rose-petal-strewn gravel drive of a wildlife sanctuary and misty-eyed wank that was Norton I could barely even write my name.

Julia's beautiful *corps de ballet* head turned on the beat of me delivering my bombshell.

'I don't understand,' she said.

'Which bit of it do you not understand?'

'What exactly did Patrick say?'

'I've just told you. Please don't make me repeat it. Believe it or not, it makes me no happier than you.'

'Not finished . . .' She pondered. 'Light? You said to me last week it was finished. You said yourself, in this kitchen, that it was done. "It's done," you said. "Finished. I feel it's finished."'

'Do you have a transcript of the whole conversation? What I said makes no difference. If Patrick wants another . . .'

'Who wrote that wonderful collection?'

'What?'

'Who wrote it?'

I sighed.

'Julia . . . please don't start playing good cop bad cop linguistic tag with me. We know I wrote it. And if you start to say I should have the courage of my convictions, I swear I'll eat the microwave.'

'If you wrote it you know when it's complete.'

'Sorry, did you not understand the joke about the microwave? I don't want you to say that.'

'You don't want me to say how wonderful your work is?'

'Yes, but I don't want you to say the obvious.'

'It's not obvious. If I didn't like your stories I'd tell you.'

'I don't mean that. I mean the obvious . . .'

'I know you and I love you,' she said. 'And I know you play the blustering hard man. But it's just a cover. And when you get criticised, you just buckle.'

'Ah, thank you, doctor. Next!'

'Now is the time to stand firm. To believe in yourself. Tell Patrick you have finished the collection, and he can like it or lump it.'

'Any more clichés? That's what James Stewart characters say

in Hollywood movies. Then, to the audience's great pleasure the publisher goes on to publish the brave writer and a classic is born. In reality they just put the manuscript in the bin and move on.'

'Well, I don't know anything about James Stewart ...'

'It's just an illustration.'

'What do you mean an illustration? We're talking about books.'

'Julia ... why are you so dim? Fuck this ...'

'I'll ring him up and say it's finished. And don't start swearing. You swear so much these days. You even swear in your stories.'

'Oh, so I'm so sensitive in my writing, but you don't like the swearing. Has it ever occurred to you that I only swear in character. It's the narrator that swears.'

'Hmm ... I'm not sure about that.'

'The narrator is a different character in each story.'

'Yes.'

'What do you mean "yes"? He is.'

'That narrator-as-character. I'm not sure if it works. Readers just want a narrator. They see themselves as the narrator. They don't want different—'

'Why are people queuing up to destroy my confidence? I could just stand on street corners reading out my work and have the public give helpful suggestions about how it might be improved.'

The *corps* made a thoughtful progress round the kitchen and came to rest by the sink. I could see the Fairy Liquid peeking over the beautiful nape of her swan neck. How did my life come to place such beauty beside such prosaicness; such desire besides such irritation? I could see tears weren't far away.

'I love you,' she said, reaching for her more valuable chips as I shuffled and re-dealt.

'Right,' I said.

'And I think you are a wonderful writer. All I want is for you to feel confident and happy.'

'Then give me more sex and less criticism. That's a joke.'

The tears were getting closer. She kept tears back for when the 'I love yous' failed. It was for such wagon-circling moments as these that I lived. Watching her cry was like being on heroin. I just sank back into a warm haze of self-reproachful bliss. Her tears made me want to kill her, of course. But as they came, so I felt my strength – the strength I would need to throttle that beautiful neck – ebbing from me. I would have to wait for it to return, and in the meantime feel the ecstasy of her misery.

But we hadn't yet gone far enough. I saw her pull herself together and try to smile at me. I needed to play for higher stakes.

'Anyway,' I said, 'the upshot is that we can't go to Norton. I'll have to work here over the weekend. Patrick wants the new story quickly.'

'Not go to Norton?' she said. Her smile faded and her features actually seemed to ripple like a wave as true pain moved over them like the wind. My heart beat faster.

'You know I can't work there.'

'But we were always going to Norton.'

'I don't quite understand the grammar of that sentence.'

There was a long pause, and I took in the final, fugitive ecstasy of behaving badly. It was like a spring breeze laden with the scent of wild flowers. It was why I was born.

'You go,' I said.

'You know I can't do that.'

'Why?'

And she looked up at me, to see if I really was going to go too far.

'Because I can't drive,' she said, simply.

'Oh yes.'

Still the tears didn't come. She sat down at the table. She was calm. It was different, this take on things. I was a little alarmed. Normally by now we would be screaming and her face would look like she had had a particularly abrasive facial scrub. But she was pale. As if she were about to dance a moving, consumptive *pas de deux*.

'I love August Bank Holiday there,' she said. 'I suppose it's because when we only went there in the holidays it was always August. The long summer holidays. Daddy was always frightened we'd be bitten by snakes, so as soon as we arrived he would get the mower out. Whenever I smell cut grass I think of how that smell heralded the holidays. Even when I smell it now life suddenly feels so full of promise. He cut the grass while we unpacked the car. That's why I loved the grass being cut in that story of yours. Makes me think of Daddy.'

'Call him Dad, Jules, you're not a girl any more.'

I had to put a stop to this. This calm relating of the past could go on all night. I'd lost all purchase on the situation. Instead of a fight she was going to appease me. The ecstasy faded. The clever bitch was going to be nice; she was going to open her heart. It had happened once before, years ago. We'd been up all night talking about her friend Anna whom she had been rude to when she was eighteen and never seen again. All night.

'I can't write at Norton,' I said. But it lacked conviction.

'No,' she said softly. 'You hate it there.'

She was challenging me. She was throwing down a creative gauntlet, and I was a creative person. An unpleasant but creative person. And I was damned if I was going to be nice like some little bourgeois house-husband when there must be so many more subtle, innovative – even artistic – solutions to this stand-off. I had to be nice to her, but not because I loved her. (And please remember I did love her.) But because the *challenge* was to be nice. That was the provocation. If I had been horrible I would have lost points for being obvious. I wasn't going to have her unhappy and without her orgy of past associations. I hated her for it but I wasn't going to see her do without. Why get married if you are going to deprive your spouse of their despicable habits?

But I had to write. And the thought of her wounded swan neck lapping up the past and crying over the kitchen table at Norton while I was upstairs writing was too much for me. The guilt I would feel would be insufferable. I hated guilt and hated those who made me feel it. Not least because it made me hate myself. I had to have another story. And this one would have to be sharper. There was a limit to how far cats and undergraduates and fishing trips were going to get me. I needed something with 'cunt' in the first sentence.

And so – in an act of imagination so intimately bound up with the creative process that I stood back from it a moment and looked at it, leisurely, like a critic – I had an idea. I would ask Alex. For the weekend. He was modern. He was sharp. And he was a cunt.

Alex was one of our oldest friends. I don't know which of us met him first. He was one of the first friends we made as a couple. He floated freely into our lives, in and out, not bound to one or other of us, and therefore not subject to the possessiveness and potential jealousies of having once been owned by one of us individually. He was also the most successful of our friends, and since his success we saw less of him. But he and I met still to play tennis. Once we had argued about politics. Now we just played tennis. In my mind, playing tennis against Alex was a political argument carried on by other means. He played a left-wing game; mine was free-market tennis. I believed that whichever of us had been looking after himself the best would win; I was able to watch the result with Darwinian detachment. He never seemed to care who won, but insisted we were of equal ability; he put victory down to social forces and his own failure to engage. The game, the process, like the Revolution, would yield a winner. Our little Mixed Economy made for some good games and some spectacularly disputed line-calls. Underneath it all, much like Joe Stalin, no doubt, he loved winning.

Alex was a TV chef. In spite of his rat-like, unwashed, Irish-tenement features and implausible stubble, and the fact that until he went for his audition with the TV company neither Julia nor I had ever seen him cook so much as an egg, he was a runaway success. He specialised in Special Occasion cookery. His programme covered Christmas and Hogmanay and children's birthday parties. It was advanced stuff. How to boil an egg was taken as read, which was probably a good thing, because I doubted he knew how. Julia watched his programmes and even wrote down one of his recipes. I gave her a hard time about that. I suspect she did it because she didn't actually like Alex that much. Over the years she had gone quieter and quieter with him, as he and I screamed more and more personal insults at each other. I think she tired of the *faux* testosterone-driven verbal wrestling. She felt excluded. So she wrote down his recipes.

He got me going, he got me talking and fighting and engaging. And he was Irish. Something had to happen if he came to Norton.

'What da fock are you callin' me at ... what does the clock say? Fock! It's six fockin' dirty! *Wanker!* There was a pause. 'We haven't got a fockin' court booked, have we?'

'That's next week, you Irish twat. Do you want to come to Norton?'

'What?'

'Norton. Today. For the Bank Holiday. Weekend break. Do you want to come?'

'That gaff in Suffolk?'

'That gaff in Suffolk.'

'It's so fockin' airly ...'

'Just say yes or no.'

'Well ... Will I have to cook for you?'

'No.'

'I have dat many conts with country houses invitin' me for da weekend expecting me to cook me ahsse off ...'

'Spare me your sob-story, you ugly, overpaid Irish stereotype and say yes. There's a tennis court.'

'Ah, go on, then.'

'I'll pick you up at lunchtime.'

'Christ, I need me sleep ... We only finished filming late last night. This second series is a focker ...'

'Haven't you run out of special occasions yet?'

'We're on to Thanksgivin' and bleedin' bar mitzvahs ... We're all Jewish Americans now, ye know ...'

'We'll be with you at one.'

'Alex?' said Julia to me, when I told her. She was sitting at the breakfast table, childishly dipping a soldier into a boiled egg.

'That's right,' I said.

'When?' she said.

'What do you mean when?'

'When have you asked him to Norton?'

'Sorry. You've not grasped what I am saying at all, I'm afraid.'

'Then start again.'

'I'll start again,' I said. 'Alex, Norton, this weekend. Clear?'

'I don't understand.'

'Let's take it slowly, shall we?'

'Please don't be ...'

'What?'

'Cruel.'

I sighed.

'Did you boil me an egg?' I said.

'No. I'll do one for you right away.'

'I don't want one.' Pause. 'Look. It's a compromise. I thought you'd be pleased.'

'*This* weekend?'

'Julia ...'

'He won't be free.'

'I've already asked him. Look, I'll come to Norton, but I have to write. He'll keep you company. He'll cook for us, he won't be able to help himself. Please try and understand it all from my point of view.'

'OK,' she said, very softly. Then she got up, came over to me and kissed me on the forehead. Then she looked down.

'He hates me,' she said.

'What?'

'He hates me. Alex. He thinks I'm a posh English girl. I know.'

'Rubbish.'

'No. Posh.'

'Well, you are a bit posh. But only nicely. You've got yolk down your dressing gown.'

We drove through north London in the heat. Everything was hot metal and glass; the inside of the car smelt like a plastics factory. I liked it. Only the thought of all that green countryside all so pleased with itself made me furious. I felt like someone was forcing a drink or a drug on me. Of course Alex wasn't ready. Julia and I stood in his kitchen while he pottered like an itinerant Irish wanderer from room to room, picking up underwear and magazines. I felt as if the entire trip was being staged for him, now, as a kind of birthday present. I didn't know how my life had come down to this. We got him out the door, I nearly ran over one of his neighbour's children and then Alex realised he'd left his tennis racket behind. I drove on. I'd have to play with the old Maxply and he'd have to play with mine, or I'd never hear the last of it. It was three by the time we hit the motorway.

Alex was sitting in the front with me, smoking.

'Could we open a window?' said Julia. I knew she'd be feeling sick.

We passed a service-station sign.

'Pull over,' said Alex, 'I need a fry-up.'

'It's half past three,' I said. 'They won't be serving fry-ups.'

'What century are you living in? They serve fry-ups twenty-four seven. I know, I did a programme on them.'

'What glamour. Don't tell me – the symbiotic relationship between the proletariat and greasy food, or Why We Have Heart Attacks Not A Revolution. I should have thought fry-ups were to the great unwashed what the potato famine was to your nearest and dearest.'

Alex took a long drag on his cigarette and turned round to Julia.

'This undercurrent of right-wing Anglo-Saxon gobshite ... does he mean it or is it a pose?'

'Both,' she said, and coughed. '*The window*, please.'

'Service stations,' went on Alex, turning the steering wheel for me as I drove and diverting us down the slip road to the Lodge, 'are in the noble tradition of food and travel. They go back to the old coaching inns. Travel and food are deeply connected. It's a paradigm of life. The quality of your passage trew life. Signposts. Nourishment.'

'Bollocks.'

We parked the car.

The swing-doors of the service station swung open, and Alex entered, a mixture of John Wayne entering a bar to lay down the law to a recalcitrant frontier town and a modern Jesus going to preach to a disco; he leaned into the tide of people as if they were his destiny. The vast hotplates and stainless-steel vats of beans and chips, the gleaming contrast of sharpened utensils and mushy bubble-and-squeak, the starched chefs' uniforms like fancy dress and the tattooed, recently unemployed workers who wore them: all of this seemed awaiting his blessing. An old lady recognised him and said 'Hello, Jamie.' He didn't care. He smiled his little rat-like smile, reassuringly. Her children and grandchildren would be free to eat at the trough of populist culture, even if she herself had been made to scrape a living all the years of her leisure-less life.

I steered Julia away from the grease stalls and towards the coffee bar. Alex was off scoring cholesterol. We looked at the board with all the different kinds of coffee you could have. There were different methods of making it, different coffee beans, different milks, different strengths of caffeine. It was dizzying, like a vast departure board. And as I noticed it I instantly thought that it was just the kind of modern phenomenon that got written about; some dreadful Sunday-supplement piece – it was just the sort of detail waiting to find its way into a story, so we could sit back and reflect on the progress of our world and the fascinating contrast between the lowest common denominator all-day breakfasts and the capitalist paradigm of infinite choice of kinds of coffee. It's the stand-up comedy school of writing, the 'I recognise that cute contradiction.' It's Ben Elton in bed with Martin Amis. Fuck Patrick, he'd got me competing. I felt like writing a story about flower arranging. I'd give him *femme*. And then I'd slit my wrists drinking a skinny-double-whammy-post-Marcos-Nicaraguan-latte.

Of course politics was the problem. If you said you hated politics, which I did, you were making a political statement. There was no escape from the circularity. It was me and Alex playing tennis all over again. Everything was fucking politics. But the fact that it was politics wasn't empowering, it still didn't mean that it led to a picket line, or sanctions, or even a meaningful exchange in the Lower House of one's own intellect. Somewhere going down the hill the chain had come off the back wheel of political consciousness – you thought your well-meant pedalling was adding to your progress, but it's an illusion. Politics got you nowhere, nowadays. When there was a game to be played, you got on with it. Why? Because there's a limit to how far thinking about anything but food and money and winning the game will get you.

I would have liked to have talked to Julia about all of this, but by the time I had thought it, and the metaphorical dust of all those metaphors had settled, she'd ordered. She was clearly fluent in coffee-bar Esperanto. She got what she wanted.

In a rare and misguided protest I ordered a cup of plain filter coffee. It still took me at least a minute turning down all the things I didn't want. No extra hot water, no hot milk, no sugar, no pastries. I don't know how long it had been sitting at the side of the *Blade Runner*-inspired cappuccino machine slowly evaporating down to the cocktail of aluminium and caffeinated carcinogens; it looked like molasses and smelt of those organic feeds you put on grow-bag tomatoes. Julia and I sat together; she sipped her choice like a Roedean coffee-monitor. I scowled. I wanted to be writing. I could have written there. I could have gone to the bogs and written a short piece out on lavatory paper and stuffed it in my inside pocket, like having a furtive wank. I could have scrawled something in the back of the new AA road map we had in the back of the car. I could have written anywhere. But not at Norton. I was being led to writers' block as to the scaffold.

Before I had reached halfway down the thickening gloom of my coffee, there was Alex coming towards us.

'Kedgeree! *Kedgeree!*' he shouted, to anyone who cared to listen. 'They even do fockin' kedgeree. I fockin' love it. Once upon a time the only people who got kedgeree were Eton fockin' scholars. Let's hit the road.'

'I thought you wanted a fry-up.'

'I don't want to eat this shit. I'm a fockin' gourmand . . . I swill it round me north and south and spit it out. Drink up. Give us a swig o' that coffee. I'm that parched . . . *Jasus*, that tastes like . . . !'

Just beyond Colchester we stopped at a Waitrose. It was an education to see him work the place. He roughed up the manager celebrity style, charmed the checkout girls, promised them a mention on his show and got ten per cent off. There were more old ladies, and none of them called him Jamie. As I had guessed, he had no intention of letting us cook. He put two hundred pounds on my credit card.

At around six thirty we pulled off the main road and up the gravel track that led to Norton. There is half a mile of chestnut trees and then the edge of the house. Only as we got closer, only in the final seconds did I become fully conscious of Julia again. I had kept her out of my mind all the trip. I had been aware of how she hated Alex smoking, hated his swearing and baroque Irish excesses; aware, probably, of how much she simply hated him. But I had no room for her unhappiness in my head. Not when I had the incipient panic of not being able to write nagging at the muscles of my right arm like tennis elbow. Now, as we turned the corner, though, I felt my feelings join hers, and in spite of myself, her pleasure became my pleasure, and I guessed that her unhappy silence had been replaced by a happy one.

But this emotion by proxy scared me. I felt it had the power to consume me. I had always kept it at a distance – particularly as far as Norton was concerned – partly out of sheer selfishness, partly out of the squeamishness I have already mentioned about other people's pasts. But mostly because I was always fearful that over-identification with other people's feelings was unmanning. The idea of becoming a satellite to Julia's grand rapture seemed to me a kind of death. It was like watching a firework display from a distant field, listening to the oohs and ahhs of an audience one is not a part of, an audience whose slavish devotion to the details of the display is so given away by their unsophisticated responses. They would be my responses if I was a part of the audience, but standing in a dark corner of some foreign field

– it's just embarrassing. You're left to guess another's ecstasy, and it makes you baulk at the idea of ecstasy itself.

We negotiated the pot-holed drive. I sensed her in the seat behind me, looking at the dusty drive and the untidy shrubs that spilled over the dry grass banks towards us. I remembered the photographs I had been shown at her family Christmases of her as a girl in the garden there, on the same drive, by the same shrubs; her, dressed to go riding; her, proprietorial of the flowers and the trees; her, mistress of a garden less untidy, of a drive less pot-holed. She looked at them all now, and I didn't know, nor, I suppose, would ever know, whether she was revisiting a neater, more beautiful past, or silently lamenting her husbanded, bickering present. Or both. I certainly felt her caught between the two, and that I was the thing that held her to that unsatisfactory present, like a kite, being blown back towards happiness but imprisoned in my unworthy grasp. When I tried to see her as a free thing, out of my hands, I wanted her cut loose, to be blown back to Norton, to be a young girl, again. Not so much, though, I am afraid, because I really appreciated her freedom, but because I wished that the place that held her here, in the unsatisfactory present, was not so identifiable with me. Her existence seemed leased to me, and I wanted to give up the lease; if only to have her again, freehold.

'Fockin' Manderley,' said Alex, and whistled softly to himself.

'Norton,' she said, softly, and I gagged at the indulgence of the hushed invocation of the name. I loathed her. I wanted to vomit.

We drew up to the house, Julia opened her door, got out and went into the orchard at the back of the house, without so much as a word. It was what she did.

Alex and I started to unpack the car.

'Ah,' he said, as if he had read my mind, 'what it is to have a past. Me parents couldn't afford a past for me, so I had to have hand-me-down pasts from me older brothers. But they never quite fit. I'd have 'em for a while and then hand 'em down to the next in line. Eh? Gobshite? Laugh.'

'Ha ha. That sort of post-colonial class-conscious satire went out with Thatcher.'

'Thatcher, my dear boy,' he said in imitation posh English, 'is with us for ever. She is the trodden-in turd on the beige carpet of liberal England. She is unremovable. And we all owe her a living.'

'Speak for yourself. The mass media may have taken her shilling, not I . . .'

'Gobshite,' he went on, Irish rat, again. 'Der is no media dat is not mass. Make your stories as short as you like, you will never escape Our Lady of Grantham. Self-interest is her Immaculate Conception.'

'Fuck off.'

But Alex only rifled through the Waitrose bags in the boot.

'Tank fock for that, I taught I'd left de rack of lamb on the checkout, bot it's here. Lead the way, cunt. Trew yonder ivied door.'

I left Alex in the kitchen sweeping dead flies off the sideboard. I put my head in each room upstairs, half expecting to be assailed by hornets or squatters. The house seemed aggressively similar to the last time we had been there. How could it so effortlessly present itself to you just as you had left it? It might at least have changed itself a little, in the interim, made a second draft of itself. So lazy.

I was in a state. I went to the room laughingly referred to as 'my study', and sat down. The window that looked over the garden was half obscured with creeper, and the garden beyond was exaggeratedly green and pastoral. I sat down at the desk. The tennis elbow seemed to make writing unlikely. I was enraged with that bitch and her bliss. Any second she would come walking beneath my window like a bloody troubadour and start reciting Edward Thomas poems.

Right, I thought to myself, I will write myself out of this. I will make myself alone. I will *write myself* alone.

I took out a pad of A4 and started to write:

The two of them had a silent lunch together, were civil, drank wine, and she got up to go.

'I'm glad I came to see you in your rural idyll. The house is picture-perfect. For one,' she said.

'Is that a criticism?'

'No. An architectural observation.'

'Don't be bitchy,' he said.

'Why not? Your life is what you have always wanted – it belongs in a Sunday supplement.'

'I came,' he said, 'to be a part of the countryside. Is that so pretentious?'

'Which part?'

He looked at her, and her finely made face, and wondered why they had never been lovers. All of their mutual friends had assumed that it was merely a matter of time until they slept together. They flattered one another, each acknowledged that the other was attractive, but both held off. In London it had been easy. There were lots of people, and there were lots of things to do other than sleep together. But now he had moved to Somerset, and she had come to visit him, it highlighted their individuality.

As they had parted the night before, each to their separate bed, the moment had presented itself to them. But nothing had happened. Now, just as she was about to go back to London, they had come closer to having a real argument than they had ever done before.

If he had been honest with himself he would have had to admit that he feared his move out of London was the biggest mistake of his life. Having lain in bed and fantasised about solitude, he found the fact of it dreadful. He found even such simple things as wasps and rain and unfriendly village locals so distressing he wanted to run from them. He had grown up in the countryside, and had loved it. But its terrors were revisited upon him as a grown man, and they seemed absurdly magnified. What once had been a feeling of abandon and release in the details of country life, in hedgerows and in paths that skirted the edges of great wheat fields, now seemed to him gone, replaced by indifference; urban life – perhaps just grown-up life – had destroyed the difference between looking at a misty panorama of green fields and staring at expensive wallpaper.

And then the girl had come, the girl who had been only a friend, and who now, with her soft skin and linen skirts, her deft, merciless plucking of flowers on the walk they made together, and her ironic take on his newly found, almost adolescent adventure, was tugging at him every which way.

She stood, about to leave. She had pulled up, on the Friday night, in front of his cottage. Now they had finished Sunday lunch, and she was off. They had sat out the back. It was still overgrown. She had said the nettles that arched their heads towards them looked as if they might bite. He said he liked them. He said he liked the Edward Thomas poem about them. 'Tall Nettles'. He had found her the poem and read it to her. She had just stared at him. When he came to the last rhyme, which he liked particularly, his throat had contracted with emotion and he had thought he might cry. She looked away, and he thought she looked amused, as if *she were laughing at him and his new, country sentimentality. Soon after they had gone out to the car.*

'I ought to paint your portrait. Call it BMW in clover,*' he said.*

'Something to remember me by?'

'Why? Are you never coming back?'

'You come to London,' she said, imperiously.

There was a pause.

'No,' he said.

'Don't be stupid. You obviously hate it here. I can tell. I know you.'

'I love it,' he said.

Some rooks that had nests high in the trees above the house cackled their rich, ridiculing cry, and he felt even Nature saw through him.

She looked up, too.

'It's all go, here, isn't it? 'Bye.'

She got in the car and drove off. He heard her change gear badly going up the hill out of the village. He went inside.

The instant he was in the house alone, again, he felt a dreadful, aching desire in his body for sex with the woman who had just driven off. He wanted to re-run the entire weekend and end it by taking her to bed. He felt he had got everything wrong. His desire was so strong he felt his sheer will might drag her back down the hill into his house, into his arms.

He went through to where they had had lunch. As he passed the clock in the hall he saw that it had stopped. He rang the speaking clock from the phone in the hall, wound the clock and reset it. Then out to the table. Her napkin was on her plate, and he saw it had lipstick on it. The nettles nodded in the breeze like old friends. Their pointed leaves were reassuringly distant. Beyond the nettles was a view over the fields.

He'd given up cigarettes when he had moved to the country. He was proud of his abstemiousness. Now he went back inside to the sideboard and found the one, unopened packet he had, tore off the cellophane, found matches and went back out. He poured himself the last of the wine they

had left un-drunk and took a drag. The nettles nodded more emphatic-
ally. The wind was getting stronger.

It is hard to say definitively at what point he realised there was about
to be a storm. It seemed to join and run in tandem with his confused
feelings with such ease that he felt an almost superstitious feeling of familiarity with it. He walked out, through the undergrowth, trampling nettles
and thistles underfoot, their stings and thorns tickling his feet, till he
reached the boundary of his little garden.

There was the view. On clear days you could see Glastonbury Tor
rising out of the intricate patchwork of fields. The clouds moved over
them, highlighting for a second a field of rape, winking like a beacon in
the sunlight, then suppressed. He sipped his wine. He tasted the strange,
musky bitterness of good wine, and his head throbbed a little.

When he looked up from his glass the sun had gone. He looked behind
him, and where it had been was a curious bruise-like cloud in the west. The
thistles shivered in the breeze, and he felt it, too, like a cool, feminine hand
stroking his cheek. Over the fields that had lain in sunshine only moments
before there had slid a long, grey, slate shadow. The patchwork of fields gave
up their design, as if sacrificing their invention to the simpler, duller puri-
tanism of the sky. What had been a landscape in oils now seemed a dull,
half-wash of dreary watercolour. His heart sank. But it was soon clear that
this was only a temporary lull in the drama. Strange purple clouds, some
deep grey and others rimmed with sickly sunlight, rose up from behind the
house as though from a distant explosion. It seemed inconceivable that the
sky could make such drama unprovoked by the ground beneath it.

What was it about the girl who had just driven away, he asked himself.
Why was he so miserable? The failure of love, of indestructible closeness?
A failure of will?

In the time it took him to think these things, the storm began. Only
one small break remained in the curtain of grey above him, through which
a parody of sunlight struggled through. All around, a conference of noises,

from the grass to the upper reaches of the trees, shook in accompaniment.
He watched, fascinated.

The first drops of rain fell on him, seemingly hesitant, inarticulate, as
one might guess what is going to be said, but refuse to credit it until the
torrent has come, the true reproaches, the unconsidered communication:
the storm.

It grew darker. Not the dark of night-time, but a new, enforced dark-
ness, the darkness of eclipse, or the closed curtains of a child's bedroom,
sent to bed before true night. In their own time, the clouds above his head
turned and turned, taking each other's places in slow, considered compe-
tition to empty their rain on the landscape beneath. Something cracked,
something split, something as old as memory gave way brightly, and with
the lightning, in a trick of timing almost too perfect to be real, the rain
poured down. He stood there, fascinated, his imagination high above him
and fully realised, all his frustration with life turning with the clouds in
fugitive ecstasy, while the wild, unkept garden around him nodded and
swayed in the wind, and delivered the water off its leaves on to the parched
earth beneath.

In the early morning he woke, and lay a long time listening to the sounds
of his house around him, creaking like a ship, adjusting to the stillness.
Only the quieter than quiet drip of the water off the eaves echoed through
the empty house. He slept another long, deep sleep.

He never saw the woman again.
He still lives in Somerset.

I put my pen down and stretched my back where I sat. Then
I re-read it. It all seemed pretty much a waste of time apart
from the storm at the end. You couldn't just put together two

events – the girl coming to stay and the storm – and call it a story. Or could you? Life was about our brains making connections, wasn't it? If he feels they are connected, so as far as the writer is concerned, they are. He sought release, and he found it; it was offered him. And he had the sensibility to feel it vividly. He was alive, again. It needed more sex, though. Maybe it was all about sex. The storm as sex. I'd wanted him to go and have a wank when she left, when he was wanting her, but instead he goes out and has a real moment. Is that me or the character? Would it have been more real if he had had a wank? He could have had a wank and then the storm. Would that have made for a different storm? A wank *during* the storm. Why was I always desecrating my feeling for Nature? Why was irreverence so irresistible?

I looked out of the window at the garden. The shadows were longer. Time had passed. I had written something. A fragment from which I might keep a third or less, to integrate into a larger narrative.

But would I? I didn't believe in transforming moments like that. I wanted to, because I wanted one myself. I wanted a storm. But the truth was that I found Nature's excesses engendered in me an instinctive frigidity. And descriptions of Nature always bandy about its transforming power, whereas most of the time it's the writer tarting around the transforming power of his own prose. If it has any. It's about the power of the writer.

Well, I was sick of the power of the writer. I was sick of having it all my own way. I wanted a fucking storm. Of course Julia would disagree with me there. She thinks I get nothing but my own way and that I love it.

'Gobshite, will you get your airse downstairs!'

I would work on it. I would find a larger narrative.

'Coming!' I called, suddenly better disposed towards the idiot cook.

'The lady you are fockin' locky enough to call your wife has just bin tellin' me de deal . . .'

I found Alex marshalling his foodstuffs and Julia looking disdainfully at the cigarette hanging out of his mouth. I don't think that kitchen had ever seen a cigarette.

'She says, cunt, that I'm to cook and you're to write, and she's to be grateful. If I could drive I'd be tempted to get in your car, run you over, and drive back to de fockin' smoke.'

'I knew you'd see it from my point of view,' I offered.

'Chop this,' he said and pushed a tray of mushrooms at me.

'No,' said Julia, 'I'll do it.'

She took the tray and began cutting, methodically. She wouldn't look at me.

'All right, love?' I said.

She turned her head very slowly; it arched gently, as if she were drawing me up like a fish she was landing, as if she were purposefully drawing her beautiful head back as slowly as she could, dragging her very beauty through the briar patch of my cruelty to her, so that I might see the scratches, see the blood.

'Yes,' she said.

'What have you been up to?'

'You started,' she said.

'Started?'

'Writing.'

'Yes,' I said. 'Just as you went straight to the garden, so I went straight to my desk. The past comes to you unbidden, but I have to make my present. It happens at the end of my pen. It requires effort, and a desk, and solitude. And unlike the past, they pay me for it.'

Alex turned and attended to something, humming quietly to himself. I knew that kind of pompous bollocks was just playing to his strengths, but I was past caring.

'What have you been up to?' I went on.

'Swapping childhood highlights,' said Alex.

'Ah, Dublin tenement meets *Brideshead Revisited*. I should have stayed down here, got a ringside seat.'

'Yes, you should have stayed down here,' said my wife.

'I covered that in my last reply.'

'Yes,' she said.

'Pardon?' I said.

'I just said yes,' she said.

'Mmm . . .'

'Listen, you two,' said Alex, taking a swig of wine. There was an open bottle of the Gevry-Chambertin on the side. 'Der's something I forgot to tell you. I have a rule on these occasions, when I'm taken away to strange houses under false pretences and made to play the Irish jester. And it's this. I don't do subtext. D'ya hear? And I don't do udder people's unhappy marriages. At least not over the Bank Holiday. I'll do 'em weekdays over a dozen pints at me local. I'll do both of you on separate evenings if you want to book yourselves in, I'll do an evening wid each of ya. But I have August Bank Holiday off. You got me here – I don't care. Der's a couple more bottles o' this in the pantry. We'll play tennis. And you'll eat well. Fock it. But I hates subtext. I won't have it in the kitchen. It spoils the food. All right?'

He said this impressively, and we were impressed. Julia smiled and sipped her water. I smiled and for a moment forgot what I had written upstairs.

'How about,' I said brightly, 'a quick set, now?'

'Only if you drink the rest o' that bottle. I'm not playin' with a fockin' handicap.'

I drank it. And beat him.

Dinner passed peacefully enough. We sat in the kitchen and Alex served us. He seemed to have forgiven me my kidnapping of him. He drank copiously and the cuisine seemed aggressively *haute*. Julia looked sullen and self-conscious, like someone unaccustomed to eating in public. She barely thanked him for cooking. It was so unlike her. She normally had the manners of a head-girl.

It was nearly time for bed.

'So what's this new collection like, then?' said Alex, reaching for the Calvados.

'Collection?' I said.

'Stories, focker. Same as the last lot?'

'Don't pretend you read the last lot. Give me some of that.'

'Well?'

'I don't do interviews,' I said.

He turned to Julia.

'What are they about?'

She turned to him, slowly, as she had to me earlier that day. As if she had to shake off her rageful lethargy just to take in what someone else said to her.

'About?' she said. 'What are they about? They are about separateness.' She turned to me. 'Isn't that what you said to me?'

She was so beautiful. When she spoke softly she put you in mind of a beautiful butterfly skewered on a pin weeping blood. Or something.

'Sounds a fockin' gas.'

'One of them,' said Julia, 'is about this house. Is about me, when my parents divorced, and my sister, with whom I was extremely close. It's about a little girl wandering around this house, from place to place, and not understanding people's behaviour, because in fact the parents are about to leave the house, and the grandparents are going to leave it, and everyone is acting strangely. But the little girl only gets told this right at the end in a long scene with her older sister up in the attic.'

'Did ya tell him it all, then? So he could pinch it?'

'No. He guessed. He's good at guessing. And I loved him for writing that story. So it's funny he hates it so much here.'

'Actually,' I said, 'I invented it. The details.'

'But you guessed right,' said Julia.

'Lucky guess.'

There was a long pause. I noticed Alex's rat-like mouth had turned into a little rat-like smile.

Soon Julia went up to bed. I played one game of backgammon with Alex and then went up.

We lay under the eaves.

'I would like to do something,' I said, in the darkness, 'to make us happy again.'

There was silence and I wondered if she was asleep. For a while I pondered the difference between speaking to a conscious and an unconscious person. What did words mean, anyway?

'Would you?' she said, eventually.

'Yes.'

'Then send that disgusting man back to London.'

'Why?'

'He's . . . a wanker.'

Julia never swore. She laughed, sometimes, when I swore, some-times she looked like a head-girl, but she never swore herself.

'All right,' I said. 'It'll never happen again.'

'Think of something.'

'What?'

'Anything.'

'You're not serious? You mean really send him away? But I only just got away with asking him here. I'll never get away with sending him home.'

'Why not? This is my house.'

And she turned and went to sleep.

I woke early and left Julia sleeping. I went downstairs. The kitchen looked like it had been the victim of a particularly enthusiastic amateur burglary. I made myself a coffee and closed the door on the pots and pans. Someone else could do them. I needed to marshal my creative energies. I had two issues that required my full attention.

The first was how I was going to get rid of Alex. I now felt that he had virtually invited himself, that it took a bloody nerve, and I wished he could cook something simple for a change. What were my options? Julia and I could stage a fight or I could turn even more unpleasant, and he would say something about 'fockin' subtext' again, and he'd stomp off. Except it was Sunday, and he couldn't drive, and there were barely any trains. I mean, people who don't drive – and I was stranded in Suffolk with two of them – intend a form of violence to other people's peace of mind.

I could pick a fight with him, except that both of us had long ago become inured to real insult. I stood a better chance of getting rid of him telling him how fond I was of him. But that, as Patrick would have said, was too *femme* for me. It seemed an insoluble problem.

The more pressing issue was the story. I re-read what I had written. The storm had no real context, and I had to make one. Otherwise I might as well be writing reports for the Met Office.

I wrote.

A couple of hours passed.

At some point Alex and Julia appeared on the lawn beneath my window with tennis rackets. They practised volleys for half an hour. They didn't look up to my window once. Julia was quite good. I'd forgotten she could play tennis. Growing up with a court in your back garden does wonderful things for your game, I suppose. They seemed to be getting on all right. At least with tennis you don't have to talk to each other. Presumably she hadn't asked him to leave.

I wrote on, and when I looked up again they had gone.

I wrote some more, and a short time later I heard music start up in the living room. I recognised some of Julia's favourite records from her stash of scratchy vinyl. It started with the theme tune from *Elvira Madigan* and soon deteriorated into *Ballet Classics*. Soon after I saw Alex with a fag in his hand walking the garden path. Poor bastard, he was getting the full treatment. Perhaps she had beaten me to it. Perhaps her psychological warfare of uninterrupted Tchaikovsky melodies would drive him back to Islington single-handed.

And suddenly I began, in spite of myself, to like this little crow's nest room, with its view over the garden, the distant noises and the imagined awkwardness of those I supposedly cared about, beneath. For ever this had been Julia's place, this house. It was true, I had written about it, but I had never owned the present here. I'd borrowed a past. But this room was the present, and I was writing in it. I was safe, now. Even the little window and the framed, pastoral miniature of landscape beyond seemed quaint and capable of being possessed. I would finish the story by the end of the day and give myself tomorrow, the Bank Holiday, off.

I broke briefly for lunch and worked all afternoon. Alex and Julia came and went on the lawn beneath, sometimes together, sometimes alone.

Around what I guessed was seven o'clock I stopped writing. I had nearly finished, but I wanted to hold off. I went downstairs and crept out of the back door as silently as I could. It was a beautiful evening. I slipped out of sight of the house and into the vegetable garden.

Nothing had been grown there for years. The beds were still divided up by faded gravel paths, but they divided uniform blocks of weeds, not vegetables. Only a patch of mint had survived. Where it poured on to the paths and was trodden on, it gave off its fresh scent.

I felt a bit sick, and slightly hysterical, as I did after finishing a story. Even the vegetable patch seemed to be about the story, about what it was to write things and give them up to be read. I liked the little uniform paths and the raised beds. Everything was so ordered.

At the top of the path I looked back at the house, which I could just see over the fruit trees. There, framed in the kitchen window were Julia and Alex, arguing. She hadn't got rid of him, and he was lecturing her about something. He was such a soapbox bore. She was running her hand through her beautiful hair distract-edly, and he looked sweaty and tired. I guessed he was talking just the kind of tenacious blarney she despised in him.

Yet how neat they seemed, framed in the kitchen window, a little emblem of domesticity. How ironic that she hated him and he thought her such a snob. I thought over the things I had written and thought what a softy I was at heart. Why did we not all get on better? Everything I had ever written was really just an injunction that we all get on better. Surely there wasn't really any other point, was there? That *was* Western, liberal fiction, wasn't it? So I was in good company, wasn't I?

I went to my wife's rescue.

Inside, Alex was frying something. Neither of them remarked on the fact that I came from the garden, not my study. Alex turned, with the frying pan circulating a delicious smell through the kitchen. He looked at me, as if concerned for my well-being. He seemed relieved that I was all right. Julia looked up at me, too, with the same concern. As if I had just got back from a particularly dangerous trip. I was flattered and surprised.

'How are you, lad?' said Alex, with deep-voiced, Irish fraternity. I'd never heard him speak like that, or show concern about any living soul.

'Good,' I said. 'I had to have a breath of air. You know.'

'Because you've finished?' said Julia, expectantly and gently.

'Nearly,' I said.

'Finishing touches,' said Alex, pouring a small glass of wine over the scallops he'd been frying and then scattering parsley over them. The smell was intoxicating. I don't know whether he was referring to my stories or the scallops; or both. But generosity came off the whole process in waves.

Then he turned and placed the pan on the table in front of us, poured us a very cold glass of Pouilly Fumé and placed a fork by our sides. We tucked in. The emblem of the window, the lamplit domesticity, now framed the three of us; what I had seen from without I was now a part of within. I felt an extraordinary surge of happiness, of peace among friends. We ate the scallops and they seemed the most delicious thing I had ever tasted, and as we ate in silence, the silence seemed blessed.

Alex finished his food and knocked back his wine. I noticed that as he tilted back the glass he looked back along its stem at Julia. It was a hard, appraising look, a little wary; as if he judged her. Alex seemed to be in *gravitas* mode.

'We've been talking about charity,' said Julia.

'Oh,' I said.

'Yes. Did you know Alex is very active in charity work?'

I laughed.

'If you believe that, my dear . . .' I said.

'But it's true,' she said. 'Fancy.'

'Here, lad,' said Alex. There had been ten scallops: three each. He was offering me the odd one.

'Is this some sort of proof?' I said.

Alex smiled, and put it on my plate. Then he stared at Julia, strangely, as if he disapproved of her having made the charity joke.

'So delicious,' said Julia, looking out of the window, with what seemed to be a tear in her eye. No doubt sampling a fugitive memory of a childhood scallop from twenty years ago. But at least she had finally complimented Alex on his cooking. I was beginning to get worried.

Over dinner they showed such interest in my work. We talked about the novel; about what we thought it could achieve in the twenty-first century; we talked about stories, and poems, and whether short stories and poems were versions of the same sorts of experience; we talked about the effect the books of our child-hood had had on us. Alex talked about his satisfaction at cooking and pleasing people, and we compared it to being an actor, or a writer. We covered many subjects in depth from genuinely personal perspectives. The food was delicious, and we told Alex so.

Upstairs I lay on the bed, naked. Julia was taking off her make-up. She sat, in her underwear, facing the little dressing table.

'Nice talking, tonight,' I said.

'Yes.'

I looked at her long, beautiful back. I wanted to make her speak. I wanted that back, so classically moulded and so femi-nine, to speak, as one might seek enlightenment from a sphinx or a statue. I laughed at the thought of it.

'What?' she said.

'Your back is beautiful.'

She turned a little to me, turning into the compliment as someone will try the feeling of the sun on their shoulder.

She threw her cotton wool into the basket beside the table and combed her hair.

'Jules ... I'm sorry.'

'For what?'

'For being a selfish idiot over the work. Over the stories. Over coming here for the Bank Holiday.'

'I'm only glad you're finished,' she said. Then she looked down and shook her head. 'We were worried about you.'

She got up and came and sat on the edge of the bed.

'Thanks for being sorry, though,' she said.

'It's all right.'

She turned, and lifted her legs, neatly, together, like the dancer she had been, to put them beneath the sheet. As she did so, she cast a little, hesitant glance back at the mirror of the dressing table she had just left. She could still see herself. The glance was infinitesimally small, almost invisible. It was curious, appraising, a little sad, tentatively hopeful, even slightly adolescent; there was a hint of the dancer wondering at her own facility; and it was very moving. My heart went out to her. I sensed the anticipation of life, of newness and of heartbreak. Sometimes I thought the old house just made her sad. Perhaps she found it hard to share it with me, after all, especially as I now so obviously had made myself at home there. At last.

She curled up and went to sleep.

Once again I woke before anyone, got up and went down to the kitchen. It was in much the same state as the morning before. I ran a sink of piping hot water, acquainted myself with the whereabouts of all the necessary cleaning products, filled the rubbish bin, emptied it, replaced the bag, and stacked the plates on the side. I made myself a cup of strong tea and carefully washed everything, rinsed it, dried it and put it back in the cupboards. I wiped down all the sides and put new crockery out for breakfast. Then I boiled the kettle once more and made Julia a cup of tea, went upstairs, told my sleepy wife I was going to cook us all breakfast, that I was going for bacon and eggs and papers at the local shop, that I loved her, and that it was a pretty day.

I picked up the car keys on the way through the hall and went out into the sunshine. The door slammed behind me. The 'local' shop was in fact fifteen miles away. It would be my little trip; I felt like a child let out of class.

Only when I started the car did I suddenly remember that it was the Bank Holiday. The shop would be shut. This one even shut on Sundays. It hit me, with a mixture of frustration – I had wanted to do something for everyone – and ecstasy. Because this was it – the day off, the ending of work. The Ending. For once I would, I *could*, do nothing – as between two waves of the sea, the breakwater calm, the in-breath, the ebb, the silence; I could be inarticulate, again. I could give up.

I turned off the ignition.

In a curious replay of Julia's arrival I got out of the car and went, as one drawn by desire, into the garden behind the house. I disappeared into the trees. I felt her desire for the great green abstraction that is a garden that you love. I took a path that led away from the house. I hadn't been that way before. It skirted a big wheat field. The wheat had been cut but the stubble was still there, all sharp and unaccommodating. It was a beautiful yellow. I circled the field. Norton itself was lost in trees, so much so that I had almost lost my bearings, but I pressed on. As I came up closer to the house I looked under the trees and saw a great patch of nettles in the shadows. I went closer. For some reason they drew my attention and for a while I could not work out why. Something about the way they leaned their heads towards me, nodding in the light breeze, set in motion a whole string of memories. I stood, staring at them, waiting for the reason that they had arrested my attention to make itself clear. And sure enough I realised what it was. I had written about nettles nodding their heads in my story. And here they were, nodding their heads. In my waking life I had never paid much attention to them, but for some reason had written about them, and here I was, accosted by them, visitors from my own imagination, come to reinforce reality, and find in the true article the beauty I had never noticed; the beauty I only knew now because I had tried to describe it in a story. What a bizarre reversal of the normal sequence of seeing life transformed into art.

I thought of yesterday evening, of finishing the story and going out into the garden and looking back at the house and seeing those two old adversaries, Julia and Alex, in the lamplit window. Seeing those two unlikely opposites together – just like the story of the storm and the visiting girl – made one realise that they could be brought together. It was a kind of ecstasy, in spite of their separateness, to see the two framed in the window like that. The idea of reconciling opposites – not the drama of the separate heart but of separate *hearts* – that was joy. The penance is to give up the selfish side of life to suffer the moments of generous absolution – *allowing* the separateness of those we care about. I had wanted – like the man in the storm – a defining moment. What I had got was something inestimably more valuable: a vision of the value of my friends.

I left off staring at the patch of nettles under the tree and walked on. The Bank Holiday stretched ahead of me, as vast as summer holidays.

I turned the corner. Suddenly, there was Norton. I had done a full circle. There was the house, beautiful, the green creepers holding the upper storeys in a green embrace.

From an upstairs, open window, as if the house were in crisis, as if some new discovery were being made of facts unguessed at, of revelations too profound to warrant articulate speech, came cries. And I recognised the unfamiliar sound of my wife having an orgasm.

And alongside the inevitable and predictable heartache of imagining her being fucked by Alex there was – distant and faint as the consolation we feel that, had we been born in an earlier age we would have had the bliss and the benefit of believing in the Almighty – there was the thought that, at last, I had finished my collection of short stories.